BORN TO DIE

BLOOD BOUND SERIES BOOK FOUR

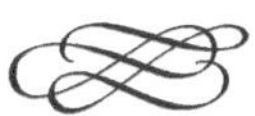

J.L. MYERS

A NEW ADULT PARANORMAL ROMANCE

MORE BOOKS BY J.L. MYERS

THE BLOOD BOUND SERIES

(New Adult Paranormal Romance)

What Lies Inside

Made By Design

Web Of Lies

Born To Die

~

OTHER BOOKS

Nerve Damage

(A Chilling Psychological Thriller)

~

FALLEN ANGEL SERIES

Ashes of Eden

Dawn of Reckoning

Breaking Lucifer

Cold-Blooded Fate

Falling Stars

Copyright © 2016 by J.L. Myers

The moral right of the author had been asserted.

This book is a work of fiction. Names, characters, places and events are either the product of the author's imagination or, if real, are used fictitiously. Any resemblance to actual people living or dead is purely coincidental.

All rights reserved

No part of this literary work may be reproduced, stored in a retrieval system, or transmitted, in any form or by any means, graphic, electronic or mechanical, including photocopying, taping and recording, without prior written permission from the author J.L. Myers.

Cover design by Digital Print Australia.
Cover art © 2016 J.L. Myers.

Visit the Website:
www.jlmyers.com

Paperback ISBN 978-0-9875653-9-6
eBook ISBN 978-0-9875653-8-9

BECOME A VIP AND GET A FREE BOOK!

J.L. Myers is giving away a free short prequel to the Blood Bound Series.

Use this link to get the your free copy.

http://bit.ly/JLFreePrequel

Dedicated to all the loyal Blood Bound fans.
YOU made this series possible.

xoxo J.L. Myers

CHAPTER 1

Blink. Blink.

The dark blindness behind my eyelids disappeared as my body took form.

Blink. Blink.

Wet tracks rolled down my face in a silent display of grief. Not because of anything happening in the here and now—I wasn't in either of those places. With vibrant green underfoot that spanned out into black nothingness, I knew this was a vision. One my mind and vampire spirit-gifted Sight had conjured. Here and now I was occupying my own body—in a future that had yet to play out. My hands were raised before me and shaking. Like I was saying goodbye to someone I couldn't touch.

And I was devastated.

With another blink, the vision warped.

Drip. Drip. Drip.

The sound came from an altar. Glossy blood had escaped a brimming chalice to drip from the altar's edges. I stood in front. Not alone. Marcus, my twin—my enemy—faced me in shitkickers and dirty jeans, his smile forced and morbid. The sight of him struck me as eerily familiar. I'd seen this. In a vision I had before learning Marcus was the damned commander.

Like before, his white shirt was unbuttoned, but the black alchemy symbol painted across his pale chest was instantly overshadowed. Beneath a blood-blooming tear in his shirt was a starburst of scarred and red-splotched skin.

I had staked him again? My damned-restoring ability had already failed to cull my twin's damned DNA once before. So why…?

The mindset change of my future self killed my burning curiosity. With no fear of the guy facing me, I was flooded with urgency while a deep sense of grief-stricken readiness almost floored me. "It's time."

Marcus joined our hands, trapping something between them. The look on his face was…compassionate? "You sure you're ready for this?"

My answer was displayed with a dance of blue sparks down my arms to our joined hands. "It's what we were born for."

Red joined the game, sparking from Marcus's chest to disappear beneath the white cotton. When the sparks reappeared from his long cuffs to meet our joined palms, our powers mingled, my blue lightning yin to his red lightning yang. Sources made for each other, destined to join—

With my fingers locked over my twin's knuckles, my body began to hum with power and heat.

The moment our voltage combined, the color changed to purple. Torture invaded my body at the same time as Marcus's—I could feel his pain somehow. Despite the strain across his angled features, his lips parted with a gurgle of blood to speak. But I couldn't make out the words as warmth dripped from my eyes, my nose...and my ears. Blood.

Unable to look away from Marcus's own bleeding eyes, I tried to speak. But the me who was witnessing the future unfold had no voice to question what we were doing or why. All I felt was the certainty that this was the only way, and...

Wait, was my heart beating?

No. It was racing. Impossible, as a vampire transitioning into a damned.

The sudden shift of power was as unmissable as it was unstoppable. Violet light split from our bodies, joining the surrounding black with a sonic boom.

One last blip and my heart stalled, freezing in my chest. My bones turned to liquid. My brain fritzed. All power and sensation fled my body.

As I fell, I felt no pain, no regret. This had been my choice. Somehow I knew that with total clarity as Marcus hit the grass beside me.

I AWOKE with a snarl that was more rabid beast than vampire. Bloodlust roiled through my body and awakened my transitioning need to kill. The heat from a living body overwhelmed me as my nails sank into thick biceps. Oh God, that scent. One that had been imprinted on my brain but that I refused to register as anything other than food.

I shoved at the pressure on my chest that kept me horizontal. Glowing red blinded my sight. I snapped my fangs over and over. I didn't need to see to find the source I longed to bite into.

A male body covered mine, pinning me with one muscle-bulging arm. "Amelia, *stop*."

I ignored the deep, strained voice. That rapid thrum told me exactly where his jugular was. And although I felt his dominant strength, a distinct twitching vibrated the bed beneath us that indicated restraint.

Too bad the concession wasn't returned.

Using my nails like talons, I tunneled deeper into his flesh. There was a grunt in reply, and heavy pressure straddled me as my legs thrashed. That crowbar arm didn't let up.

When I stabbed my nails in again, he growled. Growled? My wrists were caught in one broad, rough hand and shoved above my head. "I don't want to hurt you."

Didn't matter. I was willing to dislocate my shoulder to reach my mark.

I reared but was hauled up, sitting rather than lying down. My freed legs caught around his hips, locking him against me. Removing space between us.

Snap. Snap.

Just one more inch.

"Dammit, Amelia."

The release of my wrists had me launching at my prey, only to get caught around the neck. My head cracked into stone and I clawed at those straining biceps. His free arm swung away as I lashed out, my nails shredding the material over his chest instead. Something slid and clanked off to the side, followed by a thump and a crash. A stronger punch of blood drilled up into my sinuses.

"Drink it!"

The hold around my neck shifted, prying open my jaw. My long fangs clinked against a small, rounded rim, and then…pure heaven hit my tongue.

I stopped my attack and caught the source—a bottle—chugging down the peppery, rich blood. A steady beat took off beneath my ribs while my ability to think and comprehend rushed back. My heart reanimated…because the offering was restored damned blood, alive and pure, but distinctly different from a regular vampire's.

The haze faded from my vision then, blinding bloodlust melting into crystal-clear reality as I smelled the stale smoke scent I hadn't been able to register beyond the lure of blood. My catnap to ward off fatigue and hunger had been cut short. A twister had decimated my bedroom. Me. Atop my four-poster bed, the sheets were shredded. A spring was visible. One bedside table was knocked over, the lamp shattered and the black lace shade squashed—the thump and crash I'd heard. The photo of Ty and me about to board the cruise lay amongst the mess.

Ty knelt at the foot of the bed, cautiously catching his breath. In the fading moonlight that meant dawn was on its way, his black hair was disheveled, his cheeks flushed. He wore an expression of guarded readiness, prepared for round two if his offering hadn't satiated my need to kill. His black muscle shirt was slashed across the chest, and gleaming wetness stained the sides where my nails had claimed flesh. The furrows they'd drilled into his black-veined arms shrank, leaving only streams of crimson forking down to his elbows. Blood splatter had reached my sheets, too. All his.

Ty showed no fear or even disgust at my actions. "Are you okay?"

Me? If not for him, I'd be damned and he'd be dead.

A long-ago memory surfaced in my mind then, a life raft full of so many hopes and dreams.

With my arms coiled around Ty's waist, I forced his quaking body against mine. "Ty, I love you!" My lips connected with his, forcing them apart.

Ty struggled against me for a moment, shaking so violently it was hard to keep hold of him. Then I felt a sudden change, quick as a gust of wind. Ty's resistance stalled and his strong hands flew to my cheeks. Our kiss deepened with desperate ferocity as his tongue found mine. The cracking of his bones ceased with a single, full-body convulsion. With a rough scrape of his hands, he released my face to slide them forcefully down my back. They found my hips and his grip tightened before he slammed my pelvis against his. "Say it again."

Finding words between our connected lips and ragged breath, I uttered, "I love you, Ty. I will always *love you."*

I'd tamed the beast back when Ty had learned what Caius had done to me. But could Ty tame me? Would I even let him? Everything that ached inside of me still wanted him, loved him…*like that.* Every single part. How could I want someone so bad and feel so explicitly starved that I would end his life?

Ty watched me in that frozen calculation of his, golden-blue stare giving off a pulse. He sensed the danger and the heat. Did that throaty growl come from him…or me?

You're like a disease. I winced at my sudden inner voice. My new constant companion since I'd started the transition to become damned. There was no denying the truth. Kendrick was dead because of me. Ty had been a monster. Vanessa was gone. But physically? Drawing just enough air so I could talk I said, "I'm fine."

Drinking Ty's blood had slowed the transitioning process, kept me alive despite not having killed to complete the conversion. Being restored, it could instill me with a heartbeat and hide the traits that marked me as 'dead girl walking.' It also dulled my thirst, or at least it had. My tolerance had increased and the effectiveness of it had decreased over the past three weeks. Now what had sufficed in the start, barely kept me from taking down everything with a pulse.

Not that Ty would let that happen.

With my guards relaxed since eliminating Marcus's numbers at the hotel, Ty was now my personal bodyguard. Except it wasn't my body he was guarding. It was everyone else's.

Satisfied I was re-leashed and not an immediate threat, Ty stood up. Striding over the shattered lamp, he kept me in his peripheral even as he removed his wrecked muscle shirt. Swinging one powerful arm, the shredded material was launched toward the bathroom door. The slashes across his chiseled chest, below where his mother's silver-chained amulet hung, had already stopped bleeding. Soon they would be just another four scars added to the ones that covered his entire body. Many had been inflicted growing up through his father's harsh lycan training. Newer ones came from battling his enemies: rogue vampires, and more recently, the damned. The rest?

All me.

Ty lowered onto a curved bench against the wall, next to his utility belt full of silver stakes and daggers. The furthest point he could sit from me while still being in the same room. "In the vision, what did you see?"

Even in the seclusion of my suite, he tracked my every move. Like he expected me to bolt at any second. That look never left his tired face. Sleep was a luxury he scarcely allowed himself while keeping me in check. The blanket on the couch in the lounge where he waited out my sleeping hours hardly ever got used. No wonder he didn't want to 'start again.' Even as I shuddered at the memory of his words, I couldn't stop my gaze from drinking him in.

Not that I wanted him like that. Of course not. Wanting what you didn't deserve was pointless.

As I swung my legs over the bedside, my mind backtracking over what I'd seen, a sound registered. Heartbeats. Four. Right outside the main door where guards remained stationed while I was inside. My royal protective detail that had quickly learned to ignore the odd crash and bang if it wasn't followed up by a call for help.

Like time had suddenly skipped forward, I found myself steps closer to the foyer. Clenching my fists and every muscle up my arms, I backtracked in a flash over the debris I'd hurdled without noticing.

"One bottle wasn't enough," Ty stated as fact. Of course he'd noticed. He could read my every sinister move like a book, because he'd been what I was so close to becoming. A damned vampire. A monster with a shattered soul and no conscience.

Movement from behind didn't make me turn, but a flash of light gained my attention. In the destruction, Ty's stake had tumbled free of my bedside drawer. The same one Mr. Malau had gifted me when our hope of finding and saving Ty had dwindled. The same one I'd failed to restore Ty with when he'd captured and imprisoned me before Kendrick came to my—

Don't go there. I shook myself as the stake glinted as if to taunt me.

An unavoidable scent stopped my intent to kneel and I spun. Now a glass topped to the brim was produced.

Ty held it out. "See if this helps."

All you do is take. Take. Take. Take. Even as my sight danced from Ty's beating chest to the door, I gritted my teeth, biting back the need to tell that voice to *shut up!* Looking at only what Ty held out, I grabbed it. Drained it. Then I sank and bent. My need to suffer was granted as I swooped up the stake and the raw silver burned my skin. A damned trait that was now consistent in me. Keeping a tight grip, I faced Ty. "I want you to use this on me."

"Amelia, you're burning." Ty reached for the stake and I stepped back—glass from the shattered lamp stabbing into my feet and delivering a punch of welcome pain. "Give it to me."

"I will." With the smell of my burning flesh rising as my blood mingled with his in the air, I squeezed my fist tighter. I bit back a hiss. "I want you to keep it. And promise me you'll use it on me if I'm too out of control."

"Don't be ridiculous." He frowned so severely I could see how deep this burden was cutting him. Right through his beating heart. The one I'd brought back to life. "You can always restore yourself."

If it was even possible. "Not if I'm too far gone, I can't. But I won't be responsible for any more pain and suffering. If you can't stop me from killing, if I snap and try to take off, you *will* use this. You *will* stop me. For good."

Ty paced back across the room, hunting boots clapping against the stone with each strong stride. His fists curled to stop his arms from shaking. The look that crossed his face was tortured. "Amelia, I can't. You can't ask this of me."

Something in me tore wide open at the sight of him, but my lips formed the words anyway. "I can and I am. Promise me!"

Ty was in front of me fast as lightning, staring down at me with intensity. His hot hands clasped my neck, thumbs curled around my throat to keep my eyes on him. "This thing you're becoming is *not* you. You're doing this to save lives. To stop that bastard Marcus." His canines slid free and he released me with a shove, snatching the stake from me. He seemed to shake himself and took a step back. "I won't let you kill and I won't end your life. Even if you lose your will to fight and to save yourself, I can promise you, I won't. When this is over, Marcus will be gone and you will be restored. I refuse to accept any other outcome."

I CLOSED the door to the enormous double-chambered Baldassare tomb, feeling like I'd just stepped into my own personal hell. And not because I hadn't taken the time to pull the lamp shards from my feet. That same nausea I'd felt when I'd said farewell to Kendrick's body three weeks ago still drowned me now. Even without needing to breathe, I felt like I was suffocating. But my legs operated. I stepped further into the first candlelit chamber, stripping everything external from my mind. Still nothing could remove the memory of the moment my twin had snapped Kendrick's head sideways and severed his spine.

I swallowed down a wave of nausea, knowing what state I'd find him in. Still cold, gray, unmoving. Kendrick was dead. There was no confusing that. But he wasn't decomposing like a normal corpse laid to rest. At least not since his canceled funeral twenty-one days ago.

Oh God.

My heart skipped a beat as I let my eyes focus on Kendrick and the raised glass box he lay within, a coffin of sorts, but with upmarket features. I cringed at the repetitive wheeze of manufactured air that cooled the inside to subzero.

Biting my lip to keep from screaming, I touched the ice-cold glass. Below, Kendrick's quiet body was laid out. A pillow was propped beneath his head. Like it mattered if he had a soft place to lie on. He couldn't feel it. He couldn't feel anything. Not anymore. Even if he magically came to life…the contraption bolted below with tubes pumping freezing air into the glass coffin would keep him in this state of existence. Frozen in time.

Dead.

I sucked in air, waterworks threatening to drown me. Then I spluttered. Dead lungs didn't need air. My fingers itched to pry open the screwed-shut top as I stared at his face. So peaceful. So lifeless. So banged up. His features were the same and yet so different: strong, manly, his golden brown hair curling gently. But those cuts and bruises wouldn't heal. They couldn't. I traced the glass, imagining I was stroking his face. Imagining he was asleep and I was trying to rouse him.

The heated hand that slid down the back of my arm was all comfort. Despite the silent approach, I knew it was Ty. Still I flinched as his fingertips grazed the scars that ended at my elbow. The ones I'd inflicted to burn off my alchemist marks to connect with and warn Kendrick. Fat lot of good that had done. He'd died anyway. Now I had a permanent reminder to go with the internal agony.

Ty's hand fell away, resting in a fist beside the silver at his waist that was a constant wardrobe accessory. Had he seen the tips of my fangs slip between my lips? "Ah, sorry. I didn't..." he trailed off. There was a stiff creak as he squared his shoulders, and a cracking as both his knuckles squeezed tighter.

The silence that followed was deafening. It's not like there was anything between us. At least I knew that was true from his end. We still hadn't talked about my *relationship* with Kendrick. What we'd been and what we might still be—if he were breathing. Though Ty wanted nothing from me in a relationship sense anymore, I felt his need to know in the way he watched me now, gauging my reaction as I let my currently silver-blue eyes drift from the main attraction and through the entry to the second chamber. To the cracked leather sofa the damned I'd restored, Raven, virtually lived on. To be close to Kendrick, to fight to bring him back, to watch over him—because she loved him, honestly and openly.

Did Ty wonder if I was jealous of her dedication to the guy who'd been—was—my best friend...and had been my boyfriend? Could I honestly deny I wasn't?

Where's your head at, thinking about your love triangle while he's cold and stiff? I grimaced at the lance of pain my devious inner voice had accurately encouraged. Seriously, what was wrong with me?

The urge to take the dagger from my belt and remove my emotional pain along with the physical agony was strong, but I shut it down.

With a shake of my head, I slid a card from the back pocket of my jeans. The one Dorian had delivered under Marcus's compulsion right before Kendrick's funeral was set to begin. The scent of the calla lilies it'd been attached to invaded my nose. My breath caught as I glanced at the handwritten words, even though I'd read and reread them a thousand times over. The words my twin had arranged perfectly for the biggest punch.

Ice freezes life—and death—until blood and soul can resurrect the once living. Restore your conscience and you'll never know. Yin to my Yang, Marcus.

I'D OBSESSED over every word, and I knew a number of things. One: Marcus wanted me to remain in transition for a reason I hadn't uncovered—yet. Two: Only a frozen state could freeze life—and death—in its current existence. And most importantly…there might be a way to bring Kendrick back to life. To resurrect him from death.

The words I said were silent, spoken in my head to my soul's mate like when he was alive. *Kendrick, no matter what, I will find a way. I will bring you back—even if it kills me.*

Like every other time I'd tried to communicate with him since his horrific death, there was no response.

CHAPTER 2

A quiet rustling from the sofa tore my stare from Kendrick's frozen face, and I walked numbly into the adjoining chamber. Ignoring the scent of blood and the sound of two beating hearts was a never-ending struggle. But it was time to bring up the second reason I'd ventured down here. The same one that brought me back every single day.

With a yawn, Raven lurched up into a sitting position. "Oh, hey." The volumes of books skewed over her blanket-covered feet shifted with her movement. More littered the Oriental rug—and was that an Ouija board partially covered by the mess? Her tired eyes shone with hope—as they always did. "Any news?"

The same question she asked me every day, because she hoped a vision would enlighten our mission of finding a way to resurrect Kendrick. Having gotten through the agony of seeing him lying back there, I let my mind finally wander back to what I'd seen.

A moment later, the sound of books being shoved to clear a space on the ottoman broke my silent contemplation. As did the closer proximity of his heated scent. The leather creaked as Ty sat, his glance at me fleeting, as if holding my gaze reminded him of my most recent attack. "What did you see?"

Biting my lip to force concentration, I saw how I'd stood with my twin by choice. How I'd unleashed my power to join with his. Pain flared through my body again now at the memory. I'd felt that kind of agony before. When my father had drained the life from my veins.

Death.

"Amelia?"

I shook away the fear of what my future held. Ty was waiting, and from the look in his eyes, he expected the worst. "I combined my power with Marcus's."

Ty's jaw parted before a deep frown scored his forehead. "By choice?"

Nod. "I didn't see why." And I wasn't about to spoil the cliffhanger of me dying because…it could have something to do with Kendrick and Marcus's claim that he has knowledge of how to resurrect the dead. From the straightening of Ty's lips, he thought so too.

"So that could be the key?" Raven's hands clasped together like her every prayer had just been answered.

Her excited desperation crippled me. The truth was… "I have no idea." I hadn't seen Kendrick in the vision, hadn't felt any link to him, or even that I was there in some way for him. But what else could force me to work with Marcus? I brushed my palm over a volume that was balanced on the arm of the sofa. *Spirit Bound.* The mental link I was supposed to share with Kendrick…theoretically, even in death. "What about you?

The light to her maroon-chipped irises vanished like a flare burning out. "Zilch. Most of these jabber on about origins and past spirit-gifted vampires. There's a lot about the ways the power can manifest. The visions. The blood bond. Not that any of that even comes close to what you've mastered. It's mostly just a bunch of hypothetical guesses without proof to back anything up."

"And connecting with the dead?" Ty sounded lifeless as he asked the question. He'd been there moments after Marcus had killed Kendrick, when Marcus had used my power against me to knock me out. He knew he'd been restored in large part because Kendrick had stood by me.

"It's all speculation. Some books claim it's possible, but I'll be effed if anyone bothered to document how."

Ty glared at the wonky book stacks next to him like he could make the right words appear. "So we're still at square one." With a deep breath, he withdrew a cancer stick from his pocket and lit the end. A habit he'd started after being damned, to simulate breathing—and remind him of who and what he'd been before being turned into a monster. "Troy and Marika have exhausted all the current leads." Smoke curled from his lips as he exhaled with irritation—because he was stuck here babysitting me instead of joining them in the takedowns?

Now with the alliance, his pack was residing in a house skirting our vampire community and liaising with other packs on damned info on a regular basis. The general vampire community was edgy at the idea that wolves were now allies, not enemies, but they had no choice. The decision had been made. Wolves were protected here.

"The few damned they uncovered fought to the death," Ty added. "None were caught."

And now for the action I'd planned even before learning of our dried-up leads. I pushed the book aside to perch on the sofa's arm. "Then it's time to break out the big guns."

"We're going after Marcus!" Raven almost squealed in anticipation, kicking the books off her feet to jump up. "What the heck are we waiting for?"

Though she had spent over a hundred years on Earth, ninety of them damned, she still had the personality and naiveté of the fifteen-year-old girl who was turned against her will.

Ty stood to his full six-foot-plus height, free fist curling like he was imagining choking my twin right then and there. With the horrible acts Ty had committed after being damned by Marcus, it was no mystery why he hated my twin so much. He'd led attacks on the vampires, he'd imprisoned and tormented me, he'd...*killed.* "We're not taking off after that asshole without a plan. That'll just lead to more blood on our hands."

Like it had when I'd gone after Ty alone and without a plan.

Even Raven's excitement wavered at that. Having been damned before I restored her, the girl had executed her share of havoc on the innocent.

"Ty's right." I eased off the sofa to gain distance from the living blood bags. They were no longer monsters, but there was one in me rearing to be freed. Ty's scent flared in anger, overpowering the smell of smoke, and his corded arms bulged. I froze like a deer in headlights for too many conflicting reasons. Hunger, the need to kill, and desire...the non-murderous kind.

Ty went statue-still too.

"Five against one." Raven seemed oblivious to the tension she was third-wheeling. "We'll find him and nail him to the wall. Literally. Then we'll torture 'how to bring Kendrick back' out of him."

Raven's *run into hell without any personal concern* shocked me out of my *kill or seduce* musings. I hadn't even known this girl existed for six months while Kendrick was befriending her...and lying to me. But I wasn't dwelling on that now. "Five against tens, twenties, maybe hundreds...we don't know." Even though all but a few damned at the hotel were killed, bar the ones that escaped, Marcus would have made more. The survivors would have been tasked to turn new recruits.

"But there haven't been many reported deaths." At my raised brow, Raven shrugged. "I eavesdropped on the last boardroom meeting."

"That doesn't mean he doesn't have numbers." Ty drew hard on his cig, holding his breath before blowing the white smoke out. Through his T-shirt, I saw his back muscles tense. "Marcus had other locations. Other hideouts for his army." With another long draw, the smoke exhaled with his hardened words. "I didn't care enough then to uncover the locations. My mind was set on one task."

Yeah. Follow Marcus's lead to get to me. I shoved my guilt to the back of my mind. There'd be time for that later after we'd exhausted every possibility to save Kendrick. "Damned horde or not, we need to find him first." And now the main reason I remained in this perpetual limbo of good and evil would be put to use.

"Our personal magnet is ready and waiting, right?" Raven raised her brows in question.

It was a long shot using my connection to any damned to seek them out in hopes of finding Marcus. But it was a helluva lot better than waiting around for a breakthrough. I needed to take action, to be of use for once. "We'll seek them out and torture his location from them."

"Then we need to organize our arsenal, inform The Seven, and set out." Ty ditched his cigarette butt in the tall potted plant against the wall and got to work texting Troy and Marika. His beta and third-in-command were up for anything.

Ty was both determined and unconcerned for good reason. The first came from years of ingrained training and discipline. And the second? With wolves now aiding vampires, the strict rules had been reassessed. All royals could now leave the compound at will. It wasn't necessarily any safer here than hiding out there.

Though I couldn't see much beyond the UV-tinted windows of this candlelit tomb, I sensed the closing in of imminent sunrise. *Damn transitioning sun allergy.* We'd have to wait until sundown, the equivalent of a new vampire day. I cleared my throat. "We'll leave first thing in the morning."

I TRIED and failed to ignore the steam wafting from the cracked bathroom door as I filled my utility belt with newly sharpened daggers and stakes from my weapon crates. Dressed in fitted black Under Armour, I was physically ready. Mentally? I was a mess. It was time for me to man up and make things happen. And here I was, thinking about the naked lycan in my shower.

The pattering water shut off after barely two minutes, and less than thirty seconds later Ty emerged into my bedroom. His focus was on his phone as he texted his pack and gathered up his utility belt from the nearest weapon crate.

Mine was on his bare chest—

Until his head snapped up, flicking wet drops from his satin-black hair. But his eyes didn't remain on me. His canines lengthened right as I registered a new scent and spun to the source.

Dorian was loitering in the foyer, one foot kicked over the other as if amused at the sight of us. Something in his pose and uninvolved expression sent a chill up my spine.

Ty tensed, beside me in a flash as his weapons jangled with the buckling of his belt.

"Dorian…what's up?" Lame.

We'd barely spoken since he'd delivered Marcus's note. He'd

made absolutely no mention of Vanessa, his girlfriend who I'd revealed had been murdered. Was he suffering PTSD? Or just that doped up on mind-bending compulsion?

Dorian's dark brows hiked and he smiled. "Unscheduled board-room meeting. Now."

Minutes later I had cleared the portrait-lined corridor, grand stairs, and main hall along with Dorian and Ty. On the walk down to the boardroom, I confirmed that Dorian was still heavily under Marcus's compulsion. His lack of any personality or emotion reminded me of how Vanessa had been with Ty. I shuddered at the memory of her end, of Ty pouncing and tearing into her throat. I wiped my sweating palms on my thighs, minding the weapons still strapped around my waist. That hadn't been the real Ty.

I entered the boardroom, getting a nod from Ty, who was dressed in a T-shirt and leather jacket, his feet still bare. His gaze slid from me to my brother and promised that he'd remain close by—to keep an eye on Dorian and to bust in if I turned ripper.

Dorian watched me, his smile beaming anticipation as the guards inside closed the double doors behind me—a new precaution since the damned had attacked and locked the royal guards outside less than a month ago.

The heartbeats of five living vampires echoed against the stone walls of the closed-off room. Having trained my lungs to cooperate —well mostly—I began the unneeded chore of passing air in and out while taking a moment to clear my head. Aftermarket sprinklers now lined the stone ceiling, and large fire extinguishers flanked the doors for backup in case flames were again used to trap the royals.

I imagined Ty barging in and cracking open my head with an extinguisher to stifle the little voice that whispered, *break their necks to stop the screams and you can drain them all.*

"Oh, good. We're all here." Already seated, Uriel's greeting around the tall back of her wooden throne brought me out of my thoughts.

Weapons clanking, I slid past the solid armrest into the Bathory throne beside her. I'd been called down here for a reason, but with my own safety threat to sort out, I took the lead and addressed the three waiting council members around the round marble slab. "We need a backup measure to protect our perimeter —more than the new patrol of lycans and guards. The wards aren't enough. Marcus has a way around them, which we've all witnessed." I didn't add that his in was likely Dorian. Keeping Marcus from getting to my brother would prevent any new compulsion. "We need to take action before a new attack is organized."

In her throne beside me, Uriel inclined her head. The red chips in her irises—left after I'd restored her from damned to living—glinted as they caught the wrought iron chandelier's light. In thanks for saving her, her support of me in this room had never gone astray. "What have you in mind, Amelia?"

"Electronic sensors set around the immediate boundary, along with surveillance cameras. More camera surveillance and a mix of trip-line sensors at three intervals beyond the wall, spanning out two miles in between. A protected security station inside the castle that is manned by guards twenty-four/seven. Oh, and alerts built into every sensor that will report back instantly if any are dismantled, damaged, or otherwise lost by the grid."

"I vote in agreement," Uriel voiced without question. "With a slight rise in human disappearances, it is important we take action."

So despite the lacking leads, there was "action." Which could force the damned to close in. Vampires were their staple diet. Humans were a less sought after backup. With vamps in hiding or here, the damned were sourcing the easiest alternative—for now.

Lady Rasputin, in a lavish gown as always, scoured my black attire with a pointed look. "And the sourcing of these electronics?"

"I know of an electronics boutique in Anchorage." I hiked my chin—and forced myself not to plug my nose. "They have everything we need."

"I can arrange a guard detail and retrieve the items myself," Lord Strigon volunteered.

"With that settled…" Lady Rasputin peered across the long expanse of the table. With a nod to the guards just inside the doors, the heavy slabs of wood were drawn apart. "You may enter."

Curving around the tall backrest of my throne I saw— "Dorian?" He didn't look blank like before, instead he seemed lucid. Like himself rather than a zombie delivering Marcus's will. My eyes questioned *is that you?* But out loud I said, "What's going on?"

Dorian spared me a smile before focusing on the others. "Thank you for agreeing to see me," he said with a bow, one hand slung across his front and the other curved behind his back. "Some important information has come to my attention."

"That is why we have agreed to this unorthodox meeting." Lady Rasputin sounded as bored as she looked.

Right, I'd forgotten about the unscheduled part of this meeting. Hadn't thought for a second it had anything to do with my brother. My *what the hell?* expression got no response from Dorian.

"So this big news?" Strigon's brows rose. "Let's have it."

Dorian took a few steps closer, standing behind Marcus's old throne. The one my twin had sat in before he exposed himself as the damned commander.

A sense of dread filled the pit of my stomach. I knew what was about to be unearthed from secret. "Dorian—"

"*I* am the last Vladimir." His voice was clear, unwavering, and with no indecision. "The true heir to this throne. The child the lady birthed seventeen years ago was me. Marcus is an imposter. A wolf in sheep's clothing, even more than being the evil manipulator of the damned. He's a Bathory. Amelia's true twin and the traitor, Caius's son."

I shot up and forced Dorian back toward the tall Gothic windows by his arm. Fear of my secrets coming to light mingled with my instinct to solve problems with my fangs. *The RVC can't react if they're dead.*

My voice was a low hiss through clenched teeth and extending fangs. "Why are you doing this? Now? Here? Is *he* making you?"

Dorian shook his head, his chocolate-brown hair shifting with the movement. His hands shot up in surrender and his voice was a whisper. "No. The opposite. Marcus stopped me from wanting to come forth back when you told me. That compulsion's worn off now."

But I'd been with Marcus at *Bite* when we'd confronted Dorian. How had he compelled my brother without me knowing? Was this a ploy too? His voice was normal, clear, unzombied. His unmasked expression proved that he knew where he was and what he was doing. "But you wanted nothing to do with being a Vladimir. You didn't want to be restricted or caged."

"You know me, Amelia. I never shy away from a challenge."

"Ah hem."

With a genuine smile from Dorian, one I hadn't seen since before I took off after Ty, I released his arm and faced the others.

"Amelia, is Dorian's claim incorrect?" Uriel questioned, curious more than anything.

I wasn't sure if this was him or Marcus pulling the strings, but the cat was out of the bag. Denying would only lead to investigation. "It's true. At least I think it is. I saw Caius switch Lady Vladimir's dark-haired baby for a blond one. One he called 'my son.' "

"He was there during the birth," Uriel admitted.

"The late lord requested his presence with his wife after being called away last minute on a damned threat in Russia," Lord Strigon added.

Lady Rasputin said nothing, but eyed Dorian and me with suspicion, one after the other. "You saw this in a vision?"

Dorian filled in the blanks before I could backpedal. "One she had before Marcus was even outed as the damned commander."

My head snapped sideways to stare at my brother. "I—I—I didn't see if the other baby survived."

Dorian was all cool, calm, and collected. "I realize we should have come forward sooner, but we want to set things straight. We want to prove our suspicion."

"How?" Uriel looked back and forth between us.

Dorian was all smiles as he toyed with the carved edge of the throne and delivered his answer. "Amelia can use touch to see the events from the source—Caius."

"And we should simply trust this sudden new proof?" Rasputin demanded, grasping her glass to take a sip of thick blood.

I remained mute, fear of conjuring a vision and my resulting hunger making my mind race. Not to mention Dorian's friend/foe actions.

"Don't take our word for it." Dorian shrugged. "Exhume my late father. His blood won't lie. But at least find out if there's any need to go to that extent first."

"I see no harm," Strigon surprised me by saying. "If we're all in agreement?"

There was a confirming nod from Uriel, and then Rasputin who waved a hand at the guards. "Escort the traitor here."

As the guards left, Ty strode in, eyeing Dorian as he flanked my side. "Don't worry. I'm right here." His hand touched the small of my back. With his lycan hearing, he knew exactly what was minutes away from happening. "And I'm not going anywhere."

My fake breathing threatened to turn to hyperventilation. If I was on the verge of losing it, or if my transitioning traits began to show, he'd take action to keep the possible victims alive. But I knew what was coming and I knew what my reaction would be. Refreshed starvation. I brushed my hand past the stake at his waist, my pleading eyes meeting his. "Keep me in check."

"This is a private meeting," Lady Rasputin all but barked as Ty's jaw clenched. Of course she had an issue with a lycan being in her space.

Ty, however, made no apology. He made no move to leave as he addressed the others. "I will not leave Amelia unguarded if the traitor is being brought here."

More like them unguarded with the hunger-stirring vision I was being forced to conjure.

Lord Strigon stroked his goateed chin in contemplation. "From the restored damned who tried to infect her after setting the damned on us all. Funny how allies can shift."

Ty flinched, and I knew it was because he had succeeded in infecting me. Guilt had his gaze dropping and fists clenching. A low rumble rose up his throat.

"And now he's our ally, among the other wolves," Uriel added, once again the voice of reason and understanding.

The next few minutes passed, Ty keeping Dorian in sight and the others debating the wolf's presence. The vote tied as the guards returned, forcing Caius through the open doors. Shackles with a connecting chain joined his wrists, but his feet were unrestrained. After surrendering to be captured and after I'd restored him, they'd minimized his security measures.

"My daughter!" The old vampire's brows shot up almost into his hairline. "You made it out alive." His expression of what seemed to be shocked relief twisted into distaste. "And with the *wolf*."

He hadn't known the outcome of the attack at the damned hotel? Though clearly he'd known I was in danger. "I did."

Caius made no other mention of Ty, and I had a feeling he was holding back. Instead, he regarded me with curiosity, patting down his rag-reduced suit as if trying to make himself presentable. "My dear, Amelia. It is truly a blessing to see you." Like they didn't even exist, he spared no glance at the other council members. And was that a hint of gratitude mixed with relief in his dull gray eyes? "To what do I owe this pleasure?"

"You are here as a conduit." Uriel rose from her throne to close the space between them. "Unless you'd like to reveal who Dorian Lamont really is?"

"Even if I wanted to…" Caius addressed me alone, a clear warning in his eyes. "I am not free to part with those words."

Marcus had compelled him to keep quiet on anything relating to him and being the damned commander, which clearly included his true identity. But was that warning for my benefit, or his?

"Not that your words would be taken as gospel." Lady Rasputin blew air through her nose.

Uriel spoke before any more snide could pass the eldest royal's lips. "Are you ready, Oracle?"

The beat of my heart chose that moment to drop fractionally. Undetectable to the other members, but a warning I'd learned to notice. Ty's supplied blood was beginning to wear off. Bringing on a vision would speed up the process, petering the organ out to silence again. And then my sinister need to kill would redouble with a vengeance. The thick veins that hid beneath my skin would return. I groped for control as I nodded to the waiting royals and tugged on Ty's sleeve. "Give me your jacket."

Whipping it off to drape around my shoulders, Ty leveled a glare around the table that dared anyone to challenge him. "One vision. One confirmation. Then we're out. No questions. No conversation."

Eyebrows rose at the alpha's no-nonsense conditions, but no one argued. Even Caius seemed to regard my protector with respect. He held out his hand, hanging chains jangling in response. "Ready when you are, my dear."

With a nod from Ty, the guards tightened their hold on my father's arms. I approached, getting close enough to reach out and touch him. Despite our rocky history—and the fact that he'd tried to kill me—I no longer held any fear for the old man before me. Yet as I cupped my palm over his weathered, dirty hand, I hesitated. I certainly wasn't a pro, and I didn't want to risk bringing on the wrong vision. "Dorian, I need you too. It'll help." I hoped. I was kind of winging it. I had never brought a vision on using two people before.

Dorian regarded me with suspicion then shrugged to take my hand. "Do your worst, Sis."

With Ty guarding, the RVC watching, and my father and Dorian to either side of me, my lids slid shut. The dark void rushed in and split from the center in a straight line, like a theater curtain parting to reveal the action on the silver screen.

Inside the Alaskan cabin I'd grown up in, my mother held a baby in her arms as tears tracked down her splotchy face. Her eyes were vampire silver-blue but bloodshot. Her body trembled so badly, her green armchair shook along with her. "Where is my son? I need my son."

Caius knelt before her, desperation across his tired face. "You have no son. You only had one baby. A precious girl."

"No, no, no!" She shook her head, disheveled blond hair flying back and forth. "You're lying. You took him. Bring me my son!"

The channel switched.

Caius entered the Bathory suite, going to the bedroom. His bedroom, decked out with dark wood and clothed antique furnishings. A duffel bag was placed on the bed and the zipper parted. A dark-haired baby was extracted. With pale ivory skin, the tiny chest inflated and deflated with breath. The baby Caius had taken from Lady Vladimir had survived. But why wasn't he awake and crying? "She needs you, boy. Lamayli needs a son. I will take you to her soon…before the anesthetic wears off." He went to the walk-in wardrobe and, when he came out, that blond baby I'd seem him swap was in his arms. "This is the only way you will be raised as my own. Ready, my son?"

Switch.

Caius walked through the door to the cabin, stomping snow from his boots. In his arms the tiny bundle was beginning to wriggle, waking as if for the first time. When he reached the lounge room's entrance, those little lungs sucked in deep and let out a wail.

Across the room, still in her green armchair, Mom's drooped head snapped upright. Even though she'd been asleep, I was cradled in her arm. Her puffy eyes grew wide at the ongoing cry. "My *son?*" she barely managed to choke.

Caius came to her, his eyes locking on hers as he began lowering the wrapped bundle. "This is your son, Dorian. Your perfect dark-haired boy."

I growled and snatched my hands away as the last of my vision vanished quick as a flash. Red invaded my sight and as I spun towards Ty, I saw black veins forking past the cuff of Ty's leather jacket I wore. There was the sound of chains as Caius was pulled back by the guards, and footsteps as Dorian back-stepped to the table. And beating hearts all around, pumping fresh, intoxicating blood.

How long does it take to drain a body? I dug my nails into Ty's side. *So much to do…so little time.*

"Rein it in." Ty's body tensed but he didn't jerk or restrain me.

Grinding my molars together, I managed only a few words as Ty kept me facing away from prying eyes. "It's…true. Caius switched Marcus…for Dorian. He's the true Vladimir."

Ty's strong arms caught me and held me against his broad chest. "I have to get her recovered." He didn't ask permission. And he didn't wait for any objections. Instead, I felt him swiftly move toward the double doors, knowing I was about to lose it. At him. Knowing those black veins would be tracking up my neck as my heart fought its last dying beats.

"Which makes Marcus your twin," I barely heard Lady Rasputin spit over the blood rushing through my ears. "Until this is proven, I vote the relevant parties remain on grounds."

Still clinging to Ty's side, my nostrils flared and my fangs throbbed. I was so tempted to take her out first. And yet some small part of me knew I needed to shut those impulses down. "Get me out of here," I rasped as the vote was affirmed. The rosy haze to my sight turned a deeper shade of crimson, and I released one set of nails to touch the stake I'd returned to him. I hissed at the sting of silver contact. "Or I'll stake myself."

CHAPTER 3

"No you won't." Ty caught my wrist as the words escaped his mouth in a growl. He left my embedded nails in place as he forced me past the guards. Mounting the grand stairs, his nostrils flared as his hold on me tightened. He mumbled as he picked up speed down the corridor toward my suite, "Guess our mission's on hold…for now."

Though I heard the words over the rush of his racing pulse, I couldn't care less. The slamming of my door had my mind on a one-track loop of blood, death and…*lust.* God, I wanted him. Blood, sweat, and tears. I wanted to touch him, to dig my nails in deeper, to scour his flesh, to strike with my fangs, to trap his body with my own…and let all my pent-up energy go in an uninhibited primal rush.

The tight hold around me released. Now in the lounge, Ty's stare was dangerous in the moonlit room. "You need to *refuel.*" As my reddening sight fell to his neck, a rumble vibrated up his throat. Had Ty's body inched closer? His hot breath ruffled my lashes.

Spellbound, I wrapped my hand around his throat. My thumb curled over his jugular, my fingers falling along the crook of his collarbone.

Ty recaptured my wrist, stalling my parting mouth as I leaned in. "*Amelia*." The "stop" was unspoken.

"Your smell…" I inhaled deeply, taking in all I could of him. A mix of the old and new: rich peppery blood and that musky scent that clung to his V-neck. Memories of Ty damned and using my attraction for him against me rushed to the forefront of my mind. How he'd pressed his body into mine. How he'd kissed me hard and soft. How he'd trailed his fangs down my body. How he'd broken my skin to taste—more than just my blood.

Kendrick's.

My clinging fingers splayed out straight, no longer gripping his jugular. I turned my head away. My fangs pressed into my lips with throbbing need as I clamped my jaw shut. "Sorry."

Ty released my wrist and backed away, wary eyes following my every move. "Me too."

Ouch.

Tightening every muscle in my body, I forced myself to perch on the arm of the couch. I tracked his movement as he went to the cabinet below the TV. I didn't need X-ray vision to know there were veins tracing up my arms and legs beneath my jeans and Ty's jacket. Those black tracks, like roots under my skin, almost hummed as they grew. Ty's back was to me, the muscular build of him clear even through the layers of his clothing. Tightness up his neck hinted at the readiness of his whole body. The twitch of his ears was proof enough that he was tracking any sudden movement I might make. A clink sounded, followed by an increase in the scent of his blood—blood that regenerated super fast due to his hybrid, restored-damned DNA. I clutched the armrest, nails slicing small crescents into the material. That unnatural filter over my vision intensified as my hunger peaked. My heartbeat failed. Dead as a doornail.

Looks good in red. Doesn't he?

As I thought *hell, yes*, I imagined how red Ty could become. A deep nick into the right arteries and a whole lotta red would come pouring out. Enough to paint every inch of him, and then extra to lick off…for the fun of it.

"Amelia?"

I blinked slowly, then flinched when I registered Ty standing right before me. So close.

His narrowed stare seemed to read my devious thoughts, while the topped glass he held made my mouth water. But he didn't hold it up for me to take. "No more visions."

I wondered how much would spill if I snatched the crystal—but if I spilled any, I could pounce on the living source to replace—"What?"

Ty stepped back with the glass. "It's too dangerous. You know it is."

His unwavering eyes, with their sun-speckled ocean coloring, said the words that didn't pass his lips, words I spoke for him: "Too dangerous for you and every living being within a mile's radius of me."

Ty bared elongating fangs and canines—the dental enhancements that marked him as a rare hybrid glinting as the dim moonlight grew with shifting clouds. "Too dangerous for you." His free fist clenched. "We both know what they do to what they fear."

My hunger was momentarily distracted. Ty was talking about my race's deadly actions, which had killed his grandfather and made the wolves our enemies. The feud had started over fear of what his grandfather had done—love and impregnate a lycan. Ty's grandmother.

We'd come so far since those long-ago centuries, but I couldn't voice a reply as my gut suddenly squeezed with hunger. I slid off the couch and crept forward. "I can't control my visions," I hissed.

Ty was in front of me in a flash, that full glass still held away from me. His arm came up horizontally, pressing me back. "Not the unexpected ones, but the conjured ones…" His chin jutted and a muscle ticked in his jaw. He held the glass closer, just out of my reach. "You can't bring any on until Marcus is stopped and you're restored. Agree to this, or I'm out."

I didn't want to agree. My visions could help locate Marcus and stop him. Not that they had, yet. They could give us insight to his plans and incoming dangers. But without Ty as my donor, I'd have no option but to restore myself—and lose my ability to locate the damned. Even as I grappled with my options, I realized I was clutching Ty's arm. Blood welled around my nails and, as my mouth opened with a hiss, my tongue traveled over my lower lip. *Strike, taste, kill.*

Ty tore his arm from my grasp. And as he held the blood-filled glass a fraction closer, I reined in the shred of conscience I had left to save me from going for the kill. "You win."

Ty exhaled a long breath through his nose. He flipped his phone from his jeans. "I'll inform the pack and Raven of the setback." His nostrils flared as he held out the glass. "Take it."

Those two simple words struck me like a truck as I took the glass and downed the offering and my heart pounded back to life. The same words Kendrick had said to me, in this very room after he'd become my donor.

In that not-so-long-ago moment, I'd succumbed to my mixed feelings for my best friend. Before believing Ty was truly gone. I'd kissed Kendrick back, my tongue licking over his. He'd tasted like…home.

Now he was dead.

Ty was alive.

With me in transition, his blood was now keeping me in line. Just. But I'd moved on with Kendrick. Forged something new with him that had forever changed our friendship when I should have known better than to ever believe Ty was 'gone.'

I gritted my teeth, my hand around the crystal squeezing harder and harder. The fortuneteller had lied to me.

"What is it?" Ty hung up and replaced the phone in his pocket. "More?" He reached out to collect the empty glass as it shattered in my palm.

"No," I hissed as I recalled standing behind that star-embossed curtain in a black room lit by dozens of candles. Madam Rosalie's beady eyes had glanced from Kendrick to me—with empathy. *"The boy you love…he no longer exists."*

I shook my head and removed Ty's jacket, throwing it at him as I slumped back onto the couch's armrest. "Madam Rosalie lied about you being alive. Later, she said restoring you would trigger a chain reaction. And something about a cost to people in the crossfire."

"So many died during the hotel battle." That muscle ticked in Ty's jaw. Did he blame the deaths of those people, and all the others he'd hurt or let be hurt while he was damned, solely on himself?

"No. That's not it." That slide of eye from the old woman to Kendrick then me had been a clue. Ty's blood gurgled in my gut, churning with suspicion. "She knows something about Kendrick. And she's going to tell us, whether she likes it or not."

I pulled my iPhone out of my back pocket, ready for my thumbs to do the walking. Sudden fear of what Madam Rosalie had withheld made me stop dead as my heart suicide-jumped into my gut. Was Kendrick running out of time? Was there a limit to this possible resurrection that I didn't even know about? I shuddered at the thought and blinked back bloody tears to thumb the screen.

Ring. Ring. Ring.

The incessant sound went on. Madam Rosalie didn't pick up. Neither did voicemail. "Dammit!"

"No answer?" Ty had taken up residence on the wing chair, tapping a scarred hand over his knee. For once he wasn't watching me with that waiting readiness. Like he could sense as I paced and redialed by the moonlight terrace doors that I wasn't a 'killer' threat right now. Instead, his jaw was jutting and slightly off-center. Deep in thought?

Unlike last time, I couldn't summon her if she wouldn't pick up her damn phone. As the line rang out again, I resisted the need to crush the rectangular disk. "We'll need to go to her." I'd been to her shop once before. With Kendrick. My best friend, who'd always had my back, and died after helping rescue the guy he'd battled my heart for. *Life comes at a price.* That horrible inner voice was right. Ty had been brought back to life. Now Kendrick's heart was still. The world found balance in everything. Life and death were the tipping scales. "She's in Boston."

"Amelia…" His deep-in-thought expression turned to contemplation as Ty studied me from head to toe. "We're grounded, remember?"

"Shit." Damn RVC and their voting power.

Ty folded his jacket over the armrest, got up, and skirted the coffee table. "Besides, it's too far. Too dangerous. And it's not—"

Anger spiked in my veins—at them, at him, at myself. "Because I'm a freaking liability?"

"What are you two doing here?" The unexpected frail voice shut me up fast. "Where did you come from?"

I spun at the sound, whirling so fast my surroundings blurred. There was no one but Ty and me here. "Did you hear that?"

The sight of Ty made me freeze. He was rigidly still, black-veined arms rippled with muscle. Strain overcame his face that pinched deeper before his lids flung open…burnt gold. "It's not necessary to travel," he grated between clenched teeth.

"You're not really here."

I balked at the flickering figure who suddenly filled the wing chair Ty had left his jacket draped over.

Madam Rosalie searched the lounge frantically—and froze at the sight of us. "The boy…you succeeded." Her eyes boggled at our black attire and the deadly silver weapons strung around our hips. Her bony fingers with their many rings clutched the armrests. "What have you let him do to me?"

"Amelia, I've never done one like this before. Not with two people." Ty grimaced, his molars grinding audibly. "I can't keep it going for long."

I knew then what was happening and how the fortuneteller was suddenly here. "A dreamscape. How? You've never even met her—"

"I saw her," Ty grated. "At the psychic fair. I followed you after I…I just needed to make sure you were okay."

After he'd transformed and accidentally cut me with his sharp wolf claws. I absently touched the long scars on my non-burned arm as I marveled at Ty's power. But I couldn't dwell on it. Not now. Time was precious. "You're asleep," I addressed the old woman. "As soon as we're gone, you'll wake up. And if you cooperate, that'll be sooner rather than later."

"What do you want to know?" Fear now gone, Madam Rosalie's stare challenged me. She was far from clueless. But she was clearly going to make me work for her words.

"You knew Kendrick was going to die. You saw it happen when I visited your shop."

"Making this boy's heart beat triggered a chain reaction of events. Crossfire was and is inevitable."

That was the closest I was going to get to a 'yes.' "Why the hell didn't you warn me?"

"It would not have changed the outcome. Life and death is a balance." I'd thought the same. "Though you should know, Amelia, the path is not complete. Others hold the possible future of the lost in their hands. You have seen part of the outcome, have you not?"

"What's she talking about?" Ty snapped, his eyes squinting even further.

"Combining my power with Marcus, right?" After her cryptic and frustrating words, a sly nod was returned. So it did have something to do with Kendrick. I knelt before her and gathered up her thin-skinned hands. Without a scent to smell or even a pulse to hear, she wasn't a temptation. Ty was in control of this dream…for now. "Is that what I need to do to bring Kendrick back? Is it even possible?"

"Possible?" Madam Rosalie glanced out at the rising moon. "I believe it is possible. Though I cannot see the how of it, or even if it ever happens. I do know, however, that when life and death are in question, a great sacrifice must be paid. There are no refunds."

I shot a glance at Ty, whose tan skin had begun to pale. Hands planted into the wall above the long cabinet, his claws scraped into the stone. His legs were shaking.

"You can reach him."

My attention snapped back to the old woman. "Kendrick? Like talk to him?" True hope soared in me for the first time since Kendrick's death. I was spirit gifted, which included the power to see and speak with the dead. Something I'd never thought I'd ever want. But now? This old woman was claiming I could connect with Kendrick…see him, hear him…after all the times I'd tried and failed. "Tell me how."

Madam Rosalie's form flickered, and she began to bleed color in a counterclockwise swipe.

"Amelia…I…can't." The dreamscape was failing. Ty was—*oh crap*—I rushed to catch him as he fell to his knees and the merry-go-round spectacle cranked up to full speed.

That crackly voice reached us through the spinning vortex as the woman's form sucked in on itself. *"Look for words that cannot be spoken."*

Draped over my lap, the weapons around Ty's waist that dug into me were no deterrent. My focus was set as I picked up his scent mixed with burned tobacco. I couldn't look away from Ty's face. Lids closed, lips parted. All I needed was to add a shitload of blood to turn us in the here and now into a long-ago memory. When Ty had died in my arms at the Portsmouth Vampire Council. *That could easily be fixed.* "Shut up!" I spat at my inner voice. But even as I hissed my disgust, I couldn't help envisioning how easy it would be to take him like this. To sink my fangs in deep and drink my fill… until that irregular lycan heart gave out. For the second time. Not that I was hungry, but easy prey…

I licked my bottom lip.

You're not a monster.

I jerked at the unexpected words, head snapping up and eyes darting to find the source. Even in the lacking light, my transition senses linked every shadow back to its origin. The lounge, bedroom, and foyer were clear, only furniture filling those spaces. The main door was shut. And I hadn't heard those words, had I? Split personality much? Unless…

My senses heightened further. *Tasty blood, steady pulse—up for the taking.*

As my need to kill resurfaced, I ignored the beat of my heart. Minding the silver chain that disappeared below Ty's V-neck where those black veins grew darker, I inched closer, baring my fangs. But I couldn't forget those words or the sense of right and wrong that was still welling up inside of me. "I won't hurt you," I heard myself say as my fangs throbbed in protest. "I…" I forced my back to straighten, to put distance between my ready lips and Ty's hot flesh. "I…won't."

Ty's lids cracked opened then, thin slits revealing red-veined whites. "I knew you could resist." His voice was raspy; the smile across his perfect lips was full of pride.

"You were testing me?"

Ty lurched upright, abs flexing as he moved off my lap. Positioned between the coffee table and cabinet, he levered one hand back onto the rug and shrugged. "You're not the monster you think you are. No matter what happens, what you think, I know it's true. There's still so much of *you,* the real *you* in there."

He placed his free hand over my heart. So close to the place he'd bitten and drawn my blood from. The memory of that intimate dreamscape made me shudder with hunger and disgust at the same time. Even without being fully turned, I was as bad as the creature I'd left him to be. I opened my mouth to argue against his unwarranted belief in me—when a light bulb went off in my head. "I'm not a monster."

"Amelia, you're…wait, what?"

"When I thought you were passed out." *And I imagined making you bloody*, I thought but didn't say. Propping my elbows back, I hoisted myself up onto the couch to put some separation between my fangs and his veins. I grabbed the pillow Ty hardly used and clung to it to give my hands something other than flesh to focus on. "I…I heard—well, not a voice." Which was true. I'd felt the words rather than heard them. There'd been no assignable accent, age, or even gender. Now I knew the truth. "I felt those words. Inside of me. Like they were my own, but not. Like they were spoken *to* me."

Ty almost groaned as he got up, his muscles twitching and weapons clanking at the strain.

He had really drained himself bringing that dreamscape on with two people simultaneously. Still his power had grown while he was damned. I'd seen the past proof when he'd rendered me suddenly unconscious without me even knowing. When he'd created a sub-reality to taunt me in. To tempt me.

That was behind us now. "I didn't know you could do that," I said quietly. "The dreamscape. Not like that."

Ty's maroon-chipped gaze darkened as he went to the cabinet. One hunting boot caught on the rug and forced him to stumble the rest of the way. "I learned to test my limits when I was damned," he said as he rebalanced.

He filled two glasses with the stocked human blood in the mini fridge. Returning with calculated strides, he handed me one. Despite my hunger, my heart was still animated. I didn't need to tap Ty. But being a hybrid—and after feeding me, followed by that dreamscape —he clearly needed the boost.

"The voice." Looking down at me, the shadows under his eyes made it look like he'd been awake for weeks. Well, I guess that was pretty much true, with him keeping a constant eye on me. But they were worse since his impromptu dreamscape. "You think it's Kendrick, don't you? Talking inside your head?"

"Talking inside whose head?" Raven called as she rushed in from the main door without knocking. With her utility belt brimming, she was armed and ready. "What is going on here? Aren't we taking off?"

"I didn't get around to calling Raven after Troy," Ty answered before I could ask.

As he went on to fill her in, I couldn't help thinking back to all the conversations I'd had with Kendrick through our connected minds when he was alive. We were blood bound. Even in death. I hadn't felt his presence since then—had assumed he'd been gone in every sense, especially since he hadn't answered me any of the times I'd tried to talk to him. But had I been wrong? Shortly after waking and remembering Kendrick had died, I'd been creeping like a lion toward the main door—and the guards outside with their veins full of lifeblood. A sudden image of Kendrick's face had flashed in my mind, spine jutting out and purple welts twisted sideways. That unexplained image had stopped my hunt in that moment. Then I'd attacked my unsuspecting Mom with the intent to drain her to death. I almost had. Until unspoken words, ones that had come from somewhere deep down inside of me had risen. *Don't give in to the monster.* I'd thought that a glimmer of my conscience had shone through. But what if it wasn't my conscience?

"Amelia, hello?" Raven waved a black-veined hand right in front of my face. "What do you think? Is Kendrick talking to you?"

Still holding the full glass, I adjusted my grip before I spilled it down my tank. I wasn't one hundred percent sure. Far from it. But if I were going to believe in something, it would be this. "Yeah. I think he is."

"So talk to him already." Raven threw her hands up. "Find out if he's okay. Ask him what the heck we're supposed to do to save him."

I threw back the glass of human blood. Yuck, dead blood. The daunting task of trying to communicate with Kendrick when all previous attempts had failed felt like I was planning to pull off the impossible. "It's not that easy." I discarded the empty glass.

"Because you've already tried and failed." Ty's face was a mask of hidden feelings. A puzzle I couldn't decipher. We hadn't talked about Kendrick since his death, but with how closely Ty watched me, he'd have clued in if I'd been able to bridge that ghost communication gap.

"Yeah." I'd pleaded for Kendrick after Marcus snapped his neck. Supported his head and pressed my ear to his chest. There'd been no rise and fall of breath. No heartbeat. No verbal response. Bloody tears welled at the memory while an internal fight rose up. I'd given up on Ty, and I wouldn't do the same for Kendrick. I was spirit gifted, for God's sake. Bound in blood by body and soul, in life *and* death.

I hurdled the back of the couch and paced to the terrace doors. "Look, I don't think this'll work. It hasn't before now. But I'll try." Facing the glass, I glanced out at the night-darkened gardens, seeing the fountain to my far left. Where his mother had died. An ache took up residence in my chest, remembering the pain he'd felt from that loss. *Kendrick...are you there, somewhere?* Long seconds dragged on with no response. *I need you. Please.* Nothing. *We want to help you.* Nothing. I pressed the heel of my palms over my sockets, bearing down. *Speak to me. Say anything. Say you hate me. That it's my fault you're dead. Yell at me. I don't care. I can take it. Just say...something.*

Nothing.

As every pleading word registered in my mind, nothing was returned. I faced Ty and Raven. "I need some time...alone."

Raven nodded and made for the door, but Ty hesitated. With one hand in his pocket, he eventually nodded, too. "Okay." Then he was gone.

I spent the rest of the day between meetings and training trying to bridge our spiritual gap. When I slipped silently back into my suite almost ten hours later, I leaned into the door, letting my head fall back on the carved wood. Seven in the evening with sunrise imminent in the next hour. And I had jack shit to show for it. I was alone in body and mind. Visiting every location within the Armaya's imprisoning walls to trigger a reaction had done nothing but exhaust me.

All those times he'd shut me out when alive…was Kendrick doing the same now? Was this silence a big stuck up middle finger?

Was it my answer?

The sound of the mini fridge opening pulled me out of my depressed thoughts. I trudged into the lounge, my hold on the box under my arm tightening.

Ty was on the couch, his chin in his hand and elbow resting on the armrest. His eyes were tired but alert. He'd heard me come in. Been waiting since I'd taken off to visit Kendrick in the Baldassare tomb. He pulled his other hand from his pocket, seeming confident in my control as he flicked a cigarette from the soft pack he held. "How'd it go?"

The clink of glass on glass stalled my reply as Raven twisted up from her crouch before the fridge. Her hopeful expression fell at the sight of me, while I registered what she held in her hands. A bottle topped with blood. But it wasn't just any regular glass bottle like all the ones our community was stocked with. This one was more cylinder shaped—to prevent knocking and breaking when he'd carried them in his backpack, for me. "You got nothing?"

Raven lifted the bottle towards her lips and I dropped the box to shoot right before her. I shoved her as I snatched the greatest link I had to Kendrick back. "What the hell is wrong with—"

Hot flesh clamped around my neck. Ty's arm, and he was pulling me back as Raven stumbled, her backside hitting the cabinet. "Sorry, I should have known." His breath was hot in my ear. "Just rein it in. I know you can."

Given my nature, his assumption was more than fair. Still, I couldn't deny the sting. "I'm not hungry." Ty stalled when I tapped on his arm rather than clawing into it. His hold released. "Raven, I… you were going to drink *his* blood. The last bottle."

"Oh, shit." The shock on her face melted into understanding. "I didn't realize." Then her focus zoned in on something behind me. "Where did you get that?"

I took the cap from her extended hand and secured it on the bottle before turning around. The cardboard box I'd dropped had cracked open on impact. A folded board stuck out, made of varying shades of brown with black lettering. "I saw it yesterday in the tomb. Have you been using it?"

Satisfied I wasn't a threat, Ty slouched into the wing chair and lit up a smoke.

I knelt by the fridge, replacing the last bottle of Kendrick's blood right in the back. Unlike human blood, his, being pure, wouldn't go bad if kept out, and if I ever planned on drinking it, chilled after dropping from body temp was best. But no one would ever get to drink this. The last thing I had of him.

"I've been trying to connect with Kendrick myself," Raven said, her gentle steps quiet as she moved to pick up the contents. "It didn't work, you know."

I swiveled back upright, putting all my remaining faith in my next words. "Maybe it will now."

Raven's youthful voice radiated hope. "You're not giving up?"

"Never." Kendrick could hate me all he wanted. He was dead because Ty had lived. That I now knew for sure. Though indirect, Madam Rosalie had confirmed it. Chain reaction. Crossfire. Game.

Set. Match. But I'd never give up in this. Whatever it took, I'd find a way to reach him…to bring him back. I'd do anything.

I had to.

Raven placed the cardboard box on the coffee table. "You're all spirit gifted and shit, but maybe we need to open a door. From the living to the dead."

"You're seriously going to use that thing?" Ty rested his lit cig in the potted plant on the table and donned his leather jacket. "An Ouija board. Really?"

"You got a better idea, half-breed?" Raven knelt and lifted the lid, setting up the board and that heart-shaped piece of wood with a glass circle at the pointed end. She picked up a white candle and held it out to Ty. "Light?"

I didn't question it as Ty lit the wick before pocketing his Zippo and reclaiming his cigarette. After all my failed attempts so far, I'd go skydiving if I thought it'd help. Without warning, I shuddered at the thought of using the board. The hairs across my nape stood to attention. Was it suddenly cold in here? "It's worth a try."

"Then let's go."

Raven moved in closer, but Ty stayed put. "I'll keep watch from back here." Superstitious? I'd never expected him to be. Although, after losing his mother to a violent death, maybe he feared connecting with her after all this time.

I knelt beside the coffee table and propped my arm on the white-painted top.

"Put two fingers on the planchette," Raven said as she put hers on the heart-shaped wood and waited for me to do the same.

"Now what?"

"I've seen this in that movie, *What Lies Beneath.* Michelle Pfeiffer, Harrison Ford, and a ghost hell-bent on unearthing the truth. It's my fav post-damned movie."

One she'd watched with Kendrick between snowboarding vids? I instantly chastised my petty jealousy. This wasn't the time or the place.

Raven cleared her throat and closed her eyes. "We wish to commune with the dead. With the spirit of Kendrick Baldassare. Kendrick, can you hear us?"

Deafening silence answered back, interrupted only by the sound of my blood rushing in my ears. "Kendrick, are you there?"

Still nothing. More questions were fired from Raven, asking where he was, if he was okay, if he could 'give us a sign.' There was no response.

My voice made another appearance as disappointment rained on me like a cloud. "How can we help you? Kendrick, how can we bring you back?"

As silence stretched on, all I could hear was our heartbeats, the guards' outside my suite, and the breath that passed through Ty's and Raven's lips. Raven's was shallow, desperate and waiting. Ty's was steady, resigned to the failure of our task.

A distinct tingle vibrated from my two fingers connected to the planchette. Like an electric wave, it swam up my arm to my shoulder then struck into my heart.

The planchette shifted.

It jerked left then right, making Raven gasp. Ty sat up straight at the sound. "What is it?"

Frozen in disbelief, I stared at our pale fingers on the disk. "It moved—"

The planchette shifted again, cutting me off. And this time I felt something else—the weight of a broad hand holding mine, keeping my connection to the disk. On a steady crawl, it slid across the board, stopping briefly with the round glass over a single letter before moving on. L…E…A…V…E… A vivid flash of the moment

Marcus ripped Kendrick's head sideways stole into my mind, neck twisting, spine cracking. M…E…

"Are you doing this?" Raven sounded half terrified and half excited.

I felt sick to my stomach. And not just from the reenactment, but rather from morbid anticipation of the next word and who was delivering it. Kendrick. No other spirit would have brought on that one, horrible memory. "Tell me you are."

"No way."

The planchette didn't stop its course. D…E…A…D…

Ty crept forward, squatting beside the table as the disk stopped. "Leave me dead. Why would he say that?"

Before I could utter a word the planchette shot out from under our fingers down over the GOODBYE—

The terrace doors flung open, closed drapes flapping in a sudden whipping breeze. Raven cried out as I tipped back, my arm knocking the lit candle off the table.

Then the wind stopped.

I went to rise but Ty grasped my scarred forearm to haul me up and away from where I'd fallen back. He pointed down. "Look."

I couldn't help but do so as Raven slowly rose too. The hot candle wax had splattered across the dark stone to form messy white letters.

"Or you will be?" That sick feeling in my gut intensified. "Will be what?"

Raven's voice was hollow. "If Kendrick lives again—one of us will die."

CHAPTER 4

"You're honestly going to prove that hocus pocus wrong?" From the wing chair, Ty flung a thick volume out across the coffee table. One boot was kicked out onto a wonky stack, the matching one swung over the first. The unlit cigarette he held made it to his mouth again, before being swiped back out. "Go to whatever lengths, risk your life, to maybe bring him back."

I couldn't hide my cringe at his spat words. After a day of research—and finding nothing much on the resurrection front—Ty looked as tired as I felt. The memory of our ghostly message hadn't left my mind for a second. *Leave me dead. Or you will be.* I glanced over the countless books we had delivered from the library that cluttered up the couch on either side of me, the rug, and every flat surface. The message hadn't been as definitive as Ty's assumption, and we needed something, anything to go on before there was even a reason to start this argument. "I'm not going to risk anyone. But my life is my own."

"And you're willing to give it."

Behind the challenge in Ty's eyes, an unasked question shone, one that sent my defenses on attack. I loved Kendrick. Had loved him in ways beyond our complicated friendship when he was still alive. I'd given part of my heart to him. And I'd had no right to. But that wasn't why I was hell-bent on uncovering any way to bring Kendrick back. Even if we'd remained platonic, at least from my end, I would go to the ends of the earth to find a way. Kendrick was dead. A consequence of my restoration of Ty. A consequence of who I was and who my twin was. The damned commander had wanted my distractions out of the way. Marcus had used Ty to try to sway me. He'd tried to eliminate Kendrick. More than once. Eliminated Kendrick's only family, his mother, to weaken him—or had that been a ploy to ensure he'd come for vengeance. Only to be served up to death.

"Yes. If that's our only option—"

Ty was in front of me in a flash, calloused hands pulling me up from the couch by my shoulders. He gave a little shake. "There's always another option. *Always*."

I gasped at his closeness. His scent drilled right up my nose into my brain. My toes curled with restraint. My lips parted, desperate to taste his…lips. Instead, I forced words out. "Until there's not."

Ty's fangs lengthened while his canines remained retracted. "That's called giving up—"

The creak of the main door swinging in and then shutting cranked Ty's head around. But it wasn't Raven returning with more books or a breakthrough in the research she was carrying out in the tomb. It wasn't even Ty's pack with an update on their damned leads.

The familiar person that skirted the granite foyer table to enter through the archway wore an expression that tweaked his facial features in all the wrong ways. It was too hard and devoid of his natural charisma. "Sorry to interrupt your little spat, but…" The smile that flashed Dorian's white teeth was cold with malice. "I wanted you to hear it first, Sis."

I stepped back from Ty, glad the guards out in the corridor hadn't seen the way he'd been holding onto me. We didn't need an *act now think later* scene with what I suspected my brother was about to divulge. "They've proven you're a Vladimir."

That cold smile widened. "And now…" Dorian's hand lifted, tremors quaking from his fingertips up his arms—at me.

My lungs squeezed in my chest and my mouth gaped. "Dor—ian." I coughed despite not needing to breathe. It felt like my insides were being wrung out like a sponge. Compacted until…

I spluttered and red sprayed from my mouth at Ty.

"What the hell are you doing?" Ty was between us in a flash, but the body block didn't help as ice inundated my bones, bringing me to my knees. "Let her go."

Dorian bared his fangs in satisfaction. "Make me."

The lycan's growl was a prelude to pain as he caught my brother around the neck and threw him back. The wing chair's crack was loud as a clap of thunder and then Ty was on top of him. He grabbed Dorian around the throat and squeezed.

"Ty, no!" I choked out as his clenched fist wound back—

The main door flung in and belted into the wall, delivering my worst fear.

Guards swarmed in, swords slicing the air when they saw the hybrid attacking the newfound royal heir.

Just as Dorian had planned.

In a split second, two things happened. One: The guards registered the blood around my mouth and the spray that dotted Ty's face and upper chest. Two: Dorian barked his command, "Restrain him!"

I struggled to gain footing, ice slowly thawing from my bones as Ty leaped up. "No, stop!"

But it was too late. Acting like I wasn't even in the room, the guards went for Ty. Sword-free hands catching at him, he bucked and growled. Stumbling over the broken chair and into the couch, Ty fought back. But he was only trying to get free. He wasn't fighting to hurt anyone.

From my utility belt I uncoiled my whip, ready to fling it around the sword-holders' necks. The same one Ty had gotten made perfectly to fit me. The one that now had a rubber grip over the silver butt. "Dorian. What the hell are you doing?"

As sword hilts batted Ty's face, turning him bloody, his body began to tremble. His inner wolf was rearing to break free—and so help any vampire who got in its way.

Now back on his feet, Dorian put himself in Ty's glowing line of sight. "I wouldn't do that if I were you, wolf." A term Marcus had used when Ty was his damned hybrid and second in command. Dorian's hand by his side shook with power.

"Dor—" My mouth and tongue suddenly froze as a blizzard chill swamped my marrow. Almost inaudible cracks rang out as my bones began to splinter. The whip fell, clattering to the ground. I barely stopped my fall by gripping the table by the archway as my hand froze.

Ty head-butted a guard blocking his view, and his feral gold stare found me through the re-crowding guards. The agony he saw across my face had his body vibrations giving out. He grunted, reigning in his inner wolf as the assault of six guards brought him to the ground. The other two pointed their swords to that soft spot under his throat.

As he kept his eyes on me, panicked at my condition, the ground vibrated with tremors. Earthquake? But there wasn't time to dwell on that. His words, "Are you okay?" had a sword tip breaking his flesh and adding to the scent of his spilled blood.

My hunger rose—but my anger at what they were doing to Ty grew like poison in my freezing veins. Electricity brewed beneath my skin, dancing down my arms. My hand was holding my rigid body up, but I'd break the damn thing off if it meant using my power to save Ty. "Hurt him and I'll put you down," I spat, despite my numb tongue. "Every single one of you!"

A few of the guards balked at the deadly promise in my voice. But none backed off. Instead they hesitated, looking to Dorian for instruction.

"They won't hurt him." All calm and collected, Dorian leaned against the archway opposite me. His shitkickers were crossed at the ankles—like he couldn't possibly be more relaxed. To them he nodded, "You have your orders."

As the ice in my bones began receding—was Dorian's power draining?—a glass syringe was freed from one guard's pocket. It was handed over to Dorian who bit the plastic cap between his teeth. The chamber was empty. They weren't injecting Ty, they were…

I went to snap the syringe from Dorian's hands as he strode forward but I froze. Beneath my ribcage, it felt like a hand of ice was squeezing around my heart. My heart that was animated by Ty's blood and wanted to continue beating. The shock of resulting cracks had my electricity retreating. "Dorian, what the hell—"

The standing guards with swords parted for Dorian to pass. Ty didn't fight back, seeing only the way I clutched at my chest.

"That's a good wolf." Dorian bent beside the complying hybrid and nailed the pointy end into Ty's arm. Pulling back on the end, the vial was filled to the max…with Ty's blood. "Release him now."

The guards hesitated.

Dorian flashed his fangs. "You heard me. Release him."

All the arms on Ty let go and the guards made for the door.

Ty scrambled upright, seething through fully extended canines. "Your council's going to give you hell when they learn you challenged the wolf alliance."

Dorian back-stepped around the foyer table to the door. "I'm only operating under their approval."

The ice around my heart thawed and it let out a shocked beat. Relief and fear drowned me as Ty came to my side. He was okay but… "Dorian, what the hell have you done?"

My brother smiled, body half out the open door. "You'll see."

SAFELY BEHIND THE UV-PROOF GLASS, I paced back and forth, glancing out each Gothic window as I passed. Twilight was here, with the promise of skin-igniting sun that would arrive in, oh—about thirty minutes. And still I wanted to be out there, clearing the closed-up shops and houses that kept the light out.

But Ty wouldn't have it.

He wouldn't risk me with my sensitivity to sunlight.

So I waited, feet refusing to quit that back and forth. They would be here soon and then everything would change. After Dorian's actions at the RVC's hands, it had to.

If the vamps wanted to challenge the alliance they'd only weeks ago instigated, they were going to reap the rewards of their deception. The inevitable confrontation kept my animated heart racing, and distracted my thirst for any nearby guards. Including my own, which I'd left around the bend to the boardroom.

Sweat bulleted my skin.

With the sun's arrival, I'd be stuck. Trapped. Here without my donor—without Ty—when things turned ugly. My life was about to free-fall once again.

And where was Dorian, the guy who'd been my brother for the first sixteen years of our lives?

Waiting in the boardroom with the others I'd summoned.

Not that I blamed him for what had happened. Not really. Marcus had to be behind this stunt. It didn't do him any good to have our races aligned. Reigniting the hate between our kinds would stall the combined efforts we'd arranged to kill or catch his damned minions.

When a formidable trio appeared up the main street, I neared the closest window to the guarded doors. Ty led the group, all leather and directionally planted hunting boots leading the way. His hard features promised action, but the strain that pinched his brow showed worry and fear. As he mounted the castle's steps, his nod was a question of my readiness. Of if I was sure about going through with this.

There was no uncertainty as I nodded back. My allegiance was to the people I loved. And I wouldn't have Ty bend to a race that had made his people slaves—and then declared war, because their one-minded rules had been challenged centuries ago.

Behind Ty, his pack of two was ready as they cleared the steps to the large landing. Troy's brows arched, his canines glinting through his lips. Happy at my support and rearing to act since our damned seek-and-find had been put on the back burner. Marika's eyes glowed intensely gold and the gentle growl in her throat demanded subtle attention.

Just as planned.

The guards manning the tall, iron-braced doors tensed at the closing-in pack, hands going to their swords. Ty and I moved without warning, Ty in front and me from behind, striking out to knock each one unconscious with dagger hilts.

I got out of the indirect but growing light that pricked my skin as Troy and Marika dragged the two inside and closed the doors. For the moment, the order was not to kill. Just to disarm.

"I wish it didn't have to come to this." Ty looked like the Hulk, except for the missing green skin, but his words were sincere. Despite his ingrained hatred and mistrust of my kind, he had been open to this alliance. "But they've shown their hand. I just hope they don't force a retaliation."

Ty didn't want a bloodbath. He didn't want another revolt like the one his grandmother had led. Disgruntled divergence was better than all-out war at this stage. Numbers—on both sides—were still first and foremost in the war against the damned. If we all killed each other today, the damned would win.

"Me too." Without any outside breeze, I could scent their lycan blood. I could feel his swimming in my veins and pumping my heart, too. Swallowing down my always-present hunger, I began the in-out routine to hide my transition. We were on the precipice of something game-changing. Something we wouldn't be able to go back from. Fear of the unknown had me desperate to wrap my arms around Ty one last time. Not to taste, but just to hold. To rest my head on his chest. To feel his constant warmth. After all we'd been through, if this was the last time I ever saw him? I settled for a smile. "We're in this together."

Side by side, we owned the hall as we cleared the pews and corridor to the boardroom doors. The royals' loitering guards were dealt with in the same manner as the first two, though not quite as quietly. The temptation to leap onto the unconscious guards was so strong, but then Ty's fingers touched my hand. "Ready?"

Unable to talk—because I needed to keep my fangs trapped in my mouth—I nodded.

The door was opened in on a stunned room of royals as Troy and Marika dropped the two guards inside. I clenched my fist at the assaulting scent of built-up blood.

Uriel stood up first, wide-eyeing the threatening display before noticing the out-cold guards in a tangle beyond the open doors. "Amelia, what on earth is going on?"

Ty took the spotlight, stalking further into the room. "You commanded my blood be drawn with force. You've violated our alliance and I won't stand for it."

"Violated?" Lord Strigon tabled his glass, the crystal clattering at the fast release and blood splashing over the rim onto the marble slab. "No. That's not what happened."

I reached the alpha's side, glaring at the others as I faked being alive. "So you didn't send Dorian with guards to my suite after Ty?"

My lips curled over my fangs as my eyes settled on my brother. That smug smile as he glanced between thrones at me was all Marcus. Those steepled hands before him as he occupied the Vladimir throne were my father and twin incarnate.

Lady Rasputin had turned sheet-paper white, and her *I'm better than you* voice shook as she spoke. "We ordered the retrieval of the lycan's blood."

Accusation tainted Uriel's voice as she turned her head to Dorian beside her. "Lord Vladimir was assigned the role of informing and collecting. Force was never ordered."

"But it got the job done." Dorian smiled, taking clear pleasure in the confrontation he'd instigated. His shrug was full of innocence as he faced the others.

"Amelia, we meant no harm." Uriel vacated her throne and

walked over. Troy growled and Marika tensed, but the royal didn't stop or flinch. "We only sought the truth."

Ty stepped closer to her and Marika and Troy stuck to him like glue. He was their alpha. They protected him above all others. But Ty almost seemed at ease, curious more than ready to teach someone a lesson. "The truth about what?"

Dorian slid his throne back so he could throw his legs up onto the tabletop. He sent a smile our way. "About who…or should I say *what* your lycan is."

The world stopped spinning. I swear my heart stopped. Then it sped up, pounding in my ears like a drum. No. He hadn't. He couldn't have. But that calculating look across my ex-twin's face said it all. "You told them…?"

"That Ty's a hybrid, one of two in existence?" Dorian shrugged again and that little voice in my head tempted me to make him stop moving and speaking for good. "They had a right to know."

"You'll never find him." Ty's dangerous whisper brought me out of my head. His statement was true. Harper had been sent away after the hotel battle to a lycan pack overseas that would keep him safe. The RVC would never find him. And neither would any damned. He came face to face with Uriel, bright and challenging eyes trained down at her. To her credit, she didn't budge. "As history is the best indicator of future actions, we'll be leaving now. Try and stop us? You won't like the outcome."

The alpha turned to leave, but I stayed put, waiting for their backlash.

"We don't wish to break the alliance."

Uriel's words and the conviction in them surprised me, and I wasn't the only one. "What?" Dorian spat, his perched feet falling off the table as the alpha spun back with a growl of distrust.

"What do you mean?" I demanded.

"The alliance still stands," Lord Strigon said. He pulled a handkerchief from his sports jacket and dabbed at the blood he'd spilled. "From our end, we have no wish to sever it."

"But you're right." Ty showed no fear, but a hint of confusion shone through. "I am a hybrid."

"Descended from the heir we burned at the stake." Dorian's eyes narrowed with scheming intensity. "His grandmother turned the wolves against us. Took our guardian slaves from us."

Troy and Marika bared their canines, edging in close to my brother with clear aggression.

I snapped my dropped jaw shut and blocked their way. He was provoking a war. Turning our races against each other. Which is exactly what Marcus wanted. But there was more than simple compulsion going on here. To keep acting this way, Marcus would have to have anticipated each race's reactions and added back-up compulsion to keep him stirring the pot. I fought the temptation to rat out my brother and the influence he was clearly under. The risk of him being imprisoned and tortured—or worse—by the RVC to gain information on Marcus was far too great.

"Our primitive ways have evolved," Lady Rasputin said with disdain. She'd clearly approved of the old ways and wished she wasn't dealing with an enemy race for the good of her kind. "We allowed the lycan residence in our castle. With one of The Seven no less. Unguarded, but for Lady Bathory's discretion. His pack lives in our community. We have proven our loyalty in this joining of races."

I glanced around the room at the other royals. "The truth can't be your only motive." I strode to Ty, not touching him but standing close enough to feel his heat and readiness. His scent made my mouth water and I punched my nails into my palms to keep my mind from bloody thoughts. "What do you want from this?"

Uriel smiled, genuine and non-confrontational. "Ty Malau traces back to the Ruthaven line. A line that was killed off after the burned heir's sire passed. He never repopulated, too ashamed by his son's affair with the lycan. Now we have a descendant. The eldest and rightful heir to the Ruthaven throne. Ty Ruthaven, we wish to crown you."

"Are you kidding?" Dorian threw his questioning glance around the table. Clearly this wasn't what Marcus had expected to happen. "He's half wolf. He can't be crowned."

"Times have changed, Lord Vladimir." I cringed at Uriel calling Dorian that. It made him seem too much like Marcus, even though my twin was God knows where. "We can crown him…and we will."

I could swear heads were rolling. Mine included.

"I don't want your throne," Ty stated, meeting the edge of the table and pressing one finger into the marble top. "Alliance or no. After everything your race has done to mine, I don't trust you. Not now. Maybe never. I won't follow your rules. I won't be restricted by expectation. I am a wolf. First and foremost. Regardless of what my blood says. My allegiance runs with them. You can keep our alliance. And we *will* stop the damned." Ty flashed a look of triumph behind him as the guards in the corridor began to stir. "But things have now changed. The only protection Lady Bathory needs is me and my pack. Her grounding will also be lifted immediately if you want us to continue fighting your battles with the damned."

Silence settled over the boardroom. Dorian tapped the table, eyeing the key players like he was at a boxing match and waiting for the two sides to recover for round two. Troy and Marika kept their focus locked on the two eldest royals, ready to pounce at a moment's notice.

I reminded myself to breathe, realizing I'd stopped.

No one seemed to notice, too keyed up for the next move like me. Ty was either very smart, or he'd just pushed a bunch of stuffy vampires too far.

"Very well." Uriel shared a look with her colleagues who all nodded, except for Dorian. Then she extended her hand to the alpha. "Our vote is cast. The alliance between vampires and wolves will continue. Your demands are met, and we will not force any other change."

Ty's nostrils flared. Satisfied, the alpha faced Uriel and clasped his broad hand around her small one, almost swallowing it whole. "Then our alliance stands. For now."

CHAPTER 5

I revved my Ducati while wind assaulted my braided hair and flailed my hood behind me. After almost two hours of driving in and out of small towns, the confidence I had in locating any damned was wearing thin. Ever-present hunger surged my irritation and tempted me to switch plans. It would be so easy to pull over with the pretense of having found a lead—and let loose on the living bodies that filled Ty's bright blue WRX tailing behind me.

My idea of riding ahead to take away the cat-and-mouse of tracking them was beginning to fail. The need to use my spidey senses to detect some damned action was becoming a distant memory. *Pull over. Take a break. Have a snack.*

Being around half past ten at night, the road I was on was quiet and lit up by a half moon. But the trees siding the road would provide enough shelter to act out—

As my hold on the throttle loosened, my killer thoughts stumbled just outside of Wasilla. That strong internal pull that had led me to Uriel before I'd restored her reared its demanding head. Like hands inside my guts, the pull was sudden and impossible to ignore. I'd once thought the pull was Kendrick trying to connect with me. My heart had broken a little more when I realized the true nature of the pull. This wasn't him now, either. It was the connection I had to the damned, the one that alerted me to their whereabouts.

Back in control—I hoped—I tapped my brakes. The signal to let them know I'd picked up something.

Plugging into the sensation, I kept moving on the Parks Highway until I passed the *Welcome to Wasilla* sign. Through the town's center, I hung a left at the intersection, but I didn't get far before the internal pull lured me down an Avenue I didn't catch the name of. Houses were set back from the road, not packed in tight, but not spaced-out, either. This couldn't be right. Too high a chance of human interference.

The WRX's high beams flashed behind me. Apparently Ty felt the same.

But then the number of houses dwindled and the road dead-ended. Or not.

With my navigation tugging at me relentlessly, I killed the engine and rolled down a sloped gravel driveway. In neutral behind me, Ty killed the lights and let momentum keep him rolling. Moving to the sidelines, I nodded the WRX on. We weren't there *yet*. There was movement in the cab, but I couldn't make anything out through the dark tint.

After the next bend, the driveway continued through thick lining trees into darkness. Ty pulled up while I dismounted and flicked down the kickstand to prop my Ducati upright. He emerged from the sports car, his potent scent finding me in the crisp night air and making my fangs peek from my gums. His eyes as he tracked over my covered arms were intense. But as he pulled his hand from the pocket of his jeans, he didn't question my control or hunger. Instead, his lips curled, revealing both fangs and canines. The anticipation of battle thrilled him. His maroon-flecked irises caught mine, and he tipped his head as if to say, *got your back.*

With a stake in one hand and dagger in the other, Raven jumped out of the sedan next. Her expression was a mix of *oh, shit, it's time* and *let's do this.*

"We're close." I yanked my dagger free. "I can feel it."

The WRX vibrated, shadows moving behind the midnight-black tint. And then *I* stepped out of the car, followed by a random damned. "Good idea, Amelia," my likeness said to me. "I'd rather look like the untouchable one over the tasty lycan."

Posing as a damned, Troy quit testing the sharpness of the blade he held. "I feel like a disgusting leech. No offense." He eyed me. "Can we move already?"

Exactly what I'd been wondering. With two of the four having unmasked scents, I was getting twitchy just standing here. That tugging didn't help, either. I turned to lead the way. "Let's go."

When the driveway appeared to be coming to an end without any sight of a dwelling, I suddenly stumbled. Another sensation joined those hands inside my guts. One I hadn't felt for weeks. I gasped as Ty caught me. "What's wrong?"

Joining the pulling was a feeling of recognition—of my soul recognizing its other half. But it wasn't my soul's mate, my blood bound connection to Kendrick. And the sensation was starting to fade. I pushed free of Ty, because of his closeness, and because of what I felt, and forced my feet to keep on silently. "Marcus is here. I think he's getting away."

As we cleared the bend, I wanted to hurl.

This was the right place, all right. A cozy cottage, double-story with a wraparound deck. Blackout curtains prevented seeing in through the many windows. No cars were parked outside. The damned moved faster than human automobiles. Faster than us.

Ty took the lead while I crowbarred my stomach against the increasing damned pull. At the same time, my sense of Marcus dwindled. Mounting the steps, Ty's boots were soundless. The weapons around his waist and the big dagger strapped to his thigh didn't clatter. How he kept his jeans from making that swishing sound was beyond me. Lifelong training in stealth. Without his jacket, his black muscle shirt left his arms bare. Even with the potential danger, my stare lingered. The eye contact over his shoulder snapped me out of it. In his hands were a dagger and a stake. Just like the rest of us. Splitting a look between Marika and Troy, he then nodded to Raven.

The plan had already been set, regardless of our location.

Troy bared his canines and Marika nudged Raven to head around back. They were charged with her protection and keeping any damned from escaping. Take down if possible, with the intent to interrogate and restore, otherwise aim to kill.

Moving with the same stealth, the trio dispersed. With her weapons at the ready, Raven shadowed Marika. Troy looped the opposite way to complete the circle and meet them around back. Each and every move they made was silent.

Something unsaid hung in Ty's unwavering stare as he looked at me, but I couldn't decipher it. There were too many conflicts to puzzle out. "Ready?" he mouthed without sound.

To stalk into hell with you? Always. I flashed my fangs in answer.

Ty balanced back on one leg, his other foot tucking up as he angled himself in a karate-like stance. He booted the door, cracking the wood in two. The splintered sections catapulted in, the sound a definite alert to our arrival.

Ty leaped inside and I shadowed. Another split of wood rang out as the others broke down the back door. Inside wasn't dark like I'd imagined from outside. Large flickering candles around a lounge area on the bare wooden planks highlighted everything. Damned crowded inside in three circled groups of five or more. Their disgruntled faces cranked around at the noisy entrance. And then the smell hit me like a semi.

Blood.

Each group was circled around a human victim that they'd been devouring like a pack of hyenas. With bloodied faces and long red-painted fangs, they dropped the dead bodies. The smell of blood drowned the air, filling my senses and hijacking my thoughts. I went to kneel in a puddle of pooling red…

"Amelia, get with the program!" Ty snapped as the damned leaped for him.

The hiss and sudden attack of the damned shook me out of my haze. Grip tightening around my weapons, I joined the assault. The next few minutes whizzed by in a blur. The damned were all fangs and nails, speed and ferocity their main weapons. More than half shot down the hallway toward the sound of our oncoming trio. The rest took on Ty. Six-to-one. I went to continue the assault, my mind taking a second to realize that none were advancing on me. I was still on the protected list, because Marcus had deemed me so.

Ty was not. And yet my intent to help him stalled.

Instead, I refocused on the victims and their leaking blood. *Such a waste. Unless you make use of it…*

I shook my head at my inner voice, forcing my eyes to focus on Ty and the fact that he didn't need my useless help. He was awe-inspiring in battle. Flinging one stake, he dusted the first damned, exploding it in a rain of ash over the twisted bodies on the ground. A second was nailed to the wall with his dagger, kicking out a few lit candles as he stumbled. Light became scarce, but Ty didn't falter. A larger dagger was freed from his thigh holster. Slashing out while minding the dead at his feet, he sliced a third damned's neck to the bone. The body fell, black blood spraying over a red puddle and skull hanging by a thread.

I could see why Marcus had been intent on turning Ty into one of his damned—into his second in command. He was magnificent. A God in the art of battle.

While damned, had he been holding back when he'd attacked Kendrick at the hotel? When I'd attacked him to get free, had he drawn on the sliver of conscience he'd had left not to kill me? The answer was clear in his lethal ability.

I couldn't tear my eyes away. Couldn't move.

A fourth sprang at Ty, going for the jugular. He ducked with time to spare and a replacement stake was tugged from his ankle holster. He was as fast as them. One scarred, muscle-popping arm wrenched up, exploding the damned into a shower of ash overhead. Four down. One of the last two went to run, and Ty nailed the same stake through its back. It fell but didn't disintegrate. Its screech pierced my ears as it writhed to reach the silver in its back.

Ty had missed?

Before another second could pass, his long dagger sliced through the torso of the other as the one nailed to the wall got free. It was coming for Ty from behind, with Ty's dagger.

"Look out!"

I ran to cut the damned off, but Ty was like lightning. With a spin, he drove his elbow into the damned's temple. Like he'd done to me after I'd discovered Marcus was my twin. The damned was quick, too. Fool me twice? The damned struck Ty in his upper arm with Ty's own blade, digging in deep. His blood free-poured. He didn't react. One hand caught the damned's assaulting one. The long dagger Ty still gripped stabbed through the damned's gut, coming out the other side. A wrenching twist up cut off its cry and turned the soulless damned to ash.

Ty yanked the dagger from his arm and spun in a blur to face me. His chest pumped with ragged breath. "Can you still feel Marcus?"

But I wasn't tracking. With the action now over, one thing dominated the space. Blood. A blend of black rotting berries, and tempting fresh and peppery red. Ty's and so many others'. It puddled on floorboards between the dead and damned remains. It speckled the walls and curtains. The writhing damned was covered in the stuff.

Something—no, someone—blocked my view of most of it.

Ty. He came closer, seeing me flinch and the way I stared at the slowing leak from the gash in his arm. There was no fear. He could dispatch me as easily as the five damned he'd already put down. "*Amelia*, is he here?"

My stomach ached in hunger as I focused on Ty's face. My gaze shifted to his neck. No, I wouldn't give up my control. I forced my eyes back to his face. And there was the answer. In all the action, that sensation inside my body had been forgotten. Easily done, despite the distractions…because it was no longer really there. Just a watered-down sensation. One that I knew meant he was out of reach. I tried to blink the rising red away and shook my head. "He's not here. Not anymore."

I turned away from him as two of our group rushed in from an adjoining hallway—Troy and Marika now back in their own skin. Looking worse for wear, they both sported gashes and bruises. Their fighting gear had been rent open, the black material damp with blood.

So much blood. *Mesmerizing, tasty blood.* So red, so glossy, so pungent.

Though they all stood stationary, the space between us shrank, getting smaller and smaller. The cooling bodies on the wooden floor behind me were forgotten in favor of the live sources I neared. But then a body stepped between me and them. All raw muscle and strength and heat. *A volunteer?*

I tracked one taut, black-veined arm as it slowly reached up, getting higher and higher until…he gently cupped one side of my jaw. "Amelia."

That deep and understanding voice registered, and I flinched as my vision regained focus. Ty. Over his shoulder, I couldn't miss the looks on the others' faces as they took in my unharmed clothes and lack of injuries.

Troy sneered at me. "Since when did you become a flake-out, Barbie?"

Marika didn't add her own smart-ass comment. Instead, she looked disappointed…and on edge. Like she wondered if I'd swapped sides for good. Like she would regret having to take me down.

"They wouldn't fight her," Ty said, his look at me questioning my state of mind, his words keeping the part out about me standing around like a zombie while he took out six…

My mouth opened then shut. My need for blood didn't budge, but that sliver of my conscience was in full operation. I glanced bashfully at the others. "Are…are they all dead?" I questioned as a shuffling sounded behind me. Without captives, we had no one to interrogate, and no one to restore and bring back to the Armaya. All those lives…gone.

A patter of ballet shoes shot down the stairs I only just now noticed. "That one's still alive." Raven strode over blood and bodies and kicked at the damned on the ground still clawing to pull the stake from its back. "Upstairs is clear."

"We put down the rest." Troy shrugged unapologetically. "We didn't have a choice."

Marika looked down at herself and the healing cuts up her black-clad arms and torso. "The second they smelled my blood, they knew I wasn't you."

A wolf imprint only changed the person so they appeared different on the outside. It couldn't alter their blood or DNA. All abilities had their weaknesses and setbacks, and I reined in my own weaknesses to ignore the scents and sights around me.

A ringing started up in my ears, and I barely heard Ty order his pack and Raven to start disposing of the human bodies. There was movement around me, hefting and sliding as the action was carried out, the bodies being carted out the front door and away from me.

Ty threw his Zippo at Troy with a nod. "Not a trace."

I turned to glimpse the writhing damned. Marcus was gone, but I wasn't going to leave here with nothing. No freaking way.

Shoving one Van into the damned's back to hold it down, I bore down on the silver that was so close to its spine. My palm sizzled at the contact, but as Ty came closer, no doubt to take over, I held up my hand. Speaking to the creature beneath me, I said, "Where's Marcus gone? Where's his main hideout?"

The damned's body turned rigid to keep the silver's damage from spreading. His hiss was my only response.

Loyalty or compulsion?

Cracks rang out beyond the cottage's blood-splattered walls, branches being ripped off trees to no doubt create a peaked cover over the dead. Right now with my gut squeezing and the last of those not-quite-empty and cold bodies being carted away, I didn't care what the damned's motivation was. I didn't care that what I planned to do would cause him more pain, either. Turning my need to feed into anger, I pulled the stake back two inches—then nailed it back in on an angle.

I spoke through gritted teeth over the damned's wail. "Are you new? Were you already turned at the hotel invasion?" With few vamps going missing since then, finding out where these damned were coming from was a step to help us stopping new recruits.

Ty said something as my hold on the stake clamped tighter. The smell of the damned's and my burning flesh joined the scent of blood. But I wasn't listening. At least not to him. *Teach the leech a lesson. Take your fill.* And why the hell not? I was part vampire and part damned—even before my transition, after my father's actions to infect me.

"Answer me," I grated, scenting acrid smoke wafting in through the open door. My blood felt like it was boiling. The earlier red from my sight started to cloud my vision.

"Screw you, bitch." The damned twisted his head so his gray cheek was smooshed in a red and ashy slick. "Go to hell!"

Something in me snapped, the thin control I was losing vanished. I tore the stake from the damned's back and flipped him over. Ty's hand on my shoulder was met with an elbow as I picked the damned up by his shirt and pinned him to the wall. "Wrong answer." Mouth splitting wide, my fangs hit bone as they sank right above his collarbone.

And then I pulled on his vein.

Black blood slid down my throat like an oil slick, creating a chain reaction in my body. That watered-down link to Marcus vanished. My heart gave out. My vision turned ruby red. And my hunger increased ten-fold.

I drew harder, reveling in the power of losing control, in

unleashing the monster within. Supporting the damned's weakening body, I spun, searching—

Ty shot up behind the damned I clung to with my nails and fangs. Then the cold gray body came alive with heat. He turned to instant smoldering coals that singed my clothes and my skin beneath, my mouth and my tongue, as he collapsed into a pile of hot ash.

Ty holstered his stake. "Amelia, rein it in."

Reasoning with a monster? I almost laughed. But as I readied to pounce, that ringing in my ears stopped. The sound of heartbeats replaced it. And not just Ty's or even the three living beings outside where a raging bonfire plumed smoke up into the sky.

This one was quieter. Weaker. Not in this room, but still in this cottage. The last beats of a heart that was about to fail. An easy target.

Booting a foot into Ty's stomach, he flew back, shattering a window. With seconds on my side, I shot down the hallway and a set of stairs, blasting through a cellar door. Inside, silver chains hung from a bolt in the ceiling, sizzling against the wrists they trapped. Suspended by them was a girl covered in fresh blood. Vampire. And now dead.

Perfect.

I pounced, fangs bared and claws clenched, ready to hang from the still-warm blood bag and drain the contents.

But I never got there.

The arm that swung in front of me was thick and covered in black veins. And it didn't strike out to attack. It lined up perfectly, taking my thrusting fangs deep into that tan skin. The pull I took was mechanical—primal and without thought.

The coming-to-life of my heart as his chest connected with my back shocked me out of my attack.

Ty. And he was feeding me by vein. His other arm clamped around my waist, holding me close. I hissed as the red bled from my vision, my urge to kill replaced by something stronger. Heat, attraction, yearning, and desire. Thoughts of tearing clothes away, of using my mouth for so much more than biting, inundated my mind in a rush…but as I saw without blinders the girl hanging before me, that too melted away.

Ty spoke as I pried my fangs from his flesh. "Are you okay now?"

After what I'd done to him, that damned, and had intended to do to this girl who just died in this lightless, blood-reeking cellar? "I… the damned's blood. And then I heard her. She was still alive."

"Marcus left her for you to find."

Before I could ask, Ty's extended arm pointed at the stained concrete below the hanging girl. Paintwork married with old bloodstains. Except it wasn't paint. The poor girl's wrists had been cut so that red streamed down from her suspended arms to stain her white dress. My twin had left her here like this. And I knew why. It was clear from the message he'd finger-painted with her blood onto the concrete floor.

Finish her off for me, twin.

Marcus had been here. He'd felt my approach just as I had felt his presence. And he'd retaliated.

CHAPTER 6

Poised on my throne in the packed main hall, I awaited the scheduled proceedings, anxiety raising my pulse at the events that would formalize the RVC's findings. I felt naked in spite of the many heavy layers of skirting in the extravagant black and gold gown I wore. One reason had to do with not wearing my usual weapons around my waist. The other reason related to Ty's eyes. I felt his gaze on me like a flesh-burning laser. The intense way he watched me made my body hum. But there was no desire in his unwavering stare, only the rigid strain of muscles bunching in readiness to take action. Even with my need to kill numbed by his supplied blood, it was never gone.

And he knew it.

Arms crossed over his chest, Ty kept watch from beside the stage, armed to the teeth. Not that he'd even need all those weapons against me if I lost control. Yesterday I'd seen him dispatch six damned with deadly precision. Almost without breaking a sweat.

With seven thrones lined up on the stage, five were now occupied. The Paole throne would remain empty. None of them wanted to take on the honored role. Or the danger that came with being in charge. It was no wonder, after all the past deaths. Whole families had been targeted. But the aim was to wipe out the rulers. Taking the throne put an *x marks the spot* over every crowned royal's head.

Kendrick's throne, positioned on the end beside mine, made my beating heart ache. I felt like I was suffocating, which had nothing to do with the tight bodice that strapped my chest. A flash of him lying frozen in that glass box inundated my mind. Until he was breathing again and beside me, nothing in this world would feel right. Thank God for Raven who was now nose-deep in book stacks in the tomb, determined to find something to help after our failed mission.

Finding Ty's unmoving stare, I knew I wasn't all that held his focus over the many gathered formally dressed royals and turned vamps.

Forcing my thoughts to the guy on my other side fed the growing tension roiling through my muscles. Dorian, though not crowned yet, was right beside me, calm and collected—because that's what this get-together was all about. Hand loose on the Vladimir throne's armrest, he surveyed all who'd come to welcome him as one of their new rulers. I itched to question him, to find out how exactly Marcus was getting to him here in our protected community. Any interrogation died on my tongue though. There wasn't any reason to think he'd reply with honesty or even have the capacity to.

"I thought it was for the best."

I stiffened at Dorian's unexpected words.

"Revealing Ty's bloodline." Dorian met my eye as he glanced up through thick black lashes and the hair that hung over his forehead. "I should have come to you first. Given you a heads up. I guess I just knew you'd refuse. But we could have had another throne. Another voice. Another vote."

Ty's growl was low but clear over the din of the growing crowd.

I studied my brother's face. No shifty eyes. No haze. No pursed lips that were a tell of his scrutiny to my reaction. He wasn't gauging if I was buying his words. He believed them. Had Marcus compelled Dorian's actions to gain Ty's blood, then his words that tempted a revolt in the boardroom? All signs pointed to yes. Which reinstated one thing on my to-do list. I had to find a way to break Marcus's hold on my brother. Before Dorian's forced actions set something horrible in motion.

Patting his hand, I faked a smile. "Everything'll be set right, Dorian. I promise you it will." If I couldn't find a way to prevent Marcus's manipulation, I'd have to inform the RVC. Force them to imprison my brother until Marcus was stopped. But right now, I stood and smoothed down my gown before going to the table siding the thrones.

Ty beat me there, picking up the gold ceremonial chalice and making the audience hush at his unexpected presence on the stage. He paid none of them a glance or even acknowledged the RVC members who raised brows at him. His cautious expression as he held out the jewel-encrusted cup voiced an unasked question. *Are you sure you can handle this?*

Pursing my lips, I grasped the chalice and nodded. "I'll be fine."

Right now, he wasn't worried so much about Dorian, but more about my ability to perform the blood ritual without turning lethal—and revealing my true colors.

I nodded again. "I can do this."

Trusting my word, Ty returned to his post, while the many other guards lined the hall's perimeter.

I reached down to the crimson silk over the table and stalled as a hand grasped the hilt of Uriel's wavy-edged silver sword. Dorian raised the weapon, then brought the blade down in an arc—to hand me the gold-plated hilt. Taking hold, my voice projected for all to hear as the crowd quieted. "Lord Dorian Vladimir, you are summoned here today to stand before the Royal Vampire Council to be recognized as one of The Seven. Have you come of your own free will,"—*likely not*—"ready to take your place as the living heir to the late Lord Vladimir?"

Unlike my crowning, Dorian showed no nerves or reservations. He bent at the waist in a bow before rising. "Yes, Lady Bathory. Of my own free will, and ready to take my rightful place imposed by my blood."

Anxiety rising, I swished past my brother, barely noticing which royal I stopped before. A woman's pale arm was extended—must have been Uriel, with those black veins and green gown. I lifted the weighty sword and cut fast and deep along her wrist. The sudden well of crimson and punch of blood had my knees going weak. The crowd noticed, their quiet chatter filling the hall. The trickle followed by the *drip, drip, drip* as the cut healed itself had my sight frozen on the pool that had collected in the chalice below.

A cleared throat from across the stage had me blinking and moving on. After the wash and repeat on the last two royals, my legs were shaking as I returned to the table and lowered the cup.

Ty was there waiting, and took the sword from me. "You're doing great."

I didn't reply, keeping my long fangs trapped in my mouth. The silver burn that sliced over my wrist had my stare lifting from that pool of delicious, warm blood.

When my donation was complete, I reclaimed the sword and gold cup, repeating in my head, *don't drink it,* as I returned to Dorian and faced the crowd. The bright chandeliers hanging from the Gothic rib-vault ceiling highlighted their confused and even disgruntled expressions. They feared the lycan when they should have feared me—and the guy I was about to make one of their sworn rulers. Dorian raised his arm up, but I couldn't complete the cut to add his donation. I wouldn't.

As quiet discussion rose up from the pews, Dorian leaned in to whisper in my ear. "In case you feel like informing the RVC of anything, just know, the moment you do I will use that blade in your hands, or any weapon I can get to,"—his intense and unwavering eyes stared into mine—"on myself." A dangerous smile curved his lips, one that was so like Marcus. "I'd have no other option."

As he went to take the sword from me, I held up the chalice. I had no clue how Marcus had anticipated this, or when he'd implanted that little ditty in my brother's mind, but I sure as hell wasn't going to test his threat now.

Dorian offered his wrist with a triumphant smile, and slow seconds later the chalice was full. Feeling dead inside, I said what was expected of me. "Kneel before your people and repeat the sacred oath."

Dorian's voice was loud and strong. But I wasn't listening. My brain was stuck on how Marcus was pulling this off. While I stood there all zombie-like, I was vaguely aware of the loud applause from all around. Then there was movement. Everyone dispersing through the iron-braced doors.

My eyes regained focus as Dorian appeared right in front of me. "You did well." His smile was Cheshire cat wide as he gripped my arm. "Besides, I'm not the monster here, now am I?"

Ty's warmth bloomed beside me with a growl as Dorian released his hold. "Don't think you can blackmail me like you did her. I won't let your crap slide."

I didn't question how Ty had heard Dorian's threat as I watched my brother stroll from the stage stairs. "Next time, wolf."

With Ty busy watching after Dorian as he meandered toward the grand staircase, I heard the RVC members' quiet footfalls down the corridor followed by the stomp of guards. Something in me changed. Like the power had just been sapped from my body, my predatory side rose hard and fast. Black veins forked out over my exposed arms like rotting tree roots. My sight blinked from multicolor to vivid red.

I was ravenous.

I vaulted off the long stage in a single bound, tearing down the corridor.

My mind had shut off. My ability to see any wrong in what I planned to do lost to my burning need to take a life. Through the red, all I saw were the backs of guards and the three formally dressed, easy targets in front of them. All I could smell was the rich scent of lifeblood that filled each living blood-bag's veins. The sound of each of their heartbeats was like drums in my ears.

Boom-boom. Boom-boom. Boom-boom.

A maddening repetitive noise that needed to be stopped. Permanently.

I pre-planned my zigzag through the guards, ready to render them unconscious. Ready to pick off the unarmed targets in all their extravagant attire.

Fists clenched to bash skulls, my fangs throbbed with greed.

I struck out—

A quick, calloused hand caught my neck with a punishing grip. And then I was flying back in a semicircle. *Oomph.* Air burst from my lungs as my back hit the corridor's stone wall. A body draped in the heady smell of smoke pinned me and the Cinderella gown I wore in place. A corded arm across my throat forced my face to angle up sideways.

In my thrashing to get free, I almost missed the punch of blood that stained the air. Until hot drips pattered my parted lips. From Ty's wrist raised above my head, torn open from his bite.

Utter fear and determination dominated his black-veined features as he frantically scanned my face and then my neck. "They're receding," he rasped, eyes flicking up to mine. Some of that fear melted away as my view of him drained of red and my struggle suddenly gave in.

Too quickly, the action I'd just taken rushed back through my mind. Ravenous. Attacking… *Oh shit.* My heart kick-started like a stone-cold engine struggling for rhythm as I swallowed and went to snatch Ty and his leaking arm away from sight—

Too late.

"What are you doing?" Uriel strode through the cluster of guards like she was going to pull Ty off me.

"She needed blood." Ty didn't try to hide it as he released me and dropped his bleeding arm. He made no apologies, either. "Mine's pure."

"*You* are now her donor?" Lady Rasputin reached Uriel's side with a look of disgust.

Lord Strigon arrived last, tall enough to see over the women's heads. "Yet you refrained from connecting flesh to vein."

Rasputin looked like she was ready to set the guards on Ty. "Because they know it's wrong."

But she was wrong. The bigger reason was that blurring that line would do more than tempt me to the edge of taking a life. Blood from Ty's vein had never been simply about food. It never would be. Even now I recalled tasting Ty's flesh yesterday, and how it had ignited my desire—until that suspended dead body had registered.

Ty squeezed his fist as his dripping blood slowed with the closing of his torn skin. "Out of respect for your outdated and one-minded ways."

Uriel spoke before Rasputin could spew her rebuttal. "This is a council matter." She motioned to the double doors a few yards back from where Ty and I stood. "It will be dealt with as such."

"There is nothing to discu—"

"In private," Uriel said, cutting off Rasputin as she eyed her older colleague. "Right now."

Making sure my breathing was even despite the racing of my reanimated heart, I led the way through those double doors. Taking my place around the massive round table, I double-checked that my bare arms were absolutely free of black veins. Satisfied, seeing only super pale skin, I surveyed the others as they too sat upon their thrones. "Are we going to have a problem?"

Silence fell over the room until Rasputin sneered, "This cannot be allowed."

Ty reached the back of my throne, a low growl breaking the silence as three sets of eyes glanced from me to him. His hand curled around the carved backrest, making the wood groan in protest. His voice was clipped. "Thank you for proving my point. For confirming that my choice to refuse your throne and all its *privileges* was the right thing to do. You'll never change," he spat at all three of them. "Your words to a lowly lycan are nothing more than hot air. Followed so long as you need us to fight your battles. So long as we're saving your skin—"

"That's not true." Uriel stood from her throne, hand pressing into the marble slab. "At least not for all of us."

She narrowed her gaze across the table at Rasputin, while Strigon made work of filling crystal glasses from the decanter topped with blood. He slid four to the seated royals, then stood to advance on us.

Ty released my throne and faced the olive-skinned royal, staring at the glassed blood Strigon held.

"I fully supported our offer unto you and accept your refusal." Strigon offered the glass. "You drink blood, do you not?"

Ty accepted the peace offering with a tip of his head. He downed the glass then handed it back. "I do."

From my side, Uriel cleared her throat. "Back to the issue at hand, we should have addressed this sooner. Since Baldassare's…"

Strigon stalled momentarily in his retreat back to his throne. Ty tensed—I could actually hear his muscles cording. And I cringed, my heart bottoming out and sudden bloody tears welling. I blinked them back with a flutter. I saw in my mind how he lay, gray and stiff, spine jutting at the side of his neck. I feared if I let the waterworks go, they'd never stop.

A new distraction drained my tears dry as the boardroom doors opened and clapped shut. "Since Kendrick's death," Dorian finished Uriel's words like they meant nothing. Like he was discussing the moon that had lowered in the sky toward the mountainous tree line.

Ty was back behind my throne as Strigon reached his and Dorian came to take his crowned position. He hiked his brows. "Meeting without me. Should I be concerned?"

His expression showed he was anything but, and the way he surveyed the newly hung replacement portraits, a smile parting his lips at the fire extinguishers beside the doors, sent a chill up my spine. Like he was Marcus and remembering the way he'd burned every royal portrait to cinders. Like he wanted to test the extinguishers' effectiveness—with the guards locked outside for the first time since my twin's deadly attack.

I wondered manically as I stared at him what had surged my hunger in the first place. There had been no vision, no expanse of time since Ty had donated his bottled blood. Yeah, I'd been tempted by the ritual, but my control had held out. My mind had been stuck on…Marcus.

I searched my brother's innocent eyes, remembering how he'd touched me moments before. Had he somehow drained me—like Marcus had done after he'd…killed Kendrick? The most obvious solution dawned on me. A mark. If my twin had marked him with the same symbol that drained damned who broke into our community, he could suck energy from anyone he touched.

"Maybe for your sister," Rasputin's voice jarred me out of my rushing thoughts. "There was an *incident.*"

Dorian seemed to consider her words as he looked to me then up to Ty. "They know you're surviving off hybrid blood." He steepled his hands on the table. "I don't wish to create waves on my first day." He shrugged, his apologetic look at me making me want to slap the compulsion from his head. "So what have we all decided?"

Rasputin fingered the rim of her glass. "I believe I have been outvoted."

Strigon nodded to Uriel, who said, "As proof of our continued acceptance, your donor arrangements will not be challenged." She leveled her gaze at the only objecting vote. "Not now. Not ever."

Ty's reply was curt, a nail in the coffin of reality. "So long as the lycan supporters live beyond our efforts to eradicate the damned."

Not a word was said after that. There was no point arguing the truth.

SITTING beside me the following day, Uriel's head twisted my way, her maroon-flecked irises hopeful. "Have the wolves sourced any new damned leads?" The black veins from being a restored damned stood out in stark contrast against her pale flesh.

With a sigh and shake of my head, I glanced away from her—

and the vein pulsing up her neck. My sight fell on the empty thrones around the boardroom's marble slab. Paole's and…

The other council members, including Dorian, began talking about other 'important' issues. I barely heard a word over the sudden buzzing in my ears. I couldn't stop my head turning to my left. Kendrick's throne. My whole body tensed as my heart seized. Ty's donated blood was keeping it animated right now, which only exacerbated the bodily response. God, it felt like someone had stabbed the organ and was slowly twisting, around and around. I wanted to be with Raven, finding the answers to bring him back. Not here dealing with mundane council issues. Not still wondering if Dorian was marked as I suspected, all the while knowing I didn't have anyone to confirm my suspicions. Not worrying about the next move he would make under Marcus's influence—or if he'd challenge the acceptance of Ty as my donor.

After a while the words "replacements" and "refused position" made it through. I cleared my throat and forced my voice to work with my lips. "Sorry, what position?"

"For the new alchemist," Lord Strigon supplied with a nod at the raising of his blood-filled glass.

Lady Rasputin's clipped reply was joined by a hard stare. "After Vanessa Aquinas disappeared around the same time you did."

I saw the event as if on fast-forward in my mind—of the moment Vanessa had disappeared from this Earth for good. Ty leaped for her and tore into her jugular. With an agonizing roar, Vanessa's body dropped to the ground, still and lifeless. Her eyes were vacant. Ty rose, turning his bloody face to me. "Calling my bluff? You lose."

I'd fought back, injured Ty enough to steal the room's key and his Zippo. But then I'd stalled. Whirling around I saw something as shocking as Vanessa's dead body twisted on the ground. Ty was on his knees, smearing her spilled blood as he crawled forward.

Crimson tears tracked down his face. "Kill me, Amelia. Do it. *Please.* I beg you."

My hand went to my throat as my stomach's contents tried to escape. Not giving in to Ty had secured Vanessa's death and resulted in an act Ty would never forget…or forgive himself or me for. I hadn't told Dorian who'd killed his girlfriend, and I'd never informed the RVC of what had happened to their alchemist.

Either my guilt at what I had kept secret or the horror of that very memory must have shown through, because Dorian called me out. "You know what happened to her." Peering around Uriel to me there was a flash of emotion in his suddenly distraught face. "To my V-Vanessa." His stone-cold exterior took over, stripping the rising glaze from his silver-blues.

I wouldn't name Ty as the perp. He'd been damned when he'd committed the unthinkable after I'd failed to save or stop him in time. Still, I had to say something. "Vanessa was being controlled by Marcus. He used her to mark his damned. That's how they got past our wards. And…" I paused, studying Dorian's reaction to what I'd already said, wondering if he even knew Marcus had compelled him to force Vanessa to his and Ty's location.

Blank look. No recognition.

If he remembered, he clearly wasn't aware of it on a reachable level. "Following Vanessa was how I uncovered the damned hide-out…and found out that Marcus was the damned commander. Before the battle, a damned killed her. I saw her die."

"Why are we only hearing about this now?" Lord Strigon questioned, even though Lady Rasputin's hard stare seemed to say the words.

I'd bomb-dropped Vanessa's death on Dorian before Kendrick's canceled funeral to get a reaction out of him. There had been no more than he'd shown today. I'd never intended to keep her death from the RVC. "So much has been going on. It simply hadn't crossed my mind."

"I am sorry for your loss, Dorian. I know you were involved. Unfortunately, this trying report does not lessen our need for a replacement." Uriel, always backing me, gave a tight-lipped smile. "Our wards must be revised—to prevent the damned entering at will. And the marking of our guards must be routinely maintained."

Determination and grief showed across Dorian's face as he stood up. "I can step in until a suitable replacement is found. Vanessa—" He paused, frowning as a car's loud exhaust rumbled from somewhere outside. "Ah, she ah, taught me some basics—"

"What the hell?"

Ty's voice beyond the doors was a rattled shout that had my head cranking around.

"No, you're not authorized—" A guard's words cut short as the boardroom doors swung inward.

The girl who marched inside knocked the unnecessary breath from my lungs. Everyone else gasped and balked. Ty was right there too, shadowed by guards. He looked white as a ghost, unable to look away from the sapphire-blue-eyed girl with her long, wavy red hair, and pixie features. Her face couldn't be confused. Neither could her unblemished, pale skin and the beat of her heart that was racing as if she'd run from hell just to get here.

I jumped up fast. "Vanessa, you're…*alive*."

Dorian stared like he'd just seen pigs fly. "V—Vanessa!" His shock mirrored everyone else's as well as my own. "I thought you… Amelia said…" He struggled to force the words out. "You were dead."

"She was." I scanned every inch of her. Her chest heaved up and down, recovering from her sprint here. Those sapphire eyes held no flecks to suggest she'd been turned damned and restored. Black tracks didn't fork over her exposed hands, face, or throat… I gulped. The remnants of Ty's vicious attack had left a textured patch of skin on her neck that was as big as a fist. And the scent of her blood—her human blood—tempted my hunger.

Having moved to the side, Ty got a clear glimpse. His white face dropped with guilt. "You died." He gulped hard and even as I moved toward him with my hand raised, I couldn't stop the confession from passing his lips. "When I was damned…I killed you with my…" His lips parted as both his fangs and canines elongated.

My gaze shot to Dorian. There was no blink of shock or even a twist of fingers into fists. There was no reaction.

Vanessa, on the other hand, shuddered as if remembering those exact moments Ty had taken her down. Her hand rose as if to touch the marbled flesh on her neck before dropping into a fist. "Yes, you attacked me." A mash of sorrow and disappointment darkened her eyes. "You left me for dead."

A long scrape sounded as Uriel pushed her throne back and came forward. "There is clearly more to this story that we must hear. Guards, you may return to your post."

As the guards filed out, I wondered if that was such a good idea. For one, I couldn't reconcile in my head the fact that Vanessa was even here. And alive? How was that even possible? Moreover, why was she here, and under what capacity? Without being obvious, my hand neared the dagger at my hip. The same one I wore every day, along with a stake and my whip on the utility belt that fit snugly over my Under Armour gear. I didn't touch the hilt, but I was ready. If this was a trap in some way, I wouldn't let it get out of hand. Vanessa, herself or not, was not going to die on my watch twice. As I shared a glance with Ty, I saw he was equally prepared, his weapons in close range and his taut body ready to act if Vanessa was put in danger.

Uriel waved toward the open doors. "Ty—"

"I'm not leaving with them," Ty ground out.

"A lycan making demands." Lady Rasputin snorted as she clutched her full glass of blood. "See what happens when we associate with slaves—"

"I will never be your—"

"He may stay," Uriel cut in before an argument could erupt. She eyed Dorian, Strigon, Rasputin, and me. "Agreed?"

Lady Rasputin was the only one to stay her hand. Four-to-one. Ty would stay.

As the doors clapped shut, Lord Strigon motioned to the Paole throne. "Vanessa, please, take a seat."

Vanessa nodded as the rest of us returned to our seats. She walked around the far side, her movement swaying the drapes and making me cringe as she passed. Thankfully it was night beyond the cover, and the glass was UV-proof, but the transitioning instinct in me couldn't be helped. If my current state had deteriorated since being out in the garden with Ty almost four weeks ago, unfiltered sun could do more than just burn me. It could incinerate me. I shuddered. Death by fire? I'd heard the screams of damned who'd died that way. I'd smelled their melting flesh, too. No thanks.

As Vanessa went to take the Paole throne, she frowned at the only empty one left. "Where are Kendrick and Lord Paole?"

She didn't know? My throat constricted, choking closed.

"Lord Paole was lost when Marcus ambushed us in this very room." Uriel's glance at the fire extinguishers suggested she wasn't exactly trusting of Vanessa's sudden appearance—or motives, either.

Ty stood right behind my throne. "Marcus killed Kendrick at the hotel battle."

"Oh, Amelia." Tears flooded and fell. Crystal clear. No hint of crimson like a damned—like I'd seen when Ty begged for me to *kill him.* "I didn't know. Oh, God, I'm so sorry."

With all the fresh blood on offer, the leash I kept my hunger tied to was fraying. I filled a glass and downed the lot. "Marcus claims there's a way to resurrect him." I'd shared the *ice, life and death* part from Marcus's note with the RVC when I'd canceled Kendrick's funeral. I hadn't shared the fact that Dorian had delivered the note because Marcus had compelled him. Without a way to break my twin's compulsion over my brother, I wasn't risking the RVC taking extreme measures to sever the puppet act. And now with Dorian's suicide threat, there was no way they'd be enlightened on that issue.

"Wow. Okay. I'll help figure it out. For sure. We'll find a way."

"Not before you explain your return," Lady Rasputin said before taking a sip from her glass.

"How-how are you here?" Dorian stuttered. The cracks that showed in his exterior gave me hope that we could break Marcus's control over him. Especially now that Vanessa was back.

With all eyes on the young redhead, Vanessa took a deep, even breath and blew it back out. Something I still struggled with being in transition. "When I was bitten, I was infected with lycan and damned venom. I must have passed out after the attack, because the next memory I have is of waking to Marcus. Most humans can't survive a damned's bite. He told me I was dying. From the agony I felt, I knew it was true. But Ty had bitten me with his canines, too. Infected by a lycan. I was turning into a werewolf at the same time."

"But you're not one, are you?" Ty's nostrils flared as he tested the air. "Your scent is human. So is your heartbeat."

There was a mark to block a being's scent, as long as their blood wasn't spilled. But I'd never heard of one to change a being's heartbeat, which is why Ty's blood was the only way to hide my transition.

"I am human, but I wouldn't have been without intervention. Turning werewolf was the only thing keeping me from dying from the damned bite. I guess it made me more than human. It kept me alive. When the damned venom had almost worn off, Marcus gave me a vial of blood. Your brother's blood, Ty."

"Hybrid blood," I whispered, the pieces falling into place. "It cured the wolf bite." Like it had in Raven, after Ty had bitten her at the PVC battle. And like it had in Marcus, after Mr. Malau had scored a bite following the boardroom ambush.

"You still had some damned venom in you," Ty said, looking like the wheels were on overdrive in his head. "You were subhuman. If it had all burned off and you lived, you would have become a werewolf."

Ty knew more about this than me, but one thing was evidently clear. "What Marcus did kept you human."

Vanessa glanced down as she felt the pulse at her wrist, like she still didn't quite believe it.

All of what she'd explained so far made sense. But surviving was only half of this confusing puzzle. "You were under compulsion. How did you escape?"

Vanessa glanced up at the wrought iron chandelier, the candlelight dancing over her face. Her gaze turned distant as if in memory before refocusing. "After surviving the infection, it was like some of the haze in my head lifted. I was compelled to mark the damned. But never *not* to mark myself. In between his minions being sent in, I slowly managed to tattoo myself."

She rolled up the sleeve of her red leather jacket to expose an inked mark along her inner forearm. It was similar in design to the mark Dorian had used to try to break the compulsion that kept Caius from revealing the damned commander's identity and his location. The one that had conveniently failed. Except this mark was black—

not gold. Black like the ones I'd seen her give Ty as a damned. Was that why Dorian's had failed? Was this unknown substance needed to mark the damned the one thing missing when we'd attempted to break the damned compulsion Caius was under?

"This blocked any new compulsion. So when Marcus compelled me not to escape after moving me to another residence, that was the first thing I did after he left." She almost smiled up at Dorian. "In your M5."

That explained the engine rumble moments before she'd burst in here.

"This residence," I said with raised brows and more than a little suspicion. "You could lead us there?"

"Absolutely." Vanessa showed no reservation or indecision. "Though I'll need to backtrack on a map to pinpoint the exact location."

Although everything she'd said and how she appeared and acted made sense, I held on to my skepticism. I'd been duped too many times in the past. Trusted when I shouldn't have.

"Looks like our search for a replacement alchemist has been answered." Dorian clapped his hands together like this was a done deal.

But I wasn't having it.

"You can't know if you're clean, Vanessa." I kept my tone sympathetic, even though I felt anything but. "Old persuasions might still be affecting you."

Vanessa nodded in total agreement. "I still want my old job back. My life. But I agree. I can't be certain my mind is clear of all of Marcus's compulsion."

"Then I vote reinstatement as our acting alchemist," I stated. "But only under twenty-four-hour surveillance."

"Amelia."

I continued over Ty's objection. "And total lockdown until further convening on your condition is agreed on." I leveled narrowed eyes at her. "Do you have any objections, Vanessa?"

She shook her head gently back and forth. "I don't want to compromise the Armaya. I just want to help. Whatever the conditions, I accept them."

Ty spoke before I could, saying almost word-for-word what I'd had in mind. "Amelia will set off with me and my pack on the new lead ASAP."

A discussion broke out as everyone mulled over Vanessa's claims, my security measures, and Ty's proposed infiltration. In the end, the vote was unanimous. Vanessa would be guarded and reinstated as the castle's alchemist. And our team would set off to the place she'd escaped from as soon as Vanessa pinned down the exact address.

Which gave me just enough time to do some investigating…

CHAPTER 7

I left the meeting in a rush, winding through the castle's back corridors toward the prison cells. Ty stuck with me, so close I could feel the heat coming off his bare arms. The hunger I'd felt earlier had my stomach clenching with demand, but I couldn't wait a minute more to find out if my suspicions were true. Especially while Dorian was holed up reuniting with Vanessa. Could we use her escape method to our advantage with my brother? I was still reeling over her sudden return from death and I wanted to believe her story so bad. But her reaction to Dorian's demeanor would speak volumes.

With each quick step my Vans slapped against the ground beneath me. The repetitive noise joined the constant beat of Ty's heart, a sound that drummed in my ears, tempting me.

With the way Ty kept his eyes on me, he knew his earlier supply of blood was wearing thin. And yet he said nothing to deter me. His need to keep me from killing was constant, but the strain across his angled face was deeper than usual. "I…I still can't believe she's alive. I mean I knew she wasn't dead after I…but still, she wasn't far off."

Aside from believing her story, it was clear he blamed himself for everything she'd suffered.

I paused in my stride and touched Ty's scarred forearm. Without permission, my gaze tracked the highway of black veins up his arm. Apart from marking him as a restored damned, they clearly illustrated the juiciest lines to tap. I licked my lower lip. Sinewy muscle bunched under my palm, highlighted in light and shadow from the flaming wall lanterns. He stepped back quickly, breaking the connection. The rejection stung, but I understood it. I wouldn't want to be touched by an almost-damned who was vying for blood, either.

"You had no conscience, Ty. It wasn't your fault."

Ty blew air through his nostrils as if to say, *sure, whatever.* The look he gave me was dark as he started in the direction we'd been heading. "After I infected you, I dragged her body down to the cavern. She disappeared after Marcus returned. I thought the damned had emptied her veins and she'd been disposed of…like the others. I never imagined…"

Around another bend, we reached the gated entrance that led down to the cells. "You want to speak to her? Say sorry?"

Ty shrugged as we descended the stone stairs. "Like that'll ever be enough."

I tried and failed to ignore the collective smell of live blood that permeated the air the lower we got. A dry swallow allowed words to leave my mouth. "She knows you weren't you then. She won't hold it against you."

That doubtful expression didn't leave his face as we cleared the stairwell and entered the circular room surrounded by locked cell doors. "Which one is his?"

Guess we were done with that discussion. I nodded to one of the prison guards. I swear I wasn't tracking that vein up her neck. "Unlock Caius's cell."

The guard moved without question to unlock the steel door. A moment later we were inside, the door closed to the prison guards. The punch of blood lessened, but my thirst for it didn't vanish. *Focus, dammit.* Clenching my fists, I ignored the quieting beat of my heart. With a single bulb lighting most of the space, Caius was easy to spot. Rather than hiding in the shadowed corners, he was standing as if in wait. His old suit was more tattered than the other day, and the silver he'd been restrained with in this cell while in transition had been replaced with marked iron.

"Amelia, how nice of you to pay me a visit." My father—by blood alone, because he'd never be more after trying to exsanguinate me—glanced from me to Ty. Did he think Ty was here to exact some kind of personal revenge?

"So the whispers *are* true." Caius scanned Ty before leveling his eyes at me. "The wolf has been granted permanent access to our restricted community. Your actions have had them reinstated as our *guardians?*"

"We are no *slaves* to vampires, old man." Ty bared his fangs and canines collectively. "We are equals. Assisting to eradicate a common enemy."

"And our powers know your lineage, *hybrid?*"

"They do," I interrupted the escalating testosterone as Caius stepped forward. The breath that I forced through my lips was making me twitchy. Though Caius didn't seem to notice any abnormality.

Instead, he smirked. "I noticed you saved my former colleagues from losing another crown…after *he* already snuffed out Lord Paole."

I had no reason to deny it. The proof had been all over Uriel's black-veined skin when Caius had been summoned for my forced vision. "Yes. Uriel was restored."

But he'd alluded to more. Ty picked up the second line of questioning. "You said *him*."

I hadn't missed that part, either. Which brought me full circle to why I'd come here. "You still can't say Marcus's name?"

Caius strolled back to the wall, wrist chains clanking with each step. He leaned his back into the stone, lips pressed together as he shook his head. "The strongest of damned compulsion prevents me speaking his name."

"Who's?" Ty half growled. We both had the same suspicion, and being the strongest? It had to be…

Salt and pepper brows popped and he spoke through clenched teeth. "*His.*"

That was as close as we were going to get, because… "The compulsion Dorian couldn't break, because he wasn't marked with black ink."

The old vampire seemed almost impressed at my assumption. "My clever daughter. But why the sudden interest…" He stroked his face where overgrown stubble was fast turning into a beard. "Ah, you know."

"That Marcus is compelling Dorian," Ty answered. "Yeah, we know."

A flash of disappointment? Caius sighed. "Like a puppet master, *he* pulls the strings."

I came forward, fangs sliding free in spite of my struggle to retract them fully. Ty stuck by my side. Fearing what I'd do or what Caius might? Either way, it didn't matter. Vanessa's story's credibility, along with our next plan of attack, hinged on this old vampire's reply to my next question. But would he tell the truth? Could he? "If that symbol Dorian tried on you had been in black ink, could it break Marcus's compulsion?"

Caius's dry lips opened then shut. Opened then…another sigh. "It is the only thing I know that could combat it."

BACK IN MY LOUNGE ROOM, Ty kept one hand in his leather jacket's pocket as he eyed the veins growing up my neck and across my cheeks. The twitch of his ears made it clear he was listening to the slowing beat of my heart. His jaw clenched as he held out a glass topped with his blood. The *take it* was implied by the sharp look in his eyes.

And I wasn't going to argue.

Coming closer, absently skirting around a wing chair, I had to fend off the instinct to snatch the crystal from his hand…*and throw it aside so I could flatten him on his back and tap the living source.* God, he smelled good. Too good. Any thoughts of our mission-to-come fled my mind. My resolve to save my brother from Marcus no longer existed right now.

"Vanessa's mark checks out," Ty grated, tightening his grip on the crystal he held. Keeping me in his line of sight—as he always did—he perched on the edge of the cabinet and tapped the open book beside him. "It can be used against Marcus's compulsion."

I stepped closer, desperate for a real taste of what was on offer. My reaching hand snagged a belt loop, ignoring the cooling glass in his other hand, pretending my sight hadn't just glazed red.

"Then it'll work on Dorian."

Ty's head twisted to the female voice and the sound of three sets of feet approaching. And three steady-beating hearts. I released Ty and snatched the glass, downing it quickly. The retreat of black veins hummed over my skin and I spun slowly to see Vanessa in the foyer archway with two guards behind her. "I'm sorry." She shrugged, eyeing our closeness and the empty glass. "I didn't mean to interrupt anything."

The same words Marcus had said when he walked in on Kendrick and me kissing. And I had just been—doing what exactly?

"You can wait outside," Ty directed the guards, shutting the book. "Your protection's not needed in here."

The guards didn't budge.

"It's fine," I tried not to hiss as I faked normal breathing and moved to perch casually—I wish—on the furthest away wing chair's arm. "We'll call you when we're ready," I said, tabling the empty glass.

With a bow to me, they retreated, but I didn't speak even after the door shut behind them. With my hunger now locked down and the beat of my heart steady again, my lack of words wasn't caused by punishing self-control. Vanessa was alive and breathing and the mark proved she could block Marcus's orders. But that didn't mean she wasn't under orders made before her escape. Ty's mind seemed to be on another topic entirely.

"Vanessa, I—" Ty stood, but he seemed unable to move. His voice dropped low and quiet. "I'm fucking sorry. Nothing I say or do can ever make up—"

"I don't blame you." Vanessa came further into the room and leaned into a free wing chair. She sighed slow and hard, lids sliding shut. Her lips twisted and she shook herself as her eyes reopened. "Even at the time, I didn't. I know you, Ty. I have for most of my life. Even when you were…damned, you fought to keep parts of your old self alive." As Ty ground his teeth like he didn't believe a word she was saying, Vanessa went to him and clutched his arms. "Stop beating yourself up. I'm here. I'm fine."

"And now…" I watched as Vanessa returned to the wing chair and assumed the same position. I'd planned to seek her out once I was back in relative control—to get the address, but also… I moved so fast I was over the coffee table between us and behind Vanessa in a blink.

She spun with a startled gasp as Ty tensed, hand on his dagger and ready to act. "What the—" No breath passed my lips and my chest turned to stone. "You're…"

"I'm in transition." This was a test of knowledge…and of loyalty. "And no one outside our circle knows about it."

Vanessa's mouth gaped in horror—but not fear. Looking to Ty, her voice was quiet. "You did this." When he glanced away in shame, she faced me without flinching. "And you're choosing to stay this way. Why?"

"I can track the damned. Which will hopefully lead me to—"

"Marcus," she interrupted. "I get it. And if that's what you choose, I'll back you…"

She accepted my choice? I really hadn't expected that. I thought she'd take the stand Marcus had, and 'encourage' me to remain an almost monster.

She frowned suddenly, staring at my neck before grasping my wrist to lay a thumb along the thickest vein. One-two. One-two. "You have a pulse. How is that even…?"

"My blood." Ty eyed the glass on the coffee table but didn't move. "It hides the traits."

"Oh good. At least one thing's going right for us. But…" Without concern for turning her back to me, she coasted around the wing chair and slumped into it. "Dorian's not okay. He's not himself. There's something fundamentally wrong with him."

Coming around to sit on the coffee table's edge, I studied her worried face. Time for test two. She may not have known I was spying that day I was following her to Ty and Marcus. But she had to remember what Dorian had done to her. "Vanessa…" Breathing through my mouth, I took her arm, rolling her sleeve up. I felt Ty watching me, waiting. Good thing. As that pale flesh was revealed, for a second I only saw the bluish veins that ran below the surface. My tongue tapped the tip of my fangs that refused to retract.

Ty cleared his throat.

I shook my head to clear my mind, my hold on Vanessa's scarred arm squeezing tighter. "Who did this to you?"

Vanessa stared down at her arm with perplexed confusion, seeing the long, nasty scars that covered her inner forearm. "I have no idea. I keep trying to recall, but there's just a black hole."

Suspending his watch over me—though not entirely—Ty came closer to inspect the healed damage. His eyes, which had turned the color of a sun-speckled ocean after I'd restored him, lifted to his old friend. "They were new that day you led Amelia to us. I didn't care to know how they'd happened back then."

I released Vanessa and put a few feet of space between me and them, lowering myself onto the sectional's armrest. It was time for the reveal…and a little wordplay to source motives. "Dorian did this. The day he compelled you to take his car and go to Ty. The day I followed you from the Armaya to the damned hotel. I don't know if it was the first time—"

"Because I was marking the damned. Even back then." Vanessa's candid interruption cut off my sentence, and the planned test I'd had coming. "I remember it. That's how they got onto the compound. How Ty did, too." Her eyes rose with crystal-clear tears. "Marcus was controlling me through Dorian, wasn't he?"

Ty went to touch her shoulder, but changed his mind. He stared down as he spoke. "It…it was my suggestion to use you both to get hold of Amelia."

Vanessa sniffed back her tears and caught Ty's hand with a look of hope. "Now we're all here and we have a chance to fix everything. What's our next step?"

"We know the black ink you're marked with can block Marcus's compulsion," Ty said, the guilt across his face paling with raw determination. "If you mark one of us, we'll be able to break Marcus's control over Dorian."

"Well, yeah, in theory. But—"

"Then all we need is some of that black ink." I clasped my hands together and squeezed, my suspicion of Vanessa morphing into anticipation. "You can use it on me."

Vanessa shook her head and her red hair followed the movement in a shimmy. "It's not that simple. I never knew the alternative substance existed before Marcus made me use it on his damned. I don't know how to make it. And the only place to get it from—"

"Is Marcus," I cut in. My eyes narrowed. "But you have the address, right?"

Vanessa nodded and pulled a folded piece of paper from her skinny jeans. "Absolutely. It's in a town called Hope."

I snatched the paper and held on tight. We needed all the hope we could get. "You were marking them there, so the ink should still be there. We just have to get through the damned without obliterating our one shot at freeing my brother."

Ty took the note from me with a frown. "Hope? That's a good three-hour drive."

Reality hit me. I'd be in a car with four living blood bags on a mission to source a substance from an enemy who'd have to know Vanessa, their secret weapon, was missing.

Ty said what I hadn't been thinking. "It's too close to sunrise. We'll have to wait until nightfall."

"Great." This was going to be a blast. "Guess he'll be expecting us then." He just wouldn't know what we were coming for.

I GROUND MY MOLARS. "Are we there yet?" The link I'd picked up on the damned a few miles back had dulled as my hunger for blood continued to rise. We'd been on the road for over three hours. Together. Ty, Raven, and me, trapped in the cab of Ty's WRX. Thick trees surrounded the thin road we were on. The scenic surroundings hadn't changed for the past how many miles. Since we bypassed Anchorage and left the Seward Hwy for the Hope Hwy, they'd only become more and more remote.

In the passenger seat, cool night air through my open window cleared the smell of their blood out. It batted my eardrums too, interrupting the sound of their strong heartbeats. Mine was holding out for now, after doubling up on Ty's blood before leaving. The internal fantasies, however, were a din I couldn't quiet. For the hundredth time, I saw our bright blue car front-ending a tree. Next second? Screams and explosions of blood painting the insides of the windows.

"We're almost there." In the driver's seat, Ty's hand left the gear shaft and reached my way. Like he had in the distant past when we'd been together in his car. As I tensed at his nearing touch, he retreated, as if remembering who we both now were to each other—and what I was. With a quick scan over my non-veined arms, he rubbed a hand across his chin. Under his breath, he added, "I hope we're almost there."

Lights flickered through the rear windshield from Troy on his motorbike. Marika rode passenger behind him, and both were armed to the teeth. With the first promising damned lead they'd had in ages, they were rearing to take action. And with our arrangement with the RVC, apart from Ty, they were my only guard for this mission. When the headlights flashed from his bike again, I knew they were getting antsy for our arrival.

"I still find Vanessa's escape kind of *miraculous.*" Raven had been quiet for most of the ride, nose buried in a book she hoped would have some clue about resurrection. No luck so far, or she'd have screamed the roof off.

After revealing all that had occurred yesterday, it seemed she more than had reservations. I still did too. I glanced through the gap to the backseat, my brows rising in a *soon we'll know* kind of way… because speaking would show my fangs and let my tongue taste the blood I smelled on the air.

A sharp turn onto a gravel road had me facing forward as they killed the motors. A moment later, we were pulling up to a log cabin buried inside a thick layer of surrounding trees. I leaped from the car, thankful for the fresh air that cleared the smell of blood from my nose.

Raven and Ty were out of his WRX too, but only Ty came around the car to face me. "What are we dealing with?"

The plan had been set before our departure. With all the time that had passed since Vanessa's escape, someone would have noticed. Marcus, or at least his damned, would be expecting us. If we couldn't sneak in and steal what we needed, we'd fight to take it.

Except I couldn't sense the damned at all. "I…"

Gentle cracks were audible as Troy and Marika left his bike and strode toward us. In the few steps over, their exteriors transformed, pallor graying and irises turning from gold to red as they morphed into damned they'd previously taken out.

With their scents masked and Raven only now coming around

the car, I managed to whisper, "I think my link's short-circuiting. I can't really feel them."

Suspicion rising, I shot forward, unable to see through the boarded-up windows. The others were behind me in a flash. Together we surrounded the wooden verandah that stretched around the entire dwelling. Ty and I at the front, Raven, Troy, and Marika spaced out from the side to the back. The only sounds were cicadas resuming their song and wind sweeping through the long grass and tree branches.

On the other side of the front door, Ty met my eye with a frown. The plan had been to wait for the others to sneak in the back, but then Ty gripped the door handle and pushed down.

My "*what are you doing?*" was ignored as Ty pushed the door in and stole inside. Right behind him, I smacked into his back as he pulled up short. The smell of him distracted me, making my long fangs ache in want. My hands rose, ready to take hold.

A door slammed, jolting me out of my dangerous train of thought. We were in the entryway, the living, dining, and kitchen one big connected space. My jaw gaped at the sight. The whole place had been ransacked. Obliterated.

"It's the same for the bedrooms." Raven kicked a mangled lamp as she appeared from the hallway with the damned lookalikes.

Marika scanned the rest of the damage as fresh cracks returned her and Troy to their normal selves. "This must have happened after Vanessa escaped."

Troy growled, canines long and deadly. He stalked over the rubble like it was nothing. "Gonna check outside—just in case there are any lingerers."

Feeling less out of control with a steady breeze wafting through the door after Troy left, I checked out the area. There was nothing that resembled the equipment Vanessa used to do her craft in between the wrecked table and splintered chair. "There has to be something. Somewhere. We need to search the place." The others nodded and got to work weeding through the mess. I got to my knees, gradually clearing some floor space from larger furniture fragments. I lifted a small round tabletop and glimpsed below. More rubbish: a smashed glass, broken porcelain…and a spray of black. "I found ink!"

As the others rushed over, Marika's words squashed my hope. "Vanessa can't use that. It's mixed with dirt. It might not even be ink."

Honestly, it looked more like blood, all glossy but without a shimmer.

Ty leaned down, grasping a chair leg that was perched like a starter log over kindling. "We'll just have to find the ink some other—"

The chink from glass-on-glass contact had me diving over rubbish to catch…

Raven edged closer. "What is it?"

The jagged edge of the bottom of a vial jutted from my grasp. Fingers pinching the rounded tip, I held it up. Black ink residue colored the clear glass. "It's not enough—"

My words cut off as a little tug pulled at my insides. Ty noticed instantly, pulling me up by one hand as his other delved into his pocket. His scan of me and the lack of threat I posed put him on edge. Body snapping tight he whipped out a stake—as a bark cut through the cicadas outside. "We're not alone anymore."

There was a split second of silence. And then the sound of hissing and feet pounding dirt filled the air.

Troy shot in through the open door. "The damned. We're surrounded." His body trembled violently as cracks rang out from him and Marika. Growling as they fell down on all fours, their forms changed and grew in record speed. As their clothes shredded and their weapons fell with a clatter, fur sprouted, covering their now-wolf forms.

"Kill or be killed," Ty barked, freeing a dagger. They raced for the door—and the damned crashed in through the boarded-up windows.

CHAPTER 8

I freed my dagger. My other hand wrapped around the vial, feeling the cut of glass as I squeezed. I commanded my mind to lash out at the countless damned flooding in. But I couldn't move. Vision failing, my eyes rolled and my knees gave out.

I fell like a stone, something stabbing into my back as I flattened a pile of debris.

I gasped, suddenly upright and seated. A *drip, drip* brought my eyes down—to the silver blade I'd just dragged along my inner forearm. Or not. The bone structure was different, more masculine. The fingers that curled into a fist were pale and long. A pot on the floor below caught the trickle of red blood that escaped the gash.

A car exhaust rumbled and the eyes I saw through looked up to the only door. A male damned entered and stepped close enough to hand out a vial. "My blood, Commander."

My real body where I'd fallen must have jerked in surprise, even though I had no control here. I was in a vision, inhabiting my twin's body.

Marcus took the vial as the gash slowly pulled back together. "Get out." The damned was gone in a flash and then my twin was tipping the damned's blood into the pot with his own. A knock on the door was met with a snarl. "Not now!" With one finger he mixed the two, the black swirling around and around until it ate up the red.

That knock came again. More persistent. Louder.

Marcus swooped up the pot and yanked the door open. "Someone better be dying or so help me—" His verbal assault stalled at the damned's terrified face. "Speak before I really lose my temper."

"She's gone. In that sports car."

Marcus flung the damned into the wall and raced—into the same room I'd just blacked out in. Beside a vacant upholstered chair, a small table was set up with a tattoo gun, a glass of water, and a pot with gold liquid.

More damned stood around nervously, glancing from the empty seat to their commander…their commander who often killed without a second thought.

Inside Marcus's shell, I shot across the room. He upended the table with a scream and threw the blood mixture down on the ground. The one he'd concocted for Vanessa to use in marking? The ceramic pot shattered and black sprayed out. The substance I'd found. "Call the others in and tear this place to shreds. We're going after her."

My lids flung open and I bit my tongue to keep from groaning at the broken glass that impaled my back. The sounds of battling penetrated the walls: bodies colliding, paws and feet pelting hard ground, a weapon connecting as it cracked bone. Ty's pack and Raven were out there, still fighting off the damned.

But that didn't mean I was alone.

A damned flew backward through the air, hitting the wall and landing on its feet.

Ty stood on the other side of the wreck of broken furniture, cuts seeping blood along his face and down his arms. Ash covered his tacky skin that was marbled with black and red. He smiled at that final damned, kicking at a pile of hot coals—once a fellow damned—as the noise outside began to die down. "Last but not least."

The scent of Ty's spilled blood assaulted me as my stomach clenched with sudden starvation. *Not least, indeed,* my devious inner voice taunted. *Get it while it's hot.*

Ty launched at the damned, going for the kill. But I couldn't let that damned become ash. "Don't. I need him." My rasp brought Ty's head around—and the damned clawed into his stomach.

Red invaded my sight. My heart stopped dead. But I couldn't lose control—I just needed a dose of reality. And I knew exactly where to get it.

Shoving my cut-up hand behind me as I levered up with a cry, I yanked the glass shard from my back. The pain cleared my head a fraction as I jumped up.

Ty was up on top of the damned, stake driving down.

"Don't kill it!" I moved without thought, without plan. Landing on Ty's back, my fangs sank into his neck—and Ty's stake plunged into the damned's chest, missing its heart.

Ty stood fast, lifting my weight with ease. Now that I had him and that potent flood of his blood was filling my mouth? Shocks sizzled from my fingers and he stumbled on wood fragments, falling down to his knees. I wasn't going to let go. Bottled blood was nothing compared to this. As I pumped more voltage to keep Ty from fighting back, the cabin vibrated, remaining jagged glass falling from the smashed windows. My skin sizzled where it touched the silver chain around Ty's neck. But none of it registered beyond a slight annoyance, like a fly buzzing around my head. I bit down harder and drank deeper.

Ty struggled to get words out. "The damned's a-alive. You—you needed—it a-alive."

The damned on the ground turned from shades of red to gray and black as my vision corrected itself. Its hand was curled around the stake in its chest, sizzling as it slowly drew the weapon free.

My heart let out a beat then raced to life. *What the hell am I doing?* My fangs disengaged and my voltage receded. I caught Ty before he face-planted a pile of shattered glass. "Oh shit. I—"

"Why?" Ty threw a shaking hand out, but the look on his face wasn't judgmental, angry, or disappointed. "Why do you need it alive?"

"I..." I cut the guilt crap—there'd be time for that later—and scrambled to the damned, bearing down on the stake that instantly burned my palm to immobilize it. "I know how to make the ink. I need its blood."

MY HAND SQUEEZED around my dagger and I pulled the blade free with a slice. The sting was met with a trickle of blood as I clenched my fist tight over a glass beaker on the long stainless steel bench. Fed and in relative control, my mind kept on track as I watched the blood level rise. After what we'd gone through and my vision yesterday, everything was riding on my hunch. "You really think my blood will work?"

I'd seen Marcus bloodlet into a pot before adding damned blood to the mix. When he'd found out about Vanessa's escape, there'd been a pot of normal gold ink out on that table by that tattoo gun.

"You're twins. Both with altered DNA." Vanessa came around the workbench, plucking a test tube topped off with black damned blood from one of the many rows of varying liquids. She shrugged. "Short of going after Marcus, this is our best bet."

Thinking past what I could hear coursing through her veins, I studied her focused face as she tipped the tube's contents into my donated blood. I'd learned more than the ingredients to recreate this black ink yesterday. I'd seen Marcus's reaction to Vanessa's escape, his ire at losing his alchemist. Everything Vanessa said had been true. Her survival. Her escape. Located down a back corridor of the castle, I glanced around the alchemist den lined with cabinets and shelves full of metals, wood, books, weapons, and cork-stoppered bottles. An alchemist's dream. "I…I'm sorry I doubted you."

Vanessa glanced up at the closed iron-braced door. The one that locked two guards outside who were ordered to watch over her actions—before I'd shut them out for our experiment. She shrugged. "I don't blame you. I would have done the same. Besides, I kinda feel safer with someone watching me."

"In case an old compulsion pops up?"

Vanessa shook her head, brow creasing with worry. "No. In case he comes back for me himself, or through…"

"Dorian." I mixed my blood with the added damned blood using my finger like I'd seen Marcus do. Despite Ty's pack wanting to put down the damned, Ty had been on board with returning it to the RVC. Proof the lead had checked out and that the wolves were holding up their end by returning any captured for restoring. Not that I was in any state to use my power to turn the damned back into a vampire, currently. But being a full damned and not a transitionee meant there wasn't a time limit for saving that one lost soul. A damned couldn't die from blood deprivation, only a transitionee could.

Vanessa took the beaker of combined blood and tipped a little into the gold liquid. "I never knew what the black liquid was, but I saw him add it to my marking gold. It didn't seem to be a measured science."

"Let's hope not," I said as she used a glass stick to mix the substances, turning that vibrant gold into a shimmery black.

She plugged her old tattoo gun—which Troy and Marika had commandeered—into a socket on the bench. With a flick of a switch, the machine rattled to life and she dipped the tip into our mix. "Fingers crossed."

I offered my arm, wrist-side up, and leaned back into the workbench. Unlike the last time Vanessa had marked me, the drilled-in ink didn't fade as that needle drummed into my skin. This time, as the gun moved in her expert-steady hands, delicate black lines and swirls were left in its wake. The symbol slowly came together, a large outline of an eye around a smaller one that existed within its intricate pupil. The same mark Dorian had tried to use on Caius—made with the wrong ink.

Vanessa put down her customized tattoo gun and wiped the excess black from my arm with a wet towel. "You're good to go."

Getting the gun from my brother's house along with her old equipment had been simple. When he'd moved into the Vladimir suite after his crowning, all his and Vanessa's old stuff had been left there. Plus Dorian was MIA again. Still, the ease of Troy and Marika getting in and out, of everything he'd left behind, had instilled me with growing worry. What was Dorian up to now? "Where do you think he is?"

Vanessa couldn't hide her worry as she placed her gun into a drawer under the bench top. "Wherever Marcus wants him to be."

"Then we'll have to find him."

The door swung open then, and Ty strode in. He tracked me first, scanning my arms and neck like he expected his blood supply had begun to fail. His nostrils flared as he reached the opposite side of the central bench. He frowned after a split-second scan of the den. "Vanessa, where are your guards?"

"What do you mean?" Vanessa said.

I glanced at the open door. "Aren't they…?" Beyond the opening, I couldn't see her two standing watch. "The guards aren't out there?"

"Not anymore." There was a *clap, clap* of boots, and then Dorian stepped into the doorway. "They won't be back for a while."

I slid off the stool and chanced a step closer. "We want to help you." Like dealing with an unpredictable wild animal, my hands rose, open and palms forward, non-threatening. Another slow step. "We can, now."

Ty hadn't moved an inch, but I could feel the ready tension radiating off him. Every muscle under those black veins had snapped tight, twitching to strike. A warning growl filled the silence.

Unconcerned, Dorian grinned, white teeth flashing and smirk sinister. "Didn't know I needed any." He cleared the threshold and tugged the door shut behind him. "But if you're hell-bent…"

"Dorian, wait—"

Cutting Vanessa off, his hands strained, one pointed toward her and me. The other trained at Ty who'd gone to race around the bench. Behind me, Vanessa cried out, stumbling off her seat as Ty fell to his knees, wheezing for air. Distinct cracks rang out from Vanessa's body—so different from when a lycan imprinted or changed forms. These were quieter, more subtle, a sound I'd heard and watched before. Like a winter's sudden cold snap to a lake, Dorian was freezing her. From the inside out. Ty fumbled to get up, bracing on a stool as he coughed crimson. More blood streamed from his eyes, nose, and ears, gushing like tiny waterfalls. He snarled and staggered, the stool tipping and taking him down to the ground.

Overcoming the shock—and knowing Dorian had his hands too full to use his ability on me—electricity flooded my palms. Throwing them up, I unleashed forking streams of blue. Bullseye. One to his heart, the other to one wrist. Focus lost, his hold on Vanessa was severed and she listed sideways, hitting the ground and banging her head on a bench leg. Panic swept through me, and I rushed to help her. The last being I'd seen Dorian freeze had been kicked into a million frozen pieces. Vanessa was human. She'd be long dead before freezing through.

"I'm fine," her voice was a rasp. "Stop him."

I went to lash out again—and stalled before I could let loose more voltage. Blood. So much blood. And not just anyone's. Ty's. I'd seen it flooding out. Now I couldn't rid the smell from my sinuses. Couldn't quash the thought of tasting it—all of it. Of licking it from his hot skin as I pinned him on his back…

Spinning around, I became the danger, the predator, eyes tracking and stance primal.

Behind me, Vanessa saw the change as rose-color stained my sight. "Amelia, no!"

My irises were bright red. The monster was breaking free. Ty pushed up to his knees, fighting to get vertical. That delicious red kept on running. Tracks reformed down his cheeks, chin, and down his neck. They stained that amulet chain and melted into his T-shirt. Small puddles had formed on the ground where he'd been crouched. *Such a waste.*

"Amelia," Ty choked out, spitting blood. "Control it."

I could barely hear him past the sudden buzzing in my ears—could barely care that Dorian was still standing by and watching. He made no move to stop me. Why was he here again? "Do it already."

With those words, that free-falling blood poured out faster. Irresistibly. My victim's body tried to rise. He didn't get far as I closed the gap, hauled him up, and drove him back into the cabinet, rattling the contents. I trailed my tongue up his face. God, that taste. His black-veined hand shot up and Dorian laughed as I went to restrain—

He didn't touch me. Didn't even attempt to throw me off or fight back. Instead, his raised hand trembled. The walls and ground shook as if in fear. Stones punched up like whack-a-moles in the ground and hit the workbench's legs, rattling all that glass on top. Dorian went to yank the door open as the stainless steel bench flipped. But instead, he got pinned against it with a crash and a splatter of equipment and concoctions.

At the same time, my victim bucked and threw his elbow into my jaw. "Snap out of it."

Stumbling back, I hissed. The blood leaking from my prey had stopped. But I didn't care. I stalked forward—

You're not a monster.

Those same words stopped me in my tracks. Stripped my need to kill more quickly than any beating ever could. *Kendrick.* With my sight still red, I saw the bleeding guy pinned against a cabinet with total clarity. "Ty, shit." I released my clawed hold, despite how much my clenching stomach protested.

Any apology died on my tongue as Dorian's banging to get free brought me around. Vanessa, now thawed, raced with Ty to keep him pinned as the barricading bench lost its driving force. The force Ty had conjured to move stone and hurl metal across the room.

"You have a connection to earth."

Ty glared at me. "Not the time, Amelia."

"And you're a bloody bomb with the pin out." Vanessa's look of betrayal was directed at both of us. "What the hell?"

Neither of us had detailed the unpredictable danger I could be. And when you compared apples to apples, was I any less of a threat than my brother?

"Argh!" Dorian bucked harder, trapped hands flexing and fingers trembling, trying to conjure his connection to water again.

Operating past my lingering bloodlust, I rushed over and clutched his cheeks. My eyes drilled into his, red lenses fading as silver sparked in my eyes. "Override Marcus's compulsion. Ignore everything he's compelled you to do. He has no power over you anymore."

Dorian's fight died down and he began to… *Laugh?* Ty and Vanessa released him and we all backed up. He shoved the workbench off, then used a booted foot to force the table back to an upright position. "Fun time catching up." He opened the door wide.

Ty leaped for him but Dorian spun, freeing a dagger from a forearm holster that had been hidden below his long sweater. He pressed the sharp edge into his own neck and a line of crimson appeared. "How easily you forget my threats." He'd been compelled to kill himself if we revealed him to the RVC. Evidently, that threat was a fail-safe to get out of any tense situation. Dorian's dangerous smile remained as he backed up. "Until we meet again."

And then he was gone, out the door and down the corridor. I shuddered as his last words and the way he'd said them triggered a memory. When Marcus had rendered me unconscious after killing Kendrick. *Until we meet again, my sister.* My twin was still controlling Dorian, somehow. Which meant… "The mark you gave me didn't work. It didn't break Marcus's compulsion."

"No shit." Ty scrubbed his face. "And our lips are sealed."

Vanessa just stared through the empty doorway like she couldn't believe someone who had once loved her could come so close to killing her. "What do we do now?"

The sound of footsteps had all of us gawking through the open door. Vanessa's guards resumed their watch like they'd never left, and like they were blind to the destruction in the den. Dorian had compelled them, despite their repelling marks. But I couldn't give up on him. "We'll find another way."

CHAPTER 9

Hours later, I found myself down in the Baldassare tomb. I was alone—at least in body. But spirit?

Was that you in my head? Are you still here, somewhere?

Staring down at Kendrick's entombed body through the glass, I prayed for a response. But there was no twitch of his eyelids. No tension returning to his grayish flesh. How could there be? He was as dead now as he'd been the moment Marcus had snapped his neck. The freezer chamber had stalled any process of decomposition. It had frozen all his injuries, too. The puffy bruises across his face, the cuts over his knuckles from fighting my twin—and me—the purple-blue stripes diagonally across his throat from that fatal twist.

"Dammit, Kendrick. I need you. I'm failing at everything. Freeing my brother. Saving you…"

Even if you don't want saving. I shuddered at the sight of the Ouija board in the adjoining chamber. Fear more than temptation kept me from trying my luck on the spirit board again.

Still, no words sounded in my head. No reply through our bond.

I was alone in this candlelit tomb. Had been for the last twenty minutes. Talking to a ghost—I wish. Raven was down in the library, rummaging for new books. So far, she'd found nothing of use. Ty was seeing to his pack, working to organize some raids on possible leads Mr. Malau had provided. Vanessa was down in her den, poring over old volumes for a solution to Marcus's control over Dorian. She couldn't understand why the mark she'd put on me hadn't worked. The whys were pure speculation: Either my blood wasn't a good enough substitute for Marcus's, or we'd used an incorrect mark to sever old compulsion compared to Vanessa's which blocked new compulsion. Whatever the problem, I was stuck, up shit creek without a freaking paddle. Failing at the most important tasks of my life—saving the people I loved.

Still, I couldn't forget that internal voice I'd heard down in Vanessa's den. *You're not a monster.*

Was that you? Or just my fading conscience.

I scanned the empty tomb, past the walls of pigeonholed remains that were covered with concrete plaques, praying he'd magically appear. He didn't. And there was no reply.

Running one hand down the glass cover, I couldn't hold back the memories that flooded to the surface. I touched my lips, feeling that kiss Kendrick had laid on me as we'd watched The Vampire Diaries. The way he'd pushed me back on the couch sped my heart up now. I'd kissed him back. I'd kept the heat rising. He'd kissed me again in raw hopelessness before his mother's funeral, before making his demand to be with me. Soon after I'd seen Ty. I'd chased him down and found Kendrick at the Gazebo. I thought I was losing my ever-loving mind. I made a choice that night, one that had caused then—and still did now—so much pain. I'd started something unstoppable with Kendrick. With my best friend—who I'd been falling for.

As my eyes squeezed shut now, I saw the first time I took his vein, tempted to take so much more than his blood. Kendrick had let me, had wanted me to take everything. *"Soul and blood, I'm yours. Always."*

I'd been ready to start my life with him, my best friend. To go on without Ty, with Kendrick by my side. Which is what he'd always wanted. To rule by my side, to share our lives, a bed.

I'd ripped that all away with my deception and betrayal. With the times I'd let Ty get to me while he was damned.

And Kendrick had still come to my rescue. Still helped me save Ty. One life restored, the other now frozen in perpetual death.

Heart aching like it was being twisted in half, I wiped a crimson tear from my cheek. Unable to look at Kendrick's beaten lifeless face, I laid my head down on the freezing glass. Time passed as I wept, losing tangibility, spanning out before me. But I couldn't stay like this forever.

Straightening from my lean over the casket, I swiped away my tears. The silence was deafening as the round of steam left on the coffin's glass by my breath shrank smaller. My hand went to my heart—still beating, and aching like I'd been shot. I squeezed my eyes shut.

Finding that place deep in my chest, I sent out a message. *Kendrick, please. I need to know if you're still out there. Your spirit. Your soul. I don't care what happens to me, but I just need something. I understand if you hate me…*

Something light as a feather brushed over my cheek and my eyes flung open, searching. No one was here but me. But candles on the candelabras were flickering as if someone—or something—had disturbed them. I touched my cheek. I hadn't imagined that… I glanced back down at Kendrick's face—and gaped. The round of steam hadn't faded. It had grown, not on the outside of the glass cover—but on the inside. And that wasn't all. Clear as if a finger had traced them were letters spelling out two words.

Blood Bath.

I blinked hard and reopened my eyes, residual red tears sliding free. No letters and no message. No steam.

But I hadn't imagined those words…or that slight brush across my cheek. Kendrick had sent me a message. He had answered my plea. But in what capacity?

Were his words a clue…or a warning?

Mind racing with the possibility of what those two simple words meant, I turned to run. Whether a clue or a warning, action needed to be taken. But who to seek out first? Ty and his pack, or Raven down in the library? Racing for the only exit, not knowing where to head, I tugged the door in—

And slammed right into Raven. The tower of books in her arms hiccuped, then tilted, swaying side to side. She scrabbled to steady the stack. "Thanks for the heart attack." She showed no concern of my demeanor possibly going south. Instead, she pushed past me and stalked to the adjoining chamber. "Wanna tell me what's up?"

I followed her in, eyes vacant. Hands clasping and unclasping, I barely registered her carefully sliding the fresh stack onto a side table, or the old scattered books that fell to make room for the new.

"Because I can see from here that your hair's not on fire." She careened around and stalled at my closeness. "Oh, I didn't hear…" She frowned. "Actually, you look seriously pale. Like worse than norm—"

"I think Kendrick's trying to communicate with me," I rushed over the sound of my racing heart.

That shut her up. Made her mouth gape, and then shut. "Think?"

I kept the touch across my cheek to myself and went straight for the big guns. "A message on his coffin—written on the fogged-up inside."

Wheels turning behind her eyes, she dropped onto the sofa and grasped her pillow to her chest. "What did he say?"

"Two words. Blood bath. I have no idea what it means, and I don't know how to explain it, but I'm sure it was him. It could be a warning."

"Or a clue."

Of course Raven would take that line of thought. She was in love with the guy, had devoted all her spare time to finding answers to bring him back, while I was busy with obligations, my own issues, and helping Dorian.

It could be a clue. But if it wasn't… Walking back to Kendrick's coffin, the glass was only a fraction cooler than my fingertips as I traced the line of his face from above. "Either way, we need to find out. If it's not a warning, it could be what we need to bring him back."

"I'll get onto it." Raven got up to snatch the first few books off her new stack before returning.

I was already backing up to the open door. "I'll be back soon. I need to make sure it's not a warn—"

A sudden and unyielding sensation tugged at my insides. "Oh, shit." I spun to race out the open door and pulled to a halt.

Ty had just shot in. Panting like he'd sprinted here, his eyes scanned me like he thought I'd lost control again. "What's going on?" He eyed Raven, brow creasing at the sight of her safe and unharmed.

"We got a clue from Kendrick."

I quashed Raven's hope with rushed words. "It's not a clue." I was sure of that now. Staring past Ty into the dark of late vampire night, that sensation didn't let up. "My spidey senses are on overdrive," I said as the intensity soared. I darted around Ty, scaling the tomb's exterior to get a better look. Ty was up beside me in one bound, eyes darting with mine over the graveyard's tall walls, the busy streets and open shops, the trees that led to…

"Something's coming."

I spun to see Ty pointing between wind-swept trees to a section of the far-off stone and marble-columned wall.

And that's when I saw him.

I stared at the spot that was visible every half second as tree branches danced. Dorian was at the outer perimeter, a sledgehammer in his hands. He looked behind him—pausing as he caught my eye. With a smile he peered up to the swirling ashen clouds as they collided and…

Crack!

The connection as he swung the sledgehammer at the warded wall reverberated with the strike of lightning that streaked across the sky. The tomb shook as if in terror. The deed was done. Protection down and us now sitting ducks, I knew what was coming. And as the alarm wailed, triggered by the damage, I knew the wards meant to weaken and slow the damned had been disabled.

"The damned are coming!" I screamed over the wailing alarm. Adrenaline pumping, I went to jump down to the ground. The anticipation of their speed and ferocity filled me with terror. Distant movement stalled me mid-action.

Damned spilled over the twenty-foot wall like a menacing black and gray ocean. Right over the damaged wards Dorian had disappeared from.

Ty caught my bicep, his bulging as he freed his dagger. In a voice half animal he growled, "They'll head for Main Street. We need to cut them off."

And the street was packed.

Leaping together, we hit the gravel running. Raven was right behind us. “Time for action.”

As we cleared the headstones and tombs, a garden path had us bursting onto the road the castle steps led down to. The castle’s iron-braced doors flung open and countless guards filed out, armed and ready.

Ty forced his dagger on me as I screamed up at them. “Damned have broken the barrier!”

“They’re heading for Main Street,” Ty barked as cracks rang out, the sound of his bones breaking fast like a nail gun. “Attack to kill!” he grated through lengthening canines. With a roar of power and pain, his body beefed out, fur sprouting mid-stride through shredded clothes as his weapons fell and he landed on all fours.

The shocking display tore a startled cry from Raven. “Little warning next time.”

The guards hadn’t moved, mouths gaping as the giant wolf beside me snapped his jaw and remnants of his torn clothes fell away. He was ready.

And so was I. “Raven?”

“Let’s shut this down.”

The sound of screams cut through the wind, countless and coming from the city center. Getting over the sight of a wolf transforming, the guards pelted down the steps as we took to the streets. We didn’t get far. Damned drove up Main Street like a plague, a bottleneck, keeping us from the cries that split the air behind them. But they didn’t individually attack to kill the scurrying civilians. Instead, each vampire in range was caught and thrown back into the mass like an offering, a shared kill.

Ty leaped into the mass, sharp teeth bared to shred flesh. I didn’t try to follow. With the erratic way he’d be cutting down our enemies, I’d just get in the way…and likely get bitten. Instead, I kept to the outskirts with Raven and the guards, picking off damned one by one as we fought to drive them back down the street. With our daggers and stakes and the guards' swords, damned exploded into puffs of ash and live coal. We were making slow ground, the training the guards were now subjected to amping up their skill.

But something didn't feel right.

More than the fact that the damned were steering clear of me. So many guards had swarmed out with us and they were all equipped. Yet only a few guards had been taken down—most only injured, and only one I'd seen actually killed. It was almost like the damned were taking it easy on us, despite being at full strength and speed. Focusing on slowing our push down to the city's center rather than taking our lives.

"They're keeping us from the city center!" I screamed over the many cries that still cut through the air. I didn't know for what, but I couldn't see Ty. Oh, God. "Take them down, now!"

With Ty's roar through the damned that clung to him like parasites, the battle forged on. Black sprayed out, painting the cobblestone road and windows of the shops where scared vampires hid, as we pressed further down Main Street.

The barricade of damned thinned suddenly, each soulless male and female quitting their attack to speed down the street. Ty reappeared as they dispersed, black fur tacky with blood but steady on his paws. Thank God. He snapped his jaw at me as if to say, *I'm fine,* then wheeled around to chase after the retreating damned.

Right behind him, I stopped abruptly as I reached the city center. Raven stalled with me. Half the guards kept after Ty and the damned across the field, the others stood back, weapons ready. At the various streets surrounding the city's central fountain, more guards stood in dumbfounded silence, swords ready but still. Troy and Marika were among them, blood-covered but standing in wolf form. With Troy scenting the air and a jaw snap from Marika, they took off in Ty's direction with the other lycans who must have rushed in from their guard posts around the perimeter. To protect vampires.

Still, the fact that they'd all worked together and fought off a common evil wasn't what drew every remaining silver-blue eye.

"Oh my, God."

Attacked vampires, civilians, and a few guards were strewn about the cobblestone like discarded rag dolls. A few floated in the massive fountain, some hung twisted over the side as red-stained water rained down on them. But they weren't dead. Twitching, each one slowly corrected their crooked limbs and got to their knees. Facing me. Their throats were shredded. They'd all been bitten. Infected with damned venom. The smell of it drilled up into my nose, but something else I saw kept my devious thoughts silent. Glossy black stained their mouths, dripping down their chins. Their hands rose, palms forward.

Surrendering?

Returning from across the field, Ty morphed back into human form. He swiped a shred of cloth up to cover his manhood. Troy and Marika were right behind him, remaining in wolf form as the lycans and guards with them fanned out. "They escaped over the wall, had cars and motorbikes waiting to remove them." He eyed the kneeling people and saw my stunned expression. "What's going on?"

I stumbled on my words, thoughts dissolving at the sight of his scarred, naked flesh. He was magnificent. And uninjured, bar a few cuts—which I considered racing over to lick—that zipped shut as I stared.

"They've all been…" Raven couldn't get the words out either. But not for the same reason.

"Infected," I blurted, realizing how inappropriate and just plain wrong my thoughts had been. Ignoring the warmth that bloomed over my face, I strode forward to the closest one. I clutched the man by the cheeks and forced his face up. I clenched my teeth to keep my growing fangs in check. "Why?"

The man's eyes rolled back and tremors overtook his body as he turned limp. Like dominoes tipping over, the others fell too, one by one. Almost twenty in total, some writhing on the ground, some out cold. Like I had been. A few screamed—the burn of blood and bite mixing as sweat sprouted. Over the sound of pattering water, I heard a change. The lessening noise of heartbeats.

Their hearts were stopping.

Across the city center I met Ty's stare. Now I knew the 'why' behind the attack. "They're all in transition."

Even naked, he didn't hold back from taking charge. "Restrain them all and secure them in the cells. Treat them as if damned until the RVC convenes."

Despite his words, I knew the outcome. I wouldn't have it any other way. Restoring these transitionees was the only right thing to do. I wouldn't let them suffer as monsters, and I wouldn't have them put down. Or worse. Die. They were innocent. And the consequence of using my ability on so many? I guess I was going to find out. My life was not above all of theirs. No way.

The guards were still gaping. They hadn't moved to follow Ty's order. Fangs elongating fully, I shouted. "You heard him. Take them down to the cells!"

CHAPTER 10

I watched from my throne as the rest of the RVC entered the boardroom and took their seats around the marble slab. After yesterday's attack, I'd made a decision to use my power to restore each of the nineteen infected vampires, and called this early morning meeting.

The idea filled me with a sense of purpose and dread at the same time. My legs wouldn't quit twitching under the table. My hands shook with nerves around the glass I'd just emptied. The rise of living scents in the room registered through my internal panic. Was I doing the right thing? I already knew the answer. Knew it as I imagined those poor civilians and guards suffering as they became what I fought to keep contained every day.

Their lives mattered. Their souls.

I couldn't let them die or be put down. I wouldn't.

"Seems as though we have some important matters to discuss," Dorian's statement pulled me out of my head a fraction. Sitting on Uriel's other side, he retained that sparkle to his eyes. That devious intent. He was up to something. Seeing the white shirt he wore with the top few buttons undone made me cringe. It was something Marcus would wear. "I can't imagine how Marcus is gaining numbers with so few reported deaths," he went on. "But after yesterday's attack, we must decide on a course of action for the infected."

Staring out at the dark mountainous horizon of early vampire morning, I had a strange suspicion Dorian knew exactly how Marcus was rebuilding his army. There had been a rise in disappearances, Ty had told me after the catch-up yesterday with his pack. But calling Dorian out wasn't an option. Glancing to the portrait on the wall behind him, to his blooded father, Lord Vladimir, I knew it was a risk I wasn't willing to take.

"I want to restore them," I heard myself say as if someone else were speaking. Leaning forward to grasp the decanter, I refilled my glass. "It has to be done. And I have the ability."

Uriel went to pat my free hand as I threw back the blood, and I flinched at the warmth of her touch. A little blood spilled, dripping down my chin before I swiped it away. "Sorry, I…"

"We can see you're nervous." Uriel's gentle voice was all warm and understanding. But it wouldn't be, if she realized my stare at her hand was tracking that central thick vein all the way up to her neck. Compared to Ty's blood, human blood was little better than water. A Band-Aid on a severed limb. "Twenty-plus transitionees—"

"Nineteen," I interjected.

"Nineteen to restore is too much to expect of even a gifted vampire, when time is a matter of life and death."

Uriel's smile was somber, yet it was Lady Rasputin who answered. "We will not make allowances to *feed* the infected to keep them alive."

Lord Strigon's face hung with guilt. "Despite my suggestion, I agree administering blood to them is too dangerous."

Good thing they didn't know about me. I'd be good and truly dead. The power Caius had engineered me to possess, which gave me the ability to help others like me, would be lost. Reminding my lungs to continue inflating and deflating, I absently scanned the portraits around the room. Twelve lined the curved stone walls, the one behind me of Erzsebet Bathory rather than my traitorous father. Transitionees only lived as long as their bodies could handle the infection—or until they consumed a vampire's lifeblood. Without blood to sustain them, they could last a few days if lucky, a week I was betting at most. One a day would leave the majority of the infected dead. And I couldn't live with that. I wouldn't.

"I think I can restore three, maybe four a day." I thought of Ty and what I was deciding without his input or permission. Being an advocate for the innocent, I hoped he'd understand, because, without him, there's no way I could pull this off. He was my comedown from those murderous highs, and if my hopes were right, a battery pack to recharge not only my body but also my electricity.

"We saw the toll it took when restoring Uriel," Strigon pointed out. "More than one, maybe two per day will not be kind on your body."

"And we have seen the impact a vision can have." Did Lady Rasputin sound concerned for my well-being? "Restoring a life must take a greater toll."

"Unless she recharges." Dorian's quick words stalled Rasputin from raising her glass to her thin lips. "On the hybrid, right?"

Narrowing my gaze, I nodded, wondering if he was about to push the donor issue again. "That is my plan." Having let the damned in without the weakening effects of the wards, did he know what Marcus's intent had been? Obviously turning a bunch of our community. But to what end?

Dorian rose, throne legs scraping. He strolled to the first window with its open drapes and smiled at his reflection. "Well then, I hope your plan works." He spun to face us all. "Though in the event you cannot restore at that speed, it is not unforeseeable that some lives may be lost."

Words Dorian would never string together in that way.

My suspicion and that sense of dread deepened as Uriel questioned, "What are you suggesting, Dorian?"

That horrible smile parted his pale lips. The one that belonged on Marcus's face and not my brother's. "I propose we give our people hope. Show them the lengths we are going to in order to save all that we can."

My heart skipped a manufactured beat as I dared to ask. "How?"

"By Amelia performing live restores before the town's people. By revealing the power of our weapon in our battle against the damned."

"No." The glass I still clung to clanked on the marble as I let go. He was trying to expose me. "I can't do that. I'll perform the restores in the cells. It's safer—"

"Seeing the act and repercussions to Amelia will help our people understand why not all can be saved," Dorian spoke over my rebuttal. "It will prove we are not favoring ourselves over them."

"It will nullify any blame for the lives that will undoubtedly be lost," Rasputin added thoughtfully.

"No. No." My mind raced with my heart. If this were forced, I'd risk outing what I was. I'd lose my link to the damned, my only means to track Marcus down, any hope of freeing Dorian from his control, and discovering how to resurrect Kendrick—because staying in this state was the only way Marcus would reveal how to bring him back. So why was Dorian pushing for this? To test my resolve, my dedication, or just to make me suffer? "The act is too draining. I…I'm not myself straight after. I…" *Dammit, think.* "I don't want to be seen in…in that state by our people. They already fear my power."

"That is true." Uriel had been there when I'd accidentally zapped a training room full of vampires. "We don't want to elicit more fear in our shaken community."

Strigon nodded at his colleague. Good, this was good.

"Amelia has much better control than before." Dorian reached the table's edge and leaned into his hands on the top. "And I believe in you, Sis."

I wanted to launch at him, forgetting he was my brother and treating him only as Marcus's sick puppet. I clenched my fists instead, and pinned my lips shut. All this arguing was raising pulses, spiking the sound and the scent of blood in this enclosed room.

Uriel went to pat my hand before deciding better of it. "I believe we can come to a compromise."

"One restore a day?"

I bit my tongue to keep from hissing at Rasputin.

"I was thinking one in total." Uriel filled her glass, then mine, sliding it closer to my clenched fists. "It will still deliver much-needed hope. No one could doubt that, even from a single display."

"It will also illustrate our efforts and our ability to fight this war," Strigon added.

I lifted the glass before me and did well to drink the blood without spilling, despite the tremors up my arms—from fear *and* growing restraint. Continuing to argue wasn't going to make this go away. And with one public restore instead of nineteen agreed to by two of our five, doing so may just hike that number up. Gulping down the last drop, I spoke carefully, keeping my growing fangs hidden behind my lips. "One public restore. Today. At two a.m." I needed time to prepare and inform Ty and a little planning to lessen the threat of me outing myself or worse. Turning ripper on the royals and a full hall of unsuspecting civilians and guards.

The vote was almost unanimous, excluding only Dorian. "Agreed."

~

"This is a bad idea, Amelia." Ty was far from happy about the decision I'd made without his input. Yet as he glared at me over his shoulder, the slice on his arm continued to fill the glass on the boardroom table. "What if your eyes shift to red? If those black veins sprout out all over your skin?"

I had to admit, I was terrified about the approaching audience. Ty's concerns were totally valid. But there'd been no getting out of this. The RVC wanted to prove that we had a way to fight back against the damned, to save ourselves from eternal damnation. It wasn't a bad idea. Though given my state of being, it was a huge risk. A risk Dorian had instigated.

Even now as I paced, dressed in black gear and Vans pattering with each forceful step, I worried over his intent. Over Marcus's intent.

He wanted me to remain in transition. Did he hope forcing me to out myself would drive me straight to him—and away from a community that feared too fast and understood too late?

Maybe.

I took hold of the glass and stared down at the glossy red that filled the crystal to the brim. This was my third glass of Ty's blood. It would have to be enough to keep my transitioning traits hidden. "That's why I'm throwing back your blood like a drunk."

"Live blood would do more," Ty said with a glare, clearly seeing no comedy in my words. Making for the doors, he mumbled under his breath. "If you weren't so stubborn."

I pretended I hadn't heard him, though we both knew I had.

Again Ty was right.

Even as I mentally acknowledged that, my gaze went to his throat and that thick vein. If I started, I didn't think I could stop. I saw again a flash of when I'd attacked my mom, ready to take her life to fill the void of my hunger. Plus… "I can't use you in that way." It wasn't fair, to either of us. He didn't want me, and we couldn't be what we had been before. Besides, he'd given enough of himself already. He was harboring and assisting a monster in disguise…for the greater good, because in my state I was more helpful than if I cured myself. "I just…can't."

A stiff nod was my reply from Ty, as one side of the double doors opened before him and two figures slipped in.

Raven looked worried as she eyed the empty glass I tabled and the healing gash on Ty's arm. The black restored veins over her face seemed too dark against her paler-than-usual flesh. "It's packed out there. To the brim."

Knowing what I was, was she worried I'd blow my cover and her hopes of resurrecting Kendrick?

The second girl who stepped around the restored vampire had long blond hair and Under Armour gear identical to mine. She glanced around the twelve royal portraits like she was seeing everything on fire as damned attacked and she fought them off with Mr. Malau and a pack of wolves.

Marika doubling for me now had been my idea. To help welcome the crowd while I prepared—drank as much of Ty's blood as I could. And to step in again once the deed was done—and Ty had to haul me back in here.

Her being in here now meant… I sucked in a lungful of air and fought the need to cough over the exhale. "Restore time."

Ty reopened the door and muffled speech reached my ears from the many people that filled the hall. He strode out but I yanked him back, fingertips touching the stake I'd returned to him. Barely hearing the sizzle as the smell of burned flesh filled my nose, I said, "Whatever you need to do. Keep me in check."

His jaw jutted, but he didn't argue, removing that silver contact as he continued to the main hall. I trailed behind, passing him as he positioned himself beside the stage and I mounted the steps. Already being two a.m., seated and standing vampires left barely a square of space visible.

The royals were waiting on their thrones. Including Dorian, who, as he watched me, seemed entertained at the events to come that he'd put in place. With one hand propping up his chin, his smirk was on show. I was certain my suspicions had been right. He wanted me outed and driven away—right into Marcus's hold.

The din of collective speech quieted as I reached my throne, and I shuddered. Not because they were watching me in suspense, but because Kendrick's throne was still positioned next to mine, ending the line of seven. Too many images rushed through my mind, and I sat quickly to redirect my focus. Still, as a door opened and chains rattled, I went to grab the hand that used to be there. Was no longer there. Because Kendrick was cold and stiff in that freezer coffin.

I'm not giving up, I declared internally as two guards forced a shackled transitionee onto the stage.

The male vampire was dragged to…

I jolted. A huge wooden board stood erect beside the thrones with eyelet hoops for securing chains to. I hadn't even noticed it before, but couldn't look away now as the transitionee was secured, legs tied down tight and arm chains strung through, ready to be pulled by the guards at the right time. The silver sizzled against the transitionee's flesh. Allergic to silver—like I now was—with his flesh being melted away.

There was talking, from Uriel I think. I couldn't tear my eyes away to make sure. She was announcing the phenomenon to take place and quieting the lingering chatter.

Ty mounted the stage then, holding out his inscribed stake as I faced the transitionee. Even though his arm restraints weren't tight, he made no attempt to lash out. I took the smooth length of silver, the sound and smell of my flesh burning obscured by the sizzling transitionee. Breathing through my mouth, I stepped closer, gathering blue voltage across my skin and down to my weapon-ready hand. Still, the transitioning male made no move to strike out. Instead, he reached up to tear open his shirt and expose his chest. Then he held out his arms as if the chains had been pulled taut, even though they still hung loosely from his wrists. A sacrifice offered up. "You will restore me. He promised."

That same monotone voice that was almost robotic. A result of compelled action.

With the burn of my hand intensifying, I lunged forward and the guards tugged the restraints tight at the last nanosecond. But they hadn't needed to. The man put up no fight.

The tip drove into his bared chest.

Bullseye.

Light and power exploded, and the man's head slumped as the stake came free and I staggered. Vision hazy and bones feeling like jelly, Ty caught me, his broad body keeping me from view of the crowd and crowned royals. Snatching his stake from my burning hand, he all but pushed me down the stage steps. He called over his shoulder as the seated watchers jumped up and cheering ensued, "You've had your circus act."

Two steps further and my full-body drain switched gears as thick black roots forked up my arms. Still smelling all those bodies of blood behind us, I hissed and stomped my feet down like anchors.

"We're almost there," Ty grated.

But I didn't care, the guards lining the hall were closest—and easier prey compared to my protector. I could hear their beating hearts as mine faltered. If I knocked Ty out, I'd be on them before they could comprehend my actions. I twisted to get free, nails biting flesh as I tried to remove Ty's trapping—

Something hot and sharp punched straight into my side.

My hiss turned guards' heads as the door creaked open and swung shut behind us. And then one hot and one lukewarm set of hands took hold as my vision bled red. I thrashed as they restrained me, knocking into thrones and walls. A portrait fell to the ground.

There was a trickle of blood filling a glass, and the uncontained scent sent me crazy. Then a smoldering body trapped me against the wall. That sharp burning like a poker in my side shoved in deeper, the burning stake parting my lips with a cry—

Hot blood poured into my mouth, the cool rim of a glass meeting my lips as my fight gave in. My heart roared to life and color and definition crept through the red. The two sets of hands restraining me let go.

Ty stepped back as I took the glass, putting distance between his body and mine. Making me hate that all our physical interactions were to stop me killing, over something else.

Really? I was really thinking about that after what I'd just done?

"The transitionee," Ty grated through rough breath, moving to right a throne as Marika nodded his way and slipped from the room to take my place. "What did he say?"

By the door Marika had just escaped through, Raven was panting from the struggle of restraining me.

With my glass empty, the guilt rushed in. "Raven, Ty…I'm sorry."

Raven shrugged. "When you're evil you do evil. When you're good you do good." She didn't tend to sugar-coat or get bogged down with sentiment or guilt. From the day her existence had been revealed to me, she hadn't spoken of the crimes she'd committed as a damned. From the look on her face though, she understood my ongoing torment.

"What did he say," Ty demanded.

The intensity in his eyes jump-started the train of thought I'd have started, had my murderous hunger not interrupted. Moving to sit in my throne, now facing out from the table, I recalled his words. *You will restore me. He promised.* Like my brain had suddenly rebooted, I understood his statement and what it'd meant. Yesterday's invasion had been warfare of a different kind. Instead of bloodshed and death, they'd created a problem that would need to be fixed. *By me.* It wasn't just about trying to out me and the monster inside. To drive me away and into Marcus's hands. It was a way to monopolize my time. To keep me from being able to free Dorian of Marcus's control and find a way to resurrect Kendrick.

"It wasn't a blood bath," I whispered, piecing what I'd thought and what I now knew together. My restored silver-blue eyes shot up. "Raven, you were right."

Rehanging the fallen portrait, she looked surprised. "I was?"

I may be stuck restoring another eighteen vampires, but I wasn't a one-girl show. "Blood bath *was* a clue."

"It wasn't the attack." Ty has just reached the same conclusion I had.

"We need to—"

"I'm on it," Raven tugged the door open, hope dancing in her eyes. "You two focus on those transitionees."

The door all but slammed shut and Ty met my eyes. "Guess we've got a job to do."

Together and in secret, while he struggled to contain the thing inside of me. But the sooner this was over, the sooner we could help Raven figure out this clue.

"No rest for the wicked." Or the good, it seemed, in his case.

CHAPTER 11

Four days had passed, and every hour seemed to drag on even slower than the last. I entered the cell of the next transitionee I was meant to restore. Every one of my bones ached like I'd been strapped to a torture device that slowly but surely pulled your arms and legs clean off your torso. My muscles twitched, fighting to hold my weight up. My vision was free of red, but blurry, that fuzz you got when first waking, but in this case it never cleared. I kept my lips clamped to keep from groaning.

Across the dim space, the female transitionee bared her fangs, thrashing against the silver that kept her strung to the wall, starving like the others. And not just for a sip. The bloodlust had already started. That blinding hunger I knew all too well. This one had murder in her eyes, the need to complete the conversion and become fully damned.

She was number twelve on my "to restore" list.

Dragging my tired feet, my Vans scuffed the uneven stone

ground and I lost my balance. Great. Awesome! Just what I needed. Stupid *can't perform basic motor functions* feet.

Ty's calloused hand caught around my slight arm to steady me. I'd been trying so hard to hide my increasing hunger, fatigue, and loss of vitality from him more than anyone else. As if I could fool him. The way I'd taken to staring at him and every tappable vein had increased to the point that I didn't even realize I was doing it most of the time. Each and every clearing of Ty's throat had become a constant, *hey, you're eyeing me like I'm your next meal ticket.* Though he never said it out loud. Through clenched teeth, he grated, "You can put this one off until tomorrow."

Not a suggestion. No way with the tightening of his heated grip and that unwavering stare.

Despite the command and the unwanted irritation I felt at being ordered around—like I was one of his pack—I considered the option. Yeah, I could put this one off. But each remaining restore meant more time taken away from finding a way to free Dorian and resurrect Kendrick. Too much time had already passed on those two fronts. The consequence of one was hissing and spitting on the far side of this cell.

The chains rattled as the transitionee's stance became predatory. She strained against her bonds, red stare trained on Ty and hands reaching out toward him. Unlike the one I'd restored on public display, all the others had put up a fight. Not towards me. None had dared strike or lash out at me. But Ty, who accompanied me for every restore and kept any guards and royals away, was more than tempting to their hungers. The struggle for me to hit the right spot with silver was getting harder and I was being worn out right along with Ty.

A loud grumble reverberated off the stone walls and floor. Not from the transitionee, but from me. That sick feeling that came after already restoring—was it two?—was gaining momentum. My sight unfocused further. Was it hot in here? I shucked off my hoodie and fought with my tripping feet again. I really didn't feel up for this. "Maybe I should wait until—"

The restrained woman began to thrash—no, not thrash. A seizure. Her whole body was shaking, suspended off the ground as her legs bent and her arm restraints kept her aloft. Choking gurgles tore from her throat. Her eyes pinned shut. Her mouth twisted open in agony. The beginnings of black veins that had marred her skin grew like living vines over her exposed flesh. Like they were alive and consuming her body, squeezing the last of her life from her. When red froth spurted from her mouth, I knew what would come next.

Unlike me, none of the transitionees had been given blood. It was a call I hadn't agreed on. The RVC wanted them kept weak. To protect the castle, the guards, and everyone inside our walls. To prevent further infection. And now…

This woman was on the verge of death.

Her transitioning body was giving out. Without taking life, its animation without a heartbeat was failing.

I dropped my hoodie. "Restrain her!"

Ty hesitated, horrified conflict in his eyes as he looked me over. "You're too weak." When I tripped to get to the woman, he bared his canines and blocked my way. "You need to recover first."

He was going to stop me? Even before being damned and coming back, he'd cared about all innocent lives. Werewolf, human, even vampire. "There is no first." My fangs slid free in agitation. "My life is not above hers." Blue lightning swarmed down my bare arm to my hand. "You can't really let this innocent woman who has a life and family die like this. You won't."

Ty looked behind as more red froth stained the front of the

woman's white blouse and one shoulder dislocated from the violent shaking. He ground his molars, a screech ringing out. With a growl, he marched to the convulsing woman and pinned her to the wall. "Hurry the hell up, then."

Shooting to his side, I snatched his stake from his belt and drove it home. Blue light exploded and the force propelled me back. The woman sagged as I hit the deck, my butt crying out in pain. I'd lost weight in four days? I blinked hard, dropping the flesh-searing silver. Had the light gone out?

Ty was kneeling by my side in an instant. I knew because I could feel his heat. There was a rustle of his leather jacket as he produced a thermos and shoved it into my hands, directing the rim down to my lips. With one hand around my nape, he tilted my head up.

I drank with greed, Ty's blood spilling down my chin as I swallowed as fast as I could.

Light crept back in gradually, rosy light that painted the gray cell in red tones. The restrained woman was hanging by her chains, head dropped and body limp. But her heart had started back up. She was alive.

"It's not working." Ty's grated words made me look at him. Worry pinched his brow and his lips were tight.

I followed his stare down to my bare arms. Black veins. Everywhere. They weren't fading, and neither was the red lens from my sight. Wetness trickled from my nose, and my gut backflipped. I curled over, clutching my arms around myself. I was starving. My insides felt like they had turned on themselves and were devouring me from the inside out.

Ty swiped my hoodie off the ground and pulled it around me fast. He went to swoop me into his arms. But I had other plans.

Half in his arms, my nails dug in deep, refusing to let go. My fangs ached for flesh.

Throwing him down, I landed on top of him, straddling his hips. I struck out to claim my prize as Ty's hand came up to catch—

I didn't feel his grip on my neck. Didn't see what came next. Sensation seeped from my body, and my vicious hold on Ty loosened. My hands fell. My lids slid shut.

My body had given up.

I CAME to with groggy grace. My lids were heavy. My limbs felt like my bones had been replaced with putty. A slice of panic set in. Where was I now? Where had I been? In a rush, I saw that dark cell. The transitionee dangling suspended after my restore. And then… flattening Ty on his back. Going for the jugular. *Oh, shit. Ty.* The groan from my lips was hoarse as I ratcheted upright—on a soft bed.

Blink. Blink.

Back in my bedroom—had to be. The Three Days Grace posters plastered to the walls became clear. Ty had carried me back here? More blinking. And more. Faster and faster. Crap. Everything was still tainted red. Which meant my irises were still blazing. They hadn't returned to silver-blue. Fan-freaking-tastic.

"You're still covered in black veins, too."

I jumped at the voice, my beating heart amping up before I realized who had spoken. Ty. He was perched on one of my weapon crates, watching me with clear intensity. The utility belt I'd had on was draped over one side.

Looking down, I saw he was right. Those black veins hadn't receded like they normally did. More foggy memory returned as I raked my gaze over Ty's neck. No pinkish healing flesh. My fangs hadn't reached their target. My consciousness had given way. "How long was I passed out?"

" 'Bout sixteen hours, give or take. How're you feeling?"

Shifting to examine myself, I paused. A drip was attached to my arm from a long tube that retreated back to a bag on one of those hospital stands. "Your blood?"

Stiff nod. "I had you hooked up to my vein for a while. Thought it would do more. Not that it really did much to lighten the veins. They darkened right back up when I unplugged the live stream." A cigarette found its way to his lips and a moment later it was lit with a flick and roll of his Zippo—the same one I'd stolen to set an indoor bonfire to burn marks from my arm…to open my mental communication to Kendrick. To warn and save him. The first time, when I had succeeded.

Ty's gaze dropped—because I was stroking the marbled length of my forearm in distant memory. His jaw tightened as that muscle ticked up its length. "You seem more in control."

It wasn't a question, but it was clear he wanted an answer as he drew on his death-stick and blew out. Minding the needle taped to my hand, I ran my palms over my shoulder and down to my stomach. I watched their trail as if touch would give me the answer. But what I felt inside was the only answer I needed. That devouring itself feeling was gone. I wasn't about to launch across the room and attack the one living blood source in my suite. I wasn't even tempted to snatch the baggie off the pole and sink my fangs in, forcing the contents down my gullet in a rush. The hunger wasn't gone. It wasn't even ignorable. But it was leashed…for the moment. "Yeah. I am."

Shrug. Drag. Exhale. The rich smell of tobacco smoke filled the space between us and clouded the smell of his blood.

Reaching for my robe, I pulled it around my shoulders and swung my legs over the bed—

Movement through the foyer had my head cranking up and sideways.

At the same time, Ty growled, fingers squeezing the butt between them while his free hand clenched. "What do you want?" he snapped, smoke puffing out with each word.

Wearing that cold but devious smile, Dorian entered the room without concern. Even as Ty and I both shot upright and I tore the needle from my hand, he strolled in carelessly.

Ty blocked his way, palming the butt of his dagger. His canines lengthened. "Answer me or get out."

"I come bearing gifts." One hand swung out from behind Dorian's back.

Stepping up beside Ty, I felt a chill at what my brother held out. A petite box tied with a white ribbon and a small square of cardboard attached. A name tag, written in flowing cursive.

Amelia.

"What is it?" Fear stopped me from finding out firsthand. Dorian's last delivery had been a note from Marcus, full of promises and threats. I had no doubt this one would be the same.

My brother hiked his brows, eyeing the black veins that peeked above my robe and struck over my hands. How long would clothes hide the veins?

Dorian shrugged and went to turn away. "If you don't want it—"

I snatched the box from him and pulled one end of the ribbon. The petite bow came loose as Dorian continued on his way, the door shutting behind him as he exited back through the foyer.

Ty drew hard on his squished cigarette, ash falling as I wriggled the box's lid free. "What is it?"

Sitting back on the bed, I took the folded card from inside as Ty sat beside me. Having Ty this close, his radiating heat penetrated my chilled skin and spiked my pulse. I cleared my throat and quickly unfolded the plain note. It was the same as the one delivered with the bouquet of calla lilies before Kendrick's funeral. My breath hitched out of human reaction and I coughed at the rush of unneeded air.

After all that restoring, thought you might need these…
Marcus.

Under the card was a plastic container with two round lids. Unscrewing one I found something I never thought I'd need. "Silver-blue contacts." Just like the ones Marcus had worn to hide his damned side. He knew I'd been doing everything in my power to restore the vampires he'd set his damned on to infect. "Dorian's been reporting the restores to Marcus."

Ty touched my hand, the hot connection rippling goosebumps up my arm and down my body. "I think it's time the RVC knew about his control over Dorian. We can't keep going on like this. Your body can't handle a repeat infection—and what if even more are infected next time?"

I pulled away, because the warmth was doing more than just heating my hand. And because… "No way. We're not telling anyone. You know he's compelled to kill himself if we do."

Ty's lips twitched in irritation and he stood up. Striding back to the crate, he butted out his cig in a glass dish. "He can be imprisoned until Marcus is stopped. Until we find a way to break the compulsion. Restrained for his own safety."

"You think Marcus won't find a way to make good on his threats?" Unable to sit still, especially with the challenge in Ty's eyes, I got up and began pacing. I imagined Kendrick then, lying stiff in that glass coffin. I raked my eyes over Ty and those black veins. One was dead; the other had been made a monster. "He got what he wanted with you and Kendrick. He only strikes harder when we best him."

"Then we allow him to continue to let the damned in." Another cigarette came out and was lit up with the flick of Ty's Zippo. Harsh draw in. Out. "We continue to let him report to Marcus?"

"Ty, please." I stopped pacing and strode over to kneel before him. My hands went to his knees and squeezed—a little too hard. Tobacco and blood. It was the new norm, and one I was growing attached to. My reddened eyes lifted to his. Even through that rosy tint, that combination of colors was beautiful, gold, green, and blue; a sun-speckled ocean with maroon flecks. Proof of how much he'd been through and how he'd survived. How he'd changed. "I—I can't risk Dorian. Not after…"

"Kendrick." Raven's voice had me jolting upright to see her loitering in the foyer. "We will find a way to free Dorian. But in the meantime—"

"Not happening," I snapped. "But I agree we have to do something. We can't compel the guards on his rotation to keep him from leaving the compound or to report any meet-ups. He damaged the wards, and not a single one of his guards was anywhere to be seen. He's controlling them—he did it again with us in the den last week."

Raven came into the bedroom, hands folded over her chest. "But he can't control someone he doesn't know is tailing him." Her smile said plenty.

"You want to spy on him?"

She shrugged. "I've had a lot of practice with stealth." Yeah, like ninety years. Her smile fell. "Besides, I've hit a wall with resurrection research. I'm waiting on a bunch of books from other councils to be sent over."

I pursed my lips and raised my brows at Ty. "What do you think?"

"Fine." Smoke curled from Ty's lips, but the argument was gone from his deep voice. "But if we find nothing…"

I didn't want to, but lives were at stake here. "Then I'll tell the RVC myself."

WITH MY HEAD twisted over my shoulder, I stared at that last transitionee I'd just restored. Finally the last. After three more days that brought me closer and closer to the point of no return. Even with my silver-blue contacts on I knew my vision was red. Everything, from the dark stone lit by a single dull bulb to the man hanging limply from shackles, was a vivid shade of red. My hoodie and jeans covered most of my flesh, and makeup kept the black veins that now forked up my neck concealed.

What lies inside? A wolf in sheep's clothing. Or should I say a transitioning damned in vampire disguise.

"Amelia, come on."

Ty was waiting by the door, a full thermos of blood ready in his hand. It was time for me to follow him back up to my suite so he could fully refuel me. Like he'd done after every restore by bloodletting into a glass for me to drink—which had needed refilling four times of late. His stare on me was intense. Even with my face turned away from him, I could feel his eyes drilling into me. I could sense the readiness of his body, could hear the creak of his joints as his muscles tensed around his bones.

The utter starvation that wreaked havoc on my body never faded. It was attacking me from the inside out, right this second.

He held the thermos out. "Amelia. Let's. Go."

The sharp edge to his voice was received, but the restoree's pulse had just started up. Their heart raced at the shock of being given new life. I was closer to that man than I was to Ty—or the offering in his outstretched hand. And the man was fresh, easy prey, still restrained by silver that sizzled. *Screw that dead crap. Fresh is best.*

I shot forward, ready to take what I wanted. What I needed.

Ty was on me in a flash, hand squeezed around my nape, and face up in my grill. "You're coming with me *now*." He shoved me around toward the door as I hissed. The thermos found its way to my hands as he grated in my ear, "We're going up to your suite. If you push me I will take you down. Guards watching or not. What do you think they'll do to me then?"

I saw a flash of their swords poised at his jugular when Dorian had threatened me to provoke Ty. The images culled the spitfire response of my inner voice like a hot poker being dipped in icy water. "They'll…kill you," I said as he forced me out into the open circular room.

The guards looked disturbed by Ty's hold on me that swiftly switched to an arm around my waist. They should have been more threatened by me and the way my hidden red eyes zeroed in on their tappable veins. "I…I just need to rest."

Ty all but hauled me back up the prison stairs, spitting words at the guards marking the exit. "Give us space."

They stood back as Ty flung the gate open. My thoughts tempted me to fight back as he directed me through the labyrinth of corridors. I unscrewed the thermos lid instead, and the blood was gone too soon. My hunger remained. Biting down on my lip, I couldn't stop my arm from twining around him, or my nails from punching through his T-shirt to score his flesh.

"We're almost there," he growled.

Almost there. Almost there. Almost there. The main hall and grand stairs whizzed by in a blur, and I wasn't sure if it was Ty driving us on, or if I had taken over. *Get him alone. All to yourself. Shut everyone out.* "Shut up!"

Ty spared me a frown as we cleared the corridor and burst into my suite. The door slammed behind us.

"Hey, you're back. Good, I've…shit, you look even worse. Are you *okay?*"

Raven with her blue-black hair and black-veined hand that held a novel—The Secret Garden—entered the foyer. But I saw none of it. The sound of her steady heartbeat drummed through my ears. Acting before any thought could weasel its way in, I head-butted Ty and launched over the central table. Flattening Raven to the ground, the book she held went sliding. I snapped my fangs, hissing and snarling.

"Amelia!" Her forearm pressed against my throat, her free palm pushing against my forehead.

I was getting closer.

A sound behind us alerted me to Ty's intervention. My bent leg kicked straight behind me and connected with his stomach. I heard rather than saw him fly back and hit the door. My sight—flaming red now—wouldn't leave Raven's jugular. My jaw stretched wider. Just one more inch.

"Amelia, stop it!" Raven was doing well to hold me off. But I was in transition. She was a vampire. I was stronger, and I would win.

Hearing Ty clamber in his boots, I shot a spark behind me. The hit sounded with a thump as his ass hit the ground, weapons clanking against stone.

"Amelia, rein…it in." Ty was struggling back to his feet, and *reasoning* with me? Good luck. "This isn't the real you."

Wanna bet? Despite his words, I didn't give a shit. Not anymore. I needed to feed.

Right. Now.

Clenching one fist, I drove it into Raven's cheek. Her forearm holding me back lost its strength. The inch I needed. My parted mouth snapped shut on—nothing.

Raven was no longer beneath me. She was just…gone.

CHAPTER 12

Blinking over and over, I let myself see what I'd been too blood crazed to notice. My nails were embedded in dirt, not in the stone of my suite's foyer. Not in Raven. Had I killed her? Oh, shit. Had Ty come through and killed me? As my heart raced, I couldn't reconcile the lack of pain or white light and weightlessness. I'd always expected heaven to be that way. Except the air here wasn't still. It was moving and warm. I was outside.

Sudden trees sprouted up around me like I was watching hundreds of years of growth all at once. A sheer mountainside appeared to one side of the green and a new shower of water plummeted over its edge and down into a tranquil lagoon.

Elevating onto my knees, I saw Ty perched on a large flat rock. His muscled arms popped with tension. His glowing eyes were… disappointed. "I thought I could always talk you down. Never thought I wouldn't be enough. That our past wouldn't be enough to sway you…"

I'd been here before.

With Ty.

So this wasn't heaven. I wasn't dead. My hunger was gone and my sight was clear. And I knew why. Ty was always one step ahead, always a hero waiting to pull a move to save the innocent. "We're in a dreamscape. *You* did this." To stop me from killing in cold blood. "You brought me here."

"I didn't want to."

Ouch. The truth hurt. Like hell. But of course he wouldn't want to bring me *here*. The place we'd found together on the cruise and shared intimate moments wrapped in each other's embrace, pulses racing, breath quickening. Oh, God, I could remember the feel of him against me, his bulge below the surface of the water, the way I'd warmed and readied for him. *Don't go there.* I shut the memory down and shook my head. "Then why bring me here?"

Ty gazed at the waterfall as mist dusted our bodies. "Thought it would calm you down. Serenity and lack of temptation."

Guess not. "Oh." The only temptation was Ty, here and now. And not his blood. He'd muted the smell. But that and my starvation would return as soon as I woke up. "What about when we come out of the dreamscape?" I cringed at the thought of what I'd done to Raven. "I'm going to be homicidal."

"You're going to take my vein."

"What?" I shot upright and my lips parted then shut, parted then shut. Damn, that was a seriously enticing visual. One I could easily evoke after all the times I'd fed from him in the past. "I…I can't do that. I can't use you like that." What I really feared was not being able to stop. Not wanting to.

Ty stood and came my way, stopping a foot away from me. "I'm offering…and you will stop," he said as if he'd read my mind. "I don't care what you are, I know you. You *will* stop. You will."

Ty's faith in me was unwarranted. I'd come so close to killing, even before today. Him, my mom, and now Raven. When did it end? When it was too late? And how could I do this, and not blur the lines between us? Ty didn't want me, and I didn't deserve him. I'd given up, cheated. Kendrick's body was frozen and he would be coming back. I couldn't do to him what I'd already done to Ty. "Ty, I..."

"No. You don't get to refuse me on this one. You need live blood." Ty looked sidelong at the gushing waterfall, then back at me. His voice lowered. "Like you were getting from Kendrick."

Without invitation, I remembered coming up behind Kendrick in the training room. My hands on his shoulders had stopped him from filling a bottle with his blood. "That's not what I had in mind," I'd said. And those few words had changed so much. Taken what we'd already started and amped it up.

The memory fast-forwarded.

My voice had cracked as I spoke. "I do love you. You know I do."

"But you're not *in love* with me. You never have been and you never will be."

I barely refrained from clutching my chest at the sudden strike of pain. Damn, that hurt. In my foyer, Kendrick had relived my dreamscape with Ty. My actions had shattered him. Broken his heart. Broken us.

And now what Ty was suggesting would be like a repeat of that. A fresh betrayal. I couldn't...I just...

"We'll find a donor, then. You'll supervise."

Ty growled. "Taking from someone else just risks exposing what you are. It has to be me. And after everything I did..." He gulped, the threat across his face melting. "To my brother. To you." His eyes squeezed shut so tight that frown lines creased his forehead. "To Vanessa. Fuck. If I don't keep you in check it will be my fault. I infected you. You are what you are because of me."

Just like he'd become damned because of me, because of our involvement together and my insistence on coming out as the Oracle. I'd failed to save him in time. I'd angered him by moving on with Kendrick. I'd refused him when he was damned.

"I get to make up for that, in whatever way I see fit. And this is it." Coming in closer, he tilted my chin up, forcing me to look at him. "You can't stay the way you are and stop Marcus, free your brother, and bring Kendrick back to life. It's already gone on way too long, and I won't have it for another minute. Agree, or something else has to give. Continue as you are—on my vein—or restore yourself."

An ultimatum, just like Kendrick had given me to get me to agree to drink his blood. Restoring myself—if it didn't kill me—would kill my link to the damned. Prevent me from tracking them to get to Marcus. And I'd been warned by my twin. If I stopped the transition, I'd never find out how to resurrect Kendrick. And Dorian? I had no doubt he'd join Kendrick with Marcus's help.

But could I do what Ty was asking of me?

When we resurrected Kendrick—and we would—he'd be angry at my choice, but he'd be alive. Now I was justifying? I squared my shoulders. "Ty, I can't—"

The streaming waterfall slowed its free pour. Ty's heartbeat, erratic and elevated, seemed to get louder. Heat dampened the air, raising the temperature and spiking the scent of...blood. Ty's.

Hunger rekindled in my stomach, a furnace in need of something to devour.

"Let me do this for you." Ty's eyes cast away, staring at the lagoon as the ripples dulled upon reaching the grassy shore. "For Dorian, our people...for Kendrick."

Somewhere in the back of my mind—past the throbbing need my fangs were daring me to take, I knew Ty was right. Something did have to give. And I couldn't let it be them. I knew what live blood had done for me before. Would it do what I needed it to now? Contain my inner monster long enough to save them all? There was only one way to find out. "Okay."

At my quiet acceptance, our surroundings distorted before coming back into focus. The serenity was gone. The waterfall. The trees. Lying on the ground in the foyer, a hand reached down to pull me up. Broad, scarred, and traced with black veins. Ty's. I accepted, the soar of his scent making my fangs punch fully out and dizzying my head. A quick look and listen revealed we were alone. Raven must have taken off. But I couldn't dwell on her…or anything else for that matter. Saliva pooling, and stomach squeezing like a wrung towel, my red sight locked on Ty's throat. On that thick vein and the pulses of blood that filled it.

"It's okay." Ty stepped closer, one hand going to my arm as his head tilted with invitation. He unclipped the silver chain from his neck, tucking his mother's amulet into his jeans. "When you're ready."

The fear I felt at what was coming paled with the sluggish tightening of my veins. My still heart wasn't circulating the fuel that kept it beating, that kept me and that sliver of my conscience in check. And I was ravenous.

A hiss escaped my lips. My sight remained locked on its target. All restraint gone, I pressed right up against Ty, levering higher on my toes to reach the source. Grabbing the back of his neck, I struck hard and fast. A viper on attack. And then I was sucking. Drawing on that pulsing stream that exploded with pure bliss inside my mouth. Hot, alive, euphoric…oh God, I remembered his taste, how it stripped all thought from my mind and touched me deep inside. Now was no different. My thoughts were gone, MIA as my free arm went around Ty's waist and yanked him closer, clanking our weapons and locking him against me, trapping his muscled body. The growl up his throat tickled my lips. Made me drink faster. Greedier. There was movement between our bodies. Lower down. Ty was turned on.

The thought and rush of his blood filling me warmed my icy skin. Warmed my insides too. Made my brain and anything outside of this moment flee my mind. Right, wrong. Good, bad. None of it mattered anymore. None of it even registered.

The one thing I knew as a hot hand gripped my waist, was that Ty wanted me. Good, bad…monster. It didn't matter.

And I wanted him. Here and now.

Releasing my fangs, I licked up his neck and shrugged off my hoodie. "Come with me."

Ty resisted my backward step, keeping me close…until I bit down again. The groan that escaped him was full of pleasure and want. This time when I pulled us back, Ty moved with me. One step, then another, and another and more until I fell back on my bed with Ty on top of me. One of his hands released his utility belt, flinging it over the edge with a thump while the other bent my leg up. Ty filled the gap. His bulge pressed into me and my fangs broke free with a hiss. And then Ty's mouth was on mine, hot, hungry, and tongue lapping.

"I want you." With my fingers threaded through his hair, I reached down his body to his waistband and tugged. "I want to feel —" I hesitated, my mind kick-starting while my lips took those punishing kisses. Something wasn't right.

I'm not your boyfriend. I never really was.

I felt those words like they'd been spoken to me. Kendrick had made the declaration to get through to me. To help me save Ty.

Because he was over your shit, my darker self spoke. I saw the moving image of him, sweaty and wrapped in Raven's exploring arms in that training room. The way renewed anger blazed in his eyes. His hiss cut off as he tugged her closer, kissing her hard.

In my distraction, Ty broke away, breath ragged and face flushed. His eyes were luminous in the dim room where the only light shone through from the foyer. His face dipped, lips parting to reclaim mine, but at the last second he pulled back. "I…can't do this. We can't…" He hovered above me like he was having trouble forcing his body to do what his lips had said.

The sight of Raven locked to Kendrick's lips invaded my mind again. My hiss now—of pain and anger—was met with a growl. And then that space was gone. Breathing hard, Ty's lips reclaimed mine, hot and hungry. And for a moment, I got lost in him. His taste. His scent. His hands on my body. My heart had come back to life—and with it, my sense of right and wrong surged.

An earlier memory came forth, one from before I'd broken us. The mess of Kendrick's blue and orange striped bed was behind him. The one he'd watched vids with Raven on. Kendrick's strong hand cupped my nape. *"I love you. I was wrong to give up so easily. To act like I didn't care if you went back to Ty. I do. I want you."*

I'd said those last three words minutes ago to Ty—on my bed.

As my exploring hands on Ty's muscled back stalled and my lips gave up their rigorous kissing, the last thing he'd said that day invaded my mind. *"I'm not giving up on us. On this. Not until you tell me it's over."*

Ty felt the change and pulled away, my no-longer clinging hands falling to my sides. "I…I…" Horror at what I'd just let happen stole my words. Regardless of my actions—and the retaliation I'd driven him to, even despite his words to ensure I saved Ty from being a monster for the rest of eternity—I'd never said we were over. I'd never made a choice.

"I shouldn't have done that. I—I got carried away." Ty

dismounted the bed in a rush, frowning down at the tousled sheets. He swooped up his weapons. "It's been a while…"

I felt a physical jolt at his admission. *Been a while.* Since he'd been intimate with someone? Because he had when he was damned? I scrambled up quick, covering my heart that felt like it'd been daggered. Knowing I had no right to my feelings after what I'd just let happen…and all I'd done while Ty was damned.

"This"—Ty motioned back and forth—"between us. It's just blood. A means to an end. Nothing more, nothing less. We have our roles and missions to execute. And I'm sorry. I won't let it happen again."

A means to an end. That's all I was to him. All I'd ever be. Whether his body lusted after me or not. Glancing down and hating myself, I saw the black veins speeding their retreat up my arm. And come to think of it, that rosy tint was completely gone too. Taking Ty's vein had worked. Which meant feeding from Ty would have to continue. But I had to be better. I would… "I won't let that happen again, either. It's just blood."

CHAPTER 13

I went to the graveyard alone, despite Ty's concern for imminent twilight. For one, I needed space after our heated interaction. Keeping in time with my heartbeat, my lips still throbbed from our rough kisses. My body thrummed even now. And I hated it. What I'd done. What I'd wanted. How he'd responded. That it had worked—the blood drinking, not my disgusting seduction. My hunger was satisfied almost fully for the first time since I'd been infected. For the moment, as I cleared row upon row of headstones, I felt in control.

And so completely not. So confused. So divided. What the hell was wrong with me? Evidently, so much more than being in transition.

Now I had to survive on tapped-vampire—or should I say restored hybrid—vein. Like I had with Kendrick. It didn't seem to matter what I was or was trying to stave off becoming, I was still a monster, in body and mind. Blood was my fix, and it had to be from the vein.

Secondly, I had an apology to make. One that couldn't wait for the rise and fall of another day's sunlight.

Clutching the book Raven had dropped when I attacked, I entered the Baldassare tomb. The Secret Garden—a book Kendrick had given her while she'd been hiding down in the catacombs, before I knew of her existence. Kendrick had kept the proof secret to keep my damned-restoring ability from me, for my own safety.

I couldn't tear my eyes off the ground as I passed his coffin. Not after what I'd just done with Ty. So much more than use his vein for a greater purpose.

I found Raven in the adjoining chamber, wrapped in her blanket on the sofa. For the first time as she looked up from the books across her lap—no doubt on death, life, and resurrection—she seemed wary. "Feeling better now?" Her eyes shifted over my shoulder. "You're alone?"

The step forward I took had her hand going to the crease in the sofa. The shiny tip of a dagger poked out from the end of the cushion. I stopped my advance and held out her novel. "I'm really sorry, Raven. All the restoring sapped me. But I'm better now. I'm in control."

She snatched the book fast, total suspicion scouring her face as she studied me. "How?"

There was no point lying. "I took Ty's vein. Will continue to, until all of this is over."

"You mean until we find and stop your twin." At my nod, she relaxed a fraction, though even when she glanced down at the returned book she clutched with both hands like it was a lifeline, it was only for a nanosecond. "I came to see you before, well… because I have news about Dorian."

"Oh?" I moved slowly to keep from startling her or amping up her dagger-in-reach hand. Perching on the arm at the other end of the sofa, my heart had sped up in anticipation. "What did you find?"

Raven shook her head, short black hair swaying. "Absolutely nothing. Every day, he trains his ability at twelve a.m. But that's it. No phone calls. No secret meet ups. I even checked security footage. He hasn't even tried to leave the compound. The one time Dorian ditched his guards, he just went and lay centered in the field on that scorched patch of earth."

Where the slaughtered and beheaded had been burned to cinders.

But something wasn't adding up. "Marcus had to be in contact with Dorian to make him deliver those contacts."

With all the security cameras mounted to the perimeter, any being coming or leaving beyond the wall was captured. "The old footage should have shown something."

"But they never met," Raven pointed out what she'd already reported, sliding the books from her lap. "Or don't you believe me?"

I had no doubt Raven was being honest. She'd never been anything but. "No. I do. But I…"

"What?"

I saw in my mind all my recent interactions with Dorian. The way he spoke. His mannerisms. The expressions that were not now —nor had ever been—his. The way my hunger had unexpectedly surged after his crowning—when he'd touched me. When he'd drained me? I'd felt that drain before—but with a shitload more burn. From Marcus.

"Oh, shit. I think…" But thinking wasn't enough. I had to know for sure. "I have an idea." And I needed a prop. I stood up and strode to the door. Outside, the stars were dimming, the hue of twilight turning the dark of night into a fleeting deep blue. I turned back. I didn't have time to waste. "You coming?"

Raven was right behind me in a flash and a few minutes later we'd returned to my suite's bedroom.

Ty shot in from the lounge room at our entry, but he seemed unconcerned for my demeanor. Instead, he averted his gaze from me —and my bed that I'd closed in on. His hair was tousled, like he'd finally been catching up on some Z's. "Uh…everything okay?"

"It will be, I hope." I went to my bedside and grabbed the latest card Dorian had delivered days ago. It was because of Ty's ultimatum to take his vein that I thought I could pull this off, and why I no longer felt bound to the promise I'd made to him about conjuring visions. Not that that excused everything else that had happened. But now wasn't the time. "Fill him in, Raven."

"With what?"

"Just what you know. I'll have more"—I hope—"soon." From the drawer, I retrieved Marcus's other card hinting at resurrection.

Ice freezes life—and death—until blood and soul can resurrect the once living. Restore your conscience and you'll never know. Yin to my Yang, Marcus.

A fresh ache started up in my steady heart, and I didn't try to ignore or push it away. Instead, I held on to it, blocking out Raven's explanation as I sat on the bed. Forcing my mind past recent events as I felt the disheveled bedding, I shifted back to the center, crossed my legs, and closed my eyes. With a handwritten card in each hand, I kept my focus on their words and the person who had written them. Marcus. The delivering hand, I hoped, would join me to both the instigator and his puppet. Dorian.

Soon enough, the void rose up and those black slinky shadows swam around me. Keeping my focus on what I needed to find out, I dared the right shadow to respond. And then it did. One remnant slinked around my bicep, curling around and around as it descended my arm to my wrist. When it slid around my hand, my fingers splayed and caught the slimy length at its middle.

The vision that flooded in felt like a blast to my heart, one that had me ducking like I was trying to evade a shower of spearing glass shards. I'd felt that punch of power before. When the damned had first invaded the Armaya and run riot in the streets. But this time I wasn't scrambling upright in the main street, watching the damned cut down their prey after shop fronts had exploded with fire. I was in a house. Dorian's.

Now I knew. Those explosions had been Marcus. A diversion.

Standing in the entry to the joined kitchen and dining areas, the scene made me gape. The kitchen was banged up, water sprayed from the faucet. Smoke billowed from the snapped dining table. Vanessa was unconscious by that table, just like we'd found her. But the rest wasn't the same. Instead of bleeding out on the ground, Marcus had Dorian up on his feet, clutching his torn, bloodied T-shirt. My twin, and the one who'd been a hero that day. Who'd saved my brother's life. Or so I'd so easily believed. "You may as well give up. You're as good as mine."

"You'll never fool them—"

Dorian went to swing, but Marcus clawed into his side and head-butted my brother's beaten face. Blood spurted from Dorian's nose and his head lolled, eyes rolling like marbles. He was close to passing out, the injuries he'd sustained weakening him after the battle he'd just been in. But not with a damned like we'd been told. And Marcus wasn't saving him. Striking to kill, he buried his fangs deep in Dorian's neck.

Marcus was sucking the life out of him.

Out of instinct to protect, I went to lunge. Fat chance. I was glued to the linoleum.

Dorian's body turned limp as my heart drummed so hard it felt like it was going to punch a hole in my chest. As Marcus lowered my brother down on his back, all I could do was watch. Using the tip of a stake that was suddenly in Marcus's hand, he pricked his own neck without any reaction to the silver contact. Then he drew my brother up so Dorian's gaping mouth lined up with the gush of blood. Time passed in slow-mo. Nothing changing. No movement. Then Dorian shifted, catching Marcus around the neck and gripping hard. There was a noise of sucking, followed by swallowing. And then—

Boom!

The sonic boom—the same one I'd felt in the streets—plowed into my body, knocking me back. I'd felt that kind of body-slam before. When Kendrick had given me his blood to bring me back to life after Caius drained almost every drop from my veins. My suspicions had been right. And I knew why Dorian had been allowed to survive Marcus's vicious attack.

I shot upright and scrambled, shocked at my sudden ability to move. I swiped the dagger from my waist.

"Amelia, it's just us! You're back with *us*."

Ty's voice broke through as my sight cleared. I was back on my bed, covers even more of a mess. Raven was standing back by the window where dull light grew around closed drapes. Ty waited by my bed. His whole body was stiff, ready to take me down. And who could blame him? After most visions, I lost complete control and went psycho monster killer. But not this time. My heart was racing from what I'd seen, and I *was* hungry. Though not in any way that made me want to forget who or what I wanted to be. Ty's *live* blood was still keeping me in control.

"I'm okay," I said quickly. At Ty's raised, uncertain brow, I said, "I am."

Ty narrowed his eyes, hand delving into his pocket. No cigarette was retrieved and he must have believed me because he stood down and let me help myself off the bed. Good, I needed to burn off the jittery energy from my body at the revelation that was crowding my mind. I was spirit bound. Marcus and I were, as he called us, "two halves of a whole." He had a variance of my electricity, able to sap my power to feed his own. He could implant visions into my mind through touch. "Same boom. Same take and give of blood. Only in reverse. Dorian had been the victim. Not Marcus like I had been."

"Amelia, what are you rambling about?" Raven chanced a few steps closer.

I stopped pacing and faced Ty and Raven. I knew how Marcus was controlling Dorian even without being in physical contact. No wonder the compulsion-breaking mark had failed. "That first time the damned attacked here, we thought Marcus saved Dorian's life. And he kind of did. But not before almost taking it."

"You're not making any sense, Amelia. And I wasn't there. Were you?" Ty shared a look with Raven who confirmed she had no idea what I was on about. Ty came closer. "What did you see?"

It all made sense now. "Marcus is spirit bound. He's bound to Dorian."

"I STILL CAN'T BELIEVE they're bound to each other." On the other side of the workbench in her den the following morning, Vanessa suddenly stopped scanning the page of a thick volume. Her teary eyes lifted with a sniffle and her hand curled into a fist. "I remember that night like it was yesterday. A damned breaking in and Dorian defending me, the weak human. Me getting knocked out. Then waking to you all there and Marcus having saved him. How could I have been so wrong?"

From the look on her face, she blamed herself for believing a lie which had set us back in finding out how to sever Marcus's control over Dorian.

"It's not your fault, you know." I understood her guilt all too well. But unlike me, she hadn't done anything wrong, hadn't made any decision to impact the demise of others. Unlike me, she was innocent in this. A stack of discarded books was lined up beside me, and an untouched one was mirrored on my other side. We were on a mission now: read every word available from the Armaya's library to find a way to break a spirit bond. We'd resort to electronically scanned books and importing from other councils, if we had to. "Marcus's compulsion is second to none." I'd been on the receiving end myself. "You believed what he wanted you to."

"Yeah." The single word held no belief. "Sure."

Vanessa's guard—now down to one since proving her loyalty—who'd been switched out for a new one, returned and positioned himself against the jamb. Eyes and ears and all and not wanting info leaked, our talk was cut short.

The guard didn't utter a word. He was only there to make sure Vanessa wasn't under lingering compulsion that could threaten security. And in this one-exit, stone-walled, and windowless room, he didn't need a front-row seat to do his job.

Fake breathing, I got up off my stool and motioned the guard out into the corridor. "Stay watch out there. I'll call out if there's any issue." Though he looked conflicted at the order, the guard nodded his head and closed the door.

"So, is it hard?" At my raised brow, Vanessa clarified. "The faking it."

Since she'd discovered I was in transition, we hadn't spoken much about it. Though she seemed unworried, she clearly had her usual alchemist curiosity for anything out of the norm.

I shrugged. "Less than it used to be."

Vanessa went back to her book, finger moving from left to right and down a fraction at a time. Quitting the fake signs of life, I followed suit, pulling the next book down from the stack and cracking the cover open.

After a few pages, I felt like I was reading the same thing over and over. The other books on spirit bonding and bonds had been much the same. How the bonds are created. How they operated, once created. None mentioned anything about breaking a bond.

Once created, a blood bond cannot be severed. And, *Even in death, a spirit bond cannot be broken.*

I was getting really sick of those lines and every variance of that wording. Kendrick had told me the same—when he was alive and breathing. But if that were true, why hadn't I been able to reach him? Why couldn't I speak with him? Why couldn't I see his ghost? That was another perk of the spirit ability, and one I'd never thought for a second I would want. Or need.

Now I prayed Raven, who'd gone back to researching the *blood bath* message I'd seen, would find a way to connect me to him. To bring him back to life, not just in an ethereal not-flesh-and-bone way, but permanently, flesh, bone…beating heart. I'd give anything to find a way, give even more to make it happen.

I glanced up when I felt Vanessa watching me. "What?"

"Ah…" She glanced down to the book in front of her then back up. "You seem to be doing okay…"

"Yeah…" I noted the continued lack of black veins up my bare arms. Though I could scent her easily from across the table, that killer instinct was—well, not dead, but—hibernating. A dull ache compared to what it had been before retaking Ty's vein this morning. Was she worried I might get hungry soon?

"You haven't been tempted to…I mean, like, complete the process, on anyone?"

While that little voice tempted me to think her concern was an invitation, I recalled all the times I'd almost crossed over to the dark side. On my mom, Raven, Ty more than once… "I won't lie. It's a struggle. When Dorian *visited,* I wanted to…you know…on Ty. He wasn't the first. And…" if I was being totally honest. "I can't say he'll be the last."

"But you continue to stay this way despite the risk?" she whispered.

The risk to everyone I cared for was greater if I went against Marcus's orders outright. I shrugged and kept my voice low. "Right now, I don't have a choice."

I was just about to go on when the next book on the stack caught my eye. The title *Blood Bonds and Compulsion* in gold lettering had a light bulb going off in my head. Turning the pages, the text went into control being abused through a bond. It was almost unheard of, but in the event that one of the two bound held a far superior aptitude for compelling, they'd have the ability to telepathically compel their soul's mate—in whatever way they saw fit. Even to the point of meshing their thoughts and desires with the being they were bound to, making them almost the same person but in two different bodies.

Which explained a hell of a lot.

Like Dorian's behavior at *Bite* when he'd effectively cheated on Vanessa by using a blood donor at the club. Like how he seemed so shut off and remote, so unfazed even when he learned Vanessa was dead. Like the glimpses of him that shone through before the calculation and threat crept back in.

None of it was my brother. He was trying to fight it.

And failing.

"He's powerless to refuse any demand sent through the…*link*." I kept their names out of it as I whispered to Vanessa and slid the heavy book across the table to her. The guard was outside that thick wooden door, but he was still a vampire with super-human hearing. "No matter how hard he tries, he can't refuse."

Vanessa's brows drew together in a tight frown and she scanned the page, then the next and the next. "It doesn't say anything about blocking the compulsion. And I already used the best mark I knew of on…*you*." She sighed hard, breath catching as she exhaled. "Leave this with me. I'll check it word for word. Maybe there's another mark or some other way to tackle this."

Leaving her to it, I went back to my towering stack. When I'd been through another eight books of much the same, I stared at the last in the stack. Cracked leather-bound cover in forest green, and thick as a tree. *Blood Bound.* About halfway down the contents page, a subtitle jumped out at me. *Breaking a spirit bond.*

"Hey, I think I might have something."

Vanessa came around the workbench as I read the passage in my head.

The bond between a spirit bound and their blood companion cannot be severed. The connection is everlasting in life and in death, though reports connected to the afterlife are thin at best and not proven…

The typed scrawl continued down the discolored page, detailing how unbreakable the bond was believed to be with reports of those who'd been bound and how they'd remained that way until both parties had passed on. My hope at that title died as if it'd been shot.

"This is just a recap of all the ways you can't break the bond," Vanessa pointed out. Yeah, that was totally obvious. She sighed and moved back around the workbench. "And there was nothing in that other book about a special mark or any other way to block the compulsion. Nothing in anything else I've read through, either."

I turned the page—and my eyes bugged. "Hold up." Vanessa was back in a flash and I read the last sentence out loud.

"Although a blood bond cannot be severed, it is believed that a new and perhaps stronger bond could take its place, thus rendering the previous bond nullified by the new one."

Vanessa snatched the book from me, bringing it up close to her face. "You know what this means, don't you?"

Unfortunately, I couldn't mistake it. "To free Dorian from Marcus's hold, Marcus would need to bond with someone else...*like me*."

LYING on my bed in the dark of vampire post-midday, I was almost in a trance. With one hand across my chest, I could feel the strong drum of my heart. My free hand went to my lips. Warmth radiated from them, remnants from whose flesh they had been planted against. My fangs tingled in lustful memory.

Ty had left through the foyer, in a rush. Like the suite had been on fire and I was stoking the flames.

Standing in my lounge room—because that was neutral ground compared to my bedroom—his blood in my mouth had been pure heaven, velvet heat that had filled me up and drowned my homicidal urges. The sense of achievement I felt warred with a tinge of regret. With all my strength, I'd stopped myself from grabbing onto his taut body. Stopped myself from turning our feeding into a kissing frenzy. From throwing him back on the couch he hardly slept on, with its strewn blanket, and pinning him down. It had been almost as hard as not killing, and so much more tempting. The smell of him, the feel of his hot, scarred skin at my mouth… And he'd been into it, too. Hard…like last time. Though he'd tried to hide it. Had done his best to keep inches of space between our bodies. Had even turned to the side to put more space between us.

His body wanted mine. Like mine wanted his. God, the things I'd imagined doing with him…to him.

But our heads knew better.

We were a train wreck waiting to happen. A train wreck Ty had suffered through long enough, and one I'd brought Kendrick into the middle of.

"Argh!"

I ratcheted upright, pillows flying and hands dropping from my chest and lips. Kendrick was dead. And what was I doing? Fantasizing about Ty, the guy I'd broken his heart for. Kendrick had given everything, literally, to help me save the love of my life…because he was the best guy I knew. Selfless. Honest. Everything I should have cherished and kept safe.

The door to my suite opening and all but slamming brought my head around. My first thought was that Ty had come back, been powerless not to return and finish what we had been so close to starting. But then Raven jogged in from the foyer and smashed that imagining to smithereens. The guilt that swamped me for even continuing that train of thought clawed at my stupid heart.

"I'm a genius! And feel free to tell me so." Raven's expression was alight with excitement, her eyes bright and a teeth-flashing smile parting her lips. Held close to her chest was a wound-up scroll. Around her clutching arm, I could see its age from the tattered and frayed edges, and the stained effect that looked like it'd been attacked by tea bags. "I've finally found something."

Like I'd just been zapped by lightning, I sat up straighter and pushed my guilt aside. "About Kendrick? About resurrecting him?" Oh God, please say yes.

Raven came to my bedside and handed over the scroll, unwinding the cracked leather tie that released the discolored length. "Not quite." The ink inside was handwritten in a calligraphic scrawl, the letters so flowy they were hard to separate into legible words. "It's a blood ritual."

From all the closely joined letters, three words jumped out at me. *Bath of blood.*

I saw in my mind again the seemingly finger-painted message on the inside of Kendrick's glass coffin. My voice was hoarse as I touched the rough curling sheet. A chill cascaded up my spine. "Blood bath."

"It's to connect a spirit-bound vampire to ghosts."

Keeping my grip gentle, I used my forearm to support the scroll's length and stood up. Pacing around, because sitting still right now was impossible, I made sense of the scrawling words.

Only a blood ritual can fully open the door between life and death, effectively creating a link between those of the living and those who have passed beyond. A full break of the doors that separates both worlds is not an easy task, nor is it advisable. Once a door is opened, it may never be closed...

I traced an intricate symbol blotted into the stained cream paper, turning away from the dead end—the window—I'd almost walked into.

"That mark's supposed to open the door between a spirit gifted and one deceased."

"Kendrick," I breathed. "I'd be able to communicate with him?" Just to hear his voice again…

Raven nodded, her arm twining and untwining around one of my bed's four posts like she was having trouble keeping still, too. From the hopeful gleam in her eyes, I could tell she hoped like me that communication would give us the next step to restoring him.

I read ahead, seeing the description for the mark Raven had just recapped and then getting to the actual ritual part. *Blood sacrifice. Submerged.* Images of Erzsebet, my damned grandmother, with girls strung up and bleeding out over a bathtub came to mind. I saw their almost naked flesh, the torrents of red streaming along their upside-down bodies to flow into a wooden tub. Trickling, dripping. I cringed at the thought, at the imagination of the sounds. My mouth watered at the same time. Not a monster? Yeah right. I wanted to be just as bad as the Countess whether I deluded myself into believing otherwise or not.

Forcing my dark thoughts aside, I made myself talk around… yep, lengthening fangs. I stopped moving and faced Raven. "Ah, sacrifice…submerged?" If this all came down to taking innocent life…even though it could connect me to Kendrick…I didn't think I could do it. And if I did? How the hell could I live with myself? Was Raven so focused on bringing Kendrick back that she'd take someone's life to do it? "Whose blood would we need?"

Raven took the scroll and pointed further down. "The spirit gifted needs to be submerged in blood for the ritual to work… damned blood."

That image of Erzsebet rose and changed. No longer with young girls stung up and crying as their lives bled out from their veins. Instead, I saw thrashing damned. Black oily blood spattering a castle chamber while the rest collected on the Countess in the barrel of a tub below.

The folklore I'd read on her had been from human sources. A story of a monstrous woman preying on innocent girls. Vampire records hadn't mentioned the act, because killing the damned in any way would have been applauded, not made into a horror story.

Problem now was? We needed a shitload of damned blood.

And I'd just restored all the captured transitionees. Not that their blood was damned. That change only happened once they'd taken life. Apart from Uriel, no other damned had been captured since the hotel invasion. They'd all been disposed of, bar the few who had fled. And the single one we'd transported back from Hope was not going to be enough.

Raven turned the scroll over for me to see an image of a bath with only hands emerging from the endless black puddle, clinging to the edges. Someone was submerged below the surface. "A heck of a lot of damned blood. And…"

In the image, a man was bent over the bath's edge, liquid streaming from his slashed wrists. "That's the sacrifice?"

"It only says they must sacrifice their blood until the ritual takes effect. It says nothing about them having to die. But…"

The drop in my gut had everything to do with the way she'd said that last word. Total dread made my heart skip with anxiety as she pointed to a single line in the text. I read the passage out loud. *"The live sacrifice must be offered from a pure source without coercion. One that has known total darkness, but now walks in the light."*

Raven spoke the instant conclusion I'd come to. "It has to be a restored damned."

"I'll do it."

I spun around to that deep voice, knowing exactly who it'd come from. Ty strolled in from the foyer. But he didn't ask questions about everything we'd uncovered. The look on his face—the same one he'd worn when feeding me—screamed at his guilt. For what we'd done in this room yesterday? The split-second slide of his eyes to my bed screamed, *hell, yes.* For what he still imagined doing now?

But he didn't owe me that. Or even Kendrick. I had pushed the boundaries, gotten lost in a confused state between lust and bloodlust. He'd been caught in the middle. "You don't have to do that."

There was no sign of wavering. "I want to. It's my choice."

"Then I'll be back up." Raven rerolled the scroll with soft hands. "Now all we need is gallons of damned blood."

"Who's up for a scouting mission?"

Ty was on the same wavelength as me, but getting a bath's quantity of damned blood wasn't going to be a cakewalk. It's not like the damned would happily offer themselves up for the cause. So we'd have to take what we needed. And hit a bunch of them all at once. Taking days, even weeks to source what was needed so I could finally communication with Kendrick? Not if I didn't have to. But the wheels were spinning. I knew what we had to do. "We need to hit a larger population." A place the damned would be running rampant without vampires to pick off.

"More humans have disappeared from Anchorage than anywhere in Alaska."

Ty's input set the scene, and I almost smiled. "Then if your pack's in?"

He nodded while Raven added, "Count me in."

Good. And thanks to choosing Ty's vein over restoring myself, I still had the ability to track down and pinpoint a soulless horde. Maybe Kendrick would find his way to forgiving my slip? But I didn't let that thought linger. Not now.

There was too much to plan out before nightfall tomorrow.

CHAPTER 14

"Are you sure this will work?" I asked as Ty pulled his WRX up into a dark alley. I didn't like the idea one bit. Even though I'd been the one to suggest it. We needed the upper hand, the element of surprise. This was going to deliver dropped bodies like a train wreck. I only wished I could be the one taking all the risk. The temptation to reach out and touch his scarred hand to show my fear for him was there, but I didn't dare. Not with the sound of his steady-beating heart, the collective smell in the air—and the audience taking up the back seat.

After a few hours of travel, we were in Anchorage. It was after midnight, the street light beyond the alley not reaching where Ty's car idled.

Ty didn't meet my worried gaze, keeping his focus on the busy club entrance as cars whizzed by on the main street. "That pull still full-on?" At my nod, knowing he was asking about my connection to the damned that twisted up my insides, he showed no uncertainty.

Reaching through to the back, he pulled up his sleeve to expose his scarred arm. “Then I guess we’re about to find out.”

And we would. Damned were in there, all right. And from what I could feel, I expected at least a dozen.

In the back seat, Marika jabbed a syringe into Troy’s bulging arm and dispensed the contents. When she withdrew the needle tip, his lips curled back from lengthening canines. “Two down…” the beta rasped. “You’re up.”

One last silver-filled syringe was lifted from Marika’s lap. “Here we go.” She bit the cap and freed the needle. A flick to Ty’s inner elbow, and then the sharp tip was inserted into the juiciest vein. She repeated the process on his other arm, then recapped the needle and waited. “How do you feel?”

Ty squeezed his hand into a fist, and then flexed his fingers out. He was immune to silver like any lycan, but unlike his pack mates, he was still part vampire. A side of him that had been reestablished after I restored him from damned to living. “I think I’m good.” He twitched as though what had been injected was creating some discomfort. But he wasn’t screaming out in agony…or dying on the spot. So I guessed he was right. Meeting my eyes, he nodded. “Ready?”

Garbage bags full of stacked black buckets, empty and clean gallon jugs, and too many funnels to count filled the trunk. We had what we needed. But was I ready to take off to our destination and leave Ty and his pack to lure a horde of damned to us—all the while wondering if they’d be killed outright before having the chance to get to us? Why had I come up with this plan again? Oh, right. To perform the blood bath ritual. To get through to Kendrick…to find a way to save him. Executing this plan could only be a one-off. If we screwed up and had to repeat the plan, it would just endanger them over and over, and our step-by-step would likely get back to Marcus and be put to a stop.

So I guess there was only one answer. Yes. Still, I kept from touching Ty as he twisted back in the driver's seat. "Don't leave me waiting." The look in my eyes said, *I can't keep all of this up without you.*

Ty's expression strained. He glared away. "We'll be there."

I forced myself to look at Raven in the backseat. "You set?"

She patted a duffel bag and a clink of metal on metal sounded. No blood in that bag this time. Despite her bubbly excitement, darker emotions peeked through. The plan was risky, but I didn't think she feared for herself. As she clung to the bag, I was sure her only worry was for failing to get what we needed to get through to Kendrick. "Let's do this."

Gentle cracks sounded as Troy and Marika imprinted the likeness of random vampire civilians to make them the most enticing bait in that club. Damned preferred vamp victims to human ones. They were more of a challenge to kill than the weaker race, but what their bodies ultimately needed—in the start, to complete the conversion, and in the end, to thrive.

In a matter of seconds, when the disguises were complete, they exited the back. Ty lingered, lips parting like he wanted to say something else. Or like he wanted to kiss me goodbye…just in case.

Or like he was focusing on altering his exterior to appear vampire too. Selfish dumbass. The lines that marked him as a restored were shrinking back, fading into his skin. His pallor paled from tan to chalky. His eyes blinked from sun-speckled ocean to vivid silver-blue. He shrugged on his jacket, checking his concealed and loaded gun. The same his pack mates carried. Going into a public place, their only other weapons would be a few concealed stakes and daggers. The thought terrified me.

Ty's now silver-blue gaze as he looked at me hardened. "Make yourself scarce when we get there. We don't want to tip them off to our trap."

Before I could utter *be safe,* the driver's-side door opened and cool wind swept in as Ty stepped out and shut me and Raven inside. Leading his pack through slowing traffic, they reached the club's entry, going to the head of the packed line. Proving himself vampire, Ty used his gaze to gain instant entry and a second later they'd slipped inside.

"Want me to drive?"

With the passenger door open and city air filling the cab, I hadn't even noticed Raven exit or walk past the hood and into my line of sight. "Uh, no." Swinging my feet over, I slid into the driver's seat—it was still warm—and fired up the engine. "I'm good."

Raven said nothing as she got in, noisy backpack settling on her lap as I got into gear—in my head and with the car—and pulled into traffic.

Minutes passed that could have been hours with me auto-piloting out of the busy part of Anchorage and proceeding past industrial buildings. We finally reached our destination, where thick trees strangled the parking lot we pulled into. Kincaid Park. Almost two hundred acres of mostly forest with intertwining bike paths that would be ghost trails, with it being so close to midnight.

Without pause, Raven and I got out and went to the trunk. Hearing on sharp alert, I picked up only the quicker heartbeats of animals and birds. No humans anywhere near us. Not even another parked car to suggest someone might return—except for the one we'd dropped off here before delivering Ty and his pack to the club. If all went well, we'd need the extra space for transporting the… material home. Not that we were setting up here. "Let's move our butts."

Raven nodded, and we each took two of the four huge garbage bags. Relying on our vampire night vision, we took to the shadows, darting through thickening trees. Our destination had been researched and set for a purpose. Scouted before our return. Following Ty's lingering scent from earlier, I found the spot. Heavily planted and dark, with a cluster of tall, thick-limbed cottonwoods.

The perfect suspension points.

Quickly tying the bags full of jugs, buckets, and funnels up and out of eyesight, Raven and I took to the trees like monkeys. Silver chains from the duffel bag burned our skin as we secured them to the thickest and strongest limbs that would soon need to hold a pissed-off and thrashing damned.

Securing the last tail of the chain I'd D-shackled in place—so the damned wouldn't see them when chasing their prey in—I finally returned to the ground.

Raven handed me a gun which I cocked as she loaded her own. Moving silently, I surveyed our work, imagining those blood-hungry damned suspended and bleeding out.

Hearing a noise in the distance, I listened for footsteps. But it was too soft. Like the precise running gait of a lynx.

Time seemed to slow exponentially, each second feeling like a delayed hammer to my heart. "Let's get in position."

Without further word, we each spider-monkeyed a tree. At the highest secure limb where foliage concealed my presence, I wedged back into the thick, rough trunk.

Seconds passed. Minutes.

God, the waiting was torture. Not knowing how many would be led our way, and if they'd make it here in one piece. Ty and his pack, not the damned. If I lost them—lost *him*...

A distant sound shot terror through me. Hissing, snarling, and someone being flattened to the ground. Then another. Scrambling to get up. Racing steps.

Ty flew into the area below, not because he'd run in, but because he's been thrown. Troy and Marika were next, Marika tripping as Ty's back connected with the base of the same tree I hid in, way above. The cottonwood shuddered as I clung on to keep from falling. A damned on Troy's back brought him to the ground as more damned sprang at the lycans-in-disguise.

Covered in damned that threatened to block my suspended view of each of them, Ty, Troy, and Marika didn't fight back.

I itched to take action. To intervene. To stop this. But I had to wait.

As the hissing turned into savage biting and messy slurps, I had to anchor to the trunk to keep from leaping down. Raven's pale, horrified face, which I caught sight of through obscuring leaves, brought my exact fears home. This was taking too long. They'd be dead before it worked. If it even did.

Freeing my gun, I couldn't wait any longer. Raven followed my action.

A shift in the sounds of feeding froze us both. I expected to see a damned staring up at one of us. But no. The sound had been a tortured cry of pain, followed by another and another. In quick succession, one damned after the other scrambled back off their prey —off the bitten bodies of Ty, Troy, and Marika—

To stagger and fall.

In mere seconds, fourteen damned were strewn about the leaf litter. And they weren't getting back up. They writhed on their backs, choking sounds coming from their throats.

Indicating to Raven, we dropped simultaneously to the ground, ready to take action and help Ty and his damned-bitten pack and gather what we'd come for.

A rush of fast-approaching feet halted me from getting to Ty's side. And then I saw it.

"Look out!" I pushed Raven aside and plugged a bullet into a late-arriving damned's throat.

Raven recovered with a tuck-and-roll and pulled the trigger at another. But there was no time to waste. As the first two fell and the others continued writhing, more appeared. At least another twenty sped our way through the thick trees.

Mind screaming *oh shit,* my sight darted to Ty. Of the damned that lay around him, all poisoned by silver-injected blood, more than five had bitten him. Gouges marked his neck, arms, wrists, legs, and his torso—I could see them through tears in his V-neck. His body shuddered as he tried to lever up, bringing him back down with a grunt as he floundered for his gun. His focus snapped up to me. *"Duck!"*

I hit the deck, getting a face full of leaves. But it was Raven who fired three more shots, bringing another damned down. Not dead, but writhing in gargling agony, because each gun was packed with silver-exploding bullets.

I rushed to Ty as Raven fell to her knees between Marika and Troy. "Are you okay?" The scent of his blood was potent, but the danger around us kept my mind off murder.

"Burning up," he gritted out, the evidence clear in the sheen that dampened his face. Damned venom.

Tugging Ty up, I heard Marika and Troy getting up too. They stumbled as Ty went down to his knees. But there was no time to help them back up. The damned were here.

"Take 'em down!" I screamed.

Firing off silencer-muted rounds, Raven and I hit as many trees as we did damned. The shots that did strike gray flesh didn't drop enough of them. The volts of lightning I alternated between only floored each one I hit for a second.

Raven reloaded and freed a dagger from her thigh, shooting and lashing out. My own gun clicked instead of shooting the damned coming my way. And then I was driven back, spine smacking into a tree as I dropped the new magazine. Pinned, the damned didn't attack to kill. He simply trapped me.

Thrashing to get free, my voltage was barely more than a sting. I saw the fresh horror unfolding over the damned's shoulder.

Raven's gun was knocked from her hand. With only her dagger, she back-stepped until she was surrounded. And that wasn't the worst of it. The intruding damned weren't attacking to devour the three lycans that had morphed back into their own skins.

The state of the writhing damned around them hinted to the new arrivals that the bait was bad. A trick.

"You're all gonna die," one said as the others hauled Ty, Troy, and Marika up. "Painfully." Their arms were strung out, pulled taut—

Ty roared as pressure was applied to him first, the ground rumbling as he tried and failed to conjure his connection to earth.

"No. Stop!" They were going to tear him to pieces, starting with his arms. I felt like I was going to vomit as I bucked. Would they end it by twisting his neck clean off his spine—like Marcus had done to the damned that'd had the gall to bite me?

Troy snarled as Marika yelped. A squeal struck the air as Raven was captured, a bone snapping as a damned broke her hand to drop her dagger.

They were all about to die, here in this forest. They'd come to help me save Kendrick. They'd trusted my plan.

And I would be left the only one alive, because Marcus deemed it so.

As the sound of approaching rainfall neared and the wind picked up and the ground continued to shake along with Ty's body, I let all the rage in. At who I'd been made to be. Who my twin was. At having to send my mom away after almost killing her. At losing Ty. At being the cause of Kendrick's death.

With a scream, I stopped pushing against the damned that pinned me and tugged him closer. Fangs springing free, they punched into his thick gray skin. The damned jerked and fought back, but my jaw locked in place. His rotten berry-tasting blood was sucked down my throat. And soon enough, those strong arms now pushing me away turned weak. Fangs disengaging, his body fell. Red flooded my sight. My heart stopped dead. The monster I always struggled to contain came forth.

And I let it.

Strength renewed and multiplied, blue lightning fired from my hands. One damned was shot from Ty, another from Raven. And I didn't wait for the others to act. With the most speed I'd ever sustained, I became a tornado. Circling the damned in a blur, my voltage stopped their torturous intent—and any backlash. My gripping and twisting hands finished the job.

After seconds that passed in a blur, I froze. The earlier damned still writhed from drinking silver-poisoned blood. The intruders were statue still. Their necks snapped, but heads not detached. Able to heal—but not without helpful realignment. More than enough bodies to fulfill our needs. If I chose to care what this had all been for, anymore.

I didn't.

Past a few trees, Raven was helping Troy and Marika up. Her eyes shot from me to them. "We're not out of the woods yet."

Not even close, my inner voice taunted.

But lucky for those three, someone else was closer. Just as bitten up. Just as weak. Struggling to his shaking legs, Ty used a tree to keep himself upright. Veins still coursing with delicious blood—blood that should be cured of silver after the damned's relentless draining as his body repaired and replenished.

"Amelia," Ty's voice was warning as he frowned at the state of my black-veined skin. "You don't want to do this."

Except I did. I even planned to test his blood in my mouth before swallowing. Just to be safe. Raven—who hadn't been injected—would be my backup if needed.

Rain fell, and then it started to pour.

I was before him in a blink, trapping him against the tree as one hand shoved his jaw up and to the side. There was growling and shouting—from the other's—but I didn't care. They'd soon be next. And as the rain hardened, their words of protest were lost.

"Amelia," Ty choked out. "Rein it in."

Cutting off his air supply, I could feel his body losing the last of its fight. Damn, he looked good in red. "Don't you ever get tired of believing in me?"

With a grunt and all his might, Ty bucked, my choking arm losing its unrelenting pressure. His stare turned gold and…sad. "The girl who risked her life to save my sorry ass when *I* was the monster? Who puts everyone else's existence above her own?" A shaky, rain-drenched hand came up, not to fight me off, but to hold the others back.

They were right behind me now.

Someone swooped up my gun and the magazine I'd dropped clipped into place. The round muzzle pressed into my back—not quite lined up with my heart. From the short height, I knew Raven was holding the weapon—in her non-broken hand.

"Hell, no," Ty declared, halting my intent to floor the lot of them. "In this bullshit world, *you* are the only thing I believe in."

My arm readying to stop his words and breath stalled. Something inside me—something other than the monster—had been hit hard by his claim. That tiny part of me that was good. That sliver of my conscience. The rain washed away the scent of all their blood. Still I couldn't ignore the beat of those four hearts. My shred of humanity failed. I couldn't re-cage what I'd let loose.

I knew it was true as my arm pressed into Ty's throat and fresh electric currents cloaked my body, zapping him and ready to flatten the others with a quick spin and shoot.

"This isn't…you, Amelia. I…know you."

I screamed as I tore my arm from Ty and spun. I caught the gun before Raven could fire and pulled the trigger. Once. Twice. Three times—

I cried out as the pain registered. The puncture of flesh. The burn as the bullets exploded—in my own chest.

Hunger, red sight, Ty calling my name.

It all faded as I fell like a stone.

CHAPTER 15

Fighting the weight of my heavy lids, I blinked slowly. Deep blue shadows rose before the black fell back down. With another rise, I saw his face. Free of injury and strained as he stared back at me, eyes more gold as his full lips twisted.

"You're okay."

Not a question. A statement. Those last few seconds swept through my consciousness. Me taking the gun and firing rounds into my chest. Lids losing the fight, I registered the lack of pain from silver burning through my heart. So it had worked. I'd stopped the monster in me from killing my friends. From killing Ty. And now I was dead. No longer anyone's problem.

Except…

Eyes squeezed shut in the dark, I could hear…heartbeats. Calloused, hot fingers slid back and forth over my forearm, tracing the swirls of marbled flesh like a maze. Lids cracking, I saw his face again. One of the heartbeats was his, irregular but strong. The other was…mine. Not dead.

"Hey."

My voice was hoarse as I levered upright from soft pillows, feeling a pinch halfway up my arm. Yet I felt like I'd had the best sleep in ages. Through the growing darkness of my bedroom, I found Ty in an armchair at my bedside. One that had always sat by the tall Gothic window. The blanket that was usually draped over the couch was twisted over Ty's lap and the chair's arm. And I didn't need a play-by-play to know why. Ty had brought me back here, laid me in bed, and camped out, awaiting my return to consciousness. The circles under his eyes proved he hadn't slept. The tension that melted from his face left lines from extended worry.

"Good to have you back." Ty gulped, hand slipping from my arm. "I didn't know if it would work. But you're up. You seem…better."

I noticed something then that explained that pinching feeling, the lack of silver burn and holes in my chest. And the feeling of power that thrummed through me. A tube ran from Ty's inner elbow, delivering a direct stream of blood from his vein to mine.

Ty bit his lip like he was trying not to grunt, and ran his rough fingers from my jaw down, settling across my neck that tingled with unusual sensitivity. "I…the, ah…silver. I had to drain it out." His intense stare cast away. "I didn't have a choice."

He'd bitten me and drunk my blood? Even without any recollection, I warmed at the thought. And he regretted having had to do it—because he thought I might object? Or because with our past, he never imagined he'd have to go there again? Now his blood was replenishing what he'd taken. Fixing me from the inside out. From the liquid silver I'd shot so close to my heart.

To keep myself from killing them all. To ensure what I'd become didn't get in the way of the plan they'd all risked their lives for.

The scene flooded back, and I tugged the live blood feed from my arm. The damned. The silver infection working. And then more damned. Another twenty. Before we'd even had a chance to get what we'd come for.

I swung my legs over the bed's edge, ready to get up, ready to pace. "Did it work? Did we get what we needed?" I saw those writhing bodies—and then the still ones I'd snapped the necks of. "All the damned…" I thought of how they were normally dealt with, how Troy especially, disposed of them without a care. "Are they all—"

"Alive." Ty's palms on my knees kept my butt planted on the soft mattress. "I reported their capture before we took off yesterday. The RVC transported and imprisoned every single one—with the understanding that you'll restore them when you're willing and able."

Ty had put his foot down for me? Made demands of the council again?

Yesterday?

With that growing darkness beyond the Gothic windows, it was the start of a new vampire day.

"As for the damned blood…" Ty's tired face creased with strain, but as I felt the weightlessness of my body falling back on the bed, my protest that he preserve his strength never passed my lips.

All around me, cottonwoods shot sky-high. Writhing, groaning bodies of fourteen damned lay strewn in the mud and leaf litter. Twenty lay twisted and dead still.

Ty fell to my side—not the me watching from a distance, but the me I'd shot to kill the monster. Hand raking through my long, muddied blond hair, he cradled my head. Horror was all over his face as he yelled out. "String them up and bleed them dry. And make it fucking quick."

And then he struck, vampire fangs punching into my neck.

From my vantage point, I saw Raven clamber up a tree and release the plastic bags we'd secured. "Set out the buckets. I'll drop the chains."

On shaky legs, Marika and Troy began unpacking the buckets. "Let's get this over with," Troy grated, dropping the first bucket dead center below the first chain that clanked down.

Marika spared a look at Ty who was hunched over me and starting to quiver—from sucking my silver-laced blood from my vein. "Before he kills himself."

They amped up the operation, fighting through as their wounds healed and their bodies burned off the venom of numerous damned bites, to string half-conscious damned up by their ankles. When they were all upside down—all thirty-four of them—the me watching shuddered at the visual, anticipating what was to come. With the jugs out and lined up before the buckets, crimson leaked from the damned's mouths, the silver-tainted blood some had ingested from the prey we'd offered. The amount of silver that would have made it through their systems—whether by bullet or bite—would be small, but it was doing its job. Those snapped necks did it for the rest.

The next step would only debilitate them further.

Troy unsheathed a hidden dagger, not hesitating as he moved from one damned to the next, slicing their throats open. There was a steady splatter, the free-pouring blood growing louder as it gushed into each bucket, dulling to a collection of splashes as the levels rose higher and higher.

Ty rolled off me with a tortured groan. On his back, his lids squeezed shut and his jaw clenched as every one of his muscles squeezed with strain. Lips twisted open, he gasped for breath.

I went to rush to him, but like in my visions, my ability to move freely in this dreamscape wasn't granted. Stuck to the spot, all I could do was watch, and remind myself that I knew the outcome. Ty would survive this, and so would I…because of everything he had done.

After taking my blood—most of it, judging by the graying of his flesh and darkening of black veins—Ty's body was trying to purify itself of all that silver. It was trying to heal.

Time seemed to speed up until the flow from each damned began to slow. Each bucket was shifted safely out of the way, then moving at speed, Raven, Troy, and Marika were back up the trees. Shifting from one to the next, they released those D-shackles. Damned fell in succession, heads then bodies hitting the ground as those long lengths of silver clanked down on top of them and burned. Despite the fall and everything else, each damned was still alive—in the undead way they existed—but they weren't strong enough to move. Not after the bloodletting and with the remaining silver in their systems.

Clambering to his hands and knees, Ty bit out, "Tie them up. I'll make the call."

With a nod, Troy moved the damned while Marika joined Raven to pour the buckets of blood into each gallon jug.

When the damned had been tied to the trees they'd been suspended from, Ty forced his shaking hands into his pocket, pulled his phone out, and made that call. Then he hung up, molars grinding as he got to his feet. Swooping down, he went to cradle my limp body as he stood and stumbled. Troy was there in a flash, pulling me out of the mud. As a growl of possession rose up Ty's throat, Troy helped me into Ty's arms.

"Load up the cars and get out of here," Troy barked to the others.

Ty hoisted me higher, supporting my neck to get to his wrist. Troy's hot hand stalled his intent as Ty's fangs grew long and pointed. "You're too weak to feed her, yet." Troy's expression was almost sympathetic, despite the fresh growl of threat Ty let out as his canines made an appearance.

Troy's hold tightened. "Plus the silver's still burning off, along with that damned venom. You could do more harm."

The threat drained from Ty, and he glanced around at the tired-up damned as Marika and Raven rushed back in to collect another lot of filled jugs. "Did we get enough?"

The forest collapsed around me and everyone in it. Suddenly back in my room, I knew I owed my life to Ty after everything he'd done. And yet I had to know. "Did we?"

In spite of the amped-up drain from reliving that memory through a dreamscape on top of everything else, Ty smiled. "Yeah. We did. Vanessa's purifying the rest of it as we speak."

WITH VICTORIAN LAMPS lighting up the path as we walked, the rows of headstones that were soon superseded by tombs cast long shadows. Ones I kept mistaking for people—or the dead. Not that I'd be able to see any ghosts yet. But soon…

I rubbed at my inner wrists through my hoodie's sleeve. The new marks Vanessa had given me were good to go. I kept my voice low as I leaned into her. Her current guard tailed at a discrete distance, and I didn't want him eavesdropping. Everything was riding on this, and any mistake could cause this attempt to reach Kendrick to fail. It would make all we'd been through and survived to get to this point worthless. That feeling of being about to explode on the inside soared with each of my quick steps. "Are you sure the solution was right?"

Vanessa looked irritated that I was questioning her alchemist abilities as she glanced quickly down at the marks lining my wrists, then away. "Your blood. Alchemist gold. And damned blood. Same as last time."

When I'd failed to sever the compulsion Dorian was under. And this time the damned blood had been cleansed of liquid silver.

Since we'd returned, Vanessa had been on task, purifying all we'd returned with and creating more black ink so she could mark me and Kendrick with mirrored symbols from the scroll Raven had unearthed. The symbol that would open the otherworldly door to his spirit without letting every other spook through. The machine blowing freezing air into his glass coffin had been shut off. The lid had been removed. I'd afforded myself fleeting seconds to touch his face, like I'd been wanting to do and trying to imagine every time I ran my fingers across the transparent barrier that locked him inside. He was so cold. Frozen stiff.

I'm coming for you. I'd sent the unspoken message through a bond that was no longer reciprocated. *Don't block me out.*

With Vanessa's noisy tattoo gun, the mark had been administered, the coffin sealed back up, and the freezer machine switched back on.

Passing only a few mourners at a headstone here and there, because it was still early vampire morning, just ninety minutes since I'd awoken, we kept the chit-chat down. When we reached the Baldassare tomb, I turned around and nodded to our one shadow. He'd already been given his orders prior to our excursion. Keep your distance and don't advance on or enter the tomb unless you see a damned breaking in.

Waiting for him to set off—not that he went out of sight—I mounted the marble steps and pushed through the heavy door. Vanessa was right behind me and closed the glow of Victorian lamps out.

A warm and calloused hand touched my wrist the second after

Ty's scent reached me. That erratic beat of his heart was sprinting, now replenished after his offering from bottled Pure Blood. His thumb slid back and forth as his hot breath feathered over my ear and cheek. "You ready for this?"

Through the resolve of his deep voice, I sensed something else. Fear? That we wouldn't succeed…or that we would?

Was *I* ready? I thought of what Ty had volunteered to do, how when the time was right, he'd slice himself open and sacrifice his blood to complete the ritual. To bring Kendrick back to me. Well, at least in spirit. "I—"

A lantern came to life, bathing the space in an orange glow. Ty's touch fell and he stepped back. The sudden visual stalled any response I had been about to make and stripped all thought from my mind.

A few feet from Kendrick's coffin was the marble shell that held his mother's remains. What was directly on top made my skin prick with nerves and anticipation. A matching glass coffin. It was smaller than Kendrick's, and it wasn't empty. The thirty-four-plus gallons of blood Troy, Marika, and Raven had syphoned from the damned now filled it, purified and ready for the ritual.

I wrinkled my nose at the scent of the thick black blood. Rotting berries. I knew that smell well. Of all the instances that could come back, the time Ty had trapped me in a dreamscape in one of the feeding rooms at *Pulse* resurfaced. I shuddered as the images flooded in, the way Ty had kissed down my body on that daybed, the way he'd plunged his fangs into my inner thigh. I'd been ready to give him anything, to do anything…until I'd smelled his blood. Blood he'd wanted me to taste. It had been a test to gauge my resistance to his influence over me.

He'd underestimated me.

Raven rose from her crouch next to the lantern and a cluster of blood-filled bottles. She leaned forward with her hands on the glass box's edge. With her broken hand healed, her fingers tapped as if trying to relieve nervous tension. "Of course she's ready." She eyed Ty like she'd been watching when he'd touched me moments ago. Like she'd sensed all that remained unsaid between us and didn't approve. Her gaze narrowed at me in challenge. "Aren't you."

I didn't bother answering. Instead, I made my intentions clear by stripping down to my underwear: a regular non-see-through black bra and cotton bottoms. Refolding my clothes, I placed them atop a stack of towels that were ready to dry the damned blood from my body when and if this ritual worked. Dear God, please work. Moving between the two coffins, I glanced fleetingly at Kendrick before facing the empty pool of black. I threw one foot into the thick liquid, then the other, making sure not to spill any. The level on the glass wasn't much past halfway, and I needed to be fully submerged. I couldn't waste a drop. Lowering my backside down, I stretched out my legs. That rotting berry scent stirred and plumed. Yuck.

At least I didn't have to drink it.

Like I'd done only yesterday—for the second time. And yet in those instances, the smell or even taste hadn't made me sick to my stomach. Nervous? Hell, yeah.

Vanessa picked up the delicate scroll that detailed the blood ritual, carefully unrolling the length. "It goes on about surrendering to lifelessness."

I already knew that, had read the words over and over at least as many times as Raven.

"We still think that has to do with breathing, right?" Raven said what we'd already guessed earlier.

"Except that I don't breathe." Would the ritual still work if I was already half dead?

Vanessa didn't seem concerned. "Then you're already halfway

there. But I think submerging a few minutes before Ty's part would be a good idea."

My sight skittered to Ty. Without words, the look I gave him asked the question.

Ty unsheathed his dagger and nodded, eyes locked on mine—rather than my almost naked body. "Ready and waiting. You're up." By the clench of his jaw, there was no doubt he was determined to follow through. Screw the consequences. To himself. To what we'd been so long ago.

Ignoring the feeling of unexpected loss, I nodded and leaned back on my elbows, the thick liquid rising up my back. Slowly lowering, I felt the disturbed blood lap at my skin, coating me. My hair grew heavy as it soaked up from the ends to my roots. The smell got worse. My heartbeat got quicker. Cool wet climbed up the back of my skull, the sides of my face. My lids squeezed shut. No need to hold my breath. "Ready or not…"

The tip of my nose submerged, and then…quiet. I lay still as death, the only movement internal as my heart kept up its rhythm. Time passed as if infinite, any notion of seconds or minutes lost as I waited. And waited. And waited. Shouldn't there be dripping now, the noise of Ty's blood being offered to the pool of black? My lids sprang open to…watery black. I wasn't too far below the surface.

Ty's face appeared above me, his hair hanging forward as he stared down at me. The sight of him wasn't at all clear, but just seeing him at all eased my anxiety. But then that dagger came out. *Slice. Slice.* He cut long tracks down the length of each of his inner forearms. The initial trickle became a steady flow above my face, blurring my sight and mingling with the black. The flow kept up, strong and steady, and then it was time.

Below the surface, I moved slowly to keep the pool of blood steady and unbroken, to keep me one hundred percent submerged.

My arms traveled up, keeping close to my skin, rising up and over until… My wrists pressed together, the two mirrored symbols joining line for line.

Nothing happened.

There was no light, no ripple of power, no ghostly sightings. *Kendrick, are you there?*

Ty still lingered above my head, the blood tracking down his arms to his wrists and spilling down, down, down… Was he looking pale? How much blood had he sacrificed? Had he needed longer to recover after all he'd done to save me?

My desperation rose, for Ty, for this to be over with. *Kendrick, answer me!*

He didn't.

I went to lever up and Ty's hand splayed in a stop motion. A steadier trickle joined the pool, steadier because Ty's donation was tapping out. Raven was down at my feet—not that I could see her—but it had to be her. *The live sacrifice must be offered from a pure source without coercion. One that has known total darkness, but now walks in the light.* Only restored blood would work, and the ritual never said the sacrifice was limited to one source.

I squeezed my wrists together. *Kendrick, please. Just give me a sign. Anything.*

The blood leaking from Ty's arms had become a slowing drip. He was resting on the glass edge, lids heavy and head lolling. Hands were hooked under his pits. It had to be Vanessa, because I could still hear the other trickle. It had slowed now too, and still not a—

Surging power rippled out from my connected wrists. It rocked the surface in waves that belted into the coffin's sides. Black blood crashed over the edges and my wrists split apart. Not because I'd let the marks separate, but from the sheer force. I ratcheted upright, stripping the thick black from my eyes as it drained down my face and chest.

Ty had fallen back onto Vanessa, who snatched one of the waiting bottles and brought it to his lips. "Is he okay?"

When the first bottle was quickly drained, another met his lips. A mild tint of color slowly crept back to his complexion. "He's—"

"I'll be…fine," Ty cut in with a rasp, a sharp look of inspection sliding his gaze over my dripping torso. "Will you?"

Always concerned for my well-being.

I nodded and looked to Raven. She was conscious and on her butt, the slices up her arms slowly pulling back together. "I didn't imagine that, did I? It worked, right?" She staggered getting upright, but managed to steady herself.

A full bottle tapped against my arm. I took the offering from Vanessa and handed it over to Raven. She didn't remove the cap, just waited. She needed to know.

And so did I.

Glancing around the tomb past Kendrick's still body, I waited for something to appear, a ghostly apparition, a glow, a shadow. *Kendrick?* I'd felt that power, that explosive change that had come out of nowhere. It had to have worked. "Kendrick, please." My lips clamped shut, realizing I'd said that out loud. Still, I couldn't miss the desperation in my voice. Couldn't miss the taste of the black blood on my lips, either. I reverted to silent pleading, seconds dragging on as I looked all around the tomb with its yellow glow. No movement by the closed door, none through the opening to the other chamber. He wasn't here.

I closed my eyes and hung my head. The marks on my wrist were gone, like they'd been used up. Getting free of the black-slicked bath, I couldn't hold myself back. And I didn't bother trying to cover myself up or wipe myself down. I had to know…

The air in Kendrick's coffin pillowed out as I removed the lid. His body was freezing to the touch. And I almost expected his eyes to open, or at least move behind his lids. But that was never going to happen now. Even if the ritual had worked, it was only a way to communicate with his spirit. It wasn't the way to resurrect him by rejoining his soul with his body and somehow breathing life back into him.

As Raven crept closer and Vanessa helped Ty to stand, I untied Kendrick's wrists and with painstaking slowness, eased them apart.

The marks were gone—well almost. The once dark lines were almost invisible. Not quite as totally used as mine.

My head snapped up, my skull pivoting on my spine. *Are you here?* God, please be here. Give me a sign.

Past Raven's hope, Vanessa's watchfulness, and Ty's masked expression, there was nothing. The passing seconds and minutes changed nothing.

I peered down at Kendrick. With gentle fingers, I traced the bone structure of his lifeless face. The evidence was clear. Or should I say lack thereof. I stumbled back, butt and legs hitting the marble box and the blood bath I'd risen from. With a gulp, I felt like I was trying to swallow a fist. My sight glazed with red tears. "It didn't work."

CHAPTER 16

Alone in Kendrick's suite—because I needed the space from everyone, and to get away from his frozen body—I actually felt closer to him. With Burton snowboards up against the wall in his bedroom, DCs on the floor by his blue and orange striped bed, boarding DVDs on a tallboy and more in the lounge, he felt more alive here than he ever had where his actual body lay stone cold.

Still, none of it dulled my depression. I picked up and clasped a DVD to my chest, falling back on the white leather couch. My heart was raw. My hope hanging by a thread. After all we'd fought through, after the last few people I cared about had almost died at the damned's hands, after having to all but kill myself to save them after turning ripper, *this* was the outcome.

It had been nearly six hours since the ritual. Six hours of talking to myself back in my suite. Of only letting Ty in to replenish me. Of pleading to Kendrick's ghost…and getting no reply.

I shot up, pelting the DVD down at the ground with a tortured cry. Instant guilt overcame me and I fell to my knees. "What have I done?" Grasping the plastic fragments and cracked disk, I felt like I'd just broken Kendrick. One of so few parts of him—the objects that defined who he'd been—that still remained.

Instant tears escaped my eyes, and I went to rise as sudden dull moonlight gleamed in through the open drapes. The ghostly glow crept through the lounge room, stopping its travels at a high-backed armchair—that was draped with the royal Baldassare cloak. The gold material shimmered despite the dimness of the light, almost glittering. As if it were beckoning me to it?

Without realizing I'd moved, I found myself standing right there. I reached out and slipped the cloak from the armchair's shoulders. Remnants of the last people to wear the silky-soft material filled my nose. A woman, the late Lady Baldassare; and a man, Kendrick. I clutched the length and breathed in deep. My lungs hitched, but I didn't care. Picking up his scent like this almost made it feel like he was still here somewhere.

His frozen body didn't emit the scents of life anymore.

But this material with its tightly woven strands…

Keeping the length from dragging as I clutched it to my chest, I ambled toward the dissipating light and opened the terrace doors. Stepping out onto the balcony, I reached the balustrade and—

Down in the garden a figure seemed to appear out of nowhere. The woman with long golden-brown hair stood in the fountain, the trickling water drenching her indigo gown. My eyes refocused like lasers. Something was off about her—

My hand slipped off the balustrade. I scrambled to catch myself and stared. It couldn't be. But I knew that face. Those eyes that had always looked at me with such disdain and disapproval.

Lady Baldassare.

Serafina's face lifted an inch, her icy stare settling on me. A chill thundered through my body and my mouth parted to call out—

Serafina bent backward suddenly—at an angle that was impossible to sustain. It was *The Matrix* in the flesh, contortion that was an inch short of snapping her spine. As if someone unseen was forcing her over in that way, bending her back to the point of breaking. Flesh tore away from her neck like she was being attacked. Except there was only her there. Blood streamed and her arms flailed, pushing at…nothing and no one. Then her flailing weakened and her knees gave out. Back hovering above the water, her eyes were still on me. The light faded from them like a candle snuffed.

Then her body fell.

There was no disturbance to the water. No overflow from her body to push waves from the fountain. In fact…there wasn't a body at all. She was gone. Vanished.

Heart racing and eyes blinking hard, I had to question my sanity. I half turned—

And stumbled back. My heart threatened to leap straight through my ribs.

Serafina, Kendrick's mother, stood right beside me. I scrambled until I hit the side of the balustrade, mouth gaping but no words coming out. Her flesh was a shade of blue. The gouge on her neck was raw and messy. Blood marked her from the bite and stained the bodice of her drenched gown. Even as I stared, reality edged its way into my conscious mind. She had no heartbeat, no breath…those eyes were dead-fish cloudy, but as disapproving as ever.

Legs trembling, I used the railing to get to my feet. Finally my voice worked. "You're not alive. You're dead."

The flesh-and-bone royal was right before me without even moving. Her nose almost touched mine, and her lips parted to reveal long pointed fangs. Her dead eyes tunneled into mine. "My son's dead because of you. You're a plague on everything you touch."

She disappeared. Poofed right back to nothingness as if she'd never been here at all.

My sight darted. The garden was empty, the fountain too. I was alone up here. Inside there was nothing else. No one else.

But I wasn't going crazy. What I'd seen had been real. Somehow I knew that. Which meant…

The blood ritual had worked, and not in the way we'd planned. The door to the other side had been flung wide open.

I realized then that I'd dropped the Baldassare cloak. Serafina's cloak. A talisman that had connected me to her? That had shown me a reenactment of the moment she'd been brutally murdered—in the exact place we'd found her floating. I shuddered, seeing it all again behind closed lids. This cloak had given me the ability to communicate with her, and her with me.

I didn't debate her statement. I believed it myself. I was a plague on everyone around me. But I didn't dwell on that home truth now…

I could communicate with the dead. Which meant…I could get through to Kendrick.

AN HOUR later and still moving from one item in Kendrick's suite to another, I bit back the urge to scream. Kicking at the mess of clothes and magazines scattered over his bedroom floor, I barely contained the urge to tear everything in his entire suite to shreds.

Reaching Serafina had been a shocking fluke.

Reaching Kendrick? So far, freaking impossible.

After starting in the bedroom, I'd gone from larger things like his snowboards and bindings, to Burton jackets and pants, to every piece of clothing I could find. I'd scoured his library tower and every boarding magazine up there. All these items were special to him. Some way more than others. Any of them could be talismans, a corporeal item that could link me to him.

But nothing had.

Now after passing through the lounge and sitting room, and even poking my head into the bathroom, that horrible depression returned with a vengeance. That feeling of failure that threatened to drown me. All the furniture had been here before his mother's violent death. None of it had linked me to him…or her.

I shuddered as I reentered the bedroom, shoulders creaking in response. Seeing Serafina's death played out in that way was still fresh in my mind. To die like that, slow enough to know you had no way out? It was cruel. Meeting the tallboy, I paused at the old jewelry box. It was made of solid gold with *Baldassare* inscribed into the lid. Being his mother's, I hadn't even given it a second glance before. Now I was desperate. Lifting the lid slowly, I found the inside stuffed full. I reached in and plucked out a ring with an enormous sapphire. Serafina's name was engraved on the inside. This had definitely belonged to Kendrick's mother.

Every muscle in my body tightened as I slowly pivoted, expecting to see that blue translucent flesh and those dead-fish eyes. But she wasn't there. A look around revealed she wasn't lingering behind any corners or amongst any shadows.

Despite the ring having belonged to her, it hadn't conjured her spirit. But why? The answer hit me like a brick to the back of the head. Well, maybe not a brick. Still, the realization was earth-shattering, and one I was ready to test. A quick check revealed that none of the other precious pieces brought her back, either.

Which meant…

I understood why none of Kendrick's boarding gear or menial

possessions had connected me to him. And why only that cloak out of everything in this entire suite had linked me to his mother.

Serafina's most prized possession, the one she'd left behind and—

Snatching up the cloak, I shot from Kendrick's suite like I'd been rocket launched, startling other royal's guards. Within seconds, I was out the tall iron-braced doors, racing on until I exploded into the Baldassare tomb.

As I unhooked the stiff latch, the lid to Kendrick's deathbed sprang open with a release of chilled air.

"What are you doing?" Raven rushed in from the adjoining chamber, a book slapping the ground from her leap up. With haste, she reclosed the lid. "You can't keep opening this. You're messing with the temperature control."

Having spun at her approach, I absently noticed the marble coffin now free of my blood bath. The one Ty had volunteered to clean up—while I cleaned myself up. But I didn't wonder about him now, where he was, what he was doing. All my attention went down to my hand.

Raven saw then the folded note I held, her irritation melting into curious suspicion. "What's that?"

I'd pulled it from the inside pocket of Kendrick's suit jacket just in time. The one he was meant to be buried in. My eyes darted before I replied, my soaring hope draining with every dragging second. "It's the note Serafina left Kendrick." The one where she'd expressed her pride in her son. The one where she'd told him she loved him—for the first time in his seventeen years of life. Of all the things he owned, I'd been so sure this would have been the most important. I blinked slowly, my heart shattering in my chest. "I just thought…"

"How many more missing? And only in the last week?" Ty's

deeper voice preceded him as he strolled in through the open door, his phone up to his ear. "And all human…" Remnants of black blood that I could scent dotted his skin and clothes, and he stalled at the sight of us. "Gotta go." Hanging up, both hands dipped into opposite pockets, and then his growing concern ebbed, releasing the twitching of his biceps. He nodded to the note. "What's going on?"

From the confused looks on both their faces, it was clear that at least Raven thought I'd snapped. Maybe I had. Maybe what I thought I'd seen wasn't real. That ghostly apparition could have been a delusion. But then again… If that were true, wouldn't I have deluded myself into believing I was seeing Kendrick? I was almost tempted to touch the cloak I'd dropped at my feet again to test my sanity. Instead, I spoke. "The ritual worked."

"You saw Kendrick? You talked to him?" Raven lit up like a firework, her sight darting around like she was waiting to see him, too.

I shook my head. "No. His mother. By touching this." I bent and grabbed the gold cloak. "I thought…"

Ty leaned back into the door he'd closed, kicking one careless leg over the other even as his Adam's apple bobbed with a dry gulp. "You thought that if you found something he was tied to, then you could connect with him too."

With both hands on the expensive material, I felt my body drain further—because it had already been depleted since I'd connected to her ghost. I just hadn't noticed it with the shock and my one-mindedness to reach Kendrick. But I wasn't stopping now. Heartbeat still strong, I welcomed the appearance as Serafina's ghost blinked into existence—

Crouched on her marble resting bed and right up in my face. Expression enraged, her hands reached to strangle me as she glimpsed the fogged-up glass that encapsulated her dead son.

I jumped back, knocking into and getting trapped by that chilled glass box. "I didn't kill him. Not directly. Marcus did."

Raven squealed and backed away from me, while Ty shot over like he could defend me.

As her rigid hands froze, I spoke quickly. "It's true. And I want to save Kendrick, to bring him back. That's why he's here, frozen. There's a way to resurrect him, but I need your help. Tell me how to reach him. What object—"

"You want my *help?*"

"Amelia, what's going on?" By my side, Ty had a dagger and a stake in each hand. The look on his face was utter hopelessness. There was nothing he could see to defend me from.

"I want vengeance." Suddenly on my other side, Serafina's strained and reaching hands curled into fists. She went to touch the glass cover over Kendrick's face and her digits slipped straight through. "For my son. Prove you're worthy of my help, and then maybe I'll offer it."

"Amelia!" Weapons quickly re-holstered, Ty clutched my wrist and yanked me back. But there was nothing left to defend me from as the cloak fell.

Serafina had disappeared.

And yet as a bone-deep chill struck through my marrow, I knew she wasn't gone. And she was far from done with me.

Another chill ran through me and I heard a creak. Jaw dropping, I gaped at the sound. The door had opened an inch. As if that wasn't an invitation. And what do you know, my feet were already moving me in that direction as I swooped up the cloak.

"Amelia, what the hell is going on?" Ty demanded, throwing out a hand to slow me. With wide eyes, the look on his face was one I had almost never seen on him. Fear. For once he couldn't actively protect me. "Dammit, speak to me."

I tugged free of his possessive hold, the heat of his palm remaining even after the removed contact. I didn't linger now that his scent was curling up my nose—despite how much I was tempted to. There wasn't time. "It's Kendrick's mom." I glimpsed a flash of indigo through the gap between the door and jamb. "She wants me to follow her."

As I escaped, Ty keeping close behind, Raven caught up. "Anyone else got the mega shivers going on?"

Neither of us answered as I led the way after Serafina's ghostly figure, following the swish of her gown. Now racing to keep up, the graveyard shrank behind us, and then I was flying through the iron-braced doors. Serafina's ghost moved in my peripheral to the left. I chased after her, past the grand stairs, flying down a stone corridor…that led to the offices. That flowy gown ghosted right through one of the office doors further down.

Marcus's.

Light flashed on and off from beneath the hardwood barrier.

I stalled as Ty unsheathed his dagger and a stake. "If he's in there, he's not getting away." Stalking past me, he nodded back to us, then depressed the handle and booted the barrier wide open.

We were right behind him as he leaped inside, but the blade I'd freed from my belt didn't stay out for long. The office was empty. Marcus wasn't inside. No one living was, as Serafina ghosted through the bookshelf that lined the wall. The permanent one. Not the dummy shelf that slid on a track to reveal a hidden spiral staircase down to the catacombs. Which meant…

"Is what you're showing me in this room?"

There was no reappearance or response. No poofing in or out of sight. But she'd led us here for a reason. And I was going to find out what it was.

Stepping inside and waving Raven in too, I closed the door. "We need to search the pl—"

The lamp flickered, audibly sizzling. Ty growled from beside the tidy desk. A gold pen sat off to the side—rather than propped in its metal holder on a gold-framed desk pad. "Do you see anything?"

I knew he meant *anyone*. And from the tight cording of his muscles, he was prepared to defend Raven and me from any force, whether physical or unseen.

"Not yet." The pen caught the lamplight as the flickering continued and I went to grab— The flickering amped up from consistent to manic.

"Hey!" Raven moved to the bookshelf Serafina had disappeared through. "Is it just me or is that pen super reflecting the light onto this book?" She plucked the thick spine that was catching the thin slice of light.

I took hold of the thick—not book—photo album. Inside the leather cover the first photo, a landscape shot, revealed an extensive line of vampires, an entire family. Lord Vladimir centered them all, small children in front of him and all the others teens and adults. I couldn't look away from one of the children. The little girl Marcus had slaughtered at the top of those stairs in the Vladimir manor. "This was Lord Vladimir's entire family…"

I glanced up—and all but jumped out of my skin. Standing behind the desk was the lord himself, tall, thin, and regal. His face was frozen in utter shock and he…appeared to be pinned to the covered window behind him. His eyes widened in terror, showing too much white.

"Amelia, what is it?" Ty glanced back and forth from me to what he'd see as vacant space.

Raven edged away from the bookshelf and toward the door like she could guess what had me frozen stiff, and she wanted to escape.

"It's Lord Vladimir. He's…"

My eyes widened as his face turned to the side and his neck was torn out. The event of his death, only it didn't happen here. And unlike his real death, he didn't fall in a dead heap. Ty and Raven both began firing questions at me, but I wasn't tracking. The lord remained standing, red pouring from his neck as his head twisted back and his cloudy eyes fixed on me. The movement from his mouth held no sound—because his voice box was no longer attached. Still, the slow-spoken words registered. *Save him.*

He couldn't mean Marcus, his impersonator son. And this album revealing his ghost meant *this* was his most prized possession. His family. "You know Dorian's your son and the only Vladimir left?"

His single nod and repeated unvoiced words were my answer.

I nodded back. If it was the last thing I did, aside from resurrecting Kendrick… "I will."

The lord almost smiled—then glanced down to the desk's edge. Numbers painted in the ghost's blood, separated by dots. They began to disappear with his ghost as I neared, and I dropped the album to snatch up the pen and scribble his message down.

"What is it?" Raven asked, looking edgy as she dared to come closer.

"A message from Lord Vladimir." I ignored their shared looks that seemed to question my sanity. "A phone number maybe?"

Ty came around the back side of the desk, passing straight through the space Lord Vladimir had been standing. "That's not a phone number." He whipped out his phone and keyed something into the screen. "It's a location. Coordinates to Marston Drive in Anchorage."

Stopping my twin was the only way we knew of to save the lord's true son. And to get Serafina's revenge. "Then this is where Marcus is hiding out. I'm sure of it."

"I know where that is." Raven was right next to me, stealthy as always. "It's mansion territory."

Exactly where Marcus would be. Having grown up here with all the perks of being an heir, he would never reduce himself to a dive. Adrenaline made me forget the increasing drain I felt, but it was only a few hours till sunrise.

Ty was on the same wavelength. "We'll set out first thing in the morning."

CHAPTER 17

I all but broke through the passenger door to Ty's WRX as he rolled to a stop. All the pent-up angst and anticipation bled right out of me. We were here to capture and force Marcus to reveal the resurrection details. And failing that? We'd exact Serafina's revenge to earn her help in reaching Kendrick—by killing my twin. Despite all he'd done to me, my beating heart raced at the thought.

Another reason to feel like I was balancing on a tightrope above a volcano of lava. Taking damned blood to dull my connection to my twin had been a no-go. I shuddered at the memory of becoming a deadly liability. It was a risk that couldn't be repeated, despite its advantages.

Now my hopes and fears for this mission removed all that had fogged up my brain over the past two hours, since we snuck away from the Armaya at nine thirty.

"That pull's died down." My connection to the damned had been growing stronger and stronger as we neared Anchorage. Now it was almost nonexistent. The mansion before us was pristine, all tall walls and windows lit up with glowing exterior lights. The paved driveway was empty, and I would bet that the triple garage would be too. My connection to Marcus faded like a launched rocket. "Marcus is fleeing."

Ty had been quiet during the trip here. Brooding, almost. Now he didn't miss a beat, removing a dagger from his belt. "Troy, Marika. Track 'em down."

With roars and the cracks of bones breaking, Ty's second and third in command transformed mid-leap as they pelted through the trees fringing the property.

Ty clutched my bicep, intensity firing in his gaze. "Are there any left inside?"

I shook my head. The threat was minimal, but I could free something shiny and silver from my utility belt in an instant, if I needed to.

In her silent ballet slippers, Raven bypassed us and reached the frosted glass front door in a blink. She peered inside the first tall window, a stake and dagger filling each of her hands. "Place is immaculate." Not a light was on inside, but like any vampire, night vision came naturally. "I say we search the place."

I was by Raven's side in a flash, and of two minds as I pushed down on the locked door handle. "But if Marcus is still close by—"

"Amelia!"

Ty lunged for me as the world went on a tilt. The tiled entryway was rising up—or not. I was falling. Furnace-hot arms caught me as my eye rolled back.

And then I was miles away, back at the Armaya.

"It's been nice catching up with you." Vanessa smiled as she entered her den—

At my brother who'd now closed the door on her watching

guard. The devious smile on his face made my blood run cold. Vanessa saw the change too.

Subtly grasping a sharp length of metal from atop an anvil, she backed up. “Dorian…”

And then he was past her potion and book-covered workbench, pinning her to the stone wall. Her mouth gaped, gasping as his forearm choked off her air supply. The makeshift weapon fell. Dorian’s stare was deadpan and deadly. “Where did they go?”

Vanessa tried to get free, but even with her alchemist marks for strength, she was no match. Her lips pressed together, her head shook in answer to his demand.

Dorian’s fangs lengthened. “If you really want to die twice…”

The look of horror in her eyes as he shifted his forearm to reach her neck said she remembered every second of Ty’s attack. Every second of waiting for death. “Marston,” she blurted. “To Marcus.”

Dorian’s gaping mouth snapped shut with a smile. Without warning he threw an uppercut.

Vanessa fell just as hard as I had.

But even as I feared for what else he might do to her, after we’d tasked her to keep watch on him, I didn’t wake up.

Now inside the mansion I’d passed out in front of, I stood in a girl's lavish bedroom, peering out at the clouded night from the upper level.

No longer a spectator, I wasn’t inside my own body. I was taller; masculine, but not buff. The beat of my heart was steady. Alive then, not damned, not a ghost. My pale hand came up and I saw that wrist scar—the damned commander’s—before threading my fingers through short hair. Pivoting faster than light, I faced a red-eyed damned that’d paused in the doorway. “How many tonight? Are they—”

Marcus, Amelia’s OTG. Coming your way.

Dorian's voice…inside my twin's mind. They were speaking telepathically. Exactly how Kendrick and I had when he was still alive. Exactly how I no longer could.

Marcus's words to his minion didn't resume. Instead, he huffed air as if irritated. *When did she leave? Who's with her?*

"Lord Bathory?"

Though I couldn't see Marcus's face, I felt the shift in his features, his eyes narrowing in dire warning at the damned as he held up a single directive finger.

Five minutes ago. Dorian's voice came through loud and clear, almost like he'd known to wait to reply. *She's with the wolf, his pack, and the restored. Want me to stop them?* There was no hesitation in his submission, because he was operating under the unstoppable need to complete a set task.

Sensation collected and warmed Marcus's eyes, a sensation I'd experience before. Compulsion. He was using it through the bond. *No. Let them come. They won't find anything*…living.

His connection to my brother shut off and he made eye contact with the waiting damned at the door. "I want them ready in five. We need to vacate in less than two hours. Our time to *play* is limited. And it would be such a shame to waste them."

I suddenly pitched forward like I'd been catapulted off the top of a roller coaster and was plummeting to Earth. And then my feet found solid ground. Ty's arm around my body lingered, the heat of him spiking with his scent that invaded my nose. My fangs tingled at the thought of biting into him.

Ty stiffened like he was restraining himself. He cleared his throat and released his hold. "What did you see?"

I forced my thoughts past what my growing hunger craved. *Play. Waste them. Won't find anything living.* Those few words made me cringe as I glanced up at the house. "Marcus is long gone, but the house isn't empty."

With a deep frown, Raven shoved a bottle of blood into my hands. One she must have retrieved from Ty's travel stash in his car. "Looks pretty empty to me." She peered back through the window. "But I bet they have a basement."

Most places had them, especially a mansion this big. Were the damned lying in wait, my sense of them blocked somehow? Downing the bottle quick, I choked out, "Empty of *living*."

Ty faced the front door and used his breaking and entering skills to jimmy the lock. We passed inside without conflict and began moving through the house. Nothing was out of order. Extravagant furniture and gilt wall hangings filled the living and common rooms. There wasn't a thing that looked out of place. The family who *had* owned this place evidently took plenty of vacations and loved sight-seeing in the wilderness. Maybe they were on a vacation now, still alive in the world somewhere, while monsters were playing house in their family home. If not? They were long dead and gone.

"I'll finish checking down here," Raven whispered as Ty and I mounted the stairs that arced from one side of the wide foyer to the other. Once on the landing, we split up to face closed doors on opposite sides of the hallway.

Dagger in hand, I nodded to Ty as we cracked the door we each stood before and slipped inside. The room I had entered was a bedroom, decked out with everything frilly and girlie. The lavish girl's room I'd seen Marcus in. The bed was princess style. The decorations were the stuffed variety, and clogging up the room like they'd taken over and were just now playing dead.

There was no one inside the bedroom. Nothing living. Nothing dead. Well, except for the stuffed toys. But they'd never been living in the first place.

Flicking the chandelier on, something caught my eye.

Throwing sparkling color was—a ring. Princess cut and massive. Definitely not a young girl's and out of place in this juvenile room. Sniffing the air as I knelt down, I plucked the piece up, my eyes confirming what my nose had detected. Specks of blood dotting the carpet—

Movement to my side had me leaping up and away, my dagger hand rearing to cut deep. Though the ready attack-and-defend wasn't necessary. A woman with translucent flesh was being driven back—as if someone had her by the throat. Her split lip dribbled, drops falling as she begged for her life. She kicked as she was forced down onto the girly bed, and then two punctures bloomed along her carotid artery. But the crimson didn't leak out. It disappeared. As if someone was sucking it down before a drop could be spilled. When her mouth gaped wide as if pried open, her muffled cries cut off. Her ring went flying as she clawed at an attacker I couldn't see. And then red stained her mouth—not from her split lip, but from an unseen source as if someone were pouring it into her—and the convulsing started.

I knew what was happening even as her bones knocked and her teeth chattered.

This woman wasn't just a snack, a quick and easy meal. Marcus was turning humans. Making them vampires. To create a better food source for his damned army?

When the woman's convulsing stopped suddenly, the view of her faded, leaving nothing but the spotless bed. One that must have been smoothed out after her death.

"Amelia." The shock of Ty's sudden voice had me pivoting in a flash. He was standing in the doorjamb and noticed my shaking hands and the ring I'd dropped at my feet. He tensed, sight darting as if expecting a threat to lash out. "What happened?"

"I saw a woman. Infected, but she died." Her face didn't match any of the framed pictures I'd seen throughout the house. "She was brought here." I shivered, wondering how many had been delivered here and infected only to die. About fifty percent of humans infected by a vampire lived to turn. The rest...weren't so lucky. Was this the 'play' Marcus had hinted at? "Marcus is trying to turn humans vampire."

"To give to his new damned to complete the conversion?" Behind all that muscle and sex appeal, Ty was sharp as a tack. He never missed a beat.

"I think not." Now it was Ty who did a one-eighty to face Raven out in the hall. "You both need to see this."

Given the urgency in her tone, we were back on the ground level and descending the stairs to the basement in seconds. For the location and what residents normally kept in these spaces, the brick-walled space was immaculate. No dust. Not clutter. No furniture for TV viewing, either. Not even any boxed-up possessions that were being stored just in case.

The place was far from empty, though.

Nine people were lined up against the wall, men and women, shoulder to shoulder.

They were dead. All of them.

No-longer-leaking puncture marks pin-holed their jugulars. *This* was the 'play' Marcus had been talking about. These were his victims, and from the lack of decomposition, they were all newly deceased.

Ty re-holstered the stake he'd freed on the way down and sniffed the air as I registered a scent. "They're not normal. Not human. Not vamp."

He was right. That smell, even as weak as it was, was something I would never forget or confuse. Damned blood. Looking like dirty smears, remnants of the stuff was smudged over their lips and even some of the victims' chins.

"I found this, too." Raven picked up a plastic box filled with random items: lipstick, hair clips, cufflinks, the odd shoe, a man's chain, a woman's necklace, a wallet. "There's more than the number of dead."

I went to rummage through the box and stalled as my hand plunged in. My head heated up suddenly. "Not again!" I threw out an arm as my eyes rolled and my knees gave way. If I hit the ground or not was null and void as flickering images of men and women moved straight through me. Overlapping images of each person's actions. Although I knew what I was seeing had to have happened in staggered succession, each man and woman climbed up onto the sturdy wooden table and lay down, parting their lips—

Man, woman, young and old, they all had fangs. These were the ones Marcus had turned vampire. Marcus appeared then, slashing into a damned's neck and holding the gash suspended above his living experiments. Black drops pattered down seemingly at the same time, collecting in their mouths. Some licked their lips, others forked their tongues out to take Marcus's offering. When one seemed to become dead still, throat no longer swallowing, the next became rapt with violent shaking—

"Amelia!"

Ty had a hold of me, my back to his chest and his strong arm curled around my waist. And I was tempted to spin and bury my long fangs in the base of his neck. After only bottled blood since my earlier vision, connecting to that ghost, and now seeing how many visions simultaneously, my hunger peaked. My head told me to push out of Ty's hold, to gain some distance from not only him but also Raven, who was now replacing the box with a line of others along the wall.

My body refused to obey.

Still, I somehow managed to speak without acting. They had to know what I'd uncovered. "Marcus wasn't turning humans to feed new damned. Well, at least not solely." He wouldn't waste his failed attempts that were full of fresh blood. "He was turning humans so he could infect them to become damned. That's how he's growing his army."

A hiss cut through the air of death and silence.

Ty's other hand vacated the pocket of his jeans and he tugged me back and away from the only other live source in this basement. "She needs to feed. Raven, we'll meet you out at the car soon."

That had been me? Which made sense. The hunger I'd felt now roiled my stomach like an acid wave. My free hand's talon-like nails were slicing into Ty's forearm despite how hard I tried to resist.

I spared a fleeting look at the restored damned who had narrowed her eyes in clear irritation at the knowledge of what my throbbing fangs would soon be buried in. "Then I guess *I'll* inform the RVC and your pack."

"Thanks," I managed to grate out. "We won't be long."

The way she watched after us as Ty hauled me back up the stairs in a rush said it all. She knew this feeding was so much more than blood—even if Ty and I refused to admit it—and she wasn't thrilled about it. As far as she knew—and even I knew, for that matter—Kendrick and I were still attached. Still more than friends.

I blinked when a door shut behind me. We were upstairs already. And alone. In that girl's bedroom. What I'd seen up here and the juvenile setting should have curbed my dangerous needs and helped me focus. It didn't. My senses went into overdrive in the enclosed space. The scent coming off Ty was pure aphrodisiac. I gulped at the sight of the clean, made bed. Not a single wrinkle. *But that won't last*, that little voice sniped as images of forcing Ty back and doing to him what had been done to that woman seared across my frontal lobe—before diverting to amp up the heat.

"Shut up."

Ty didn't say a word in response, but I became acutely aware of the way his fingers lingered as his hold on my arm loosened. His nostrils flared as if scenting me, too. He could tell I was not only murderous but turned on? If personal fragrance wasn't making that totally obvious, my racing heart was.

I stepped back from him to gain distance. But I didn't get far as my shoulder blades hit the closed door. "I…" God, it was hard to talk with my throbbing dental enhancements on full show. "I could find a glass."

Gold flashed in his eyes and his lips parted, his full perfect lips. Ty shrugged. "It's just blood."

That shook me out of my fantasy, which was clearly one sided. Ty didn't want me like that, at least not on a mental level. Too much had passed between us…and between Kendrick and me. Which was exactly the point.

"Amelia?"

I shook my head. "Yeah, sorry. I know. It's just blood."

Frown. Sigh of relief? Ty held out his wrist to me. "The others will be waiting."

Again I nodded. "Right. I…" Reaching up I took hold of what was on offer, drawing Ty's hot flesh slowly to my lips. My eyes lifted to his, receiving a stony-faced expression as I bit down gingerly.

Despite my resolve, the moment his hypnotizing blood hit my tongue and glided down the back of my throat, my insides came alive. Heat swamped me, working its way from my face down my body, all the way to my fingers and toes. My skin started tingling as my heart sped up even faster. The smell of him mixed with the taste was my kryptonite.

A growl escaped Ty's throat and I saw his expression change. Something fierce and desperate overtook that mask of obligation. Hard breath made his chest pump. "Amelia…your hand."

Without breaking my lip's seal, I realized my other hand was on Ty's waist. I hadn't consciously put it there, but I couldn't deny the location. Couldn't ignore the feel of his rock-hard muscles as my pressing fingertips crept beneath his T-shirt to the ripples of his abs. *This is a bad idea*, a fleeting part of my mind pointed out. But my body had other ideas, fingers straining to keep contact while I ordered them to let go. Ty's arm tugged as if trying to pull away. With a possessive hiss, my bite tightened. I managed to mumble around my fangs' hold. "Can't…don't want to…stop."

Ty caught me around the back of my neck, rough fingers threading through my long hair. He tore my bite from his wrist, and at first I expected him to push me away. But instead, he directed my face up, bringing my lips to his neck with a growl of vibration. "Take me *here*."

His husky voice tickled my lips, and damn me, I couldn't refuse. My fangs found that sweeter spot along his jugular and sank in like a bear trap triggering. Ty answered with a groan, one hand going around my back and gripping my butt to lift me off the carpet.

A few steps later we went horizontal as Ty fell back on the bed and brought me down on top of him, shoving soft toys to the floor. With our legs entangled and weapons digging in, my bite broke free and before I could think to stop, my lips were on his. Ty caught my face and kept me there, tongue delving in deep as I kissed him hard. Hands roamed and clothing was shifted. My tank was shoved higher. Didn't matter. I didn't care. But I should have. And not just that the exposed ends of silver stakes were burning my skin. I should have cared that I was roping Ty back in by using our physical connection. I should have cared that I hadn't confessed my relationship with Kendrick to him. That Kendrick was cold and stiff back at the Armaya, and I was here without him.

But I didn't.

For this fleeting moment, I had lost all connection with reality, of right and wrong.

With Ty's blood in my system and the heat between us, all I could focus on was what my lips were doing and where my hands were. One held Ty around the back of his neck, keeping our kiss never-ending and escalating with his rough breath and my lacking one.

The other hand?

Was sliding down Ty's washboard abs to his belt. Quick fingers freed the utility belt from his hips and the burn from my skin. And then the button on his jeans popped. As I unzipped his fly, a fleeting thought reminded me that this was wrong. That Ty didn't want this. Not really. That there was more than him and me that I needed to consider. But my brain wasn't working properly. It wasn't calling the shots. And apparently, neither was Ty's.

As my fingers inched below the waistband of his boxer briefs, he sucked in his breath. "I want you," Ty grated against my lips.

Our mouths kept up the tongue play and my free hand clung to the quilt. "Me too." My other creeping hand took hold, fingers curling tight around him—

A sudden creaking had me scrambling back off Ty and the bed. I hit the floor at the same instant Ty leaped up and re-zipped his jeans, hiding what I'd been gripping a moment ago.

"We're—" Raven stopped short in the doorway, mouth gaping at the ruffled bed and dislodged and scattered toys. Her shock melted into anger that flashed in her eyes. Her lips curled back from peeking fangs. "Your pack is ready, *Alpha.*" Her disgust propelled at me. She knew what she'd walked in on had been so much more than feeding. "They've decided to track the human disappearances with a wolf contingency. The RVC agreed." She turned for the door. "We're ready to leave. Now."

And then she was gone, thumping back down the stairs.

Ty drew deep breaths as he re-buckled his utility belt. He didn't look at me. "I…I shouldn't have…"

I couldn't stop my stare from going back to the bed. The bed where I'd just gotten full-on hot and heavy with my ex. The guy I'd left for dead to shack up with my bestie.

"Amelia, I…didn't mean to let that happen. I…"

"Me neither. I mean, I shouldn't have…" Not with the way Ty felt about me. And especially not while there were still unresolved questions between Kendrick and me. Rising from my crouch on the ground, I couldn't stop the guilt that trampled over my heart like a stampede. "I'm sorry. It was a mistake." But I didn't know if I was apologizing to Ty, to Kendrick, or both of them.

CHAPTER 18

I was finally back at the Armaya, lingering outside my suite after my scheduled RVC meeting to discuss our find and agree on the suggested course of action. Once again, I'd let things get out of hand. Acted selfishly and thoughtlessly. But the time for burying things was over. Scenting him in the lounge, I knew it was time to come clean. I'd put this off long enough. My fear wasn't just that Ty would hate me—not even mostly—but that he'd abandon our efforts to free Dorian, stop Marcus, and…to bring Kendrick back.

Biting the bullet, I found Ty on the balcony lighting up a Dunhill and taking a long draw. His free hand rested on the balustrade as he stared out at the serene gardens, seemingly relaxed under a bright crescent moon's light. He was anything but. The set of his shoulders was tight. I could see from the side that his jaw clenched between each fresh drag. With a long exhale, a current of smoke was expelled and carried my way on the brisk three a.m. breeze. The glass bowl beside his resting hand was chock-full of butts. "The meeting went well?"

What had happened back at that mansion hadn't been a first. It had simply been an escalation of our past actions. And there was so much that had happened while Ty was *away.* So much that I still hadn't put into words. He deserved to know the truth. And finally, I was ready to talk about it.

"I was involved with Kendrick."

Ty froze, his hand holding the cig to his lips halted before his next drag. "Amelia, I don't want to—"

"It was more than blood." Ty knew after tapping my vein while he was damned that I had been drinking Kendrick's blood. He'd tasted him in me. He'd assumed there was more. Had compelled me to kill my *boyfriend,* intending for me to take Kendrick's life. The plan had backfired because of a loophole, because Ty had been my boyfriend first and foremost. My heart had still belonged to him, like it did to this very day. But that didn't mean I hadn't given a hefty slice of it to my best friend. A slice that had made us so much more than friends.

"I thought you were gone forever. I saw it in a vision…" I shuddered at the flash of memory, of Ty convulsing until froth spurted from his mouth and his body turned limp in that warehouse. I'd seen him die too many times. I hadn't been able to continue refuting the damned's claims, the lacking proof of life. "I believed you were truly dead."

"Amelia, I mean it." Ty stubbed his cig out in the overflowing glass bowl, a few butts falling over the edge. He pulled a fresh cancer stick free and bit the butt between his teeth. Out came his Zippo. Quick inhale then exhale. "You don't need to explain anything. I don't need to know the details." Quick glance sidelong at me, then a quick draw in and out. "It is what it is."

“It never went beyond kissing.” Seeing Ty flinch reminded me of his reaction on the cruise when I’d drunk from the on-board doctor. He’d seen that as cheating. A kiss, especially with Kendrick, was so much bigger than that. No wonder he wanted that part of our relationship to die. Even if his body still had its doubts. “But we were dating. He knew I still loved you.”

“And yet he made a play anyway.”

I jolted at the edge to his voice. “No. It wasn’t like that.” The steady breeze switched direction and flung my hair over my face. I rushed to gather the length and tug it down. “I—after the vision, I lost it for a bit. The fortuneteller said you were gone. And I lost any hope. The memory of you and everything you had lived for gave me new purpose. Gave me a reason to live on. I was going to stop the damned…in any way I could. Kendrick was there for me. Supporting me. Protecting me. I…my feelings for him had changed. They grew. Then I saw you and chased you down to that gazebo.” I pointed out over the other end of the balustrade that continued around the hedged border of the castle. Past the busy town where civilians dined and shopped lay the field and that fateful spot. “I thought you’d come back. Or that I was losing it.”

“But you found Kendrick there.”

Shock at his insight thundered through me. “Excuse me?” I remembered that night like it had been minutes ago. The moon lighting the way, Ty with red eyes taunting me from the maze-like gardens. My disappointment at finding Kendrick.

“I was there.” Ty turned and leaned back into the balustrade. In his hand, his cig was smoking away, but he didn’t bring the end to his lips. His intense eyes trained on me. “I led you to him. To Kendrick.”

“You were…” Lightness overcame me and I weaved on my feet.

Hyperventilating all the fresh air that I didn't need, I felt like my head was about to explode. "Why…why would you do that?"

Now Ty looked away, staring down at his hunting boots. "A test."

To see if I gave in to my growing feelings for Kendrick? "I failed, then. That night I gave Kendrick the green light." I'd chosen him over insanity. Over death. "I chose to move on with him."

"I saw."

"You saw me kiss him. You heard what I said."

"Every word." Ty stepped forward and slid his hand down my arm, the one I'd burned after escaping him. He paused, teeth grinding, expression angering before continuing his finger's descent to touch my hand. "Amelia, I don't blame you. Or him. It was a sick thing I did. Cruel. A small part of me wanted you to be happy, because you never would be again with me." He laughed mirthlessly and turned away to stare out at the gardens. "The damned part? Wanted to make you suffer, because when you learned I was alive you'd hate yourself. You'd be more malleable to my demands because of your guilt. You'd fold to my wishes, or so I thought."

"You…" Words formed and died on my tongue. My hand fell, letting my hair flail in the constant breeze. Ty had orchestrated everything, been a puppeteer in the events of my life after his death. But I knew that wasn't him. The guy before me, with his shoulders hunched and puffing on that cig. The guy who'd taken up residence with a community of vamps to help kill their worst enemy. The guy who'd helped keep my transition secret by giving his blood, even though he knew exactly what I'd started with Kendrick. The guy who was with me in stopping the damned and resurrecting my dead best friend—boyfriend—at any cost. "That wasn't you. Those actions."

"Amelia, come *on*."

"No." I laid a hand on his shoulder that corded under my palm. "It wasn't you, Ty. I mean it. Not. You."

Ty spun so fast, my hand went flying. "What about the Armaya attack I led, then?"

I stood my ground. "What about it?"

"I gave the commands. I set the rules."

"It doesn't matter." I re-gathered my flailing hair. Ty had been forced to lead that attack, compelled by Marcus to carry out his wishes. "You weren't in control."

"Yeah, actually. I was." Ty bared his canines and fangs collectively. He looked disgusted and pissed at the same time. "It was *my* plan to set upon the Armaya. After pushing you away, I had to have you back and I didn't give a shit who stood in my way. Even the *me* side of me was in on it. Amelia, it was all me. I was never compelled."

And there were the hard truths I hadn't expected. The ones I hadn't known existed. Good or bad, I was Ty's weak spot. The thing that drove his actions. He was my weakness, too. The thing that hurt everyone else in the process because of my stupid, thoughtless—and on more than a few occasions, reckless—actions. And I couldn't let it go on. I wouldn't. I had to be stronger. To let Ty make up for what he blamed himself for—without letting it go further.

"I'll never blame you for any of those things," I whispered as I backed up, passing the terrace doors to put space between us. "No matter what you say. I've done so much wrong. Played the biggest part…" I closed my eyes and shook my head, knowing our earlier interactions would be our last. Cementing in my mind that no matter what, I would keep our roles professional from here on out. "But none of that can be changed. Only the future can be. We can make up for the wrong we've committed—made by choice…or otherwise."

Ty's downcast gaze moved slowly up until his eyes settled on mine. The look of loss across his face was a decision. "We play our parts. And when it's over? We go our separate ways."

The fact that Ty had come to the same conclusion struck me hard. But I had no right to the sudden sadness I felt at knowing our crossed paths would soon enough deviate. It was for the best. For everyone. "To it being over, then."

IN MY LOUNGE room after a sleepless night, I sat with my back to the wall, my knees propped up. My eyes were sore from crying and the tissue in my balled-up hand was red with wiped tears. Crying blood. And not just because I'd taken Ty's vein recently—without altercation. Though I had. But because I was transitioning, still hiding the monster I was becoming and would remain until this was all over.

Which, after our failed attack yesterday, could be a seriously long time. Of using Ty. Of failing to help my brother before it was too late. But the one that hit me the hardest? Of being separated from Kendrick and without any leads to resurrect him.

The recurring memory of the heat between Ty and me was like another fist to my gut. *Cheater.* The letters should be stamped across my forehead. The worst part of it all? It didn't matter what my intentions had been with Ty, I couldn't erase the way my body had responded to him. It was a poor excuse, so not what Kendrick deserved.

Which brought me full circle.

Beside the full-wall cabinet, I stretched my propped legs out and banged my head back against the stone wall. Closing my lids and shutting out the view of the white couch I'd kissed Kendrick on and the darkening sky beyond the terrace doors, vacant nothingness wasn't gained. Instead, a flurry of events flooded in, fast at first like a carousel, then slower, to real-motion speed.

I saw the fear and determination across Kendrick's face in the boardroom when he'd gone behind my back to become my blood donor. He held out the glass, staring at it rather than at me. "I won't force you to take my vein. And I won't tell them you didn't. So long as you drink my blood like this whenever you need it."

A shift in imagery took me back to the time we'd stayed up for a Vampire Diaries marathon. Half drunk, I'd run my hand down his arm to weave my fingers through his. "You always look out for me. You always do what's best."

There had been a long pause as Kendrick's chest rose and fell will deep breaths. "Not always," he muttered, then pushed me back on the couch and brought his lips down on mine.

With my eyes closed now, my fingertips reached up to touch my lips. That kiss, Kendrick's first stolen one after Ty's death…I'd liked it, encouraged it. Felt like I was home, with Kendrick, here in this room beyond my closed lids and inside this formidable castle of vampires.

I'd felt like a cheater then, too.

Before I could dwell, the scenery shifted. Beside us in the Baldassare suite, a coffin commanded attention in the furnished bedroom. Kendrick's mother was laid out inside.

As I went to turn away, Kendrick caught my arm and tugged me back against his chest. His lips crushed over mine and his hands came up to capture my face as I gasped. With eyes squeezed shut before my open ones, it was over within seconds. "I'm sorry. I…just needed to feel something. Something other than…" He threw a fist over his chest and held it to his heart. *"This."*

He'd needed me then. Needed to feel a connection after his mother's murder. Like I had, after all our failed attempts to find signs of life for Ty.

With another shift, I was standing behind Kendrick. Fresh panic almost floored me at the remembered sight of him.

Visibly shaking, he was shoving weapons into his Burton backpack. Blood-filled bottles were lined up on the coffee table. He turned on me and stalked forward, his face a breath away from mine. "So what am I supposed to do? Sit here and wallow. Follow their rules and watch from the sidelines while everyone else dies. Fuck that. I'm taking action. And if I die, then fine. I've got nothing to live for anyway."

Wet tracks escaped my closed eyes and trailed down my cheeks as I let the rest in.

Beneath the shelter of the gazebo, my hands were on Kendrick's waist. I let one glide up his stomach to his chest, reaching his face and tilting his chin down. "I'm ready."

Kendrick hadn't moved, his body turning rigid as glass. "For…what?"

I leaned up on my toes and let my mouth brush against his. "To move on. *With you.*"

Ty's test that I'd failed. The step I'd taken that had changed everything for good. I couldn't deny I had wanted Kendrick. I loved him. Had then. Still did now. I had been ready to *be* with him. Ready to take that leap. To live again.

I let the first time I'd drunk from him creep in. Coming up behind Kendrick, I put my hands on his shoulders, stalling his intent to fill a bottle in the training room we'd been sparring in. "That's not what I had in mind."

I'd gone to pull away after biting down—because I was hurting him. Kendrick grabbed my hand at his waist. "Don't stop."

There had been heat between us, bucket loads of it. Taking his vein had felt so right. Another graduating step in everything we'd been and were slowly becoming.

Kendrick had given me the hope of a future, one of purpose and happiness.

Now?

"Argh!"

Blinking rapidly, I blotted away the fresh stream of tears and the lounge room came back into focus.

I wasn't ready to give up. Until I too was cold and stiff, I would never give up on the hope of bringing Kendrick back. I couldn't. He'd never given up on me, despite how much I'd wrecked his heart. He'd always put my best interest, my needs and wants, and my happiness first. He'd always put *me* first.

And what had I done?

Let myself get carried away again and again with Ty, failed to connect with Kendrick's ghost, and found diddly-squat to resurrect him. Picking up the gold fabric folded beside me, I clung to the Baldassare cloak with both hands. "I did what you wanted. I've proven my loyalty."

"You didn't kill your twin." Face suddenly nose to nose with mine, Serafina crouched over me. Her dead-fish eyes and gouged neck made me shudder.

Despite the curl of her lip over transparent fangs and the look of murder she pegged me with, the reason I'd summoned her kept me from shrinking away. "He wasn't there. But I won't give up. I will find a way to stop Marcus. And I will bring Kendrick back to life. In whatever order that comes—only my own death will stop me."

Serafina crept back off me—then sprang forward, mouth gaping wide like she was going to tear me apart with her fangs.

I couldn't help but flinch as I scrambled upright and dropped the cloak—

Serafina vanished.

The creak I heard stopped me from snatching the material back up to plead my case and had my head cranking to the side. The door to the cabinet had opened an inch…and I was sure I hadn't bumped it. Dropping and rolling onto my knees, I crept to the door and swung it wide. Inside was the bar fridge. And I knew what was inside *that*. A quick glance around revealed nothing and no one. Ty was off checking up with his pack, Raven was still on resurrection research, and Vanessa was down in her den working on a mark that would cut the physical tie between my twin and Dorian. Dorian was, who the hell knew. But he wasn't here. I was still alone.

As I dared to look back at the open cabinet door and fridge, my mind could only conjure one explanation. Serafina.

I pulled the fridge door open fast as if ripping off a Band-Aid. Except this Band-Aid felt like it was super glued on. I toppled back on my butt and pounded my heart as a spear of pain struck the beating organ. On the glass shelf was one item and only one item. A single bottle of blood. I'd kept it here, safe and unopened. I couldn't drink it and I couldn't bear to get rid of it. I recalled when Raven had gone to drink it…

Reaching out, I took the cold glass between both palms, keeping my grip gentle as if holding a baby bird, but firm enough to keep it from falling. The last bottle of Kendrick's blood.

"Hello, Amelia."

I scrambled around at the unmistakable voice, the one I'd known for as long as I could remember, and fumbled the bottle before clutching it to my chest. Eyes going wide, my heart felt like it was going to explode. Same golden-brown hair, same bruises he was frozen with in his family's tomb. But those eyes were dead-fish white. His almost smile was filled with sadness. *"Kendrick?"*

Standing ethereally before me, Kendrick's head twisted to the side with a crack I remembered rather than heard. His spine jutted out the side of his neck, a deadly break that despite its severity didn't rupture the skin.

And then he fell.

The horror of the tied-for-first worst moment of my life played out as if I was back in that earthy cavern, smelling the compacted dirt, seeing the flickering light from one fire pit. I envisioned my twin taking hold of Kendrick and snapping his head sideways. Sudden emotional torture made me want to fall to my knees. Or freeze in shock like I had that day.

But I refused to stall.

I forgot everything else, where I now was, that this wasn't real in a flesh-and-bone sense. Rushing forward, I slid on my knees—

Kendrick's body disappeared as I heard a clank.

The bottle. I'd let go, and it had rolled along the stone and stopped when it reached the shaggy rug's edge. I snatched it up—and had to force myself not to back away. Lying before me again was Kendrick's body. Or not. Well, not really. A ghostly projection of his corporeal form. But unlike the time when his actual death had occurred, he didn't remain dead still. Legs stretching out, his bare back—because he'd been in such bad shape when I'd arrived, bloody and T-shirt shredded from his cut-up torso—levered up off the stone until he was sitting before me. He smiled weakly as my gaze flicked back and forth from his bloodied and batted face to that jagged protrusion along his neck.

"Hey, you."

That voice. His voice. I didn't close my eyes for fear that he'd been gone when I reopened them. "It's really you."

"In the flesh—well…maybe not."

Stretching my arms wide, I flung them around him—and ended up bear hugging myself. I scrambled back with a shiver, the chill easing when I was no longer touching his form. My flesh and bone had passed right through him. So had the bottle of his blood that I still clung to. The bottle… "This…*this* is your talisman?" It didn't make sense. "The one thing that connects you to me?"

"It tethers me to this plane of existence. The one thing in this world I left solely for you. Because you are my world."

The sadness in his voice broke my heart. I couldn't help wondering if he knew what had happened since his death…if he'd seen me with Ty? "Kendrick, I'm sorry. I…"

"Shh. It's not your fault. Marcus did this because I went after him. Not you. You do *not* take this on."

So he wasn't reading my mind. And come to think of it, I wasn't getting any flickers of thought or even emotion through our bond. I studied him all over. What was it like to be a ghost? I placed my hand over his, feeling that shiver as I sank straight through to the stone. But I kept it there anyway. Maybe this was as close to touching him that I'd ever get again. "Are you in pain? Do you feel…?" I couldn't make the words *severed* or *spine* come out of my mouth, but Kendrick seemed to read my meaning from the glances I kept throwing that way.

"There's no pain. I'm…I just am." He ran a hand down his bare chest, not even flinching as he passed over the angry lacerations. His expression turned serious. "But I need you to listen to me. I don't care what Marcus promises you. What he holds over you. You need to stay away from him. No matter what. Promise me."

My grip on the bottle tightened. "You know what he's planning?"

Kendrick shook his head, the desperation clear in his see-through, cloudy eyes. "You just need to trust me. Please, Amelia. Stay away from him."

I held my tongue, glancing down at the bottle I held. I didn't want to lie, and I couldn't tell him what he wanted to hear. I'd do anything to free Dorian, to bring Kendrick back. Anything. Before Kendrick could re-insist, I said, "Marcus claims—"

"He's lying," Kendrick interrupted as I said, "there's a way to resurrect you."

My head snapped up. "He can't be. Why…?"

"To get you to go along with whatever he's planning. To force your hand." Kendrick got up, the movement fluid and light in a creepy way that raised the hairs across my nape. "There is no way to resurrect me, Amelia. I'm dead. Would be rotting, if you hadn't frozen my corpse…"

I shuddered at the word *corpse* and rolled onto all fours, free fingers digging into the rug. It felt like my chest was wired with explosives and about to detonate. At the same time, my head raced, piecing more out of his words. He knew I'd frozen his corpse. Which meant he had been watching me. All the time?

"Amelia, stop wasting your time and let me go. Turn that freezer hooked up to that glass box off and have my funeral. Mourn me. Move on."

"Kendrick, no."

The main door made a whoosh as it opened and clapped shut. Then Raven strolled in, round face tight with distress. "There's nothing in those stupid books—" She broke off at seeing me on the ground and the bottle I'd just released. The one she knew contained Kendrick's blood. "What happened? You're pale as a ghost."

Cranking my head up, I stared at the place Kendrick had been standing. The air was clear, his transparent form no longer muddying the sight of black treetops against a deepening blue-black night sky through the terrace doors. My heart sank in despair. I knew picking up that bottle would bring him back, but I couldn't bear for him to tell me to *let him go* again. "I…I saw him."

"*Kendrick?*" She rushed to kneel beside me and clutched my hands. "You saw Kendrick?"

I bit my bottom lip—to control the sudden tingle of my extending fangs at her closeness, and to fight back a fresh wave of tears. Funny, I hadn't even thought about Kendrick's lacking pulse and scent before he'd ghosted—for lack of a better word—from here. "He said Marcus is lying. He said he can't be resurrected."

"No." Shaking her head, Raven staggered as she stood. "I don't believe that. *I can't.*"

Stop wasting your time and let me go. As if I ever could. "Raven, look. I don't want to believe it either—"

"Then don't. There is a way, and I'm not giving up. And you don't get a free pass just because you're getting back into Ty."

"What?" I jumped up and clenched my fists. I was guilty of my actions, but that had nothing to do with what Kendrick had claimed. "That's not what I'm doing. I'm not saying we should give up. We just need to be prepared that what we're looking for might not exist." God, it hurt to say that. I slumped down onto the chaise part of the sectional couch, hand pressed over my heart that felt like it had just shattered all over again.

"You owe Kendrick your life. He saved you *and* Ty. And I *will* find a way to save him. With or without you." Spinning on one foot, she stalked through the foyer, the door slamming behind her.

Hanging my head, I stared down at the bottle lying on the rug. Kendrick wasn't here now, but I knew I'd see him again when I was ready. And somehow I knew he could hear me in this moment, even without picking that talisman back up. "I'm not giving up either, Kendrick. You know me better than that."

As I returned Kendrick's bottle to the fridge, using my sleeves to keep from touching the glass, I decided on my next move. We never got to Marcus before he had the opportunity to flee. But I knew exactly where to find him—to get through to him—without even leaving the Armaya. And today? I was going to demand proof of his claims.

CHAPTER 19

"Dorian, open up!"

I banged on the door to the Vladimir suite. After a failed morning search and an extended training session, his watching guards were a promise of his whereabouts that I hoped paid off. He'd been training too, on his own, and had finally returned to his suite. I hoped. This cat-and-mouse game with Marcus had gone on long enough. But I didn't need to find my elusive twin. The connection I needed to reach him was right inside this—

The door swung inward and Dorian carelessly combed his fingers through his hair. Like it needed rearranging because he'd taken a nap after training. Or had taken one of his mental discussion breaks Raven had witnessed to catch up with Marcus. "Hey, Sis. Been expecting you."

"Time for a chat—" Ty darted around me and got in my brother's face, clenching Dorian's running shirt with a growl. Dorian's rotation guards shifted, ready to stand in the hybrid's way if things escalated. Ty's voice dropped as he all but spat in his ear. "Commander."

Despite everything we'd discussed yesterday, and after revealing my first ghostly run-in with Kendrick, Ty was still backing me up, still committed to helping me resurrect Kendrick and stop Marcus once and for all. He was pretty pissed too, after his pack came up empty from seeking Marcus's next human sourcing location.

Dorian smirked as the guards went to advance, but they stalled as his hand came up in a stop motion. Tugging his shirt free, he stepped aside and motioned for us to enter. "Guess the cat's out of the bag, then."

With one hand on the hilt of his dagger, Ty stalked inside and I followed behind. My weapons were strapped around my waist, but I didn't ready to pull one free. For one, I knew no matter what was going on with Dorian, he'd never hurt me. At least not in an irreversible way. Marcus still needed me alive.

With a short directive to stay, Dorian closed the guards outside, then led us through to the library-inspired lounge surrounded by ceiling-high bookshelves and mirrors. He strode past a high-backed armchair and lowered himself into an identical one further away. He tapped the counter of a small bar with a glass-door fridge built in beneath.

"Can I get you guys anything? Drink?" He pulled free a bottle that was wedged between the cushion he sat on and tilted it our way. "Freshly drained this morning. AB negative?"

Even with that carefree and charismatic expression, it was clear the Dorian I was seeing was not entirely—or even mostly—the real deal. And freshly drained? The thought of him personally acquiring that blood made me cringe. Made my senses register the two fresher sources in this very room too.

On task, Ty bared his fangs. "Cut the BS and get us an audience."

Dorian raised a brow. "Nothing to get. He's always…" He tapped his temple, lips curving with a smile that was mischievous and somehow saddened at the same time. "*Here.*"

Aside from hunger distraction, seeing that conflict in my brother reminded me of Ty when he was damned. The things Dorian was being telepathically compelled to do and his personality transplant were not by choice. He didn't like who he was and the things he was doing. He needed our help. "Tell us how to resurrect Kendrick, *if* it's even possible."

That smirk of confidence made a reappearance. "It *is* possible." That expression alongside that voice made me shiver. It was Dorian on so many levels, and yet so alien at the same time. So much like Marcus, who never showed fear or weakness. And then Dorian was right in front of me, strong hand gripping my scarred forearm.

Ty was right there and shoved my brother, all but catapulting him back into the same chair.

But the damage was already done as that bottle shattered with his landing and blood sprayed out. Although I heard the crash, I no longer saw the book-lined lounge room. Now concrete blocks surrounded me. The ones that held the dead. On the black marble coffin before me, Kendrick's body—cut down the middle and covered in blood—ratcheted up with a choked gasp.

As I stumbled back to here and now, Ty held me upright, growling as his lips curled back from his canines. "What did you do to her?"

"I'm okay." Which wasn't exactly true. My hunger had spiked. And I had to force my grip on Ty to freeze instead of digging in further. I grated past pointed fangs, "I saw Kendrick come to life. Tell me how it's done?"

"You saw…"

"You can't think it'll be that easy," Dorian spoke over Ty's shock. "You can't get something for nothing. Everything has a price."

The way Dorian eyed me as Ty tugged free of my grasp said it all. I knew what I'd have to pay to get this information. Myself. I'd have to hand myself over to Marcus. For Kendrick, to save his life, I'd offer myself up on a silver platter a million times over. But there was more to consider. Dorian's freedom, for one. And if what I'd just seen had been real or somehow manufactured.

Ty unsheathed his dagger and got up close and personal with Dorian, pointing the tip at the underside of his jaw that sizzled from silver contact. "You can't have her."

Dorian leaned into the point and blood bloomed, bubbling down the blade.

I leaped between them and shoved Ty back with a glare. "Back off!" Controlled by Marcus or not, Dorian was still my brother. Even if by blood he wasn't. But if any more of that red spilled from his already-healing flesh, my thinning self-control would snap. With a warning look, I leveled my eyes from Ty back at Dorian. "I'm the bargaining chip, right?"

Dorian went to grab for the bottle that had been beside him, before seeming to remember and notice the splatter and glass shards. He shrugged and hitched his brows. "Correct. But…I'm not making any deals here. Marcus wants to see you. In person."

"What?" My head spun like it had just become a carousel on my shoulders. "Why now?"

Dorian shrugged. "Wheels in motion. So much to do, so little time. The usual."

Ty sheathed his dagger but remained close to me. "When and where?"

He was supporting this after his *you can't have her* outburst?

"After sundown tomorrow." Dorian smiled, pure-white fangs peeking through his lips. "I'll lead you to the place myself. It's quite public."

Public?

Dorian rose from the armchair, his hands steepled in that creepy way both Marcus and my father did. "We expect you'll bring company. Though you should know, we'll have plenty of our own. If you intend to try anything, there will be a spectacle. You care if the bovines learn of our existences. Marcus does not."

Dorian was referring to humans as cattle. Spelling out that Marcus had no concern in exposing our races to the Homo sapiens—because he was hiding in plain sight amongst them. Off our radar because the wolves sourcing leads wouldn't expect the location.

Ty gripped my bicep and shook his head. Guess he knew this could be a trap and that Marcus would have the upper hand if he wanted to force a situation. But what choice did we have? I stepped back, needing to think past my lust for his heady blood. "You don't have to come with—"

"If you go, then so do I," Ty grated out, fists clenching.

Another step back as I breathed through my mouth. The plan was set, good idea or bad, it was irrelevant. We were doing this. But we wouldn't go in blind. We'd need fail-safes and backups to help control the situation. I nodded at my brother. "When do we leave?"

"Nine p.m. sharp." Dorian's smile was goading. "Oh, and we'll need to get the guard watch lifted from Vanessa. She'll be coming with us."

"PULSE?"

I couldn't believe my eyes or the sight of that bright flashing neon sign. Being eleven at night, after two hours of travel, the place would be packed. Once a meat market for prowling vampires on the hunt for fresh human blood—though not now that the damned threat had sent most vamps into hiding or to our guarded community. Already the line beyond the bouncer-watched doors was halfway up the busy street. In the heart of Anchorage, any disturbance would draw attention of the human authoritative variety. I itched to palm the dagger I had concealed below my hoodie, feeling like we were walking into the lion's den. Full-on weapons in public had been a no-go.

"He's in there?"

Dorian tipped his head as he bypassed the bouncer without a care. His eyes seemed to glaze for a split second. Out came that cool smile. "He's waiting."

By my side, Ty headed our tribe with his pack, a few late call-ins, and Vanessa, as he faced the damned guarding the entry. "Step aside, deadbeat." Ty's lips twitched, looking like he was about to flash canines as he shoved his way inside.

Vanessa tugged on his arm, terrified eyes shifting from the damned to her friend. "We can't draw attention." Scantily dressed women, as well as men irritated at the cut-in, were now eyeing our group. "They're already watching."

"Try me." Troy snapped perfectly human teeth at the sneering bouncer while Marika stuck close to his side, hip-glued hand so close to the stake hidden beneath her long black jacket.

Every step down the black entry, I expected a surprise attack. But none came. And seconds later, our group had emerged into the belly of the club. Already packed, the few tables were occupied and the bar was jammed with people vying for their next dose of loosen up. The strobe-lit dance floor was a flurry of gyrating bodies, moving to the blaring music. The smell of human blood was thick in the humid air. Drinking from Ty before leaving was the only thing keeping me in check right now. And even then…

My eyes began tracking, discerning which out of the many on offer would be easy game. I ground my molars. *Get with the program,* I chided as Ty narrowed his gaze at me in warning.

Vanessa stuck close to the alpha's side like she expected to be jumped by a hungry damned at any second. "Can you see Marcus?"

Through the mass of bodies I'd been eyeing, I hadn't even been looking.

Ty was peering at the wall above the dance floor. "Asshole's probably spying from behind the one-way mirror up there."

I glanced around, mimicking Troy, Marika, and our extra lycan muscle. Now that I wasn't petrified about going up there to see feeding sessions, I noticed that the mirror effect continued on the opposing wall above the bar area too. "I think—"

"Come on!"

The shout carried through the crowding humans as Dorian back-tracked to us, looking annoyed as if we were holding up his fun.

"We don't wanna miss the party." He winked then jogged his brows at Vanessa. "Follow me. I'll take you to the VIP lounge."

Without another word, he spun on a dime and marched toward the left of the bar. Then he disappeared behind it. Following on edge, every one of us weapon ready, we found the black carpeted stairs behind the wall backing the bar and began climbing. Dorian waited at the top, smiling as we reached our destination. Despite the meeting, I was glad to have distance between me and all the living bodies downstairs.

As I'd suspected, one-way glass peered down over the entire club. The room had black carpet and black walls, a corridor that led to what I hoped was a secluded exit, and was furnished with red silk chaise lounges, armchairs, and…a black marble throne. The same one he'd sat in at the damned hotel in that cavern.

I clenched my fists and let my throbbing fangs loose.

The cavern he'd killed Kendrick in.

Marcus smiled from his throne, anticipation curling his lips back from long pointed fangs at the sight of Vanessa and me. His demanded guests. The glare that struck his face was directed at Ty, and his nose crinkled as if the scent of lycans was getting to him. But he only addressed me. "So glad you made it. Not quite the same as spying you through someone else's eyes, my twin."

On either side of him, damned lined the wall, their black clothes blending in while their gray flesh stood out. They outnumbered our party even with the five extra lycans, and the way they tracked those heated bodies put me on edge. Barely restraining themselves? Hell, yeah.

"We're not here for small—"

"Talk. I know." Marcus narrowed his eyes at Ty. "Such a waste you turned out to be, wolf. Under my leadership you could have been a legend."

"I'll be a legend when I kill you," Ty snapped, brandishing the long dagger that had been hidden beneath his jacket.

The damned made no move, but their red eyes slid all at the same time to Ty. They looked ready to kill and happy to make him their next meal.

Marcus simply chuckled. "Is that why you came?"

"No. We don't want trouble," Vanessa said quickly. I spared a glance at her standing back with the lycans, frozen as if in shock. She'd been through heaps at the hands of the damned. Been killed, or so we thought, by Ty's own fangs. After learning of Marcus's demands for this meeting, she had volunteered to come without hesitation. I commended her on her bravery. Guess she needed to face her demons. Or make up for the bad she'd been forced to do.

Returning my focus to my twin, I nodded. "Vanessa's right. We're here to make terms. I want to resurrect Kendrick and break your control over my brother."

"He's not your brother!" Marcus's hands clenched the arms of his throne. "*I* am."

I didn't falter. I wasn't here to make nice. "Only by blood." Two steps brought me closer to him as his face flushed, and Ty mimicked the movement. "You're a monster—one I can't save. You turned Ty and made him everything he hated. You bonded with Dorian to use him against us and our race. You killed..." I pounded my chest at the pain, fighting to hold back the crimson tears that threatened to well. "You killed my best friend. And I *hate* you."

"You don't really mean that," he said with absolute certainty. "We're blood. One and the same."

"I do mean that." Another step forward brought that rage back to his sharp features. "I tried to see the good in you. I tried to help. It may not be your fault that you're this way, but I can't fix that. And I can't have any more blood on my hands. So here I am. I want Kendrick brought back to life and I want my *brother* free of *you*. So name your price."

Reigning in his ire that had turned his face red, Marcus leaned back in his throne. "Aside from the alchemist? The same thing I've wanted all this time, since I knew you existed and since I planned to save you from our father's attempt to take your life. I want you—bound to me."

"*Why?*" Ty ran his finger along the length of his dagger, dangerous eyes flashing gold.

"It's the only way to release Dorian from my control."

For once I believed Marcus. Well, mostly. With Vanessa's help

I'd uncovered that only a new and stronger blood bond could sever an existing one. Twin to twin? What could be stronger than that? Still, I didn't believe that was the only way to free Dorian. There were always loopholes. At least I hoped there were, in this case.

"That's not the only reason," Vanessa chimed in to my surprise—and apparently Marcus's, too. "It can't be."

My twin glared at our alchemist, baring his fangs. A threat that next time he got hold of her, she wouldn't escape alive. "It is the only reason that matters. Bond with me, Amelia, and you will have access to all you need to know. Including the means to bring your dear boyfriend"—his probing gaze slid to Ty—"Kendrick, back."

A jab at Ty that, to my surprise, didn't elicit a response. And why would it? Involved with Kendrick or not, Ty wasn't interested. But he was in everything else that had been said. "Reveal the resurrection, and if it works, Amelia will give herself over to you."

I held back my gasp at Ty's unwavering ultimatum. I knew he'd never allow me to go through with it, even if we did bring Kendrick back.

Evidently, so did Marcus. "No dice."

Lycans growled and almost unnoticeable cracks sounded over the pumping music that vibrated the glass wall.

Before I could utter a halt motion, Marcus clicked his fingers and the damned came to life. Roars broke out as the lycans barreled into armchairs and lounges in wolf form, canines bared.

Ty moved like lightning, vaulting over the chaise lounge in his way. "Stop or he's dead!"

I gaped at Ty now standing at the throne. With one arm around Marcus, the tip of his stake was pointed at my twin's heart. Without my voltage, could a direct hit kill him? Though in case that failed, Ty had his bases covered. In his other hand he held a silver dagger, the blade pressing into Marcus's jugular.

The damned hissed and some twitched, frozen but ready to continue the attack on each creeping-in lycan. Troy and Marika in the fray were the only ones in human form, stakes glinting from both their hands.

Ty pressed harder with the blade and a smear of blood welled around the silver. "I'll cut his fucking head off if any of you move."

"Then do it," Marcus taunted.

A cry had my head cranking to the back of the room where light flashed up multicolored through all that dark glass. Vanessa was by Dorian's side, her hands at his throat…with blood leaking from between her digits. "Oh, God. Oh, God. What's happening?"

"Oh, did I forget to mention?" Marcus chuckled, causing Ty's blade to cut deeper.

As more blood gushed, Vanessa screamed out, "Ty, you're hurting him!"

"Aside from the blood bond, a mark binds our physical forms." Marcus's lips pulled wide with a smile. "And don't think getting out of this will give you the chance to unlink us. The mark isn't visible. See, I cut your dear *brother* open and marked him internally. With my own hands. No one knows where the symbol is. All you need to know is…so long as we're bound, if I bleed, then so does he. If I die…"

"Ty, let Marcus go."

A war of the head and heart showed in the alpha's desperate eyes. "Amelia, we can end this. End him. This war. The damned."

In my mind, I saw Ty going through with it. Clawing into Marcus's blond hair as he rushed that glinting blade back and forth. Back and forth. Like nails down a chalkboard, I could hear Vanessa's cries as blood poured from Dorian's neck. "But at what cost?" I choked out, swallowing down a rise of vomit. We may never discover how to resurrect Kendrick, but here and now… "Don't kill my brother, Ty. *Please*."

Though I wasn't looking her way, I could hear Vanessa whimpering. "Amelia, he won't let you leave without bonding to him. It could save Dorian."

Fuck that. Hand steady, I whipped out my dagger and brought it to my throat. My heart had survived silver-exploding bullets shot at close range. But even damned were snuffed out by decapitation.

"What are you doing?" Marcus croaked around Ty's blade as Ty uttered, "Amelia, no," at the same time.

I stood my ground. "Call off your damned, Marcus. We're leaving." I narrowed my eyes at Ty. "All of us."

"And if I refuse?"

"Then you'll lose the thing you want most. Me." I pressed the deadly sharp edge into my flesh. Red bloomed, leaking down my neck and over my collarbone, absorbing into my black tank. "I'm not playing, Marcus. And I'm not backing down."

A tense moment passed, lycans and damned frozen in battle-ready stances as Ty held his ground and Vanessa stood by Dorian. Then Marcus nodded. "Very well." He eyed his damned in a way that promised instant death to anyone who disobeyed. "Stand down."

The command had every damned retreating through the crushed furniture with a hiss to their post along the wall. Ty released Marcus, weaving through the mess to reach my side. He nodded to the growling wolves, then bared his canines at Marcus. "We'll be leaving, now."

Marcus's smile was pure calculation. "Until till next time. Which, I promise you, won't be too far away, twin."

CHAPTER 20

I scaled the wall from my bedroom balcony down the west end of the castle. It would have been a helluva lot easier to enter through the suite's main door. Except then any guards —who rotated on and off between all the crowned royals—would know I'd been snooping. A quick check had already revealed *his* guards were not standing wait outside the door. A half moon shone high in the twinkling sky. Being just past midnight, he shouldn't be inside. Not with his routine, solitary training…

I grabbed the balustrade edge of the last balcony, tensed my core muscles, and kicked my legs up and over. Landing without a sound, I put my back to the moss-covered wall. A peek through the window revealed a movement-free room of black-and-white high-backed armchairs siding a leather Chesterfield.

A quick window check revealed the bedroom and sitting room were vacant too.

Dorian wasn't inside.

A steady whistle from my lips was met with the appearance of a broad, muscled figure over the balustrade. Fully equipped with weapons that glinted in the moonlight, Ty had tracked me from the path below, his presence keeping any patrol guards from looking up. He met my eye for the briefest moment before prowling up to the double doors and, after a double check, opening the way. "If Marcus left anything behind, it'll be here."

Ty was downright against me bonding with my twin, and after searching the Vladimir office again, this was our next step. After living with Marcus as part of his damned army, Ty knew the guy always had an ulterior motive. Even in the position he'd been in, Ty had never known what my twin's end game was. As his second in command, he'd still been kept on a need-to-know basis.

"After you," Ty muttered, holding his arm out along the open door.

I passed with a nod, the warmth coming off his body registering as if I'd neared a roaring fire. And he didn't take his eyes off me. I had a feeling that whatever he was stewing on had as much to do with Marcus as it had to do with Kendrick. But he didn't say a word.

Peeking through to the sitting room, I tried to keep my mind on task.

At the same time, Ty completed a quick sweep through the rest of the suite, passing me with an *all's clear* nod. Striding away, he gripped the black railing to an ascending spiral staircase. "I'll take the library tower."

I watched as Ty mounted the steps two at a time like he needed to get away from me. "Oh, okay." Entering further into the room, the mirrored walls ping-ponged my reflection as I headed to the closest shelving unit siding the tall Gothic windows. A thorough check revealed a rich supply of books on the history of our race, the wolves, and the damned, and the most in-depth volumes I'd seen on abilities. The info I'd uncovered with Vanessa on breaking a bond by creating a new one was there in black and white. Of everything there, I found nothing new that could help us separate my brother from my twin. Just confirmation that a stronger bond could sever an existing one.

I turned the page on a thinner volume on spirit ability, wondering if the lack of credible info was due to so few spirit-gifted vampires having existed. If there was only one Oracle generally in existence, did that mean there was usually only one spirit gifted? One vampire to flesh out all the intricacies and secrets of this gift? I thought of Marcus's ability to steal my visions and how he'd bonded to Dorian. One—except, it seemed, in the occurrence of twins.

Refocusing, my eyes widened.

And there was my fate sealed in black and white: *Twins are believed to be more susceptible than single-born vampires to inherit a spirit connection. Their natural connection, even if unbound, trumps all other blood bonds. Once bound, their link can never be severed.*

"What did you find?"

I almost jumped at Ty's sudden voice before replacing the book on the shelf. "The same as before."

"You bonding to Marcus?" Ty growled and clenched his fists as if ready to punch something.

"It's the strongest bond." I noticed the book he held then, with its pristinely kept, brown leather cover and hanging red bookmark ribbon. "What's that?"

Ty came over and stood close, making me twitch at his proximity and the scent of him. Since my breakthrough with Kendrick, I'd kept taking his vein to a minimum, stocking up on his bottled blood in between. Now, as I heard the beat of his heart and saw the pulse of blood up his neck, I could barely think of anything else.

"It's a journal. Marcus's."

Like being cold-clocked with brass knuckles, those few words snapped me back to attention.

"It's got everything. His youth as an imposter. Knowing Caius was his father. Knowing you were his sister…"

I snatched the journal and fingered through the pages. The first entries were about being different and left out. The next were about me. He'd wanted to know me, had hoped I was like him too… because no one else was. Later, there were rants about Caius's lack of drive beyond his need to restore his family and how useful the power we'd been instilled with could be. Then the subject changed. Each day was about…*me*. Marcus had detailed his outings to spy on me. It had been him at St. Volaras when lightning had struck that tree and almost decapitated me. He had seen me with Ty in those early days even before I knew who Ty was. What he was. He'd found out after that first sighting that Ty was a hybrid, and that he was a direct descendant of the extinct Ruthavens. He'd kept tabs on our ability and combat training.

His involvement in Caius's plan to take my life hadn't gone down exactly as he'd claimed.

He'd been reporting to Caius, claiming I'd never come around, stating that they had to take my power if Caius ever hoped to save *their* family. All the while he'd planned to foil Caius's attempt to steal my power…so we'd be bound, body and soul. Forever.

After failing that, his obsession grew. It had been him who had slowed our travels to the cabin by dropping trees to block our path. He had lit the match that had burned our birth home to the ground. The cruise had all been him. He still wanted us bound. Though he never said exactly why, his desperation was clear. He needed me for his plans. Needed me alive.

The entries ended after the culmination of his plan to set me up at the Oracle ceremony. Even then, Caius had thought he was going to stage an attack to get control of me. Marcus had had other plans. If he'd gotten me then? Great. If not, that was okay too. His main focus was Ty, staging his untimely death so he could make him his own and use him as a bargaining chip against me. The circumstances after Ty's capture before that fateful ceremony had lined up perfectly. He knew I'd give Ty my blood to heal him at the very least. He knew Ty would need healing…because he'd ordered the beatings. Had he coerced Caius into infecting Ty with damned blood so he wouldn't heal, too? Yes or no, everything had played out as planned. And Caius's claims of innocence in that attack? At least in his intent of only acquiring me and not staging a massacre—had been true.

"Guess Marcus didn't count on you." Ty's hand brushed my jawline to tilt my face up. "Your strength and tenacity. Your drive to keep safe what you hold dear…"

With my face turning hot, I gently turned my head and glanced away, removing the contact of his flesh from mine. For one, the pulse at his wrist was too tempting right now. And two…the urge to do something else, more intimate and involving touching and lips connecting, was playing in my mind. "I couldn't let you live like that." I dared to look back at him, imagining stakes were driven through my feet to keep me from closing the gap between us. "I didn't care what it cost."

A sad look ghosted across Ty's handsome face. "You do now, though…"

"What?" I got his meaning all too quick. "Kendrick? You think I blame you for Kendrick's death? You think I regret saving you because of it? Ty, I don't. I could never choose between you two like that. And even if I could, it wouldn't have mattered. Marcus was gunning for Kendrick before he turned you." The next thing I said, I hadn't allowed myself to believe before right this second. "And

Kendrick would have put himself in harm's way regardless. Marcus was responsible for his mother's murder. He wanted vengeance. We are *not* responsible for his death."

Ty didn't seem able to look at me. Instead, he took the journal and closed the cover. "How is he?"

I didn't need to ask which *he* he was referring to. "He's okay." I winced at the memory of watching Kendrick's head snap sideways, at the blank look that stole his fear as death claimed him. "I think."

"But you still believe there's a way to resurrect him?"

Despite Kendrick's claim, I couldn't believe there was no way to bring him back to life. "I have to."

"So you are going to bond with—"

"Don't do it."

Ty snarled as he spun to meet the intruder and whipped out a blade.

I darted in front of the alpha before he could strike out at my brother. "Dorian…we were just looking for you."

With his hand up and palms forward in non-threat, Dorian frowned at the journal in Ty's other hand. He didn't budge from the archway to the foyer. His sports shorts and T-shirt were free from sweat. "I don't care what you were doing. I just need you to hear me out."

I froze at the urgency in his voice, at the true fear that showed across his face. Ty even lowered his weapon-ready arm, but I could hear the priming strain of his muscles beneath his leather jacket.

"Joining light and dark is the only thing that can free me from him. And you can't do it, okay? Promise you won't. Leave me like this." His hands came together, begging as he stepped forward. "Expose me to the RVC. Lock me up and throw away the key before I do something I can't take back."

Quick contemplation had my mind firing neurons of possibility.

Being physically bound, Marcus couldn't kill Dorian. Unless…he compelled him to cut out that internal mark that bound their physical forms. And the only thing that could free my brother from my monstrous twin? "Light and dark." I'd heard those words before. Were my old suspicions right? "Who or what is the light and dark? What is Marcus planning?"

"Lips sealed. I— He's back." Dorian's urgency melted as his lips curled. His fangs lengthened in threat. "Time's up, *Sis*."

I COASTED along the back corridors down to the cells, my hope surging me on after hearing Dorian's desperate break-through warning before my twin reclaimed control over his mind. I still couldn't believe it. Was so relieved my real brother was still in there. Still trying to break free. And now I knew of Caius's innocence over the Portsmouth massacre. He'd warned me about light and dark before Marcus's identity had been exposed. He'd tried to protect me. And though I had my suspicions on what it all meant, I needed clarity. Clarity only he could provide.

I nodded to the guard manning the top of the stairs before glancing back down the torch-lit corridor. Ty had delivered me here safely, dagger gripped tight in his hand. To make sure there'd be no sudden backlash—because Marcus would know exactly what Dorian had spilled. There'd been none, and now he was on task while armed guards surrounded me, catching up on *wolf business* he hadn't wanted to elaborate on.

Descending quickly below, I came to the prison waiting area. After my father had saved my life when Ty had led the damned attack in the main hall, I believed he now wanted me to survive. Maybe he was truly sorry for trying to kill me. But definitely? I was the only one alive who held the power to save his damned family. Motioning to a waiting guard with a thick ring of keys at his hip, I indicated Caius's cell. "Unlock the door."

A clank and clatter later, and the way was unbolted.

Closing the steel door behind me, I kept as far back as possible. My hunger had grown since we'd left Dorian upstairs, and though I wasn't on the edge, I didn't trust my needs not to shift without warning.

"Amelia?" Caius's drooped head lifted from his bent knees. Where he'd been asleep—because no bed or cot was on offer in his bare cell. He rubbed his eyes and got vertical, a sleepy smile warming his tired, wrinkled face. "Whatever the reason, it is good to see you, my daughter."

I cut right to the chase instead of squabbling about his title for me—which he hadn't and would never earn. "Before I learned Marcus was the damned commander you said, 'to pay the price, light and dark must first be joined.' You warned me not to join them. That it would be my end. Now I need to know. Who or what is this light and dark?"

Caius regarded me with contemplating hesitation, rubbing at his short beard. "You already know the answer, dear daughter. Even back then you did. *You*, my dear, are the light."

Just as I'd suspected. Which meant Caius was telling the truth and not spinning lies. Marcus had given me the answer before I even knew he was my twin. But he'd said my power was the light and my other half's could be the dark. And being an ingrained part of me meant…*I* was the light. "The darkness is Marcus, my twin."

"It is the way I engineered you both. So similar and yet worlds apart." The old vampire shook his head. "I regret it all, you know. What I put you through. Even what I turned my own son into. I should have hunted down and ended my family's lives when I learned of the implications of my master plan."

Implications…meaning my life to pay the price. "You wish your family dead now?"

"Oh, no. Not *wish*." Caius leaned into the wall and sighed. "Though hindsight is twenty-twenty. Saving them from a soulless existence would have been a kindness. It would not have influenced my children's lives. It would not have resulted in the deaths of so many in my plight to save a few. I am accountable for my son. He is my doing. Though there is no way to help him now. He is a monster…despite how hard he tries to hide it. He must be stopped—for good."

"How?" My hands curled into tight fists at my sides in anticipation of what I was on the precipice of knowing—and because I could scent his restored blood. "What is he planning to do?"

"I—" Caius choked, sounding like he was gagging on his tongue. "Believe me or not." He coughed, back smacking the stone wall as he hammered a fist over his chest. "I want you to know. I just cannot…"

"Marcus's compulsion still ties your tongue?"

"As well as my actions." Caius made a gesture as if writing on the air. "Though not all is locked away. And you must know, your twin—he will never die, Amelia." At my sudden shock, Caius went on. "Neither will you. At least, not without intervention. You and he are immortal. The way I altered your DNA gave you the endless lifespans of the damned."

I'd known my blood was immortal—but me as a whole? The bombshell of living for an eternity threatened to swallow me. Seventeen years had passed so far. The last few had been full of love, destruction, and death. I didn't think I could do it for an eternity. Not with the way our races existed in fear. But… "You said without intervention?"

Caius smiled as if glad I'd picked up on that mention over the rest. "You are not infallible, Amelia. You *can* both be killed. Not as easily as a vampire, wolf, or even a damned. Still, it can be done. Full draining is not a death sentence." He and I both knew that fact after he'd failed to kill me to steal my ability. "Even staking with silver is reversible." Like Marcus had laughed off after my failed restore.

I shuddered, remembering the times I'd almost ended it all. My only means of eternal peace would be a bloody and grizzly death—from my hand or someone else's.

"Though, I believe full spinal separation would be irreversible," Caius added quietly, making me wonder if he was imagining his son's death at my very own hands.

I could barely talk past the vivid imagery after Ty's threat to follow through and do just that. I gulped. "And that's the only way?"

Caius's gray eyes became glassy and his expression turned grim. "You are each at your strongest while bound to each other, and yet, at your weakest. Your minds and souls joined, able to influence each other. And once you drink of each other's blood after the bond is complete, so too will your bodies be."

Like he was now to Dorian, though that was an artificial connection created by an alchemist mark. One that if we attempted to kill Marcus, would result in my brother's death. And I couldn't live with that. Which left one clear alternative.

To save Dorian I'd have to bond with Marcus. And if he forced me to physically join our bodies before we could take his head? I would have to die too.

~

DEPRESSION WEIGHED me down as I closed the door to my suite and slumped back against it. Bonding to Marcus was the only way to free my brother. Killing Marcus after the act? I rubbed at my neck where I'd only yesterday held a dagger. It would kill me too.

For the people I loved, I'd do anything. But what else would bonding to my twin set in motion? My lack of answers made anxiety tighten like a fist in my chest.

I walked zombie-distracted around the foyer table as an almost soundless shifting of a door swinging inward brought my head around.

Ty strode into the sitting room, a lax body with dangling limbs over his shoulder. His strong strides didn't falter after he nudged the balcony door shut. "You're back already."

Already? He was executing some plan he hadn't informed me of… I registered the dangling body's short chocolate locks before I noticed those same sports shorts and T-shirt. "What the hell have you done to Dorian?"

"He's fine."

As Ty lowered my brother onto a patterned wing chair, I rushed forward and dropped to my knees, scanning over Dorian's slack features. There wasn't a scratch or bruise on him. There hadn't been a confrontation.

"The tranquilizer will wear off soon. And we need answers. Answers only Dorian will have."

I'd just positioned his head back when I noticed the butt of a gun sticking out from the holster at Ty's hip and shot upright.

"We need to make him talk."

The smell of his blood stained the air and ruffled my senses, distracting my thoughts from how wrong all of this was, too. "You want to torture my brother?"

Ty stepped close, bringing his body heat and scent with him.

"That's why I didn't tell you. But what choice do we have? I know you're considering bonding to Marcus, but I can't let you go in blind. Too much is at stake."

More even than my life or Dorian's, or what Ty and I would never be, or bringing Kendrick back.

"But if we can uncover his true motives…and where that hidden mark is that joins them physically…"

I wouldn't have to bond with Marcus to safeguard Dorian's life. "We'd be able to kill Marcus."

With my mouth watering, I snatched the gun from Ty and backed up. But I didn't point it at Ty to make him stand down. He was right. No matter how much I wished he wasn't. We needed to know all we could about Marcus's true plans, and we needed to unlink them physically. Dorian, right now, was our only hope. "I'll do it," I rushed. Ty held out a silencer and I focused on spinning the cylinder on tight. It was better than allowing my eyes to travel to where they desperately wanted to be: Ty's lips, throat…to his hands, imagining where I wanted them.

Focus!

Ty shrugged, moving to stand by the wing chair and glancing away. A cig was retrieved and lit, a few quick puffs lighting up the end. To dull the smell of his and my brother's blood from the air?

"The bullets aren't silver. They're marked to disable."

So the torture would come after. Despite my shudder, I raised the muzzle and lined it up two inches away from my brother's bicep. It was better this way. Better while he was out cold than to wait for him to come to. Enough would already have to be done once that occurred. And I didn't know if I could stand to help—or stand by and watch, either.

But what choice did I have?

Forefinger on the trigger, I squeezed off a silenced round, then another, and another, and another. One bullet to each of his biceps and another two to his thighs. Dorian didn't cry out, he didn't flinch. As I stepped back and tried not to stare at the red that leaked from those four holes, I saw movement behind his eyelids.

The tranquilizer was wearing off.

Less than a minute later, Dorian groaned. His head tilted then jerked, rocking upright as consciousness returned. "Ah…" His lids cracked open first, then they fluttered. "What the—" His head snapped up and his fingers twitched as his muscles strained. But he couldn't move. The marked bullets had paralyzed his limbs. "Amelia, you shot me? What are you doing?"

I felt terrible, but Ty was right. This had to be done. I swallowed past the scent of his leaking blood. "We've got questions and we need answers. Make it easy on yourself." And Marcus, who'd feel any and all pain my brother did. "Don't make me hurt you."

Dorian glanced around, seeing the familiar seating, white coffee table, and framed motorbike posters that made up my sitting room. A wicked smile parted his lips. "Guar—!"

Ty swiped the gun off me and pressed the muzzle to the side of my brother's neck. "Try to scream for help and I'll take out your voice, too."

Dorian's silver-blues narrowed at his dead arms before lifting to me. "Well then, *Sis*, ask away." The change in his tone was as unmissable as the cool calm that crossed his face. "Who am I to deny such hospitality…"

Still, I kept my words directed at Dorian, trying to appeal to the real him. "Tell me why Marcus wants to bond with me. I know you know the reason. You've seen it in his mind."

"You went to all this trouble just to ask us that?" A dry laugh cackled from Dorian's mouth. "All you had to do was ask."

I had, during our meeting at *Pulse,* but I wasn't going to point that out now. And *us*? Man, if that didn't send a shiver up my spine. I hated that they were bound, but I had to do this the right way.

"Then we're asking," Ty spoke, smoke puffing out with his words. "Why does Marcus need to be bound to Amelia?"

Dorian shifted his back, then frowned down at his legs—as if he'd gone to kick one foot up onto his knee and had just remembered the limb was useless. With a sigh, he said, "We want to restore the damned. All damned. That is the whole of it. Nothing more. Nothing less."

"And Marcus must be bound to Amelia to do it?" Ty pushed.

Dorian nodded. "Breaking a curse this old requires a huge amount of power."

Blue sparks danced down my arms to my fingertips as if summoned, my subconscious mind lighting them up at the thought of joining my power with my twin's. "Which both Marcus and I have."

But I wasn't buying it. Why would Marcus want to cure all the damned he now controlled? He'd lose his power over the vampire race. And that wasn't all. No being without a conscience would want to inherit one, not when that would stop them from being the soulless creatures of destruction they were used to being. Erzsebet had proved that herself. Her plight to save all the damned along with her daughters had vanished the moment she had joined them. Marcus wasn't damned, but he may as well have been. He had all their power without any of their weaknesses. He had no conscience.

The next words I said were going to do one of two things. Elicit the claim that what Dorian had said was the truth, or bring on the torture… "I call bullshit."

Dorian smiled, that *here but not here* look to his eyes coming then going as he glanced through the opening to the foyer and the door. The guards were only a shout away. And he knew it.

His lips parted.

Guess he was going with option two.

Lunging forward, I swiped the gun back from Ty and squeezed a round into the side of Dorian's neck. My hands shook and I could barely believe what I'd done as Dorian spluttered and blood dribbled out the hole. "He…he was going to scream." I'd not only maimed my brother, I'd screwed Ty's plan to get answers. No wonder he'd wanted to keep me out of this.

"Torture won't work if he can't speak." There was no blame in Ty's voice. But then his lips curved, canines peeking through as they lengthened. He dropped his cig and stomped it out with his boot. "But I think I have a way around that."

"What are you—"

"Take a seat," Ty growled, turning suddenly gold-burning eyes from me to Dorian who bared bloody fangs.

Before I could ask why, he cold-clocked Dorian in the face, knocking him out cold. I jumped up from my half-sitting position, lost in confusion at the overwhelming need to protect my paralyzed brother. "What are you doing?"

Ty gripped my elbows evenly and shoved me straight back. My eyes rolled, body losing muscle control and tipping back into the padded wing chair as Ty fell to the rug at my feet.

Groggy, like my head was filled with fairy floss, I sat up gradually. "Why'd you…what happened?"

Ty clambered off the rug that he'd face-planted onto, and eased his backside onto the coffee table's edge. "It's harder if you're both conscious."

I watched as he took a number of deep breaths. He was sitting right before me, knees barely an inch from mine. But something was different. I couldn't smell him anymore. Couldn't hear his pulse, either. "Harder?" I glanced around. Same motorbike posters, marble fireplace, and view of the moonlit gardens beyond the tall Gothic windows. "What's going on?"

Ty levered his hands on his knees, muscles straining as he pushed upright. He faced Dorian. "Wakey, wakey," he said with a click of his fingers next to the guy's ears.

Dorian jolted and his head cranked up from its sideways hang. "What…*happened?*" he croaked, shifting in the wing chair. His hands slid—*slid?*—over his thighs, which were unmarred with the blood that had seeped out from the bullet holes. Just like his biceps —and his throat. "Hey! I can speak."

My eyes were so wide I probably should have worried about my eyeballs falling out. "No shit." As my mind caught up to this reality, the pieces clicked into place. "We're in a dreamscape."

Ty shrugged. "You needed him to speak. And then…I guess I remembered the times we'd shared them…that first time you realized you couldn't feel *him.*"

"*Kendrick,*" I breathed, sudden hurt turning into realization at Ty mentioning him. The separation from the bond we'd shared because of dreamscapes had changed things between us. It had given Ty and me a way to get close when I was failing so badly at blocking Kendrick out of my mind. Which meant? "Ty, you're a freaking genius."

Ty shrugged. "I did what needed to be done." He glanced at my brother and rubbed his own neck. "Sorry, by the way. It was easier when one of you was unconscious."

"It's cool." Dorian relaxed back into the seat, looking comfortable and at ease. Looking totally devoid of all that cool calculation that was such a constant in his expression since Marcus had bonded with him. "Can't feel anything right now."

And didn't that say it all? Ty really was a genius. "You can't feel Marcus now, either, can you?"

Dorian glanced up as he considered the prospect. Then his eyes widened as he gasped in a breath. "Wow. No, I can't. It's so...*quiet*."

"If he's not in your head, he can't control you," Ty added. "Or what you do or don't say."

Dorian's mouth gaped with another lungful or air. Then he noticed the strain across Ty's face. Standing up fast he dodged around the coffee table to kneel before me, forcing Ty to shift aside. "Don't bond with him. You can't. Not for me. Not for anything."

I clasped his hands, grateful I could be this close to my brother, my real—blood or not—brother, without seeing him as a meal or wondering if he was about to deck me or someone I cared about. "Then tell me where he marked you. Once it's removed we can take Marcus out. You won't be in the crossfire."

Dorian's urgency melted and his gripping hands dropped from the wing chair.

Ty edged closer. "What's the problem?"

"Aside from needing to get close enough to behead him?" Dorian dropped from his knees to his butt. "I was unconscious when Marcus put that mark in me. And fully healed when I came to. I have no idea where it is. Short of skinning me alive, you won't find it."

I almost sighed with resignation until my lungs squeezed in warning. "Then bonding is the only way to free you from him—"

"No!" Rising back onto his knees, Dorian squeezed my hands. "What I said before is true. Marcus needs you to break the curse. I don't know how it can be done, but I know it's not in the way he wants you to think. The curse as it stands, how Marcus wants to remove it, won't restore the damned. It will free them. Every single one of them. Remove their weakness to darkness and their insanity. It will make them unstoppable. You're the only thing standing in his way."

And there was the malevolent plan I'd know existed all along. Cure the damned? My bullshit call was right on the money. This was huge. Freeing all damned in that way would make them the worst threat the world had seen. They wouldn't be restricted to darkness. They'd run havoc night and day, eternally. They'd multiply and build their numbers until humans were extinct and vampires were their controlled cattle.

But could I condemn my brother when there was a way to free him? I stood, bringing Dorian up with me. "Bonding with Marcus doesn't mean I'll follow his lead to break the curse. I'd never unleash that kind of evil on the world."

"You think he won't manipulate you the way he is Dorian?" Ty asked, though it was clear he didn't want an answer as he plucked a cig from his pocket but didn't bother to light it. "He doesn't want to be bound to you just to use your power. He wants to control you. He wants to control the world."

"I'm not new at the bond thing." Even in a dreamscape, I felt the internal blow that hit my heart at admitting that. Bound to Kendrick in life and death. God, I wished that were true. But to date, I'd only managed to connect with his ghost once. The bottle of his blood was a talisman, but it seemed I could only use it to reach him if he wanted me to. I didn't want to dwell on that heartache right now… "He won't be able to control me like he is Dorian. I can block Marcus out."

Dorian had paced over to the fireplace and spun back around. "And what if you can't?" he demanded, getting a grunt of agreement from Ty.

Folding my arms over my chest, I stood my ground. "Then we find a way to stop that from happening *before* I'm linked to him. And we source every bit of info we can on the curse." Before Marcus forces my hand, I added in my head.

CHAPTER 21

Raven exploded through the door to my suite, waving her hands and the sheet of thin paper she clung to as she reached me in the lounge. "Amelia, I found it!"

She came to a halt when she found me poring over a book on the damned curse, which so far had offered nothing of interest to help my situation since our breakthrough with Dorian ninety-odd minutes ago. Tugging the satin bookmark in place, I shoved the book aside on the chaise side of the sectional, abandoning my useless research for the hope of something I prayed had to do with Kendrick. "Show me."

The restored damned's hair was a mess. Her eyes were wide with excitement and ringed with dark circles as if she hadn't slept in days. "I resorted to the scanned files." She hurdled the coffee table to get to me and shoved the sheet into my hands. "It is possible. He was lying."

"Who?" Checking out the paper, I noticed it was wasn't clean white with black text. It was a photocopy—of an old newspaper-like report written with an inked tip. The title read: *Resurrection Success*. Head snapping up, I stared at Raven. "*Kendrick* was lying."

He'd claimed there was no way to resurrect him, but even back when this was written in the early 1600s, someone else thought there must have been. Did that mean that split-second implanted vision Dorian had delivered from Marcus was real?

"Look here." Raven took back the paper and pointed to the scrawl about halfway down the page. *"A select group endeavored to bridge the gap between life and death. With the use of immortal blood, a discovery was unearthed. The passing of another life force is needed to reignite life that has ceased to exist. Though no proof was ever provided, the group claim they succeeded in their task. One being was reportedly resurrected to a state of living. The other was damned."*

I didn't like the sound of all of that. Passing life, no proof, and damned. I crossed my legs. "It sounds like a sacrifice. The death of someone in place of life for another. And one they'd tried to resurrect was damned?"

Raven didn't lose her spark, falling back onto the couch that gasped out collected air. "If Kendrick's brought to life and damned, you can restore him. It's win-win."

State of living… That outcome didn't sit well, but I kept it to myself—like I had the possibility of Kendrick living from Raven to prevent getting her high hopes up further. Besides, there was another huge hurdle to jump before any of this would help. Frowning down at the page in her hands, I reminded my grumbling tummy that I'd emptied a full bottle of Ty's blood after his surprise dreamscape. Pressing my lips together, I skimmed over the sideways scrawl. There didn't appear to be any other detail on the 'how' of the resurrection. "We still don't know the ritual or process to even begin to resurrect Kendrick." My brows arched. "Unless there's more you haven't told me."

"Not told..." Raven smiled and slid a folded sheet from her back pocket and handed it over. "It's a photo of the group, the one who performed the resurrection."

Claimed resurrection. My frown deepened as I unfolded the paper, scrutinizing the photocopy of an old sepia photograph. There were five in the group, two women and three men.

"See anyone familiar?"

One of the men I recognized. "That's Uriel's father, Lord Aswind." Who'd been a guinea pig like me, and died from the power my body now contained. My eyes peeled wide at the blond woman standing front and center. In her full-length gown with black lace gloves, she was stunning. The set of her features were anything but. Cool, calculated, and triumphant. A mastermind at work. "Erzsebet...my grandmother." Who was still alive, according to my disgraced father—unlike Lord Aswind. I guess Caius was going to get what he'd wanted all along. At least in some sense. "We need to track her down. Find her."

This was the closest we'd come to a way to bring Kendrick back to life without having me bond to Marcus. There's no way I was about to let this gift go. If we succeeded, we'd only need to free my brother from my twin and stop Marcus without ending my life. Hey, one out of three wasn't too bad. And look at me, being all positive and shit. I didn't know how we were going to do it. I only knew we had to.

"We need everything we can find on the Blood Countess."

Raven arched a brow. "That was her title?"

"And that was before she was damned." I shrugged, not letting the earlier stories I'd read about her discourage me, since finding out her victims—as least when it came to blood baths—had been damned. "Human folklore."

"There's always some truth in rumor," Raven mumbled, but she got up anyway and clapped her hands together. "So, what's the plan?"

"Gather up anything in the library and the Bathory office on Erzsebet." My gaze slid to the cabinet where the mini fridge hid the one thing that could link me to Kendrick. "I'll, um, get what I have here all together."

Raven made for the door, a knowing and yet saddened look on her face. Before she disappeared around the bend into the foyer, she turned back. "Hey, I ah… Thanks for taking this seriously. Thanks for keeping your word."

I tilted my head to the side. "My word?"

"To bring Kendrick back. I know you and Ty—"

"Whoa, wait up. There is no me and Ty." Even as I said the words, my cheeks lit up like flares and my heart took off like a start pistol had been fired. Raven's raised brow said she didn't buy the lie either. And why would she, after walking in on our feeding session at Marcus's mansion? God, I was awful. I shook my head. "We have a past. A really messy one. It's not something we can ever move past. Kendrick and I—"

"I kissed Kendrick."

I jolted as if I'd been zapped. There was no need to question her confession. I knew the exact moment she was talking about. Down in one of the training rooms, the time Kendrick and her… I gulped. Even now, the memory scored through me like a hot poker. Jealousy rose and I shoved it back down. I had no right to feel anything about that. Not after everything I'd done back then with Ty. I'd cheated on Kendrick and broken his heart. I'd given him hope and torn it away. And I'd kept up the missteps since his death. Time and time again,

I'd let my addiction to Ty and what he stirred in me free. I was a total piece of shit.

"It never went past the kissing," Raven went on when I hadn't said a word. "I wanted it to. Go further, that is. But when I saw his expression, I knew something had happened. Kendrick wouldn't elaborate, but I knew it had to do with you. I…I instigated the kissing. I kept it going, kept him from leaving. Tried to push it further—"

"Raven, I…I don't need you to explain."

"But you do." She reentered the lounge and stood behind a wing chair, folding her arms across the top. "He stopped it. He pushed me away. Said he shouldn't have kissed me back. Said he needed to sort things out with you. That he needed time to sort out his head."

Guess I'd disappeared before he'd had the chance. As I dared to meet her honest eyes, I couldn't think of much to say, except… "Why are you telling me this?"

Raven shrugged. "I can see how much you love him. How much you care. Even torn between Kendrick and Ty…" As I went to argue, she spoke over me. "Even then, you're doing whatever you can to help Kendrick. I know you love him. And…" The smile that curved her lips was small, as if she were remembering a nice moment she'd shared with my soul's mate. "Having him alive again is all I want. Whatever happens afterward, with you, with him, with Ty. It doesn't matter. I want him to be alive and happy, in any way that comes."

Watery red glazed my vision before wet tracks rolled down my cheeks. She reminded me so much of him, my best friend. So selfless and honest. Maybe if he loved her too, he would finally have someone who deserved him. I swiped my tears away and sniffed as I stood up. "We *will* bring Kendrick back, even if it's the last thing I do."

THE MOMENT the door swung shut behind Raven, I was on my knees before the open mini fridge. The sole item inside was centered on the main shelf. The one and only remaining bottle of Kendrick's still vibrantly red blood. That he'd bottle for me and me alone. And the only means I had to connect to his ghost…if he decided to let me in.

And yet I hesitated. What Raven had told me was still fresh in my mind. Still vivid and raw. And not the part about resurrection. Guilt weighed down my beating heart. Raven had been the instigator. And Kendrick, though angered when I'd stumbled upon them, had stopped that interaction before it got out of hand. Unlike what I had done so recently with Ty, when I had grabbed…

I gritted my teeth, anger mingling with my regrets. If that report that backed up Dorian's implanted vision was true, that meant Kendrick had lied. And despite everything between us, I had to know why.

Although my voltage was fully contained, I made a conscious effort to pull back any wandering strands. The last thing I wanted was to shatter the glass. As I gently picked up the bottle, I imagined dropping it and hearing the crash as red sprayed out across the stone and rug. *Don't drop it. Don't you dare.*

Static in the air made the hair across my nape prickle. Still crouched, I spun with caution, feeling sudden relief at the sight of who stood a few feet back from me.

His lids were closed as I went to brush his translucent but tacky hair from his face—and pulled back when my fingers dipped inside his skull. The shudder that gripped me shook my hand holding the bottle of his blood. *"Kendrick?"*

His lids opened fast. His eyes—cloudy as ever—found mine, the narrowed strain in them mimicking my guilt and anger. "Hey…"

God, just to see his face again, even like this with all its bruises and that split lip… My line of questioning diverted. "Does…" I hated asking, but I hated not knowing just as much. Hated thinking that by conjuring him I was causing him pain. I motioned to his neck where his spine jutted out and stretched the skin. "Does that…*hurt?*"

Kendrick crouched down, propping his knees and wrapping his arms around them. "Told you already I feel nothing. I didn't lie about that."

But he had about something else. Something so much bigger and life altering. "You know about the report Raven found, the vision. You knew all along there was a way to resurrect you. Why? Why would you lie about that? This is your life we're talking about!"

Kendrick blinked slowly at my last shouted words. Silence stretched on, and he seemed to be deciding what to say as he avoided my stare. Eventually he said, "That report doesn't prove anything. It doesn't give you any concrete proof or even any means to attempt a resurrection." Letting his hands unclasp, one of his legs fell slack as he leaned back into the base of the couch. "Amelia, please. Just let me go. Let me be at peace."

"No. Never." I jumped up and paced beside the coffee table, cradling the bottle to my chest to keep it safe. It wasn't that I didn't want Kendrick to be at peace. And it wasn't just about not being able to let go. It was about giving up. I couldn't forget seeing the moment he ratcheted upright to gasp air. And yet the look on Kendrick's face now held an undertone of fear. "You know something. What aren't you telling me?"

Kendrick's mouth opened, then shut. Opened… "Leave me dead. Or you will be."

I shuddered, the beat of my heart faltering as I dropped onto the edge of the coffee table. The message we'd received from the Ouija board. I didn't release my grip on the bottle, but instead wrapped both palms around it. "That really was you?"

Kendrick scrubbed a hand down his face. He looked worse than death all of a sudden, if that was even possible. "You've been through so much. And I don't want anyone else to suffer to bring me back to life." He'd already known about the sacrifice the report laid out. His ghostly message from that board and candlewax proved that.

But how real was that threat?

"I had my time. I made my choices that put me where I am right now." He lifted a hand and gazed through its fuzzy glass-like texture. "I'm okay with that."

"Well I'm not." I was up again, pacing again. "I won't hurt anyone to bring you back. You know I would never do that. But you also know I *will* find a way. I can't give up. I won't. You will live—"

"You can't have new life without death." Kendrick's snapped words made me freeze. "Everything has a price. And I won't let you or anyone else pay that debt for me."

I did a one-eighty and froze. The shaggy rug in front of the couch was vacant. "Kendrick?" With the bottle still secure in my hand, a sweeping glance of the lounge room revealed nothing. He'd vanished on me. Conjuring and keeping him here…it seemed Kendrick held the power. Not me. And he'd made his wishes clear.

But he knew me and my motivations. Knew that when push came to shove, I'd do anything to bring him back. I just needed to uncover the finer details. There was no point in winning the battle if it killed me and left everyone else to lose the war.

~

Crouched with my back to the closed fridge and cabinet, I didn't bother trying to bring Kendrick's ghost back again. After how many hours of failing in between research, it was clear he'd had enough of our argument. Not that I could blame him for playing ghost. If I were dead and hoped my days, hours, and minutes were numbered, I'd want to spend them in less unpleasant circumstances. But that was our go-to, wasn't it? We disagreed, but in the end, Kendrick would back me up. And with something this important, oh like Kendrick's life being snuffed out forever, yeah, I was going to fight.

Not that the last twenty-four-plus hours of research had helped my cause.

My tired gaze slid to the stacks of books of all shapes and sizes that dwarfed the chaise. The ones Raven had delivered by the truck-load. My mind felt hazy after reading all that black-on-white text between RVC meetings and check-ups from the restored damned.

Right now, she was retrieving a new delivery of books that would hopefully shed light on Kendrick's life-and-death claim that she'd refused to accept as a dead end.

Drained by more than lack of sleep, and with Ty off checking up on damned leads, I couldn't stop my groan as I got vertical. I picked up a book from the just-as-packed coffee table and cracked the cover. If I couldn't find out what Erzsebet and her group had done to pull off a resurrection, I'd have to find the Blood Countess myself.

Falling back onto the couch, I immersed myself in the dusty stacks. There were textbooks, volumes, reports that had been compiled into protective binders and, after gathering up my stash, a number of experiment notebooks I'd unearthed. I was looking for a needle in a haystack—Raven too—but my determination wouldn't falter. Neither would hers. I understood mine and Raven's. I loved and owed Kendrick after all he'd been through because of me. Had I been able to trade places with him, I would have. Raven was in love with the guy. Despite the twinge of jealousy I felt at that fact, it also made me feel like shit. After what I'd started with him, *I* should have been the one *in love.* But no matter how much I'd wanted it to, my feelings had never developed past just love. I would give my life and die for him, but I wasn't now and had never been *in love* with him.

As I sighed and lowered the useless book in my lap, I caught sight of the charred coverless pages of an experiment book. The same one that had belonged to Caius that we'd found in the ruins of the burned-down cabin. Full of experiments he'd continued for his mother. I knew the contents. Had read what was left of the burned pages from front to back; the tests Caius had carried out and what he'd infected us all with.

There was nothing in there on resurrections, and yet for some reason I felt the strangest need to—

I dropped the book, but caught the fragile remains before it hit the ground. The sudden heat inside my head and behind my eyes wasn't unexpected. And I kept my grip on those scarred pages while giving in to the utter weightlessness, tipping onto the mound of books on the chaise beside me.

Suddenly lucid, I blinked in the darkness as creaking sounded below me. My own footfalls as I crept down old wooden stairs into a lamp-lit chamber made of logs and stone. Tortured cries and clanking sounded beyond a padlocked iron gate between the two long benches that spanned either side of the wall.

I felt the internal need to jerk or strain at the sound, but the body I inhabited didn't miss a beat. Smallish hands grabbed onto the lip of one bench to hoist themself up onto a tall stool. Through the child's eyes, I saw the pages of the experiment book, unsinged and whole. More than what existed after the fire was still intact.

Solution 1 - Combination of ingredient X mixed with silver nitrate and exposed to ultraviolet light, then mixed with Pure Blood. Will prevent infection from instilling damned attributes while altering DNA.

Solution 2 - Combination of Pure Blood boiled with silver nitrate, then mixed with ingredient X2. Will cull the subject's natural conscience and instill damned traits while keeping them fundamentally alive.

IBB seems to have delivered the optimum results. IAB has not altered subject three's DNA or altered their natural sensitivity to sun exposure.

The eyes I saw through widened as they brushed over the page with their hands, and I wondered if this was somehow me. A memory that had been stripped from my mind.

My eyes lifted to two cork-plugged bottles on the bench. One said X, the other X2. I sniffed one and scrunched up my nose. Gaze dropping to that small wrist, I stared at the pulses of blood there. "Damned blood," the voice that spoke was young, a pre-teen, and undoubtedly male. Not mine. The shoes dangling under the bench were red-and-black sneakers.

Dorian had been infected with solution one after birth. I had been infected with the same solution before my first breath.

The boy turned back a page, seeing the three test subjects, what had been done to them, and the results. I'd seen the result for one and three. They were Dorian and me.

The boy's eyes doubled back to test subject two. The section of that page that had been too badly damaged when I'd found it in the cabin ruins.

Test Subject 2/Day 7 – Infection before breath of life with solution 2 has instilled damned attributes without any change to living status to date. Bloodthirst is excessive and not easily quelled. Elixirs are required to hide traits and control hunger. Infant displays only minor irritation without adverse effects when exposed to direct sunlight.

The boy looked up from those inky words to the bottle of X2. "This is why I'm different? Why I don't belong?"

Fresh creaking brought the boy's head around to see polished shoes stomping down the stairs. "Marcus!" In a sharp suit, Caius looked angry as hell, laser stare shooting up from the photo he held in his hand—of me as a child. "I have told you this basement is out of—"

"You love her, don't you?" The boy hopped off the stool to stalk up to his father. "You wish she still lived here, with them, the family you always wanted."

"Marcus, my son." Despite his words, Caius's tone was a blade's edge. "We have talked about this. You must learn to control your outbursts."

"So I can be weak like her? Screw that. You made me this way, *Father*." He bared his fangs and snatched the photo, crushing it in his small hands. "A living damn—"

Caius backhanded the boy, smacking him down to the cold stone ground. Putting his shiny shoe down over the boy's throat, he bent to pry the crushed photo from that small hand. His shoe relented and the boy scrambled up—glaring, rather than afraid. "Toe the line, Son—or I will reveal your true nature to the RVC."

And then I was falling into a black abyss.

Ratcheting upright, my face hurt from face-planting into jagged book edges. But physical discomfort was the furthest thing from my mind. A pang of unwanted sympathy for my twin came over me like an avalanche. I'd known all along that we were fundamentally different because of what Caius had done to us. But seeing the explanation of why and how he'd been raised with the iron fist of a father who couldn't control what he'd created, brought it all home.

How easily our roles could have been switched. Marcus was the way he was because he was infected with solution two. It killed off his conscience. It made him a living damned. Gave him all the damned's strengths without their weaknesses.

"The very thing he's trying to recreate by breaking the curse," I whispered to myself, slumping back into the couch. "A race that he can belong to."

CHAPTER 22

"There's stuff to work on…" Vanessa strolled through from the foyer not a minute later, her heels clipping with each step, her presence distracting me from my revelation. In her hands she held Erzsebet's velvet-swathed notebook. The same ancient one I'd found hidden in a box below the library tower. She opened the cover and carefully leafed through the pages that held the Countess's hand-written account of her every attempt with Lord Aswind to break the curse. "But there's zilch on the actual ritual to pull any of this off. This is just a report of each failed aftermath."

All of that I already knew, as I scooted back further into the couch's cushion. From this distance I could hear her heart, and after that vision—not to mention the bottles I'd been drinking over taking Ty's veins as much—my stomach was screaming for attention. My sharpening fangs were a threat waiting to happen.

And yet, over my thoughts of which vein to take and how to muffle her screams, I sensed a deeper reason than failure informing for Vanessa's visit.

Since our dreamscape revelation from Dorian, she'd been more than willing to bury her nose in everything I had on the damned curse. Especially the old relics from Erzsebet herself. With Raven's resurrection report, I'd been happy for the help.

Now I had to ask, "So what's our next step?"

Vanessa's red-lipstick smile was as vivid as her hair. "There are pages torn out in the back." Her heel clips were lost as she trampled the rug to get closer. Ignoring my sudden rigidness, she held the notebook out. "I think you could *see* more if you were up to trying."

"A vision?" I half hissed, fangs flashing as I snatched the book to make her back off. "I can't right now. It's not a good—"

My argument cut short as my consciousness blinked out like a light. Without any control, I was transported to another place…and time, from the looks of it. Worry for my vision hunger and what would happen when I came to, vanished. Sitting in the glassless cutout of a window, my knees were propped up beneath a long gown and my head was turned. The view of surrounding countryside and mountains was stunning in the falling…twilight!

I went to scramble out of the light. Being in transition, even this low light could burn me…except it wasn't. And in fact, I couldn't move. Just like my vision minutes ago, I wasn't inside my own body. In a medieval gown, one pale and slender hand toyed restlessly with long wavy hair. The other held a quill tipped with ink that I put to the blank page of a—velvet-swathed book.

Erzsebet.

Fall, moon, and let the threat of daylight break. I tire of waiting for our latest attempt to rid our people—and my family—of this wretched curse on the damned.

The words I'd read from this very notebook flooded into my mind. Ones that must have been written after this entry, being as she was still trying to break the damned curse. Her report of her last attempt and the failure killing Uriel's father, Lord Aswind. The man who'd lived with the power I now contained. A power that had killed him. For some reason, I had a feeling that this attempt would be their last. I wasn't sure how I knew, but my insides were churning.

There was no way to stop the event. It would play out.

So why was I stuck in this vision? Why was I seeing this past moment in time?

Lady Bathory deposited the quill in a pot of ink and leaned back into the windowless frame. She sighed at the blank cover and ran her hand over the velvet. "My life's work," she muttered. "I pray this time is not for naught."

As if to pass the time, she leafed through the pages one by one. Every word was about the damned curse and the ways she'd tried to break it. Her life's ambition in words. The mission she'd devoted her life to. And the one she'd become damned for. By choice. Before their last and final attempt, the lord and Erzsebet hadn't even come close to breaking the curse.

"Maybe tomorrow we will cure you all. Then our race will be safe and all the damned will be as they once were. We will no longer live in fear of their total domination. My daughters will be returned unto their true selves."

Was that the purpose of me seeing this? To know Erzsebet did believe breaking the curse would cure every damned? Despite Marcus's true motives, was there a way to cure instead of free them all?

With a sigh, the now-damned royal flipped to the end of the notebook. The title on the last page made my eyes bug—or would have, if I'd been in my own body.

Damned Curse Ritual.

On the background behind the writing was a symbol. It was

identical to the one Caius had used in his attempt to steal my power. A jagged bolt trapped inside a perfect circle.

The Countess ran a finger over the words at the bottom of the tattered page.

Create an activating symbol with the blood of the powers at the sacred site. Once joined in body and soul inside the circle, the light and dark will unite as one, joining heaven and hell together to lift the darkness, to free the cursed forever more.

As the Countess crossed her arms over the bottom of the page, the rest of the ritual, and what would happen as a result of casting it, were blocked.

Would those actions free the damned—or restore them?

Needing to know—and feeling my time here quickly syphoning like sand through an hourglass as sharp pain stabbed at my stomach —I focused all I could on what I needed. Instead of reading the rest of the page, Erzsebet took hold and tore it free of that thick spine. "If we're doomed to fail, this ritual dies with me."

Dammit, look down. Read the rest—

A shock of blue light erupted from the Countess I inhabited. Her eyes widened, holding up the sheet she'd torn free. "What in the world—"

The dark countryside disappeared with a fluttering of her lids. Light flooded in and my eyes shut as tears sprouted from the intensity. Fighting my body's need to keep my lids shut, I blinked rapidly, shifting the haze and bringing back focus. On my back so the tears trekked across my face to my hairline rather than down my cheeks, I was back in my lounge room, draped over unyielding books.

Kneeling beside me, Vanessa held my forearm while my grip on the notebook tightened. The smell of her reached me with the sound of her beating heart. "Are you ok—"

Scrambling up quick, I pulled up my legs and wrapped my arms around them. The barrier did nothing to stop my fangs throbbing as they punched down into my bottom lip. "You need to leave. Now." My heartbeat faltered as Vanessa stumbled back, but I managed to grate out the ritual as I stabbed my nails through my jeans and into my shins. "There was more to it—I couldn't see."

"It's enough to go on for now," Vanessa said, disappearing into the foyer. "I'll see what I can find. Maybe we can alter things to our advantage. Ensure a cure."

And then she was gone, taking her body full of rich blood from the hungry transitionee. Me. As I fought the need to chase after her…

The grinding in my gut started up strong, feeling like rocks on spin cycle. Was the air suddenly dry? My throat felt like it was stuffed with hot sand. When a loud buzzing took up residence in between my ears, I couldn't hear anything else. Not the sudden slowing of my heart. Not the opening and shutting of the main door. Tingles inundated my chilled skin as black veins forked out from my chest and down my arms. My intent to find a bottle of Ty's blood vanished as my heart stopped dead. I sniffed the air and whirled, scenting what I needed. What I'd kill for.

Ty's eyes fixed on me with a measuring gauge, the sight of him with one hand in his jeans pocket bled to vivid red. He spoke quickly, expression a look of reason and threat. But every word was lost to that buzzing.

Fresh kill.

Some part of me knew he'd offer up his vein. That he'd help leash the monster. But all of me knew that even though he *trusted* me, as his life began the irreversible descent of bleeding down my gullet, preservation would kick in.

He'll stop your fun. Take those final drops and keep them for himself. Unless…

This time, I wasn't going to let him get away. I was going to take all I needed. I was finally going to become all that I was destined to be.

My legs unfurled before me to stretch over the edge of the couch. I didn't need to push up with my palms to go upright in a way that was smooth…and seductive. Stare not wavering from me, Ty's sight narrowed, hand still in that pocket. I didn't move any further at first. That little voice in my head had come even more alive, and it was talking fast. *Want. Need. Seduce.* With my fangs throbbing, all I could focus on was the smell of the alpha and the rush of his pulse. That dangerous look in my eyes was affecting him. Just as planned. And not because he was scared in any way.

He wants you, my internal voice pointed out. *You want him…to taste. To kill. Use the appeal.*

Almost as if watching a dream, I felt my lips move and heard myself say, "I want you, Ty."

Those stunning eyes flashed a bright shade of gold for the briefest second. The buzzing in my ears quieted as Ty's heartbeat jacked into overdrive. Even with the few feet between us as he stood inside the archway, I felt his body heat spike.

I took a step closer. Then another. "You want me too. I know you do." *Want me to take you for every drop and leave you with a perfect smile on your face.*

Even as the tiniest part of me wondered what the hell I was doing, now standing right in front of him, I ran my nose from his chest up to his neck, sucking his scent deep into my lungs. The need to cough barely registered, and then my hand was on his waist. He didn't pull away. I didn't, either. And God, if that didn't make my fangs throb harder.

"Amelia." The warning in his tone was clear and wavering at the same time. "You don't want to do this. Just let me *feed* you."

"Exactly what I had in mind," I practically purred, leaving any and all rationality behind. My tongue forked out, licking from the join in his collarbones and up to the cut of his jaw.

Ty shuddered and grabbed my shoulders. His arms straightened like solid bars to keep space between us. "You're too far gone. I'll get a glass."

As he shoved me back, I darted forward and blocked his way to the cabinet. His chest was to mine, and even with the lack of exertion, Ty's breath was labored. Clamping one palm around his neck, I leaned up on my toes. "I want you to...*kiss me.*"

A war waged across Ty's tan features: suspicion, uncertainty, crumbling self-control, and most of all? The heat of want and desire. He sucked in a quick breath as my lips parted, and then it was game over. His mouth came down on mine, head slanting as his tongue lapped over my own. His arms enveloped me, pulling me close, holding me tight against the hard planes of his chest. The feel of him against me could have swallowed me whole. Normally, it would have taken me over the edge. But not now. There was something I coveted in this moment—more than the promise of Ty's hands and mouth all over me.

With a shuffle, I forced Ty back into my bedroom. A rough shove had him falling down on my bed. Right where I wanted him. The look in his eyes was pure desire and hunger. The sight of his body proved he was ready for wherever this interaction was heading. At least in a physical sense.

But that mind of his was ticking. Ty went to lever up on his elbows. "Ah, Amelia, I don't think you—"

I mounted the alpha in a single bound, my legs straddling his hips as I pressed down to remove any doubt. With his digging-in weapons shielded by clothing, I ignored the discomfort. His growl cut short as I claimed his mouth and my tongue delved in deep. "I want you," I said against his mouth. "Here. Now." I kept up the kissing. With one hand on his neck, thumb over his Adam's apple and fingers curled around his nape, I reigned in the urge to pull away as I grazed the silver chain peeking from his T-shirt. Reined in the impulse to bring my free hand around the other side to grip on tight and squeeze. Instead, that free hand glided along the soft Egyptian cotton sheets, out and away from the hot body beneath me. When my fingertips reached the bedside table, they crept over the wooden top, closer and closer. The feel of cool metal registered and then I took hold.

Take him now, for everything he's got.

My slanted kiss broke off suddenly as my arm swung inward. The jewelry box neared Ty's skull with a burst of voltage. His eyes widened with perception. Too late. Even as his hand on my butt and the one creeping up my tank retreated, the sharp edge of one corner struck his temple. My electricity did the rest, short-circuiting his brain like a mental patient getting shock treatment.

Lights out cold.

With cool calm, I brought the jewelry box to my mouth and licked the corner that was tipped with blood.

"Stop." The whispered female voice brought my red gaze up. Beyond the posts of my bed, I saw the bench seat, weapon crates, gentle light growing around the drape-shielded windows, and empty archways to the foyer and lounge. I was alone. That voice came from deep down inside of me?

The last stitch of my vanishing conscience—that this time, was going to lose.

I threw aside the jewelry box and pressed my body into Ty, tongue riding up the side of his face to the small puncture at his temple. No need to rush. I turned his head slowly to the side to expose the thick vein running up his neck. Though it was a shame there was no more cat and mouse. The need for resistance while taking what I wanted was a strong and new sensation. Enjoying the chase was part of the game. Part of the kill.

But oh well.

Maybe on the next one—because there would be more. Finally I was at the point of no return. I was ready to become the thing that lived inside of me and was screaming to break free. It was my nature. My DNA—

A flash of Kendrick entered my mind, cold, dead, spine protruding. I didn't even flinch. Was his ghost trying to stop me?

It didn't matter. This wouldn't take long. This body beneath me —whose was it again? I couldn't seem to remember. Even as I stared down at the unconscious form, all I could see was brilliant red. And the who didn't matter anymore, anyway. They would be empty soon enough. Any emotion and pain would be covered up like a Band-Aid the moment my conscience died.

I licked my lips. My head dipped low. I knew there was no turning back. The monster was me and I was it. There was no more separation. Now we would be one.

My fangs plunged in deep…

CHAPTER 23

A savage force knocked me off the hot body beneath me and I tumbled with my attacker to the ground. The hiss that raked from my throat was a threat and it was met with a fist to my cheek. Sight flashing stars, I couldn't see the person struggling to catch my blows as I struck out. Even if I could have, I wouldn't have cared. They'd interrupted my feed. My kill. Now they were going to pay. Two for one. Sounded like a plan to me.

I shoved up hard and snapped my head forward. Smack! Clean in the nose.

A girl cried out and a spray of delicious blood coated my face. "Amelia, don't make me hurt you!"

Licking my lips, the drive to taste more of her surged my need to kill. Tucking my legs up, I went to kick her off me. I wasn't the one about to get hurt—

Thumbs drove into my sockets, fingers clamping over my skull to keep us together as I kicked out. The girl grunted but didn't let go.

And then we were rolling, hitting obstacles that rattled and thumped. A shift of material sent a UV-blocked blade of light down my clawing arm and up my neck. I hissed anyway, flipping her onto her back, snapping my fangs. Those blinding thumbs released my sockets and a fist smashed me in the face.

With fresh stars lighting up my vision, my head spun. I was slammed onto my back with spine-jarring force. I clawed into the girl's side and she screamed as she caught my wrist. As my other hand attacked, my restrained one was belted down into the stone ground, once, twice, three—*crack!*

Pain shot from my wrist up my arm. The bone was cracked through, my reaching hand and fingers throbbing in agony. I snarled like the animal I was. "You're going to pay for that."

My other hand caught her around the jugular and I hauled her up. Fists plowed into my gut, disrupting the ongoing grinding of my hunger. I ignored the irritation.

Through my bleeding eyes, I saw we'd made it just inside the lounge room. And then I saw her face. Black cropped hair, silver-blue irises with maroon chips. A face of innocence and youth that had been hardened by years of horror acted out by her own hands.

Raven.

You're not a monster. Control the beast.

The words were a desperate whisper, ones that weren't strong or compelling enough for me to give them any power. I kept my tight hold on Raven's neck and soon enough her punches started to lose their momentum. Air supply. You needed that when alive. I was going to kill this girl. Take the life she didn't deserve after all the lives she'd taken while damned.

Shifting my thumb, I tilted her head to stretched and expose her carotid artery. Mouth gaping and fangs long, I leaned in.

Amelia, no!

My eyes darted, scanning to find where that man's voice had

come from, even as something stirred deep down inside of me. No one was there. Not on the book-cluttered couch. Not through the opening to the foyer. Not by the swaying drapes. Only that male body was present, still out cold on the bed a number of yards away.

I hissed in threat and launched the girl like a ragdoll across the room. There was a clatter as her body collided with the full-wall cabinet, cracking open a cupboard door as she fell. Still as the dead. And soon she would be.

Prowling closer, I knelt beside her. Shifting sounds rose, not from the male, but from my new prey. She was still breathing, hands patting over the ground. Not for long.

Leaning over her, I twisted her head and licked my lips. "This won't hurt…too much." I shut my bloody eyes—

"This will." With a sizzling sound the girl shifted and then scorching pain cut through my side.

I flipped off the girl, my back hitting the stone ground as I writhed. I clawed for the burning source and hissed when it felt like I'd reached into a bucket of pure acid. The stupid girl…she'd staked me. I heard something opening and a clank as I swiped the blanket off the couch. I needed to get this damn silver out—

An elbow belted into my mouth. My feet were kicked out from under me. And then she was on top of me. The stake tore free and re-plunged into my chest, its tip just touching my heart. I stopped moving as a hand pried my jaw wide. Cool glass clinked against my fangs and teeth, and then—

The chilled blood ran like a stream down my throat. Not alive, but so powerful. So familiar. The red staining my sight became splotchy but remained, while my overwhelming drive to kill diminished with each hungry gulp. There was no reaction beneath the tip of that stake as I forced my body to go limp. The blood wasn't Ty's…

Oh dear God, *Ty*.

Dropping my head to the side, I saw my four-poster bed. Saw the second he ratcheted upright with a gasp, expression on high alert and body ready to fight. A quick scan over me drained some of the tension from his clenched fists and corded arms. Body jittery from my voltage, he barely looked at me as he came over. "Thanks, Raven."

Changing direction I saw the girl leaning over me. Her expression was one of determination, anger, and…*understanding*? After I'd tried to kill her. I noticed then the scattered pile of books. The ones Raven must have returned with after she'd taken off in search of answers on Kendrick's life-and-death claim. If not for her— "Raven, Ty…I'm…sorry doesn't even begin to—"

"You're okay now?" Not an inquiry of physical injury, but one of mental status. Of whether my kill switch had been flicked.

"I—" I registered the throbbing of my healing wrist that Raven had broken to fight me off, felt the renewed stinging in my side, and… "God, that hurts." It was a good thing my heart wasn't beating as the punctured skin sizzled around the silver length. The pulsations would only drive the stake tip in and out of the organ.

Burning her hand, Raven twisted the stake free and threw it at Ty. That explained the pure silver length over the vamp-friendly version. Guess she'd swiped it when knocking me off of him.

Without offered help, I levered up on my elbows. I licked my lower lip and remembered the taste of that blood. I shot a look toward Raven. Beside her was an empty bottle. The mini fridge behind her was open and…empty. My still heart felt like it had just exploded as a slowing gurgle of blood leaked out of my chest. "You…that…" The words weren't coming out or gelling into any coherent sentence.

"I had no choice." Raven picked up the empty bottle and stared down at it with glassy eyes.

"What's the issue?" Ty demanded.

Finally I found my voice. "That was the last bottle of Kendrick's blood." My tone became accusing and I couldn't stop the glare I propelled at Raven. "It was my only way to connect with him. What the hell were you—"

"Hello, Amelia."

I spun and Ty tensed as if he expected me to lunge at him again. Standing beside Ty in his ghostly form was Kendrick, just as bruised and battered as ever. That poking sideways spine just as obvious. But I wasn't even touching the empty bottle. "How can I see you?"

"Amelia?" Ty sounded like he was trying to get through to a crazy person.

And it was no wonder; I was staring at the empty space beside him and talking to it. Was I finally losing my mind?

It's me. You're not going crazy.

Kendrick's lips didn't move as his words reached my ears. He'd spoken through the bond, like…before. "It was you trying to get through to me." *When I was about to kill Raven,* I finished in my head.

"Amelia, talk to us," Raven added, getting up behind me.

"I can see him," I said, moving closer to Kendrick's ghostly form and evoking further tensing from Ty. I reached out and my fingertips slipped through his shoulder, tingling with sensation that had goosebumps flaring up my black-veined arms. "How can I see you?"

Kendrick glanced past me at Raven and smiled. That same smile he'd given her when I'd found them watching snowboarding while stretched out on his bed. But he wasn't just looking at her. He was looking at the empty bottle she'd picked up. "You know how."

"Your blood…" I glanced from Ty to Raven who were both waiting for an explanation. "Kendrick's blood was the talisman that tethered him to me." A nod from Kendrick confirmed my summation was on track. "Now that link is inside of me. It's part of me."

Even as Kendrick smiled my way, fear flooded my sluggish veins. Our bodies recycled blood. How long could this new connection last before new blood replaced the talisman I'd consumed? In hours, days, maybe even weeks, would my connection to him fade out?

In my head, Kendrick was the only one to hear my concerns, and the only one to answer them. *I guess in time we'll know.*

CHAPTER 24

I lowered the book from my raised knees, my not-quite-healed wrist crying out. My gaze settled on Kendrick beside me on the couch for the millionth time. I no longer cringed or shuddered at the sight of all his wounds. I knew they weren't causing him any pain in his ghostly existence. The relief at him still being beside me—after Ty had refueled me then taken off with Raven, and after I'd gotten into Raven's delivery, had some fitful sleep, and done more research till night returned—was bittersweet at best. "I can't believe you're still here." Every second I expected him to poof into nothingness. Expected the whole *Kendrick's a ghost and now we're connected by his blood* thing to all just have been a heart-breaking dream. Or a reality that was soon to fade.

"Yeah, me neither." As his lips moved, I heard his words in my head at the same time. Kendrick stared down at himself and ran his hands down his bare, lacerated chest—because he'd died that way—before staring at his palms. Was being present like this alien to him too? He reached out as if he wanted to touch my face, but then changed his mind. "It's been so hard seeing you all this time and not being able to get through to you."

My heart skipped a beat at the reminder—he had been here all this time, sending me messages, watching me. I placed a hand on the book between us. I wanted to wrap my arms around him, to tell him everything that had happened since he was taken from me. I wanted to tell him I loved him and how sorry I was…for everything: leading him on, breaking his heart, my recent interactions with Ty, causing his untimely death. But he knew my head and my heart. I wasn't blocking his all-access pass. But that wasn't the only thing that kept me from sharing my regrets. Almost hovering right beside me, his focus kept shifting to the foyer and the door Ty and Raven had left through. "She loves you, you know."

Kendrick stiffened, which was strange to see in someone that was completely see-through. "Ah…I…"

"We don't have to talk about it. In fact, I'd rather not." And not just because the color I swear I could see staining his face was proof of his returned feelings. "I need to find out how to resurrect you, and don't try to tell me it's not possible again. We both know I saw you come alive in that vision Dorian delivered from Marcus."

The conflict in Kendrick's expression melted, and his nostrils flared as he got up and clenched his fists. A reaction I'd brought out in him in life…and now in death. "Just because something's possible, doesn't mean it should be done." He came up close as I got vertical, trapping me between the couch and coffee table. Although I felt static coming off his, well…form, there was no heat from his hand that hovered beside my cheek. No breath across my face as he spoke, either. "Some things go against what is natural, what is right."

I inched back and shook my head. "You being dead is not right. And I'm not the only one who thinks so." That got me a fleeting glance toward the door again. "Raven won't stop, either. With or without you, we're doing this."

Kendrick sighed—or at least looked like he had, given he didn't have corporeal lungs that could hold air—and almost floated as he passed through the couch over to the balcony doors. From here he could just see the fountain his mother had died in, but as he gazed out, there was no sadness in his expression.

"You know she's at peace now, don't you."

Kendrick actually laughed. "Peace? More like pissed off…"

At his trailed-off words, I filled in the blanks. "Because she blames me for your death. She wants you to live again, even if you don't." Raven was back in the library now, finding more information from books and the online database. Ty was with her as far as I knew, since his pack update had revealed no clues—only a rise in human deaths surrounding Portsmouth. I sighed at the messy stacks around the room and slumped back onto the couch. If we had anything to do with it, Kendrick's mother may have a reason not to hate me so much. "If I have to read every single word on every book in existence, I *will* find something. To prove it's possible *and* to bring you back."

The look on Kendrick's face was intense, jaw set. "Stop wasting your time on me and focus on a plan to stop Marcus."

"Not gonna happen."

After long seconds of a stare down and probing my brain, Kendrick sighed, anger melting. He knew I'd never let this go. "Come with me, then."

After Kendrick's continued argument to remain dead, that wasn't the reaction I'd expected. My suspicions rose and I arched a brow. "Why? To where?"

"Just come, already." He vanished right before my very eyes then reappeared in the foyer. "Trust me for once."

"I do trust— Hey, wait up!" I called as he ghosted right through the main door. Leaping up, I raced out the door to see him almost floating past guards who were unaware of anything other than me as I rushed to keep up. Their tempting scents barely registered as I took a right to shadow Kendrick down the back stairwell to the hall of office doors. He passed straight through the closed door to the Vladimir office. To Dorian's office. I pulled up fast, not wanting Kendrick out of my sight but not wanting to stumble upon my brother. With my replenished heart racing, I listened. The only sound nearby was the flickering crackle of flames that burned brightly from wall lanterns.

I quietly entered and swung the door shut behind me. I found Kendrick standing by the charcoal-dusted fireplace. Facing him, my reflection was repeated in the many mirrors that covered the wall on either side of the mantle. But my absent transition traits didn't hold my stare. The gilt frame Kendrick tipped his head at did. One of the largest mirrors on the wall, and as I went to inspect, the question from my lips stalled. Without much effort, the mirror creaked open on two hinges like a door.

A vault-like panel was hidden behind, but there was no keyhole, dial, or number pad to punch in a pin code. Testing the edges with my fingertips, I tried to pry it open. It wouldn't budge. "You know how to open it? What's inside?"

Kendrick pursed his lips and his sight darted to the bookshelf behind me.

Marcus liked concealing things—liked his gadgets too, I'd learned after seeing that bookshelf shift sideways to tuck behind the sofa, revealing the entry to the spiral staircase down to the catacombs. A single book tilted out an inch activated the mechanics.

I was there in a flash, tilting the book back. As expected, it initiated the sequence of mechanics that sent the hidden-in-plain-sight door sliding open. Though it did nothing to the hidden compartment behind the mirror. "Is this the right one?"

Not waiting for an answer, I shifted the books to either side out of the way, fiddling with the book, edging it out and trying to tilt it side to side, too. The bookshelf slid sideways again, and my frustration peaked.

As I went to tear the book off the shelf to uncover the latches that must be getting pulled from somewhere inside it, Kendrick spoke up. "Try pushing it straight back."

I raised my brows over my shoulder to see the unexplained indecision across Kendrick's face. "Thanks." A gentle push sent the book a half-inch through the back. A click had me whirling on the spot. The vault door had swung open. Shooting across the room, I found a stack of discolored and tattered parchment sheets. From the look and roughness of them, they were seriously old. Like, centuries. The very early date stamps of the 1600s proved it. "Oh, shit." Holding the frail pages with kid gloves, I turned to Kendrick. "You know what all of this is, don't you?"

"When Marcus showed me all those resurrection experiment reports a few years back, I never thought I'd ever need or want to see them again." He shook his head, looking conflicted. "You won't find what you need there. That report was a lie. They all failed. I told you to stop wasting your time."

Needing to see for myself, I lowered the stack onto the desk and carefully leafed through each loose sheet. Each failed attempt, ending with the earliest—which had been carried out on Erzsebet's very own thirteen-year-old daughter, Ursula Bathory. One of Caius's sisters. I knew I recognized that handwriting. Lady Erzsebet Bathory. She had performed all these attempted resurrections herself. I read further down the last page, my mouth gaping as I reached the end. "Erzsebet beheaded one of her damned daughters.

She changed her experiments to try to resurrect her. She kept trying to make it work, hoping to bring Ursula back to life—so she could do the same for the other two when she finally found and killed them too."

Kendrick walked around the desk and went to pull out the caster-wheeled chair—when his hand went straight through the padded backrest. He shrugged and shook his head. "Until she realized there might be a way to cure the damned. The dates on those end before the entries start in the experiment books we found. But like I said, it doesn't tell you how, just that not a single attempt worked."

"But you know it's possible. I do—that vision of you—"

With my hand planted on the desk and those parchment sheets, I saw a flash of moving images. A split-second scene.

Erzsebet standing by her daughter's decapitated head. That young teenage body lined up below, a cut of fabric tying the two together in place. Black blood was a messy track down that body, mingled with vibrant red. "Damn you, you coward! She would have lived!"

I didn't see who the Countess was screaming at as my sight returned to the Vladimir office. My quaking knees locked in place to keep me upright, my good hand keeping my balance as pain seared my healing one. As my mind raced over what I'd just seen and what it all meant, Kendrick saw the replay.

Erzsebet knew why the resurrection of her decapitated daughter and everyone else she'd tried to bring back had failed.

"Amelia, don't."

Kendrick knew my mind before my lips could announce my plan. His groan was voiced before my words, "Erzsebet's the key to everything and only she has the answers. To stopping Marcus. To bringing you back to life. To saving the damned. And I'm going to find her."

ALMOST AN HOUR LATER, I was cross-legged on the corner of the rug, leaning back into one of the four posts of my bed. My head was throbbing and my fatigued body needed the support. Surrounding me was a scattering of all the things that had once belonged to Erzsebet. Her journals, experiment notebooks, the resurrection reports I'd found written by her own hand. I gritted my teeth and squeezed my closed eyelids shut even tighter than they already were. The printed black and white photograph Kendrick had found of a young Caius in an experiment den with his mother was pressed between my palms.

"You won't get anything off that," Kendrick helpfully pointed out. He was far from on board with my plan to locate my damned grandmother and restore her so I could force her to reveal her resurrection knowledge. After all we've survived—sort of—he wanted to protect me. But even more than that? He had this unexplainable belief that only harm to someone else could bring him back.

I blinked away the black and glared up at him. "Nothing else has worked." So far, the journals and experiment books had provided zilch on the vision scale. Either my ability was on the fritz, or those black eel-like remnants just didn't want to play along. In the past, I'd always managed to bring on something, even if it wasn't the vision I was after.

"You know finding Erzsebet isn't a guarantee of anything other than you putting your life, and others"—his gaze shot to Raven and back—"in danger."

"Here, give this a go." Raven entered from the lounge and handed me the more recent photo she'd found of the group who'd attempted resurrections. At my staid expression, she shrugged. "I know it's not a belonging of hers, but at this point, anything's worth a try." She glanced to the place I'd been glaring at, seeing through Kendrick rather than looking at him. The hope in her eyes was almost pleading. "Right, Kendrick?"

In his ghostly form, Kendrick sighed and shook his head. "Guess I'm outnumbered. Not that that ever counted in the past."

Raven scooted back onto my bed while Kendrick ghosted into thin air. With the photo I clung to bringing nothing on, I let myself think of Ty. After my Erzsebet vision, I'd found newly filled bottles of his blood on my coffee table. In an attached note he'd said he needed to tend to wolf business and had taken off. Apparently, his father was visiting with damned info, and he was helping to set up a formidable team of wolves and vampires to scope out each lead. One task that he'd be assigning Troy as acting alpha to in his absence so he could keep watch over me. Although I didn't doubt the why of his absence, I had a feeling he was avoiding me. Trying to steer clear now that Kendrick was back—in a sense—and relinked to me. Not that he could stay away for that long. After the vision attempts, even though I hadn't brought on a single one, my need for blood was growing. These bottles wouldn't last forever.

"Do you need a refuel?" Raven asked, brows furrowed at me and nibbling one side of her bottom lip. "Or I can get Ty?"

I was sizing her up and hadn't even realized it. I shook myself. "Ah, no. I'm okay for now." Which wasn't a lie. Since she'd forced Kendrick's blood on me and reconnected us, the link to his conscience seemed to be boosting mine. Not enough to make me a non-threat, but enough to curb my desire to kill, at least so far. I refocused my energy from her neck and onto the photo. My lids slid shut and I welcomed the void back. Then I waited. And waited. Just like before, there was nothing—no shadowy eels, no sudden scenery change.

With a growl, I slammed the photo down on the stack of experiment books and shot up, pacing to my bedside. "This is bullshit. I'm getting noth—" I froze mid-sentence, seeing the way my sheets crinkled under Raven's crossed legs. Like when I'd shoved Ty back onto those same covers. At the sight of a drop of dried blood, I recalled that whispered female voice I'd heard—right after knocking Ty out with… "Erzsebet's jewelry box."

"Is that the same one in this photo?" Raven asked, scooting off my bed to pick up the photocopy of Erzsebet with Caius as a child.

"It is," Kendrick and I replied in unison as he reappeared. Though I was the only one who sounded glad at the fact. It was the same jewelry box Caius had sought. It had contained the concoction he'd needed in order to steal the power he'd engineered me to receive. And it was exactly what I needed. A personal possession the Countess had used and valued when she was alive. But that female voice? If Erzsebet was beyond damned and actually dead…

I grabbed the box with both hands and eased back onto the edge of my bed. My lids slid down—then froze and flung open from half-mast as a horrible chill climbed my spine. Through Kendrick's transparent and cut-up form, I could see a young teenage girl. With blond hair and red irises, she was as see-through as he was. And then she looked at me—no—through me. Her fangs bared and her hands came up, fingers tense like weapons as she pounced.

"No, stop!" I went to rush forward, to shove Kendrick out of the way out of instinct. But as he ghosted to my side, I froze. Not more than a foot off the ground, the girl in her conservative gown stopped short. A silent slice across her throat spurted black to one side. Her mouth gaped, no sound erupting—as her head tipped off her shoulders and her body fell.

The girl flashed from two transparent pieces on the floor to whole again. "Who are you?" I demanded, keeping my grip tight on the box. If I let go, this girl would vanish too, because that hadn't been a vision. And that girl sure as hell wasn't Erzsebet. What I'd just witnessed was the second this damned girl became a ghost. I had a strong suspicion on why she was linked to this item…

"Erzsebet's ghost…I thought she was damned?" Raven slowly backed away, eyes darting from me around the chandelier-lit room. "Is her ghost damned? You can't restore a ghost, can you?"

Kendrick glared, flashing his fangs at the threat he felt on a non-physical level. "That's not Erzsebet."

"It's not Erzsebet," I repeated for Raven's benefit. Holding the gold box out, I stepped closer to the girl. Despite my suspicion at her untimely death, and that medieval gown, not to mention her age, I wanted confirmation. I wanted proof. "Tell me who you are and how you're linked to this."

The girl's guarded expression shifted into something dark and sinister. She disappeared without warning. And then she was behind Kendrick, off the ground and clinging to his back. Her ghostly fangs claimed his neck and her young arms trapped his torso.

Kendrick hissed and reached for her arms, but never got there. Silver veins that glowed forked out over his skin and he collapsed to his knees. It wasn't the same as the veins that covered a restored damned, or even the ones that covered my skin as my hunger grew. These were above the flesh, being drawn from the inside out.

I lunged over the mess of books and papers to free him of her tangled hold, but my hands passed straight through them both. They weren't flesh and bone. I had no power to stop this.

"My essence—" Kendrick choked on his words. "She's draining —it."

"What's happening?" Raven cried out. She looked completely lost, sure something was terribly wrong but unable to see the horror unfolding. A freed dagger was clutched in her shaking hands as she stared from me to the blank space I watched.

"The ghost has Kendrick." I searched for something, anything that I could use to separate her hold on him. But I knew almost nothing about ghosts. Not how to control them, or how to… I stared down at the jewelry box in my hands. "I brought her here with this. That's what links her to the here and now." Without hesitation, I threw the piece onto my bed and the girl vanished.

Kendrick remained.

But the silver essence being drained from him didn't stop.

"What the hell?" I fell to my knees before him, so badly wanting to touch him in some way. To help. "Shit! She's not gone? What can I do? How do I stop her?"

"She—wants—you—" Kendrick's apparition began to flicker, my view of him turning on and off like a faulty light bulb. I never thought anything could top watching my twin snap Kendrick's neck, but this was about to match it. And I wouldn't stand by this time and do nothing.

"Amelia, what's she doing to him?"

I lunged for the bed and reclaimed the jewelry box.

"Is he dying? Amelia, talk to me!" Raven blocked my way and gripped my arms as I stalked back across the room.

"Move, before she drains his spirit." Raven was out of the way in a flash, but she didn't go far. The ghostly girl smiled around her fangs that were still embedded in Kendrick's neck. "You want me? I'm yours. But if you don't let him go, I *will* find a way to end you. Even if I have to die and hunt you down as a ghost. Don't think for a second there isn't anything I wouldn't do for him."

The girl slowly retracted her fangs from Kendrick's neck. She was smiling, mouth clean rather than bloody as the silver being drained from Kendrick dulled. She was still keeping a hold on him with her hands. Still draining sliver currents from him. But not to the point of killing his spirit. At least, I hoped that was why there was less being sapped from him, rather than it being because he was almost tapped out. He'd stopped flickering, so I took that as a good sign.

"Anything?"

I squared my shoulders. "Name it."

"Such a sacrificing nature you have." The girl's voice was almost musical, full of gentle innocence that rivaled the monster she'd just revealed herself to be. "So much like my mother."

"Erzsebet, right?" There was no doubt in my mind. And I wasn't waiting for offered confirmation this time. "You're her daughter. The one she failed to resurrect."

"Ursula Bathory. Nice to meet you, niece." She climbed off Kendrick's back and stepped to his side. The second her touch left him, he collapsed, twitching but still semi-conscious. She pointed to the amethyst-encrusted box I still held. "A gift from my mother… before she killed me."

That reenactment of her death had been how her own mother had decapitated and killed her as a damned. Erzsebet had hoped to resurrect her after the fact, but that initial attempt had failed. Well before the many others that had followed. After my vision, I believed Erzsebet had the answers we needed. She had to. And we would find her. Somehow.

"What does she want?" Raven demanded, fists clenched like she was imagining how much fun it would be to pummel this girl's face she couldn't see. To me she added, "Is Kendrick okay?"

"He'll be alright." I opened up my arms in invitation to the ghost. I didn't know what would happen to me, and right now it didn't matter. No matter the obstacle, the people I loved came first. Being a monster, being in transition or damned, or even dead, nothing would ever stop me from protecting them. "Do what you want. I won't fight it."

"I'm not going to hurt you, niece. And if I was alive, I'd take your power myself, if I could." She came closer to me, staring up at me in defiance. "I can find Kendrick now that I've tasted him, no matter where in the world you take him. And I will kill him if you refuse. You want him alive? I want my family back. My mother and my sisters. You will find them and you will restore them."

I was taken aback at her demand. "You freaking psycho. You almost killed Kendrick for that? I was planning to hunt down and restore Erzsebet anyway. That's why I'm here trying to bring on a vision." I motioned to the mess of journals, experiment books, and sheets of parchment paper. "All I need to know is where I can find her."

"Not just my mother. My sisters, too. You will restore them all. That is the deal. Accept, and I will lead you straight to them."

They were all together, and she knew where they were. There was no point to her threat if she didn't. But to restore them all? To do so without any getting away, they'd have to be back-to-back. I'd only ever done one at a time, and even then I'd needed hours between to recover—and to refuel my power on Ty's live blood. If I had any chance of pulling this off—and saving Kendrick's ghost from annihilation to even get to possible resurrection—I couldn't do this without Ty.

"Tick-tock." Ursula went to kneel beside Kendrick's still-twitching, transparent form.

"We have a deal."

At my curt nod she smiled wide. "We're going to need a plane. Oh, and niece? If you fail to restore them all, I *will* finish the job on Kendrick. That is a promise."

CHAPTER 25

I hugged my arms around me, feeling a chill that had nothing to do with the cool pre-twilight morning air. Having finally arrived in Cachtice, Slovakia, I should have been amped with anticipation. But the town had been abandoned, flyers in windows reporting of monsters that had been picking people off gradually and without warning. I turned away from our rental car, ditched on the side of the quiet road to keep our arrival unknown, and gazed up the mountainside ahead of us. "Why would she go back to that?"

Above this valley of beautiful weathered houses and buildings, stood the expansive ruins of the Cachtice Castle below a fattening moon. Erzsebet's old home, where she'd lived, lost her children, and become damned. With crumbled towers and arches, the place looked uninhabitable—even from all the way down here.

"It's our home," Ursula answered, young cloudy eyes wide with wonder at the sight. "So long as no one's tracking them they always come back. I could see myself flitting around bends and flying out of windows"—she nodded to the amethyst jewelry box I held—"if you could hide my tether there when we're done. I'd love to terrorize tourists for an eternity or two."

"It's been vacant for over a century." Almost hovering as he walked beside me, Kendrick looked uneasily from the talisman to our spectral tour guide. "If they always come back, why did Caius never find them?"

Ursula ignored the accusation in his tone. "My mother is crafty. If she had wanted to be found, she would have been."

"Then how do you know she's here now?" he rebutted, sensing a trap he shared with me through our bond.

Ursula smiled and shrugged, full of innocence. "I can feel them."

With nothing else to go on and the threat this thirteen-year-old ghost posed to Kendrick, we had no choice but to trust her—all the while hoping we weren't about to walk into our planned deaths.

Ty appeared around a bend up ahead then, and jogged over. Dressed in all black that hid shiny weapons from any humans that, evidently, wouldn't be a problem, he looked ready to kill. And as he glared at the jewelry box I replaced in Kendrick's Burton backpack over my shoulder, he looked just as ready to protect, even from all he couldn't see. "Everything okay?"

With each step closer to me on the gravel road, the return of his beating heart and scent of his blood grew stronger. "Yeah…"

After borrowing one of the Armaya's private jets some thirty-plus hours ago, stashed bottles and Kendrick's linked conscience had kept my urges below the tipping point. But being fully charged, especially on this mission, had been unavoidable. Feeding from Ty's wrist just before vacating the Armaya's private jet had sated my ever-growing hunger and strengthened my body and ability. It had also turned what had been hot and off-limits into a seriously uncomfortable situation. Having Kendrick present and fully visible when my last feed started? Yeah, great reality bombshell. Him going ghost right after my fangs bit into Ty's flesh, just proved how much we hadn't sorted out since my betrayals and his payback with Raven. And now the hour-long car trip to this small town, while having to connect on and off with Ursula's ghost, had sapped my earlier boost. My hunger was on a steady rise. But hell if I was going to make any announcement on that issue right this second.

"There's an old track that'll keep our approach from sight until we arrive," Ty said, breaking the silence. He glanced around as if wondering where Kendrick was in relation to me.

His cheeks were flushed and his breath was slightly elevated. Like he'd followed the track as fast as possible so he could get back to me. Those chiseled pecs strained against his muscle shirt as his breathing slowed. With his scent exacerbated by his body heat, I could almost taste him on my tongue. The quick images in my head were far from innocent: flashing gold eyes, and parted lips, reddened from rough kisses. I forced myself to look away, and paused at the sight of Kendrick. And not because he'd vanished at my inappropriate thoughts. Still with his chest bare and all those wounds, his ghostly form was even more transparent than usual. "Kendrick, are you—"

"I feel strange," he said, peering down at his hand as his fingertips started disappearing.

Ty's hand hovered over the dagger at his waist. "What's happening?"

I gulped, not wanting to voice my suspicion in fear that it'd come true. "Kendrick's beginning to fade…" I went to snatch the jewelry box from the backpack. "If Ursula's doing this—"

"She's not."

A gentle buzzing stalled my retrieval, and then Ty whipped out his phone and hit accept on the call. "Troy, what's— He did what?

All three of you. And you can't find him anywhere. Tell Marika to keep looking. You catch up on the damned leads." Stabbing his finger into the screen, Ty replaced the phone in his pocket as he paced the width of the road, kicking at larger rocks. "Dorian tranqued them all."

"Troy, Marika, and Vanessa?" The three we'd left behind to keep an eye on him and pose as Ty and me while we escaped from the Armaya.

A stiff nod as his eyes flashed gold. "Dorian's MIA."

"Shit, this is seriously…" I trailed off, suddenly wondering why Ty's blood and beating heart had had such an effect when Raven was—

"Where's Raven?" Ty frowned past me as my head whipped around.

The road behind us was empty, nothing but tall trees with gentle-swaying branches. The houses further back were dark and silent, just like the whole abandoned town had been. "She was right behind me." There was no sign of movement, but then there was sound.

Appearing from around the trees lining a side road, Raven was thrust forward by her neck. "He—grabbed—me," she choked out, a cut closing along her bottom lip as a puffy bruise across her cheek faded to yellow. Her eyes were resolved and sorry at the same time.

Did she remember my threat when she'd first insisted on finding a way to resurrect Kendrick? *I won't miss a chance to finish this just to protect your ass*. She expected me to let her die? She was ready to accept that end—to give us a better chance of accomplishing what we'd come here to do—now that this obstacle of her being a hostage was tripping us up?

"I know you won't let her die." Kendrick's form returned in a blink right beside me, then flashed over to where Raven was struggling against—

The face that peered over her shoulder was far from a shock after Troy's call. Dorian. My brother and Marcus's personal puppet. The way his nails cut Raven's skin as he squeezed harder made me cringe. Dressed in all black, his deadly array of weapons glinted in the moonlight. A dagger was poised at Raven's side, a good chunk of the tip already embedded. "Hello, sister."

Pursing his lips, he let out a high-pitched whistle.

Warmth bloomed right behind me with a crunch of fast boots over gravel. Ty bared his canines and fangs in threat, shooting a glare at Dorian before returning his watch to our unexpected visitors. A quick count—twelve damned. "Let her go and I'll leave you in one piece. The damned won't be so lucky."

"With what you all have planned?" That voice sounded like Dorian's, but the inflection was all wrong. Marcus was full-on puppeteering my brother, forcing him to keep his strong hold on Raven. Forcing his fangs to slide out, long and deadly, in unmistakable threat.

I stood my ground, staring down my brother, clutching my dagger and a stake. My ears pricked, waiting to hear the sudden advance of the horde behind us. "You know why we're here, and... what? If we abort, you'll let us live?"

Dorian smiled like he thought we were going to make a run for it and sacrifice Raven in the process. "Not quite, sister." The damned stared at him rather than us, tensed and ready to pounce, restraining themselves in wait of his command. "Though stopping you all is only half the fun." His brows jogged at his entourage. "Hunt down and kill the Countess. Now!"

Our one hope at resurrecting Kendrick without me bonding to Marcus. "Shit, Ty—"

"I'm on it."

And then he was gone, through the trees and after the damned.

With a leveled stare at Raven, I nodded my head almost imperceptibly. She hiked her chin up and her eyes flashed as if to say, *get going already. I've got this.*

"No, don't leave her." Kendrick blocked my way as I turned to sprint. We both jerked as Raven cried out, that blade delving deeper into her side as she began to fight back. "He'll kill her."

But I couldn't make that choice. Ty was taking on eleven, and Kendrick's future—his very existence in any form—was at stake. If Erzsebet died, that ghost would finish him off. "I'm sorry, Kendrick," I said as I kept on right through his form that attacked my body with shivers. *Just stay with her,* I added through the bond. *I'll try to get back in time.*

A strangled expletive in Dorian's voice reached me as I flew through the trees, and I guessed Raven had turned the tables to hit him where it hurt. The fear I felt for both of them was short-lived though, because before I knew it, I was in the thicket of trees below the cliff's sheer face—where Ty cornered the group of damned and flung his utility belt from his waist. I launched the backpack into a bush as Ty's body beefed out with a series of cracks. His muscle shirt and jeans ripped as hair erupted, his body expanding and reshaping into a magnificent black wolf. For the briefest moment, I reveled in the sight, awed to see this side of him when he was on my team and not the enemy's.

But then our time was up.

The damned hissed as I abandoned my dagger and unraveled my whip. "Back down now, and I might restore you—if I have enough juice, later."

I wouldn't. In the past, more than one a day had drained me past exhaustion—and turned me from 'almost in control' into 'stark-raving killer.' But maybe we could restrain and transport them—I almost wanted to punch myself. Kendrick's conscience—not his actual wants in this situation because Raven won out over any damned, but his innate sense of right over wrong—was messing with my head and distracting me.

"Orders are orders," one damned spat. "The wolf dies and then the Countess."

"You'll be coming with us," another one finished.

The growl from Ty's bunching muzzle was pure death threat that said without words, *not on your life.*

The damned went to run, and Ty launched into action. Jaw wide, he clamped onto and ripped out one damned's throat and wheeled around to paw-drop another before the rest could get a jab in. At the same time, I sent my whip sailing. The long length circled low around the legs of three damned, inch-long silver spikes jutting out as I flicked my wrist. There was a ping and sizzle as skin was punctured and anklebones were struck. A tug took them off their feet.

Dropping the butt as I leaped, I ignored the black spurt of blood coming from Ty's direction as a damned lost a leg. Freeing a second stake mid-air, I plunged both in deep as I landed on the trio. Ash puffed up from either side of me as the piggy in the middle caught and squeezed my neck. Guess he hadn't gotten the memo. "I don't need to breathe, you idiot." I nailed one stake in. The instantly smoldering body singed my jeans and ate layers of skin off my kneecaps as I fell through the sudden ash remains.

Jumping up and holstering one stake, I caught a better view of Ty. Three damned lay scattered, various body parts no longer attached. The leg I'd kinda seen. An arm. A head. Glossy black shone in the moonlight in puddles and across blades of grass. Fully engaged, the alpha was latched on to another damned's shin as it scrambled to scale the cliff face. More floored and bloody ones leaped up to make their escape.

I wasn't about to let a single one get to Erzsebet. With a

measured roll-kick, my whip became airborne and I caught the butt, ready to—

Kendrick flashed before me, and I could swear he was even more transparent than before. "Out of time. Raven. Shit, help her!"

"Raven's losing," I called through him in a rush.

Releasing his bite, Ty barked, snapping his jaws as his lips curled back. His massive wolf head jerked. Ordering me to go.

"But—"

He launched with a rebutting bark to reclaim the damned around the waist.

The decision was made.

And I didn't wait to see the outcome. Ty was the most deadly trained killer I'd ever encountered. He'd catch up to me soon. And right now I had to save Raven—she deserved to live after all she'd done. And alive or dead, Kendrick would never forgive me if I didn't.

Sprinting back through the trees, I found them—both still alive. But not for long. At the town outskirts where houses were scarce, both were injured, their clothes torn and stained with more than dirt. Sweet, rich *blood.* Raven was on her hands and knees as Dorian held her chin up, forcing her to look at him. Red streamed from her eyes, nose, mouth, and ears, disappearing as it soaked into the dark hoodie of Kendrick's she wore. I had been hungry earlier. Now, after hours of travel and fighting the damned…my steadily escalating hunger was something I didn't try to contain. Instead, I used the sight of all that red and both their leaking injuries like a tool to unleash the thing inside of me. I licked my bottom lip and my fangs dropped from my gums. I had a plan.

"Took your sweet time."

I almost jumped out of my skin when Kendrick appeared right

beside me. "We need to have a talk about you ghosting in and out like that."

"They've almost killed each other ten times over already." He went to shove me toward them, but his hands went straight through me. "Do something already."

"Already on it." I sprang as Kendrick caught on, and called out, "Amelia, don't!"

Not seeing me coming, I landed on Dorian's back and tugged his head to the side. My fangs plunged into his neck as he jerked in surprise. Rich blood flooded my mouth and I sucked hard. Raven half collapsed and scampered back on the road, screaming something at me that I no longer cared to hear. Dorian fought back, clawing over his shoulders to try to pull me off him. But even as he bucked and twisted beneath me, breaking my flesh, I didn't let go. Soon enough he lost momentum and slumped to his knees. His pulse became all that registered in my ears. Boom boom. Boom boom. Boom…boom.

I was going to stop. Really, I was.

That had been the plan. With Kendrick's conscience now tied to my broken one, I'd been sure stopping was within my capabilities. But with each fresh draw on Dorian's vein, stopping just seemed more and more out of reach.

"Amelia." Kendrick's transparent form appeared, kneeling before us while I held my brother's body upright.

He'd lost consciousness? I cared. I wanted to care. *But you don't. He's linked to Marcus. End this now.*

"Stop, Amelia," Kendrick said in an even tone. "You did what you planned to. He's out cold. Too weak to regain consciousness anytime soon. He can't stop us from going after Erzsebet."

Erzsebet?

"Your grandmother." I felt Kendrick hesitate. But unlike me, he knew right from wrong, no matter the situation. Wanting me to forget my mission came second to me killing my brother. "You're going to restore her and her daughters…to resurrect me."

To save him, my soul's mate. To keep that vengeful ghost from draining his spirit before I even got the chance to bring him back to life.

Retracting my fangs, I slung quick arms around Dorian and hoisted him up as I got to my feet. God, I felt strong. And like every bit the monster I was as fresh guilt flooded me. It was my mother all over again. The time I'd almost killed her to feed my transitioning side. Before I'd compelled her away and to forget her children even existed. *Thank you,* I said wordlessly. *I never meant... I was going to...*

You had it in you. Your intentions were pure. You just need reminding, sometimes. Like his voice had done to save my mom from my deadly attack.

Without asking, I now knew all those instances had been him looking out for me from beyond the grave.

"He's not dead." Raven sidled up with caution, her color returning from grayish to vamp pale. The blood leaking from her had stopped. "Is he?"

"Just unconscious." *Thanks to you, Kendrick.* I fake smiled at her. "Thanks for not killing him, by the way." Before I got the chance to almost do it myself—bloody monster.

"He's your brother. I wouldn't do that." She nodded ahead, bloodshot eyes searching. "Where's Ty?"

As if summoned, Ty blazed through the trees, skidding to a halt on the gravel. No longer in wolf form, but unbuttoned jeans and a skewed white muscle shirt from the Burton backpack over his shoulder, it looked like he'd haphazardly dressed while running here. "I thought you had…" He eyed Dorian's limp body in my arms, ears twitching—to check for a heartbeat. His eyes rose to my bloodied face. “He’s alive.”

The black ash and oily blood that covered his skin stood out in stark contrast to that white material while defining the lines of his healing muscles. His labored breathing sent a thrill through me that I quickly shot down—because he’d raced here thinking I’d killed my brother. “Yeah…” I couldn’t hold his stare, hating myself for what I’d almost done as I felt my brother’s blood drying across my chin. “No thanks to me.”

“Dammit.”

Raven, who’d half limped past us, turned back at Ty’s curse. “What’s wrong?” Kendrick, who had been right beside her, looking over her healing injuries, ghosted into thin air. “You got all the damned, didn’t you?”

“No.” Ty’s next words were a growl. “I let the last few go.”

Before I could worry about Ty’s words—or that Kendrick had vanished for good—he reappeared before me in a panic. “Four damned. They’ve almost reached the castle—”

Distant cries and battle sounds erupted. The damned had found the Bathorys.

“Oh, shit.” I felt my world imploding as I froze like a deer in headlights.

Ty grabbed Dorian from me and threw him over his shoulder. The wind picked up and I heard rain racing in as dark, shifting clouds came our way.

“There’s a cave a bit up the track.” Ty went after Raven who’d taken off up the road. “Come on. We’ll stash Dorian and get the hell up there.” He ducked through the trees as I got out of my funk to keep in pace. “Raven, this way’s faster.”

Minutes we didn’t have later we’d stashed Dorian in the cave and flown up to the flatter mountaintop that accommodated the

Cachtice Castle. Up close, the degree of ruin was even more severe than it had seemed below. For the most part, there were no roofs or internal walls. The ruin was like a gravesite, leaving only a partial shell of what was once a huge stone castle. Shooting through a tall and cracked arch, we passed a soaring, roofless tower that had nothing but a hole to enter through. The Death Tower, from what I'd read on the plane. Where humans believed the Countess had drained virgins of blood. The sound of nothing but whooshing wind and nearing rain raised my anxiety as we all slowed. Eyes scanning, I felt the fear of arriving too late. Were the damned about to take us out too?

With weapons at the ready, we entered the open space of sand and dirt and shrubs that was clearly part of the human rebuild I'd read about. A four-level length at its highest point had added wooden railings above the first floor to peer down to the ground. The humans had built a sort of arena to stage swordplay before deciding the site wasn't as it seemed. Haunted, according to countless reports I'd read during the long flights here. Tours no longer ran here. The rising toll of unexplained deaths and disappearances had made sure of that.

But none of that mattered. None of it even really registered as a break in the gathering clouds shone moonlight down on the sight. Four bodies lay scattered all dressed in the damned's usual dark and long-covering clothes. Black blood sprayed like jets from the severed necks of two, one cutting off as the other petered out with a gurgle. "That's not the Bathorys."

Ty flipped a stake and pointed it to a pile of rocks—no, not rocks —*heads*. "And this isn't over. We're not alone."

CHAPTER 26

"Two visits in such quick succession." We spun to the source of the voice. The thirty-plus-looking woman exiting through the door-sized hole in the base of the Death Tower was exactly who I'd wanted to see. Erzsebet Bathory. My grandmother. With her blond hair, gray skin below a disheveled, black medieval gown, and blood-red eyes that watched us like a hawk. Her lace-covered arms went wide, almost in a show of invitation. "So long since we've had supernatural company."

A teen that was a year older than me from what I'd researched on the flight, leaped over the man-made railing of the second level down to us. She nodded over her shoulder. "Yes, kill the rest."

Except there was no one there. After centuries of being damned, that had to be a sign of insanity. But as my grip tightened on my dagger, I was more amazed by the fact that Ursula had been right. About their location. About them being together. We had two of her three-piece must-be-restored puzzle.

"You're Anna, Erzsebet's daughter."

A girl emerged down the stairs centering the long watching platform. Nine-year-old Katalin. "Pure Blood offering. Kill them. Yes, cat and mouse. Playtime. Make them red. Lick them clean."

I controlled my shudder at the young girl's words. She may have been alive for centuries, damned for all but nine years, but she looked as innocent as any child—if you ignored the hungry stare and lengthening of her fangs.

"Stick to the plan." Ty withdrew identical daggers from his utility belt so he held one in each hand. The aim was not to stake anyone into ash. He dropped the Burton backpack, which thumped with the jewelry box inside.

"Fresh meat, delivered right to our door." Erzsebet smiled coldly. "I believe we're having a feast tonight, girls."

"How is she not crazed like her daughters?" Raven whispered to me, holding her weapons tight as she navigated around the fallen stones from the crumbled ruin to back up to me.

Having been damned for close to a century, Raven must have experienced the loss of coherency that came with each full-consumption kill.

With unrivaled hearing, Erzsebet offered the answer. "An elixir before I damned myself." She paused, seeming to judge my non-reaction before adding, "My kin were not so fortunate."

They'd already been damned.

The three began to circle us with slow steps, blood-red eyes sizing us up.

Close enough to scent his blood and hear his heart pumping adrenaline-fueled blood throughout his body, Ty spoke, "We have an offer for you." He holstered both blades as if to make a point. "One that will give you everything you once wanted."

The Countess's brows arched while her lips pursed in curious-tinged amusement. Her daughters hissed, their clear need to attack held back by their mother's halting hands.

When she didn't question the offer, I laid it out. "I can restore you. All three." Wind started to whip and I was glad my long hair was plaited back. The rain was almost here.

"Feed. Kill," the girls rasped, edging closer.

"You speak lies. There is no way to restore us," Erzsebet said with finality, though I saw a slight shimmer to her reddened stare as she eyed Ty and Raven and the black veins that covered their skin. A flash of sadness? Regret? Whatever it was turned to anger. "Tricks. Which would matter not. We will not trade our immortal strength for your false promises. Tonight…" Her bone-white fangs slide free as gentle raindrops pattered down from above. "…we feast."

"I'll keep Erzsebet out of the way. You and Raven round up the girls." Ty edged closer to my grandmother. "Then I've come to take you down, old bag. Think you can take a hybrid?"

The rain blew in harder then, soaking all six of our bodies. No one seemed to even notice.

Erzsebet's smile was as bright as her gaze. "I have centuries on you, whelp. And I've never lost a fight." She moved with blurred speed, capturing Ty by the throat. Throwing him over the railing, he sailed through the opening into the rebuilt first level. Then she was gone, inside the dark as a grunt and thwack sounded.

I hesitated for the slightest moment. I couldn't make out what was happening in all that dark from down here. But I knew Ty. He could hold his own. And right now, I had a job to do.

Raven was already on Anna. She tracked her to leap over and dodge around ruin stone piles. They met on the rebuilt length of open floor that plunged down into treetops. An area for human swordplay. Which would soon enough see real blood. Lashing out with her dagger rather than her stake, Raven stabbed to cut flesh.

The aim was to weaken and debilitate. Not eliminate.

Nine-year-old Katalin smiled at me. "Time to play." And then she was right in front of me. Her small hands gripped my waist and slammed me onto my back. I gritted my teeth at the rocks I'd hit. If I hadn't been turning damned myself, I'd have been winded.

Which she realized as I struck up and cracked her in the nose. Stumbling as I winced, she bared her fangs, black dripping over her lip. "In transition," she hissed as her tense fingers twitched at her sides. "Not for long. We make her dead."

I lashed out as she sprang at me, clocking her across the face. I cringed at the sound of a crack. I never imagined I'd have to fight a child. Not that she was any less of an opponent. Before I got another hit in, she was up and kicking my feet out from under me.

Her small nails clawed into me, and I sliced at her arms. Her skin sizzled and I smelled a stronger punch of her leaking damned blood. As I kept up the fight, hers wasn't the only blood that stained the rain-cloaked air. There was mine, from her claws and her petite fangs as she broke my flesh over and over. And now? There was Raven's.

Back bent over the arena's edge and drenched, Raven was seconds from plummeting over the edge and down that sheer drop-off.

In my distraction, my back hit the rise up to the platform. Katalin bit into my side and damn her small body was strong. But I had one thing going for me. In transition, her bite didn't weaken me with the injection of venom. Only my blood loss was doing that.

But we weren't winning. As Anna snapped, trying to strike flesh while Raven held her off with her blade, we were failing. My voltage was a no-go to give us both the upper hand. I needed to contain it. To save it. Which meant things had to get a lot messier. I knew what we had to do. It was our only chance. And they would heal. So long as I succeeded.

Not bothering to tear Katalin's fangs from me, I raised my dagger and drove it down. It plunged two inches into the base of the girl's neck and came free with a well of black. As her fangs disengaged with a shriek, I threw the blade. Tip over hilt it hit my mark—Anna's back—as Katalin stumbled off me.

"Sever the arteries!" I screamed through the pelting rain that had fast turned the dirt to mud. "Biggest to smallest."

Raven was bloody and gasping as she butt-planted off the railing. Still, she leaped up with a split-second nod my way.

Freeing another dagger, I followed my advice as Katalin hissed and came at me again.

Raven got with the program, tugging the blade from Anna's back and stabbing down her forearms.

I picked up my game too, and rolled sideways when a small foot booted into me. My dagger struck out, one, twice, hitting the thick artery in each of Katalin's thighs. As she hissed and came at me, her leap brought me down into the mud. With a stab to her stomach, she recoiled and I jumped up. As she clamped her gut, I punched the blade's tip into the other side of her neck. Then a long slice was cut across each of her wrists.

As Katalin's small body fell back, I caught her around the neck and lowered her onto the red-streaked mud puddle our grappling had created.

Being forced back from the arena, Anna bled streams of black from her main arteries. She teetered from blood loss, stumbling on wet rocks. She fell beside her sister with a splash.

Raven gasped for air like she was breathing underwater. "Didn't think…we'd make it."

With enough room between their twitching bodies, I prayed I

had it in me to pull this double restore off. I palmed two stakes and they sizzled against my skin. But vamp-friendly with rubber grips wasn't an option here. I'd never done this before, but it had to work. Waiting to restore all three individually would take too long. It would risk them repairing enough to get another chance in to kill us, or more likely, give them a chance to escape. The static I'd been holding at bay surged from my chest to my shoulders and down each of my arms. I lifted my hands high and fell to my knees. Forcing the electricity into the silver lengths, I drove them both home. Blue light exploded out from both stakes, pulsating the air and blasting out the steadily falling rain.

Over the sound of the downpour, two bodies colliding brought my head up. Through the opening to the rebuilt level, I saw the horror unfold. Ty, white muscle shirt blotched red, was slammed onto his back. Right on top of him, Erzsebet went for his jugular—and hit her mark without a fight.

"Stay with these two," I said, jumping up to leap up the stairs and inside. My vampire night vision came alive, not needing to adjust too much with how dark it already was outside. I hurdled the litter of wood, cloth, and stone. Clawing into Erzsebet's arm, I launched her aside to get to Ty. He was still as death. "No, not again." But then I saw his face frozen in strain, not slack with lost muscle control. My hand went to his chest as I scanned over his body. Bruised and bloodied. My palm came away red, and it took everything in me to think past my lust for his blood, past my grinding hunger after that double restore. "Oh, thank God." He was alive. His pulse was strong and steady, irregular like any other lycan. I had a hunch. But…

Needing the space fast, I shot across the skeleton of old rock piles that had been left and furniture that was now obliterated debris, stumbling from hunger-drained equilibrium. Erzsebet lay where I'd thrown her. Draped over the top half of what was minutes ago a velvet chaise, she wasn't breathing. Not a surprise, since she was damned. Not a temptation for the same reason. I lifted her lids and found her pupils weren't dilated. She was awake…but somehow not.

"What's going on?" Raven's voice sounded over the pouring rain. "Is Ty alive?"

Racing back to Ty, Kendrick appeared beside me, making me flinch at his sudden presence after being totally ghost throughout the battle outside. "I was there," he said quickly. "I didn't want to be a distraction. He won't wake up?"

I glanced from Ty back to Erzsebet. There was only one answer to explain all of this. "Ty's trapped Erzsebet in a dreamscape."

"Why would he do that?" Raven winced as she appeared through the doorway, drenched to the bone. The smell of her spilled blood reached me now that the rain didn't separate us.

"To give me a better chance at restoring Erzsebet." I stood up and swayed. The drain of the last two restores had just hit home, not to mention the smell of hers and Ty's blood. My knees buckled, and my bones felt like jelly, but I refused to go down. I gritted my teeth, a tinge of red staining my sight. "Why aren't you watching the other two?"

"Their hearts started up, but they're still unconscious. I dragged them onto the platform, out of the rain." Raven eyed my arms, forcing me to notice the growing black veins across my skin. "How long can Ty keep her out for?"

I shook my head and hissed around my throbbing fangs. "Not long enough for my power to recharge."

"Not in the state you're in," Kendrick added. "You need blood—" He made a choking sound, hands going to his spine-jutting neck, mouth gaping but no words coming out.

And I knew why. "Ursula, no!"

"What's happening—oh, shit! That effing ghost." Evidently Raven guessed the same from my words and total fear, even though she couldn't see the spirit either. "She wants Erzsebet restored, doesn't she? She's killing Kendrick."

"Ursula, listen to me." There was no time to answer Raven. I spoke in Kendrick's direction as his legs quaked. My stomach roiled with growing hunger. "I'm too weak. If I try now, I could kill your mom." And everyone else with a pulse, which now included the two damned I'd just restored.

"Amelia, heads up!"

I saw and caught Kendrick's Burton backpack as it flew through the air at me. Kendrick fell to his hands and knees as I tugged the gold box free. Ursula appeared instantly, hunched over Kendrick and sucking the life of his spirit into herself through her hands.

"Didn't you hear me!" I screamed, baring my fangs. "I can't freaking do it."

Ursula sneered at me, flashing her own dental attractions. "My mother will run if she comes to." Kendrick began convulsing, the ghost now holding his frame in her thirteen-year-old grasp. "So you'd better find a way. Before it's too late."

"We need to destroy this box." I was making things up, praying that if I wrecked this box Ursula's spirit would have no tether to the Earth. "Melt it or something."

"There's no time." Raven was suddenly beside me in the rubble and the scent of her blood soared as she bit into her wrist. "Recharge on me. I know you planned to use Ty, but I'm restored too. This is the only way."

The image of her going limp in my grasp seared across my frontal lobe. "I—" I stopped my argument. Raven was right. This was the only way. Even as I resisted, my mouth watered and my stomach squeezed. The red in my vision flourished. But then my eyes met Kendrick's, feeling a surge of his conscience like a shot through my quieting heart. "Release Kendrick now. My bond with him is the only thing that'll keep me from losing myself. If you kill him I'm as good as damned. Just like your mother will stay."

The streaming silver from Kendrick dulled to almost nothing. Ursula wasn't letting up completely, but she wasn't trying to snuff out his spirit anymore. "Hurry up, then. Before I lose my patience."

I struck out and caught Raven's bleeding wrist, plunging my fangs in deep. She cried out for only a second, then stood her ground as I drew deep from her vein. Delicious seconds passed as the rain eased up. Moonlight returned outside, filtering through small holes in the walls to light the dark room.

When Raven staggered, I bit in harder, dropping with her on the dirt and debris as her head bobbed. "Is it enough yet?" Her voice sounded dreary, half asleep.

"Amelia," Kendrick croaked, still on hands and knees below Ursula. "You can stop. You need to. You're killing her now."

Kendrick was right about the last two points. Her heart had slowed as mine surged back to full life. The pulse of her blood had become an almost undetectable blip every few seconds. Her breathing hitched like her body was trying to compensate for the lack of oxygen that circulated it. And he was right about the first point too. I could stop. For the first time, I actually *wanted* to stop. Before I reached the point of no return. Before I damned my soul.

I disengaged my fangs from Raven's wrist and dropped the jewelry box to catch her drenched body in my arms as she tipped.

She smiled up at me. "Am I dead?"

I couldn't help smiling back. "No. You did great. Just rest." I laid her down on a soft-looking pile of wood and foam, and stood up. Concentrating my energy, I gathered my voltage. A few sparks danced down my arms. "Shit." Not nearly enough. Fear rising, I snatched up the gold box. "I tried. But it's not enough. Please don't kill Kend—"

"Use the hybrid." The thirteen-year-old ghost sneered at the only other person with a pulse who wasn't tapped out.

"Ty's the only thing keeping your mother knocked out." I dodged over the rubble, seeing red—and not because I was still hungry. Sight clear and black veins retreating, I was livid. "Don't be reckless. If I drain him, she'll wake up."

"Your hybrid can't keep that up. Not with the beating my mother will be dishing out in his dream trap." Brighter strains of silver began syphoning from Kendrick and he grated his teeth. "Get the timing right and you can do both. Don't try at all…" Ursula shrugged with stubborn indifference. "I'm sure you can fill in the blanks."

"You bitch!" I stalked forward, but froze as Kendrick cried out in agony. And what was I going to do anyway, argue with the ghost until she killed my soul's mate? I dropped the gold box. "Fine." I shot across the space, levered Ty's limp body up, and struck his jugular. I stifled a moan at the taste of him. Kendrick had seen enough inappropriate feedings since his death, he didn't need a front-row seat while he waited to see if he'd make it out of this or not. Plus I had a job to do. Focusing past his taste, I raised one hand, gauging the sparks that gathered slowly at first, and then sped up. Ty coughed, and blood spurted from his mouth. I'd punctured right through his throat? And what if weakening him like this trapped him in this conjured reality forever? But there was no turning back now, because Erzsebet was stirring. Draped over the half chaise and now coated in moonlight that streamed through the doorway, she groaned. Her legs shifted, making noise as they hit an unsteady pile of rocks.

Time was up.

I dropped Ty without care and catapulted across the room. I landed on Erzsebet, palming a stake I'd freed in my fly over. Blue voltage swarmed as my palm burned. It had to be enough. Either way I'd find out after—I plunged the silver tip in deep, hitting the mark and expelling every ounce of lightning I had in me. The resulting bright flare of light and pulse in the air was a good sign. A great one. One that had me landing on my butt as the stake came free to fall with a clatter.

And then I waited.

Off to the side was the proof of my destruction: Ty's and Raven's bodies littering the ruins of this once grand castle.

"Anything yet?" Kendrick called from over where Raven lay. In the moonlight, I could swear he looked even more transparent. But I didn't wreck his high now. Through the bond, I felt his relief at being close to Raven, felt his certainty that she was going to be okay and would come around soon.

Swallowing my worry for him, I listened, the sounds beyond a repetitious dripping outside and whistling wind that tunneled through the long rooms and corridors making my ears hum. No heartbeat. A grunt tore my head up from Erzsebet's face to find Ty staggering to his feet. With one hand on his neck, he used the other to hike up his muscle shirt to wipe the blood from his mouth. "Guess—" He stumbled over a mess of rocks and rotting furniture. Then he caught sight of Raven. Concern creased his bruise-fading face. "You took from her too?"

I didn't go into the down and dirty. It was done now. The coercion of a ghost no longer mattered. "I had to. One wasn't enough. She's okay though," I tacked on.

His ears twitched—no doubt hearing her weak but present pulse. His expression lightened with relief. Each stride my way seemed to return his equilibrium and strength. But when he reached me, I didn't miss the small sound he bit back as he knelt down on the opposite side of my grandmother. "It didn't work?" His gaze shot around. "Is Kendrick okay?"

Still right beside Raven, he remained unharmed and still visible. Did that mean…?

Boom…

Then ten seconds later… *Boom.*

The beats slowly sped up until there was one every second. Erzsebet's lids fluttered, pupils shrinking in the horizon-falling moonlight that streamed in. With sudden black veins forking out, her hand slid up her stomach to her heart where the skin was knitting back together. "What have you done?"

CHAPTER 27

Minutes later, I paced impatiently in the rebuilt dwelling, tripping every other step over annihilated furniture and rocks. Outside, I could hear quiet talking as my extended family reunited, but I didn't risk going out there. While Raven was handing over Ursula's jewelry box, Ty was hightailing it down the steep decline to our parked sedan. With twilight weakening the moon and bringing a pale hue to the horizon, I wasn't getting out of here without the pitch black of that trunk.

And yet, my clumsy steps weren't even mostly influenced by all of that. Kendrick stood by the open door to the platform, his transparency even more evident with the rising light. "You have to come to terms with the fact that what you're hoping for may not be possible."

Because after all we'd achieved, he was running out of time? My mouth parted to argue against his perpetual need to give up. But I didn't have the strength. As quiet steps neared from outside, I drew on what I did have left, so I could fight for what I wanted with the one person who had the means to deliver it.

Erzsebet strolled right past Kendrick, unaware of his presence. “You have achieved the impossible. You restored not only me, but also my daughters.” Her now maroon-chipped silver-blues searched my face. “Why? Who are you?”

The weapon she’d sought centuries ago to save her damned daughters and our race. “I’m Amelia Bathory. Your granddaughter. And I need your help.”

Erzsebet frowned as she stepped right in front of me, studying my every feature. There was no reunion of hugging and catching up. “My son, my dear Caius. He succeeded. My blood…you have the power I imagined.”

I held up my hand, letting the small blue strands I could conjure dance along my fingers. “Me and my twin. But that’s not important.” For right now, there was only one thing I needed from this young woman who was my centuries-old grandmother.

Gazing out at the long landing before the steep drop off, I heard an engine. My time was running out too. “Tell me how I can perform a resurrection. I know you almost succeeded. I know you know why your attempts failed. Why you couldn’t bring Ursula back to life.”

“You have The Sight too?” Erzsebet said with surprise. “And that is why I now breathe? Why my heart beats?” She turned away, strolling out onto the raised and sheltered area outside, looking out as the dark sky lightened further. She spun back around. “I am sure you will understand, *Granddaughter,* such precious information cannot be so carelessly passed around. Who is it you wish to bring back—for you should know, this is not a worldwide cheat for death. There are—”

“One of The Seven—since that’s all that is left of The Twelve,” I cut in as I rushed forward, but stalled beside Kendrick, eyes pricking from the impending sun's arrival. "Lord Baldassare. A worthy male our race needs. The last of his line."

"Then perhaps I could part with my knowledge." The calculation across her face filled me with unease, and with her next words, I understood why. "But information never comes cheap."

"I gave you your life back. Your daughters' lives."

The ancient-but-youthful Countess smiled with her eyes. "You did that for you, my dear."

The same way Caius had addressed me for so many years. I gritted my teeth, but my hiss cut off as Kendrick's form flickered.

"I'm just drained. I'll be okay."

Like hell. He was getting worse, and fast—and shrugging it off to keep me from panicking. Yet as my worry for him peaked, I knew there was no point arguing—even though I'd completed the job she'd tasked to her son centuries ago—I needed something, and she was the only being in this world that had the answers to my questions. Kendrick disappeared. "Fine! Whatever you want. Name your price."

Now that smile reached Erzsebet's rosy lips. "My dear son, Caius. I wish to see him."

Did she not know? I almost sighed as Kendrick reappeared, and prayed the next time he vanished wasn't for good. My words were fast. "Caius is imprisoned at the Armaya…" I told her everything. What he'd done, to me, to our race. What he'd been convicted of. Marcus's part in it all and who he was. "I can't bring him to you."

Apart from the security and the thought of breaking our laws to jailbreak a traitor, I didn't know if Kendrick would have that long.

Erzsebet's reply spared no emotion. "The royals will never accept me back at the Armaya with open arms. I was disgraced long before my heart stopped beating. And I have no wish to be trapped there."

A honk and the spinning of tires over gravel and rocks sounded. Ty was back and the strength of rising twilight was almost too much to keep my lids open for.

"So I guess you'll be sneaking me and me alone in and out. My daughters will remain here where they are safe. Do we have a deal?"

Her black-veined hand appeared before me as my eyes watered with red tears. I took hold, despite Kendrick's internal, *I don't think this is a good idea.* "We have a deal."

One I hoped we could pull off before Dorian and Marcus threw a spanner in the works.

I PACED in the foyer of my suite, running circles around the central table. After our long journey home, it was early morning twilight outside, and I was itchy as hell. Eight-thirty and we'd only just made it back before daybreak. A gentle glow snuck around the edges of the drapes in all the rooms that forked off the foyer. Not a direct danger with UV-tinted glass—unless the panes or terrace doors were opened. But sunrise wasn't the main reason I felt like I was walking on nails. I peered inside the sitting room again. Poised on a wing chair and redressed in a gown I'd pulled from my walk-in wardrobe was Erzsebet. The Countess—as she was once known—eyed me with unmasked skepticism.

I thought of my brother. In our departure, Ty had tranqued Dorian to make sure we had a few hours head start. To make sure he, on Marcus's behalf, didn't tip the apple cart and expose Erzsebet's return. With her wish to remain forgotten, dead and buried, the

RVC's knowledge of her would break my word to her. And give her a reason not to cough up her resurrection how-to.

And that was where my anxiety spiked from. My fear at coming so far and the possibility of losing our last hope.

A knock brought me out of my head and sent me wheeling around. I all but lunged for the door and cracked it open.

Right outside, Ty hiked his brows up. "Special delivery."

I almost sighed at the sight of him. Days of stubble and that look of fierce protection in his eyes—even ringed by those tired bags from not sleeping since we took off for Cachtice—was so inappropriate to be thinking about right now. Kendrick was playing ghost again, or so he'd been claiming since after those flickers had started. But that didn't mean he wasn't here. Invisible but present. I thanked God I sensed him now, as I glanced around and saw nothing. But that wasn't even half the point. Getting distracted when I had tracked down and restored a disgraced damned and brought her onto sacred vampire grounds without proper—or any—clearance? Yeah, smart move.

I mentally slapped myself and got with the program. Standing in the doorway, I lifted my chin with authority to the prison guards who stood behind Ty. "You will all remain in the corridor. The hybrid will guard the prisoner inside."

A nod of understanding was returned from the two prison guards. Then they stood aside to reveal Caius. In the same disheveled clothes that smelled of bleach, he looked as he always had, except for the hint of speculation that hardened his aged face. Chains prisoned his wrists and ankles, clanking as Ty strong-armed him into the foyer and shut the door. Into a surprise he had no idea was coming his way.

I took a fleeting moment to look him over. Seeing him now was almost strange. A four-hundred-year-old vampire with more mileage on his weathered face to prove it. And yet his thirty-something-looking mother was mere feet away.

"You requested my company, Daughter?"

For once I didn't cringe at the title. Guess I was accepting who I was and who he was to me. With my hunger quickly seen to before Ty had left to summon my father, my beating heart sped up with anticipation. The automatic breathing I'd been faking since returning kept up its measured pace. "I have something you need to see."

With the sound of our approach, Erzsebet spoke quietly. "Hello, my son."

Caius's eyes widened with wonder and his jaw gaped at the woman standing just in view beside the wing chair she'd risen from. "Mother?" He stumbled forward, forgetting his chains and almost tripping on the links. He went down like a brick to his knees. "Is—is this real?"

Coming into the room, I had to blink to believe my eyes. Caius's cheeks were wet. He was crying silent, disbelieving tears. "This is real. She is," I said quietly.

Caius spun up from his knees to his feet and then he was on me. Ty rushed in, but he stalled before ripping the old vampire away. Caius, my father, my flesh and blood, wasn't attacking me. He was hugging me. "Thank you. Thank you. Thank…you."

I pulled uneasily from his hold and stepped back. I didn't know if I would ever forgive him for trying to kill me, but I couldn't say now that I didn't understand why he'd tried to. "I didn't do it for you." He had been right in his statement after my forced move to the Armaya for the second time. In my plight to save Ty, I'd endangered the people I loved most. I'd helped get Kendrick killed. Love and desperation made you do extraordinary and dangerous things. And accomplishing the almost unachievable didn't come without consequences. "I did it for Kend—"

A knock at the door had Ty shooting over to crack the barrier open. "You were ordered—"

Dorian burst inside, followed by an army of guards armed with chains. "Seize the exiled Countess!"

My mouth gaped in shock. "Exiled?"

Erzsebet hurdled furniture to the terrace doors and threw the drapes and glass open. Unblocked light streamed in. My skin sizzled as rough hands captured my biceps and hauled me back. Barricaded between Ty's body and a slice of dark in the foyer between openings, the burn stopped. No one but Dorian had noticed. The guards were all over Erzsebet, chairs, side tables and lamps floored in their haste.

"Do not harm her," Caius spat as prison guards seized him. Chains clattered and swords were unsheathed. The fluttering of Erzsebet's gown quit, and her hands shot up. She was giving in.

"What the hell, Dorian?" I spat under my breath. We'd left him in Cachtice with little blood in his veins and tranqued out. We should have beaten him back here by hours—not minutes.

"You think I wasn't prepped for your antics if you foiled my plan." Again with that voice that was my brother's but so alien at the same time. Marcus's puppet. "Never make a move, unless you have a backup.

"He anticipated this," Ty rasped in my ear, keeping me safely behind his back as he faced my brother.

Manacles clicked loudly as they snapped tight around the Countess's wrists. Dorian clapped his hands, ignoring Ty's snarl. "Take Erzsebet to the boardroom. She's earned an audience with the rest of the RVC."

~

"THE EXILED COUNTESS, AS PROMISED," Dorian actually bowed from beside her before he entered the boardroom.

Erzsebet kept up her struggle against her captors and metal restraints, accusation in her stare that shifted from him to me as I passed through the open doors. I pulled to a reluctant stop just inside. I hadn't been able to stop the guards from dragging her down here, and now I was in deep shit. Uriel, Rasputin, and Strigon were all waiting, standing before their thrones with mixed looks of surprise and judgment. Despite the audience, I didn't bite back my words to my grandmother. "I didn't set you up. You have to believe me. I did all I could—"

"Amelia, what is the meaning of this?" Uriel was the one to speak, and the only one who didn't look totally pissed out of the three.

Ty kept close to my left, growling low in his throat. "We have the right—the freedom—to hunt down any damned leads. She's restored, one of your own."

"If we'd known you were seeking out the exiled..." Lady Rasputin lowered in her throne after Lord Strigon, lifting her chin in authority to the guards. "Secure Erzsebet Bathory. There is much to discuss."

"Her two damned daughters were also restored," Dorian tacked on as he passed close by the pulled drapes, letting slices of UV-blocked light through. A threat, because he could open those panes and expose me—or fry me at any moment. "They remained back in—"

"If you hurt them, I swear it'll be your last regret," Erzsebet seethed as four guards forced her back to the wall. Despite her thrashing, they managed to string her up from the bolts Uriel had been suspended from when damned. "Did you hear me. I will kill you—"

"Your threats are not necessary." Uriel crossed to the woman who'd used and experimented on her father, a hint of anger peeking through in the tight set of her shoulders beneath her green gown. "Your daughters were innocent before the damned turned them. Unlike you. They will not be harmed for your crimes. They are not stricken from our community. But there are things we must know." She turned back around to face the rest of us. "Please sit, Amelia. Ty, you may be excused."

"I'm not—"

"If you were crowned…" Dorian left the covered windows and moved to his throne, the one Marcus used to inhabit. "You'd have cause to stay."

I clenched my teeth at the words my brother would never actually say as I touched Ty's arm. "It's alright." Right now I wasn't a threat to anyone in this room. And so long as no one wanted fresh air, I wasn't in any immediate danger, either. "I've got this."

Ty's nostrils flared as he pegged my brother with a look that promised pain if he dared to mess with me. "I'll be right outside the doors."

With booted strides he left and the doors clapped shut behind him. I dared to enter the room further, taking my position at the table. Ignoring Dorian's drilling stare around Uriel, I looked to Erzsebet. She'd gone quiet but was seething as if planning someone's funeral. So much for my argument to release her restraints because she wasn't a threat.

Lord Strigon tore his gaze from Erzsebet to stare at me. He almost looked like he'd rather be getting settled for bed over attending this very late and impromptu meeting. "Where did you find Erzsebet and her daughters?"

"Cachtice Castle."

The lord gaped, and Uriel inhaled sharply. "You traveled there and back, all whilst restoring three damned to life."

Erzsebet smiled at me in less of a happy, but rather a cryptically pleased way. "She is even more powerful than I ever imagined when I began my experiments."

"Then your reason for going to such lengths must be great." Lady Rasputin made work of filling crystal glasses with blood and handing them out. "Pray tell, young heir, why restore them—*especially* her"—she sneered at Erzsebet—"the exiled Countess, after her experiments that led to Lord Aswind's untimely death? Not to mention every living soul in her God-forsaken castle she struck down the day she was damned."

I'd seen the aftermath of that event in a vision when Erzsebet had locked her only son away with the vials of her living and damned blood. A vision of the crimson-painted inside of Erzsebet's castle, strewn with broken, quiet bodies.

"Out of some biological need to reunite your shattered family?" Dorian said, glancing at me from around Uriel. His raised brows were almost curious, but the narrowing of his eyes was screaming, *keep your mouth shut.*

Like hell.

I rolled my shoulders back and looked to the others. They needed to know what I'd done and why. And once they knew, like when they'd forced me to restore Uriel, they'd do the same for Kendrick. He was one of us and The Seven needed its numbers back. *I* needed him back. "Erzsebet is the key to resurrecting Kendrick. I restored her and reunited her with Caius in exchange for that knowledge."

"Is this true, Erzsebet?" Uriel seemed more than skeptical, as did Rasputin and Strigon. "You have the means to reanimate a dead body back to life?"

Erzsebet flashed her fangs with a wide smile. “Now you want to know about my experiments. Oh, how the tables have turned.”

Lady Rasputin reared and threw her fist down on the marble top. “Enough games, Countess. Do you have the knowledge to perform this or not?”

“For a price.” Erzsebet jiggled her suspended arms, making her chains clatter. “The rest of my deal with Amelia. My freedom.”

“You killed my father!” Uriel was up and out of her throne, her calm control lost in raw emotion. With her face red, she bared her fangs at the Countess, the maroon chips in her eyes glowing like tiny embers. “You don’t deserve freedom.”

“Uriel is right,” Dorian said with a clap of his hands. “Freedom is not an option here. What would it say to our people? Any crime can be swept under the rug if the bribe is good enough?”

As I glared at my brother I almost wondered if Marcus was gauging whether he’d ever be forgiven for his many sins. But then I dismissed the thought. Someone who thought they’d committed no evil didn’t repent or request forgiveness.

“Perhaps we can come to a compromise.” Everyone in the room, including myself, gaped at Lord Strigon who pressed down the front of his suit jacket. “Your daughters were innocent. They will be left in peace. Allowed to come and go from our community, should they so wish. In exchange for your help in restoring Lord Baldassare, you will be allowed to live, and will not be executed. You will remain inside our walls in a cell alongside your son.” He glanced around the table to the rest of us. “What say you all? Can we vote to this?”

“I vote execution,” Dorian didn’t hesitate to say.

“I’m with Lord Strigon. No execution, Erzsebet lives.” Aside from my own agenda, I didn’t want to see anyone hurt. More than that, I knew leniency could be a Godsend. Erzsebet had once had good intentions, despite the lives she'd taken in her plight to save her family and our race.

"I second Vladimir's execution vote," Lady Rasputin tipped her head at Dorian. "We have been far too accommodating of late. I prefer the old ways."

When there was one vote left, I rose and touched Uriel's arm, causing her to flinch. "Your vote?" Now tied, Kendrick's very existence rested upon the vampire who'd had her father taken away from her way too soon. Not to mention the Countess's compliance if this did go our way.

With a deep and slow sigh, Uriel turned from her enemy and wiped an escaping tear from her cheek. "We must do this for Lord Baldassare. Agree to our terms, Erzsebet, or face execution. What will it be?"

Silent seconds went by as we all waited. Then Erzsebet lifted her head and nodded once. "As you wish."

UNABLE TO WAIT A SECOND LONGER, I all but ran through the torchlit corridors down to the cells not two hours later. Enough time for Erzsebet to be secured in her eternal residence and set up with my arranged deliveries. Which had given me plenty of time to fill in Ty, Raven, and even Vanessa. Now, with Kendrick invisible after managing a short stint of presence, I felt non-relinquishing desperation.

The knowledge that the sun was up and any care for my jetlag was pushed to the back of my mind. I could sleep when all my problems were fixed. And failing that? I could sleep when I was dead.

Now it was time to get the information I'd been promised. The information I prayed Erzsebet came through with.

Raven kept close beside me. "I can't believe you did it. Got them to revoke that death sentence. We're really gonna get him back!"

I'd kept up my end of the bargain and reunited Erzsebet with the son she'd tasked the almost impossible to, centuries ago. I'd brought her daughters back to life. And I'd voted to stave off her execution permanently—so long as she complied and kept up her end of the deal. But did she still believe I'd set her up to be caught?

Raven's hopefulness cracked as she glanced sideways at me. But as she spoke, I knew it wasn't for the same reasons. "He still doesn't want this, does he? For us to bring him back to life."

I couldn't help but think of Ty and Kendrick for the briefest second. The alpha had been pretty scarce since the shotgun RVC meeting. He'd only shown up to feed me his blood—from his wrist, while glancing away and saying nothing.

Kendrick had been ghost most of the time since then, too. What I did know for sure was that he was still against our next move in this massive game of chess. Bringing him back to life. Despite his quiet, I sensed his unfounded fear that doing so would come at a price too steep to pay. And if that fear was founded, his prediction of only life being able to reverse death? We both knew I'd pay that price. I'd do anything for him. Having both my guys alive was how it was meant to be. Deep down, I felt that in my marrow.

I sighed, still feeling that tightening of my lungs at the unwanted air supply. "Yeah. He's still against it."

"But we're still doing it, right?" Raven's hands came together as we kept on around a dark bend. "We're not backing out of this?"

Determination lit in my veins as we passed the guarded gate and descended down stone steps, my weapons clanking with my quick steps. Emerging into the circular room, I didn't waste any time. "Erzsebet's cell. Open it up."

As a guard with the keys moved to the door left of Caius's, I whispered to Raven, "Whatever it takes, I promise you this. Kendrick *will* live again."

Marching inside, Raven shut the guards out. The time had come.

Seated behind the wooden table I'd had organized, Erzsebet looked up from the scattered open books in front of her. The ones I'd found before tracking down the Countess, which included the stained and tattered resurrection reports Kendrick had unearthed from the Vladimir office. "All my resurrection experiments. It has been many a year since I conducted such a trial."

"Trial?" I came further into the room and placed two palms on the table opposite Erzsebet. My face suddenly felt fire hot, and I couldn't stop my fangs from sliding free. I'd hinged all my hopes on this woman, for Kendrick, for our race. And it was all for what? "But I saw it. You've performed resurrections. You know why they failed."

"If you can't tell us how to resurrect Kendrick, the RVC's deal is void." Raven stalked closer, maroon chips glinting in her fiery eyes. "You will be executed. I promise you—"

"What you seek? It can be done." Erzsebet glanced sidelong at the cot I'd arranged too, with fresh linens and a soft pillow. The chain around her ankle clanked, put in place so she couldn't ambush anyone entering. "You did all this, yes? You did not set me up."

"Of course not. I wouldn't risk—"

"I believe you." Erzsebet ran a hand down the open page of the new book before her that was filled with scrawling script and thick alchemist marks. The book that I'd had delivered along with the inkpot and quill beside her. "My trials revealed to me all the elements I needed to fulfill to achieve success. Recompiled for you alone to use." At my nod she added, "It can be done, but…"

"What?" Raven all but screamed. "Anything. We'll do anything!"

I nodded at Erzsebet's raised brows. "Anything."

"A vial of blood from a vampire transitioning into a damned is needed for marking. As is your voltage, Amelia," my grandmother stated as a matter of fact.

Had I just hit the jackpot? Both things I had at my easy disposal. "Consider it done…" I trailed off at the drop in Erzsebet's expression. "What?"

"A sacrifice is also needed." She slid her finger down the jagged bolt she'd drawn on the page. "The blood of a Pure Blood vampire to feed the deceased."

I shuddered at the word *deceased.* But I guess it was our reality. Though not for much longer. I was in transition, but my blood was still pure. "I'll do it. Use my blood."

Kendrick's voice rang out suddenly for only me to hear. "Amelia, no!" He appeared out of thin air behind Erzsebet as Raven skirted around the table to inspect the marks on Erzsebet's book. Terror had a hold of Kendrick's bruise-mottled and puffy face. "You can't do this. No one can. *Please*. It's not just blood that needs to be offered."

Then tell me what! My hand went to my heart, feeling the animated beats that still resonated beneath my ribs. The thought of leaving Kendrick as he now was metaphorically obliterated the vital organ like I'd just been blasted by a shotgun. *Tell me why I should leave you to rot away.*

"Ask your grandmother. She knows exactly what's needed."

I cleared my throat, interrupting the chatter across at the table. "The sacrifice, tell me exactly what I need to give…" Hearing Kendrick's prompt in my head, I added, "And what the result will be when I do."

"The offering must be without force or trickery." Erzsebet turned a page and tilted the book up to press it to her chest. "If the sacrificer changes their mind before the completion of the ritual, it will fail. That I learned on many an attempt. That glitch led me to seek curing the damned over this. One's own preservation of life is never so strong as when it is almost extinguished. The fight for survival is ingrained in all of us."

"Preservation of life?"

Raven peered up with glassy eyes, her pale face ashen. "Kendrick was right. Every drop of blood is required. To bring him back, the sacrificer must die."

I juggled with the notion of my life coming to an end. Not hesitating because of all the things I'd miss out on when gone. The rest of my immortal life that would be vacant of Ty. The possibility of having Kendrick alive, safe, and seeing him happy. But rather, grappling with how I'd free my brother from Marcus and stop the damned if I was no longer flesh and bone. Would Raven, Ty, and Vanessa take over the fight? Maybe. But there'd be no guarantees. Unless I bonded with Marcus first. With Dorian free and my life set to end, hunting Marcus down would no longer pose a threat to anyone. There'd be no reason to hold back. I felt my resolution at coming to grips with a reality I was ready to set in motion.

"Amelia, God, no."

As Kendrick flickered beside me, I knew I was making the right choice. The only choice. "If that's what it takes."

"Wastefully admirable." Erzsebet actually looked proud of my stubborn selflessness. Guess when it came to sacrificing ourselves, we had something in common.

"Death is not black and white." Wheeling around I saw Vanessa holding in her quivering hands that original resurrection report Raven had found. She'd taken it from my suite before I'd collected everything else to be sent down here? With even breath, it was clear she hadn't run here. She'd been eavesdropping. "You can still live."

"What?" After coming to terms with my inevitable death, I felt like my head had just gone full circle and my brain was no longer in operation. Asking why she'd taken that report without telling me no longer mattered. Had I just heard that right?

Raven was across the cell in a flash and snatched the report from Vanessa. "You've highlighted that line: 'One being was reportedly resurrected to a state of living. The other was damned.' What does it mean?"

"If we have damned blood and a vial of venom, the sacrificer can become damned too. Right at the point of death."

Raven shook her head. "You can't do it, Amelia."

"Why not?" Vanessa questioned as Kendrick said, "Raven's right." No longer flickering beside me, his fading fingers reached out to almost touch my elbow. "You're already in transition for one. And even if that's not a problem, you'd be fully damned without taking life. You'll never restore yourself after that—if you even still can. You'd be worse than dead."

Vanessa's narrowed gaze widened as if she'd just realized Kendrick was talking to me. Her lips parted like she was mentally piecing together what the problem could be. "It can't be done without the sacrifice. Life for a life, right?"

Erzsebet nodded back at the alchemist, lips tight.

"I can do it."

My head snapped sideways as Raven stepped back, sight unfocused as her head lifted to stare blankly.

I knew what those three words meant even without an explanation. "Raven, no. Aside from needing a Pure Blood, you've only just started living again. You shouldn't have to—"

"I want to." Eyes refocusing like lasers, she walked right through Kendrick to grasp and squeeze my hands. "My blood's pure. Traces back to more than one line. Besides, I know what it's like. I've been damned before. I won't back out during the ritual. I won't change my mind. And after, you can just restore me when it's all over and done with. It's win-win."

Her argument was solid, the process fault proof. "Are you sure?"

"Absolutely."

I strode to the table, palms pressing into the rough wooden top. "Can this loophole work?" I didn't doubt Vanessa's idea, but I needed a vote of confidence from the one woman who had the most knowledge on all things damned and dead.

"I believe it will." Erzsebet gave a stiff nod. "Though if time is an issue, you should know…the moon will not be full beyond tomorrow. A powerful requirement to evoke this ritual." She handed over the book she'd laid it all out in.

Taking the offering, I turned. There was too much to do and so little time. "Let's get—"

Kendrick flashed between Raven and me. "I don't like this. Something doesn't feel right. Hold off, at least for a week or so. Double check everything that's been said."

It had already been too long since Kendrick had died. And I wasn't risking his very existence for the next thirty days. *I will, but only until the moon is full. This* is *happening.*

Raven noticed my frown at the vacant space beside us and cleared her throat. "Kendrick, I'm sorry, but I'm doing this whether you like it or not. You can hate or thank me when your back. That's your choice. And this is mine."

CHAPTER 28

"Never thought I'd volunteer for this again." Troy growled as he shut the cell door behind him, wearing only a muscle shirt, shorts, and not a single weapon.

"You're a hero, babe," Marika said with a smile. In her hand she held a long length of cloth. "And I've got your back."

Having returned from damned leads where they'd discovered Marcus's victims were mostly homeless, the single snarling damned suspended from chains across the barely lit cell made sense. Caught on our blood-draining mission, its bare feet and inside-out, torn T-shirt fit the profile.

No wonder the leads had been hard to come by.

But that wasn't why we were here now. With my utility belt secure, my palms perspired and my animated heart raced as I looked over the fully silver stakes. The time it had taken to get this course of action RVC approved left me feeling like I had an erupting volcano to scale. After the fact? Hell yeah, I regretted following protocol. After getting what we needed from this damned to ensure Raven's sacrifice didn't kill her, I still needed to fully recharge to be ready for the main event. To be ready to bring Kendrick back—before it was too late.

But I wasn't alone in this.

Fully informed, Ty stood by the damned. From his leather jacket came an empty syringe. The sharp needle tip glinted as it caught the bulb's light centered on the stone ceiling. Clutching the damned's jaw, he turned the male's head and held it there as the damned struggled. "Looks like you won the second-chance lottery." His intense eyes shot to me with a look of mixed respect and concern. "Today you get to live."

I nodded my readiness, Marika backed up to the door, and Troy came to stand a few feet in front of the damned.

Game. Set. Match.

Ty jammed that sharp tip into the damned's neck. The damned thrashed with renewed force, but I didn't falter. With speed, I used the key to unlock its ankles, then dodged sideways to escape a kick to the face. Then I jumped up. Ty yanked the black-filled syringe free and clocked the damned in the cheek. Those wrist shackles were released as his head righted itself. Then Ty's arm hauled me aside—

Right as the damned leaped.

Flattened to his back, Troy's lungs expelled air. The damned went for a kill shot and got—Troy's thick forearm instead. Muscles taut with a clear need to fight, he accepted the damned's bite. The sucking sound was quiet over the settling clank of released chains. For a heartbeat, none of us moved.

By the door, Marika gripped that material tighter. Ty released his hold, counting in my ear, "One, two…three."

I sprang, freeing a stake in mid-air to land on the damned's back. Palm and fingers sizzling, my burned flesh overtook the smell of the dank cell. Lightning scattered over my body to where I needed it. And then I drove the stake home. Blue power erupted with the piercing of its heart. Bullseye. And then I was flying, catapulting back until I hit—

Ty caught me in his arms. But even as our eyes met, our faces and lips so close together, I managed to put our mission first. Managed to control my rising hunger as Ty did the same and let me go.

Sliding on his knees to Troy's side, Marika had already tied off her boyfriend's arm. A second syringe came free as sweat bulleted over Troy's pinched face.

Damned venom.

It was already spreading.

"Hold him still," Ty ordered Marika, who held up Troy's shaking arm. The needle slid smoothly into one puncture. With a pull back, a marbled mix of blood and clear venom filled the plastic tube.

My gut chose the second the damned's heartbeat animated to start up the grinding. I backed up, loose chains clattering as I hit the wall, starving as the restored twitched and Ty repeated the extraction on the second messy puncture. My slowing heart became all I could hear as Marika helped Troy up and they both carted the restored safely away.

My sight turned red as the door shut behind them.

Then Ty was right before me. "We got what we needed. They'll take the venom to Vanessa to purify."

I barely heard him. Had trouble remembering why I was here and what I was doing as I licked my lips. My fangs grew long and pointed.

Ty's offered wrist came up between us. "You need to recharge. For the ritual. For Kendrick."

I blinked once. Twice. My brain fritz realigned with Kendrick's conscience that I was tied to. The one I'd disregarded—because, like Kendrick's presence, it too was fading. But now we had everything, and as I took Ty's warm flesh in my hands, I knew there was no turning back. No matter the ramifications, Kendrick would live again.

I STARED down at Erzsebet's book that balanced over my forearms. A detailed sketch portrayed the scene we'd be reenacting tonight, when the moon reached the highest point in the night sky. On a long slab of stone, a body was drawn. A person crouched over the deceased on hands and knees, and even in black and white, the detail was clear. Cut from the sternum down, the sacrifice would need to bleed out over the dead. Bleed until there was no more and the marks stole their life in place of restoring the dead person's.

The deadly scene we had to recreate in real time.

A bad feeling sat in my stomach that I couldn't shake. Could I really pull this off? Resurrect Kendrick, recharge on Ty, and restore Raven, all while keeping the thing in me contained?

When I glanced up, the shudder that ran down my spine was like a shot of dry ice through my bones. A few yards away, the scene was set. Serafina's coffin, the human-size slab of black marble, looked like an altar. Kendrick's body lay there, thawing since he'd been removed from his freezer box. His spine realigned by Ty's hands—because I hadn't been able to do it myself.

Around the altar were countless black candles, setting the shape of the mark needed to activate the sacrifice. Each lit wick flickered from the gentle breeze that bypassed the open tomb door, bringing autumn garden scents of leaves and cut grass with it. The dancing candlelit pattern mimicked that lightning bolt centering a crossed-through circle. The symbol Caius had used to try to steal my power. But this time, it would use my power, not to strip the ability from me, but to tear Raven's life away and jumpstart Kendrick's heart. The same symbol marked Kendrick's entire chest, visible with his funeral shirt fully unbuttoned and parted. Inflicted by Vanessa before she took off to source alchemy materials.

"It's almost time." I twirled to see Raven. Beneath her flowy white top, her chest was inked up too, identical to Kendrick's. She looked amped up, bouncing ever so slightly on her toes as her hands clasped and unclasped.

Not for the first time, I questioned my decision to go ahead with this. When all of this had come to light, even when it had been my life on the line, I'd had no such reservations—but seeing this sketch and the ready scene brought the severity of what we were doing home. "What if this doesn't work? What if you're not made damned and you die instead?"

The bouncing stopped and Raven looked almost annoyed that I'd burst her happy bubble. "Don't you start too. Knowing Kendrick doesn't want this done is already bad enough. I need you to be with me in this. *Please*. This is what we've been waiting for. It's the only way."

I nodded with reluctance, feeling a chill that wouldn't let up. It was so deathly quiet out there among the tombs and gravestones. The graveyard had been ordered out of bounds, closed to the public when Ty's pack took off to track down my elusive brother. This ritual was not public knowledge, for good reason. In the wrong hands and without the right information, attempting a resurrection meant permanent death, and not only for the already stone-cold. This wasn't a go-to plan for eternal life.

And yet I didn't think my unease was down to my fear of Dorian getting past the wolves to mess things up. I couldn't forget his vote to approve every move I'd suggested to the RVC. To keep all but the necessary away while I acted out this crazy plan. His support didn't make any sense. It sat like a nuclear core reactor in my beating heart, ready to explode.

I glanced out the open door. The moon was rising slowly, reaching higher and higher with every minute. Time was ticking—and I felt like I was going to be sick.

"Your gut is telling you something is off." Kendrick's desperate voice registered in my ear as he appeared by my other side. His clouded eyes pleaded as his split lips moved with speed. "Something's not right. You can't go through with this. *Please.* You can't let Raven."

"He's thawed through."

I jumped at Raven's voice. I hadn't even noticed her leave my side to weave through the lit candles to check on Kendrick's body. "I…I don't know." Warmth grew behind me then, and I didn't need to turn to see that it was Ty approaching from the adjoining chamber.

"He can't be re-frozen." Ty's voice was calm and deep, and Kendrick ghosted in and out of sight as he walked straight through him. The sad look in Ty's eyes said so much about how he felt about our future now that Kendrick might be resurrected. It also held a depth of consideration and support, like he didn't want what he had to say to hurt me in any way. "A body starts to deteriorate soon after death, and he wasn't frozen straight away. Re-freezing him now could have irrevocable effects if he's brought back to life at a later date. If his brain is affected, his body and mind may not be the same again."

"I'll take my chances—"

Kendrick's rebuttal cut off. Actually, his faded form completely vanished. So did my bound sense of his existence, as I registered how on the mark Ty's words were. Even from here, I could see the slight discoloration beneath Kendrick's skin, the signs that his dead body had already been affected by time. "The plan hasn't changed. We're doing this."

"What happened? Something's wrong?" Studying my panicked look, Raven knew something was up.

The moonlight through the open door had disappeared too. "We need to get to our places. Now." Rushing through the flaming symbol, I pulled up short at the head of his body.

Ty hung back with a nod, keeping just outside the edge of lit candles that swayed with moving wind. In one ready hand he held a vial filled with black blood. In the other, a syringe stuffed with an almost clear, jelly-like substance. The damned venom we'd collected.

Raven was right behind me, and in one leap, she was on top of Kendrick, her legs straddling his hips. She pulled a dagger from her belt and kissed the blade. "Ready or not."

Damn, she was brave. God, please let this work. "Let's do this." Keeping my charged palms by my side, every muscle in my body tightened as I watched Raven slice her blade down Kendrick's chest, keeping to the jagged line of that lightning bolt. Thawed but still cold, red bloomed at the site, but only a few slow streams tracked down past his ribs. What happened next would have stopped my breath, if I'd been fully alive. Biting down on her lip, Raven took the sharp end and carved a jagged track down her chest. Tears sprang to her eyes, and with gravity in control, her blood didn't just seep out. It poured. Glossy, vibrant red flowed from her in a number of thin streams, the current steady as she squeezed her eyes shut. Her tears fell freely, just like her blood. And I waited. And waited. I wasn't hungry. Not with the top-up Ty had ordered after the set up of this tomb. But God, that rich color was an invitation to my transitioning body, a temptation that had me grinding my molars together.

Soon enough, the black veins that patterned Raven's flesh thickened, and her crouch over Kendrick's opened flesh began to sway. I grabbed her hands to steady her above him, and had to bite my lip as my fangs began to throb. The smell of her blood had stripped the scent of grass, dried leaves, and bark from beyond the graveyard, as well as melting wax and burning wicks from this tomb.

Releasing my lip, I held on as Raven's life began to slip away. "Almost there." My ears focused past the sound of Ty's bated breath, his tensing muscles, and creaking boots that were ready to drive him our way. *Beat-beat, beat...beat...* There was a pause and then one last dying *beat.*

Raven's body gave out and she fell as I shoved our joined hands between her and Kendrick. A silent prayer passed from my lips as the entirety of my voltage shot from my chest to my arms and out through my hands.

BOOM.

A circle of blue power erupted from between their bodies and our hands, pulsing out in a thick ring. The candle flames shot high into the air to be cut down in a wave as the pulse swept out.

And then Ty was above us, cradling Raven with her torso pointed up to spill the contents of the vial into her open chest. The syringe was plunged straight between her ribs into her heart.

A moment of pure silence passed as I swapped from looking down at Kendrick then up to Raven. There was no change. Not even as Ty looped his arm under her legs and lifted her off Kendrick, placing her down on the cold stone ground. Ty held her down—but he didn't need to. There was no heartbeat or movement. Raven was dead. She'd given her life, and for what? I blinked back bloody tears as I stared down at Kendrick's just-as-lifeless, battered face.

"Kendrick, please…" This couldn't be for nothing. All the times we'd almost died to make this happen. Raven's body cooling beside where Ty knelt. "You can't leave me—"

Kendrick spluttered and gasped for breath, ratcheting upright like his lungs were on fire. I scrambled around him and onto the platform's edge to see color coming back to his complexion as his bruises lightened. Rapid warmth returned to his body as his chest knitted back together, leaving only a faint scar line of where the lightning symbol had burned away. When the spluttering eased to wheezing breath, his mouth gaped as he stared down at his unbuttoned and bloodied funeral clothes. He lifted his hands in total disbelief. The shock remained as he met my eyes. "You…did it."

My arms flung around him but a nearby groan had me letting go just as fast. Raven, who'd just given her life to resurrect Kendrick, was coming around.

She wasn't dead.

And I was suddenly starving.

Seeing the sudden danger I'd become, Ty shot before me in a flash, leaning over the marble slab with his head tilted to expose his neck. "Quick! Before she wakes."

As thick black veins forked up my arms, that red hue invaded my sight. With my mouth watering and my gut in sudden pain, I forgot everything else. My deep-buried feelings for Ty. My simmering need to kill over doing what I'd planned. The fact that Kendrick was alive and beside me, still struggling to regulate his breathing and take control of his motor functions, able to see both of us and know exactly what I was going to do. Even though I perceived a nod from him, I struck hard and fast. Each draw was sweet and pure, refueling my needs and replenishing my power. When Ty's legs turned to jelly, my fangs retracted and I caught his unconscious body before he slid to the ground.

A waking hiss kept me from making his landing soft as Raven rose fluidly. With irises red as blood, her fangs flashed from her curling-back lips. She looked every bit the damned girl who'd launched to kill back at Portsmouth.

I sprang, freeing a stake from my belt that sizzled with a vengeance and had my teeth grating. Slamming Raven back into the wall from mid-leap, I drove the stake into her heart. Blue light exploded from my hand at the same instant—

And shot me away from her like I'd just electrocuted myself. I half hit the archway to the adjoining chamber and my back cried out in pain. The stake fell from my grasp and clattered across the ground.

I'd been hit by my own power. I felt it in the twitching putty my limbs had become, in the short-circuiting of my brain. I blinked over and over to keep my vision focused.

Across the space, past where Kendrick sat slumped on the altar and where Ty lay, was Raven. Standing hunched and hissing, the stake hole I'd punched in her chest was sucking shut like a sinkhole in reverse. Her red eyes pulsed as she bared her fangs, eyeing Kendrick. Like he was her next meal ticket.

"Shit. Kendrick, get away from her!" It didn't make sense, we'd done everything by the book. But the result was clear in the monster that had now replaced Raven. "She's still damned. I can't restore her."

Kendrick rolled off the altar, intending to arm himself so he could fight Raven off. But in his state, his body didn't respond that way and he tipped and hit the ground next to Ty.

Too many things happened at the same time after that. Kendrick clambered for a weapon. Ty stirred but didn't wake. And Raven pounced.

Tapping into my transitioning side, I shot across the space in a blink and caught her by the throat. Her nails clawed at me, but I drove her back until her head hit stone. This restore had failed, but Raven had somehow survived rather than incinerating. Like Marcus had. If I wasn't recharged enough, I'd have to try again. But I didn't have the strength now. "Stop struggling." My dagger came out and I nailed it right in beside her heart.

Raven screamed in protest, her nails capturing my wrists and digging in to hit bone. "Lay down and die, already."

Her return to Evil Dead was such a shock, I hesitated. Then got clocked as her forehead cracked me in the nose. Instant rose-colored tears flooded my eyes and I stumbled back. But even as the dagger slid free, I didn't drop the weapon.

Blinking fast, I saw Raven running and ducking to get past me to Kendrick. "Don't even—" I flung a leg up and got her in the throat. She fell back from the momentum, but scrambled straight back up.

"Raven, remember who you are," Kendrick croaked, working through the stiffness as he gripped the coffin's edge to get vertical. "Let us help you."

Raven faltered, an emotion other than murderous hunger shining through in her round face. I backed toward the moonlit door, ready to stop her if she went to bolt. She tore her eyes from Kendrick and took a few steps my way, that soulless rage returning to her expression.

"Raven, don't do this. I don't want to hurt you."

She smiled wide, pointed fangs bone-white and sharp. "Well that makes one of us. See you soon." Raven smashed through the closest window and I reacted too late, crunching over showering glass as I chased after her. But she was quick, her damned reflexes kicking in and driving her away from me fast—right as fatigue from my restore attempt invaded my bones. Still, I kept sight of her as I forced my aching legs to pump through the graveyard, over the stone wall, and through the surrounding trees. And then she was gone, over the warded perimeter in one bound. The wards triggered with a resounding wail that punched my eardrums. "Shit, shit, shit!"

An amused chuckle had me one-eightying on the spot. Strolling over through the trees was Dorian, looking pig-in-mud pleased with himself. "Now that those wolves are off my tail…" Red static danced down his arms to his hands. Marcus's power, which rivaled mine. "Perfect execution, by the way. The resurrection, I mean."

I stalked forward and stared through his eyes, imagining I was looking at my twin—knowing he was seeing me through my brother's eyes. "You lost one battle. And I'm not stopping until I win this war."

"War?" Dorian's smile was cold and calculated. "If that's what this is then…you should know…" He leaned back against a tree, propping one leg as if he didn't have a care in the world. "I let you have this one. Let you bring your precious Kendrick back to life."

"Get away from her!" Kendrick stumbled in, catching a tree limb to steady himself. Forever my protector.

I moved to cover Kendrick with my body and pointed my blade's tip at my brother. "What do you mean, *let me*?"

Another chuckle, even more amused than the last. Dorian's leg fell off the trunk and he smiled. He began walking backward, those red sparks a warning not to follow. "I compelled Vanessa to suggest this *loophole.* Expected *you* would be the one to take the bait. Though the substitute serves my needs just as well. You can't restore a damned twice. The only way to save Raven now is with our combined powers, which can be arranged…once you're bound to me, that is."

As I watched him disappear beyond the thick trees, I was struck by the memory of something Madam Rosalie had said. *When life and death are in question, a great sacrifice must be paid. There are no refunds.*

Present for the same memory, Kendrick's conclusion was identical. "Raven gave her life for mine." Moonlight highlighted the unmaskable grief across his handsome face. "And you alone can't change her back."

CHAPTER 29

After ordering Kendrick's reassigned guards away to stand sentry around the castle grounds, I tugged Kendrick to a halt outside the boardroom doors. With his palm against mine—God, it felt so good to be able to touch him—we had one mission. "We'll get her back," I said, squeezing my fingers around his hand. No matter what it took—even me bonding with Marcus—I knew I would find a way. I had to. "I promise you that."

Kendrick sighed then held his breath, shaking his head as he frowned down at himself. It was alien to have gone from existence as a conscious being to having a corporeal body that needed oxygen again. "I can't believe I'm back and she's now…" He trailed off, not looking at me, guilt destroying his beating—breaking—heart. "If I'd had any idea that you wouldn't be able to restore her again... I—I just had this terrible feeling something bad was going to happen. It was all too easy. Life has a price." His free hand clenched while the one holding mine squeezed. "And Raven paid it."

Exactly what he'd warned me about from the start. But even

with the outcome, I couldn't regret having him standing here with me rather than lying in that freezer box. Even with his and my guilt over Raven. Even with his obvious feelings for the once-again damned girl.

With how the events had played out, and with everything before then—the RVC meeting, securing the community, Ty making sure his pack was okay—we hadn't had a second to sort through our relationship issues. And now was no exception. But I wasn't going to start sugarcoating other things in preparation for our big D&M. "I still would have gone through with it. I would have done anything to bring you back. And I know Raven wouldn't have backed out either."

Now Kendrick did look at me, his face tense in the flickering lantern flames with emotions he kept locked away from me. "I won't swap you for her. I can't pick one life over another."

Ouch. My hand fell free of his. Like I had with him and Ty, who was now up in my suite or in Kendrick's tomb gathering up everything we'd found on breaking the damned curse. Deep down I knew Kendrick wasn't having a jab, but damn, what he'd said felt like a kick to the guts. "Hopefully you won't have to."

My phone buzzed as it belted out the Three Days Grace song, *Get out alive.* But even as I tore it from my pocket, feeling a burn as I brushed against silver from my utility belt, I knew I wouldn't cave to do what the song warned. I'd never run from any of this—not my friends, family, or danger. I'd fight till the very end.

My phone came free as Kendrick waved. "See you back in your suite." And then he was gone—not in the direction of the main hall, but down the corridor that disappeared around a bend.

Vanessa's name was across the screen and I slid my finger to answer the call. "It worked. Kendrick's back. But Raven—I couldn't restore her."

“Oh, that’s…” Vanessa’s words rushed through panting breath, her distress palpable through the speaker. “Someone’s been here. My den. It’s—”

“Who, Dorian?”

“Yes. No. I don’t know. But everything’s gone. Everything I had on the curse. All the books. The place is a bombsite. Whoever it was is long gone.”

As I imagined all that shattered glass, tipped shelves and work-benches, and scattered wood, metals, and alchemy books among spilled concoctions, my head heated up and my eyes buzzed. “I—I gotta go.” I hung up quick, my back hitting the corridor wall as I slid down. My weapons clanked on the ground as I threw my arm out to buffer my plummeting head.

A blink stole the darkness from my sight, and then I was looking through trees, bright moonlight sending long lines of black out from each long shaft. Centering it all was a raging fire with billowing smoke that stained the still air. A girl with blue-black hair and black-veined skin was throwing rectangular objects into the blaze. Raven. And those were—I’d bet my life on it—the stolen books from Vanessa’s den.

But how had she gotten them out of here, and why? Had she snuck back in before the alarm was reset? With all the guards on high-alert? Almost impossible.

The “why” was a shadow as he stepped forward, his silhouette visible between blackened trees. “Get the last books on the fire and then get to the spot.” That cold voice was unmistakable with all its detached harshness. Marcus. He’d intercepted Raven after her escape. He’d known like Dorian had, that she would be damned and un-restorable. Holding her shoulder, even from here I saw the split-second pulse of red from his eyes. “Leave the fire to burn. I won’t be long, once I acquire the items I need to break the curse.”

WITH WALL-MOUNTED LANTERNS lighting the way, I rounded a familiar bend. After my vision, I'd raced to my suite—but Kendrick hadn't been there. Neither had Ty. The thought of what 'items' Marcus was acquiring had the two of them on my mind first and foremost. Everything and everyone was a commodity to my twin. Lives were to be used at his discretion.

Now, after chugging a bottle of Ty's pre-packaged blood that had disappeared those black veins and revived my weakening heart since my vision, I knew where to find at least one of the two. Kendrick, my soul's mate, was safe. And well within my reach, as I quick-stepped down the stone stairs to that circular room. Following my link to him, I bypassed the armed guards to enter Erzsebet's unlocked cell.

Kendrick stood before the table topped with open books, hands pried into the wood as he leaned forward. His body quivered with restrained hatred as he grated, "Stop stalling and tell me how to break the damned curse."

While I'd been stuck in that vision and looking for him, Kendrick had had his own idea to save Raven. To cure her of the curse rather than having me bond with Marcus, all the while hoping it was possible without having to give me over to my twin.

Erzsebet looked past him, surprised at my intrusion as she slid off her stool. Her marked ankle chains rattled in reaction. The expression of wonder across her face made her look more youthful. "You succeeded. I never thought I'd see the day. I never thought I'd even care again."

Kendrick stalked around the table and bared his fangs. "She's damned because of you. You said that it would work."

"Who?" Understanding dawned and Erzsebet shot a look my way. "You didn't restore her?"

I could barely take a step closer, struck by my failure and the hopeless depression that ate at Kendrick's insides. "I tried. It didn't… She's with Marcus now. Somehow they got everything on the curse from the den and burned it. Marcus said something about sourcing items."

"For the curse?" Kendrick thought the same as I did.

"The chess pieces are moving, he's getting ready to free the damned." As I looked away from his diverting stare, I noticed the rough wooden crates on the ground up against the wall. Stacked with books and discolored pages, I scented the dust and mildew that permeated them. "What's all that? It wasn't here last time."

Erzsebet took a step back from Kendrick who hadn't relented in his returned, breathing-down-her-neck stance. Sliding back onto her stool, she steepled her hands in that way Caius had always done and nodded to the crates. "They are my life's recordings and research. My daughters arranged both the transport from Cachtice and the locating of everything Caius had hidden in the catacombs from his own experiments."

This was gold, but as I skirted between the table and cot to the crates, I still had to know. "Why?"

Kendrick's fists cranked tight and he punched the bench top, making the books jump as if surprised. "So you can reminisce over lives you took in your selfish plight? Over how you got everything you wanted, while everyone else around you suffered?"

"Everything *I* wanted?" Erzsebet flashed her fangs in agitation as I lifted a crate to the cot. "One of my daughters is dead. My son is rotting away in the adjacent cell. I will be stuck here until I die or the RVC changes their vote and kills me. My actions were unorthodox, I won't deny that. But everything I ever did was for a greater cause. For my family and…" She sucked in her breath and cracked her shoulders back. "I still want to break the damned curse. Now that my daughters are safe, I want to complete my life's work."

Marcus wanted the same thing. Only he hoped breaking the curse would free them of all their weaknesses: insanity, sun incineration. "You want to release all those monsters?"

"No. I want to cure them. As I always did. Permanently."

"And you know how to do that?" Kendrick's anger deflated while his fear for my life skyrocketed. "You know what the cost is to break the curse? Is there a loophole for that too? One that won't screw us over?"

His one hope to save us both.

At Erzsebet's open mouth, I filled in the blanks. "My life is the price to break the curse, right?" The price to save them all, according to Caius. But was that the only option we had? Was it the only sacrifice needed? The words, *To pay the price, light and dark must first be joined,* made me think of Marcus and the real reason he wanted us to bond. "To save them all—if it is at all even possible—I must die."

"Unfortunately, I don't have the answers you seek." Erzsebet retrieved another crate and plonked it onto the tabletop. "Not yet. My experiments are dated, and contrary to what Caius believes. My life's work calls for the exact thing Caius has created from my pure and damned blood. Your power, Granddaughter, shared between two sources. With all of this"—she indicated the crates—"I plan to work out the details, to incorporate all that I discovered in my living years with what my son furthered after my mortal death. I will find the answers, but regardless of the sacrifice, what is done with the findings will be up to you, Granddaughter." With slow consideration, she picked through her own crate and pulled out a soggy book with a dirty, blue cover. "You are but a piece in this puzzle. A large one, I admit, but still only a piece. And as for the items I believe your twin will want to procure…"

"You know what they are?" I asked as I stopped rummaging through the crate in front of me.

"Two items are needed to free or cure the damned, depending on the finer details. The ceremonial chalice"—Erzsebet opened the book cover with careful hands—"and the bloodstone." Parting the pages to a silk bookmark, she turned the book around for me to see. "I acquired it back in the late 1500s from a famous alchemist. An Aquinas descended from St. Tomas. The elements were infused inside its core and it was bound in silver to protect its power from falling into the wrong hands."

My stare didn't let up as I gingerly took the crumbling book into my hands. I'd seen this heart-shaped stone before, had witnessed it burn my twin's hand—which at the time I'd assumed was because of the silver. But now that I thought about it, I'd seen him handle silver after that without reaction—when I'd staked him. I released the book and rubbed my thumb across my palm, wondering if I'd been burned by more than the silver chain and casing after I'd started transitioning. "I know where the stone is."

Feeling an unyielding sense of urgency, I pulled Kendrick from Erzsebet's cell into the circular room. With what I'd seen in that vision, our time was limited. Keeping my voice low, I said, "If we have what he needs, we can use it as leverage to help Raven." I hated my next words, but I knew there was no way around it. "We have to split up."

Worry of leaving me alone surged from Kendrick through the bond. His healed face strained with both worry and a twinge of hope for what we could achieve. The knowledge that Marcus needed me alive swayed his decision. "Okay. You go find Ty and the amulet." He gave my hands a squeeze and turned to leave. "I'll meet you in your suite once I get the chalice—" He stopped, noticing the unusual quiet at the same time I did. The lack of bodies. "Where are the prison guards?"

A figure appeared down the curved stairwell. "You mean *this* chalice?" Dorian's face came into view in the flickering light coming off the wall lantern as he cleared the steps. Any of his usual charismatic expression was lost to the compulsion that had a clear hold on him. He passed the jewel-encrusted cup from one hand to the other and raised his eyebrows. "You want it? Come and take it."

Kendrick lunged a second before I did, but Dorian expected it and shot sideways. Kendrick hit a cell door hard, but he refused to go down. Even as his strength at being newly alive ebbed, he forced his legs to hold his weight and blinked back the stars in his vision. And then I was there, electricity preceding my driving fist.

I froze, clenched hand in the air and shoes scuffing the ground. My voltage sucked back like it had been returned on a slingshot, reabsorbing into my skin before it could break free. Pressure built like a volcano in my body and my core temperature jumped from ice-cold to inferno. Boiling, I was boiling. My mouth parted with a splatter of blood as more crimson leaked from my eyes. "Dorian…"

Vision still hazy, Kendrick spun off the wall with the help of a conjured gust. Landing a kick at Dorian's side, the hold on me relinquished.

So he could swing that solid gold cup up at Kendrick's face.

The sweeping wind circling the room died as Erzsebet called out from her cell. Chains rattled, but she was trapped. Through the sudden buzzing in my ears, I thought I heard Caius's voice too.

I staggered as Dorian palmed Kendrick's skull and drove him face-first into the wall. Once. "No!" Twice. I lunged at the third strike, freeing my dagger as Kendrick fell.

Dorian's free hand shot out so quick I didn't see it coming. His digits caught around my throat and squeezed. My blade hit his rib as I drove it in, but then it stopped. My swarming electricity didn't make him release his grip on my throat—not that I needed the breath. And then my voltage was being sucked straight from me. Like it had been when Marcus had rendered me unconscious after *killing Kendrick.* With that strong hand around my throat shaking, my body turned blistering hot again. Fresh blood spurted from my gaping mouth and boiling tears of blood streaked from my eyes down my face. More heat trailed from my nose, and as my vision went in and out, warmth trickled from my ears. Sweat spouted from every one of my pores, drenching my clothes in an attempt to cool my body. "Dor—ian—*stop*." An animalistic squeal echoed through the corridor, and it took me a second to realize the sound had squeezed from my throat. "You're—killing—"

Dorian's voice was cold and flat. "This can't kill you."

Unable to keep the tension up, my hand slipped from the hilt of my dagger. My knees gave out, but even as my brain swelled like it was hemorrhaging, my ability to think didn't falter. I vaguely registered Kendrick as Dorian kept his hold, slowly lowering me down on my back to the gloriously cold stone ground. He was out cold, but he was breathing. He was still alive. For now. And Dorian had said…*This can't kill you.* Did Marcus know of our immortality, our bulletproofness? Wow, brain seriously fritzing. With my body almost unresponsive and only feeling the burn of my blood boiling up, I focused on re-firing those neurons in my brain. If he wanted the chalice, why show up to taunt us with it? Why risk losing it?

More red cloaked my eyeballs, stealing my vision. My head tipped to the side and the buildup of blood streamed across my face. Down beside me was the chalice, still being gripped in Dorian's other hand. Just out of my reach, my fingers crept. Closer. Closer.

"Why?" I gargled, sending a spray of red across my brother's face. There were more words, but they wouldn't come.

Dorian's smile was pure evil. "You'll find out soon enough."

My fingertips reached the lip of the cool gold cup—and the burning stopped. My lids slid shut as a scene unveiled itself in the darkness. I paced away from that roaring fire, shitkickers stomping over leaf litter in the dark below tall trees. *She knows you're coming,* Dorian's words registered in my head because I was in Marcus's. *Or at least suspects.*

Marcus's voice rose, speaking for me to hear inside his own mind as his pace picked up. *Get the damn chalice, then go pay Amelia a visit without attracting attention.* There was a noisier thumping and crunching leaves behind him. He wasn't alone. *Keep her busy until I'm done. Anyone else is fair game if it means keeping your cover. Meet me outside when we're clear. Don't be late.*

As the vision melted, there was nothing to keep me from falling into unconsciousness. Into the black abyss of my blank mind.

I CAME TO WITH A GASP, hands flying up to my throat—and meeting my own flesh. Sounds registered past the ringing in my hot and pulsing ears. Shouting muffled by—my head cranked around, hazy eyes peering up the stairwell to—a solid wall of frozen water. On the other side, which must have been three feet thick, were guards, desperately bashing to get in. I blinked the blood from my eyes and smeared more from my face as I pushed myself into a sitting position. The only other exit, the gate that led down to the catacombs, was frozen up too.

The pounding of my weakening heart increased. Caged.

I noticed then a trail of water coming from the taps on either side of the circular room. Only one vampire I knew had harnessed their water ability to such an amazing—and at times devastating—level. Dorian.

The rest of the events before my vision came rushing back.

Oh, shit. "Kendrick!" I scrambled to the side and tugged him up by his burial shirt, tearing the stained material. One arm went around his nape and the other pressed to the vein along his neck. *Boom, boom.* He was alive.

His eyeballs moved behind his closed bloody lids, then his puffy eyes cracked open. "Ah…" He groaned as muscle control returned to his body and he levered himself up. "What hap—" He flat-out stopped speaking as horror widened his eyes. He caught my face between his palms and looked me over. "You're hurt? Are you okay?"

I scooted back to break his hold. Fangs peeking from my gums, that spin cycle had started up in my stomach. My sense of smell soared, but as I looked down, my transition traits didn't rush forth…yet.

The retreating bruises and cuts from Kendrick's face bashing relieved my returned worry. "I'll be…oh, shit!" Marcus's words from my vision resurfaced: *keep her busy, fair game.*

"Amelia, what? What's going on?" Even though he was just as weak as I was, Kendrick helped me up. In my steps to gain space and clarity, he looked into my thoughts to replay what I'd seen.

The meaning behind Marcus's compulsion to my brother gelled in my mind. "The amulet. Marcus is coming for it."

"Ty's in danger." Kendrick stared up at the ice wall where guards were still belting into it from the other side, then at the one blocking the catacombs. Hands lifting with tension, he nodded. "Stand back."

When I was between Erzsebet's and Caius's cell doors, Kendrick's eyes clouded. Despite how weak he was, he conjured and directed his power, forcing the air in this room to compress further and further until it was like we were in an airtight bubble. His hands came together, shaking with strain and exhaustion.

When he teetered on his feet, my fear for his well-being overrode my worry for Ty. With all the oxygen-rich air condensed, he wasn't taking in the breath his body needed. "Kendrick, it's too much."

"Shh." His hands swung wide with instant release, splitting the ball of air out in two. One blast raced for the catacomb entrance. The other shot up the stairs, the deafening whoosh of it drowning out the guards banging. They hit simultaneously, and I rushed to Kendrick's side as he staggered, knees giving out as the ice exploded with a bang.

Kendrick had done it.

We were free.

And even without my help, he wouldn't have gone down. Molars grinding he regained his balance and control of his legs. "I'm fine," he grated before I could ask. "We need to go."

With a nod, we made for the stairs, meeting the descending guards on the landing. "Secure the castle and the perimeter," I ordered the prison guards and Kendrick's who all had their swords out like they'd been chipping away at the ice from the other side. I pushed past them with Kendrick, morbid fear rising for Ty with each lost second. "Marcus has infiltrated the walls."

Instantly on task, we vaulted up the stairs, through the back corridor with Kendrick's guards close on our heels. We cleared the grand corridor in mere seconds. Ty had been retrieving everything we'd found on the damned and breaking the curse—he could only be in one of two places. My suite or the Baldassare tomb. Reaching Kendrick's suite, my open door further down the corridor made my insides jolt.

I never left my door open.

A second later, I exploded inside and almost toppled over. I stopped dead. Oh God, we were too late. The scent of blood was heavy on the air. The source wasn't a mystery. In the lounge, the struggle that had played out was all on show. Red blood splatter patterned the smashed-up wing chairs and cracked-in-two white coffee table. The wall-mounted TV was in pieces on the blood-puddled ground and soaked shaggy rug. The long cabinet was covered in dints and smears of crimson.

Beyond the carnage that told of the struggle that had gone down here, only one thing mattered. Draped over the bloodstained couch was the source of all this blood. It covered him head to toe, T-shirt and jeans lacking any other color. God, the damage, the bruises, the cuts that looked like something had torn into him. In my mind it was the PVC again, moments after Caius's blade slid red from Ty's heart and he bled out across my lap.

Not again.

"Ty!" Finding my legs, I catapulted into the room, clearing the damage to land on my knees beside him, rough pieces of debris digging in and stabbing into my flesh. It didn't register. Neither did the sound of others moving in the surrounding rooms. The blood all over him and his torn clothes did. Even as it sickened me to admit it, the sight and smell tempted me even now. But I pushed past my dark desires, holding on for dear life to my fear. "Ty, *please*."

Hand going to his neck, the instant blip I felt was a Godsend. Still alive. But he was so banged up, lacerations had not only shredded his clothes but had cut deep into his skin and through muscle. "I'm here now. You're going to be okay." So long as I could keep my fangs and grinding insides from taking what was on easy offer.

Across the room, Kendrick was at the blood-smeared cabinet and opening the door to the dinted bar fridge. Scooping up the four unbroken bottles, he came over as cool air ruffled the shredded drapes from the smashed-out terrace doors. Lucky for me it was still dark outside. Nodding to the guards that had gathered from checking the other rooms, he said, "Marcus escaped out that way. Track him down, but don't kill him." As they fled out over the balcony, their boots crunching glass, he met my questioning gaze. "I know he's linked to Dorian in physical form. If he bleeds…"

In my shock at Ty's state, I'd almost forgotten, but I was so glad he hadn't. "Then so does Dorian."

I returned my focus to Ty, willing him to come around, holding back my sinister need to just finish him off. When he remained still, the sound of a glass bottle being opened and chugged stole my attention. "What are you doing?" Kendrick was in need of more blood than he'd already taken after his resurrection and even more after the use of his power, but Ty was hanging on by a thread. And me? I was minutes—at most—from turning lethal.

Kendrick opened the second bottle. "He needs Pure Blood. Live blood. And I don't want to risk you going ripper when I'm recovering and he's in such bad shape. And yes I get the irony of drinking his blood for the cause."

His intentions became clear as he opened the second to last bottle and drained it dry. The need to keep me from losing Ty again, knowing what it had done to me last time. And the need to repay the fact that he was himself alive and breathing because of what Ty had helped me do. "You're going to feed him?"

Kendrick bit into his wrist in answer. Then he knelt beside me and pressed his punctured flesh to the alpha's bruised and bleeding lips.

I snatched up the last bottle at the added scent of him and drained it dry. Then my hand returned to Ty's neck, feeling that weak blip every other second. The trickle of Kendrick's blood was loud, becoming all that I could hear apart from Kendrick's steady breaths and the elevating beat of his heart as the bottled blood took the killer edge off.

Then the blips under my palm started to come faster and faster as the fluid leaking from Ty's wounds slowed. His eyes flung open wide, his irises shining brilliant white gold. He gasped straight after and, seeing the person his blood supply was attached to, jerked back on the couch. His bloody mouth remained parted in shock and I expected the first words from his mouth to be, *why you?* But they weren't. "*Marcus,*" he choked out.

"I know." I winced at the bruising around his neck. After the beating my twin had subjected him to, he'd been choked to within an inch of his life. "But you're okay now."

"No." He grunted and banked sideways as he coughed, spraying red over his arm. One hand clawed from his collarbone down his healing chest. When he turned back, the look of loss on his face reminded me of our first date. "He took it. He took my mother's amulet."

The second piece of leverage we could have used against my twin. To bargain for Raven's life. And yet I'd expected as much when I exploded in through the open door and seen the carnage, knowing Ty had worn it since that day under the willow tree in the garden. "I know. It's needed to break the damned curse."

The only thing going for us was the belief that both items were needed to save or cure the damned. Erzsebet had said the difference was in the finer details. So we could still use what Marcus possessed against him, hopefully without him ever knowing.

Kendrick leaned back on the broken coffee table, wiping the blood from his wrist as his skin pulled back together. "Which means he's trying to stop us at every point he can. He's got Raven. The chalice. The amulet."

"That's not all." Ty glanced over the back of the couch at the shattered terrace doors. "He didn't come alone." And that's when I saw it, smaller patches of blood in the shape of large paws. "He's got a werewolf."

CHAPTER 30

Short hours after sunset the next morning, I was in my suite and swinging the mini fridge door open. A bottle of Ty's blood came out and I twirled up from my crouch as I removed the cap. Around me, the lounge was bare, the coffee table and broken wing chairs gone after Marcus and his wolf's attack on Ty. The drapes were gone too. But aside from moonlight through the windows, no light or air traveled in from the smashed terrace doors. Ty had made sure of that. Before the sun had risen, he'd ensured my safety rather than letting himself recover, boarding up the broken doors until new sun-safe glass could be installed. Which is why I hadn't voiced my need for his blood. The other reason? The larger reason? Had nothing to do with the fact that Kendrick was alive and breathing. Nothing to do with the fact that using Ty, with everything that remained stirring between us, felt even more wrong than before. Yeah…absolutely nothing to do with any of that.

I stared at the glass bottle I held, feeling a chill come over me as my heartbeat dwindled in my chest. Feeding was even more uncomfortable now—because I still didn't know where I stood with Kendrick. With my actions re-damning Raven, I hadn't worked up the guts to force that conversation yet. And now, as I watched those telltale black veins root down my arms to my hands, as that rosy tint colored my sight, as my stomach clenched like a vice, I hoped this bottle would be enough. Hoped it would cull the simmering thoughts that tempted me to seek out something better. Something living. To kill.

With my transitioning senses on high alert, I didn't miss the quiet entry through the main door or the almost soundless steps over stone. Didn't miss the *who*, even before I saw his face, either. That scent was too unique. The irregular beat of his heart a dead giveaway.

"You need live blood," Ty said, stalling to lean into one side of the foyer archway. "I know you don't want to, but you know it's true."

From the shifting of his jaw and the look in his eyes, he clearly didn't want to have to do this. But he'd made a promise to help hide my secret and curb my murderous appetite until we succeeded in stopping Marcus and the damned. "I'm sorry." For so much that I couldn't even put into words right now. The scent of him clouded my thoughts too much.

Ty faked a smile and came over to me, sighing as he ran his hands from my shoulders down my arms, pausing with a brief frown at my burn scars. He continued to my wrists, stopping there rather than taking my hands. "Don't be. I don't want you to be." His frowned deepened as he let go and lifted his wrist to my lips. "Just…feed."

My aching fangs dropped from the roof of my mouth and I licked my lips. Bathed in white moonlight through the uncovered windows, I stole a glance at the pulse of blood up his neck. My fangs throbbed. So tempting. But I took his hand instead, bending it back to expose the veins at his wrist. To stop myself from flinging his arm away so I could pounce on that thicker rush of blood, I struck quick, tearing a hiss from between Ty's lips. The groan up my throat was unstoppable as what he offered flowed into my mouth and down my throat. His pulse entered me at the same time, spiking my dying heart to mimic the erratic and elevating beat of his. His body heat intensified.

Or had that space between us suddenly vanished?

I couldn't remember moving, but I definitely hadn't heard Ty shift an inch. And my other hand was…clinging to his side, my fingers toying with the hem of his muscle shirt like they were readying to crawl beneath the black cotton.

"Ahem."

The clearing of Ty's throat accompanied him stepping back away from me. Still hooked to his vein, another unmistakable scent brought my eyes up. *Kendrick.* And he was standing in the foyer archway…watching.

My fangs retreated in a flash and I all but threw Ty's arm away from me. Not because he'd been feeding me. Kendrick knew what kept me in check apart from his conscience, what kept my condition on the DL. He also knew this had been our first feeding since his resurrection. From my own mind, he knew I'd been putting this off. And why. But from the staid look on his face, that's not all he knew —or had just witnessed. Bond block or not, the scene had painted a pretty clear picture. A hint to all the encounters I'd let happen when Kendrick was still dead. All the encounters he'd witnessed in his ghostly state. "I—"

A loud buzzing interrupted the tension and the words I wouldn't have been able to string together anyway. Ty's phone was to his ear. "Troy. Yeah…be right there." Shoving the phone back into his pocket, Ty said, "I gotta go." His expression was stony, guarded and somewhat apologetic. "Troy's found a new lead. A homeless group the damned are tracking. We'll be securing their safety before the damned can take them to recruit. I'm going with them."

I wanted to speak, to say I'd go with him. The thought of him putting himself in danger and me not knowing the outcome until he did or didn't return terrified me. But my words stalled. Ty was already backtracking past Kendrick in the archway and following his long shadow to the door like it was his getaway. This wasn't a discussion or open invitation. He didn't want me to tag along. "Be safe," I managed to utter as the door shut after him.

"He'll be fine." Kendrick's smile was sad. "I should know. He's almost killed me and you more than once."

I went and sat on the couch stained with Ty's dried blood. How had my life become such a mess? "I didn't know you were…I mean…"

Kendrick came and sat down next to me on the adjoining chaise. "It's time we had a serious talk."

Taking gentle hold of my hands, Kendrick's eyes stayed down on them, his breath passing in and out through his lips slowly. The look on his face was troubled, his brows pinching and jaw set.

And didn't that say everything he didn't leave open through the bond.

Unlike Raven, who had only ever lightened his expression and mood, I was the stark opposite. A constant reminder of what he couldn't have fully and all the things I'd done to hurt him. A source of continual anguish that refused to let up because of who I'd failed to be for him. So unlike Raven, who he'd kissed after my betrayal with Ty—who was now permanently damned after sacrificing herself to bring him back to life. All she'd ever done was back him and offer unquestionable support and loyalty.

And what had I done?

Gone against him when he needed me to back his vengeance for his mother. Let my lost hope for Ty and growing insanity sway my actions. Offered more than I had to give in a moment of weakness. And taken his unwavering love and thrown it back in his face with every intimate interaction with Ty.

I was dirt. Unworthy of his or Ty's love.

But like Kendrick, my mind was vaulted shut, locking away everything I knew and felt. But even with his thoughts on no-access, I couldn't ignore the fast beat of his heart or the way his broad shoulders slouched with dejection. Even if he hadn't witnessed the scene from moments ago, I knew one thing for sure. "You could see me every time I fed from Ty, couldn't you?"

Kendrick's fingers holding mine flinched, tightening almost indiscernibly before loosening. His frown deepened as he blinked slowly, like he was seeing all those heated encounters right now in his mind's eye. "I tried not to. I…" He swallowed, and the sound was dry and labored. "I wasn't spying, but even without looking, your thoughts were so loud."

He'd tried to get away and couldn't? The scene of Kendrick lip-locked to Raven flashed in my mind and I pulled my hands free. I cringed at the notion of being trapped in that corridor that day and having to witness their interaction for its entire duration. God, the few seconds I'd seen had been more than enough.

"I'm sorry for what I did with Raven. It didn't go past kissing, but still, it wasn't right."

He was apologizing? Feeling his eyes on me, I couldn't look up to meet them. Instead, my gaze shot through the archway to my bed. One of the places I'd let things go too far with Ty after Kendrick's death. Way too far. And before Kendrick was murdered by my twin? Even now the memory of that dreamscape in a *Pulse* feeding room where Ty's fangs had grazed down my body, and his icy hands handled me with rough touch, ignited something inside of me. My tongue slid over my teeth and I swallowed back the memory as I shook my head. "You don't need to apologize. I broke us. Long before—"

Kendrick's hands flew up to cup my jaw, forcing me to look at him. "You didn't know that was real. You never meant to hurt me. I know that now."

I jerked out of his hold, hating myself even more because of his understanding. Ire lit in my veins that coursed with the blood I'd taken from Ty, and my heart belted in my chest. "I wanted it to be real. I wanted Ty to be real, in that moment, in the others that he manufactured." The tone from my mouth was cold and hard. I sounded so mean. But that wasn't my intention. I hated how I'd used Kendrick, how I'd betrayed him. He needed to know the real me, not this pedestal-placed figment that I could never live up to. "After you died, I tried to do the right thing, but I couldn't help myself. Even with you cold and stiff, I was going behind your back. Letting things happen that shouldn't have. You know—you saw it all. The feedings, the touching, the kissing—"

"And I hated every second of it."

The torment in his voice made me recoil like I'd been slapped. Crimson tears welled, and as one fell, Kendrick's thumb came up to wipe it away. When his hand stilled, cupping my jaw, and his forehead dropped to mine, I didn't pull away. "I'm so sorry, Kendrick."

"I don't want you to be." His head lifted and I dared to meet his eyes. There was no anger, no regret, just…empathy. "I hated every second of it—but not for the reason you think."

Now I did pull away. "What do you mean?"

"I can't say that knowing and even seeing the way you were with Ty didn't hurt me. It did. When I found you at that hotel filled with damned, even though I knew I was there to rescue you and Ty, I still held on to my hope that you would pick me. Even wished that Ty just wouldn't feel the same about you if and when we succeeded in restoring him."

Getting up, I padded past the terrace doors to the siding window. With the shredded and stained drapes gone, my view over the balcony of the royal gardens in full autumn color was unobscured. Despite the moonlight, I imagined seeing Ty bathed in golden light, watching me from the grass between manicured hedges and shrubs. My lids shut at the painful memory of him below the draping willow saying, *I so badly want to ask if we can start again. But I can't do it. I just...can't.* "He doesn't feel the same. Not after everything I've done."

"If you believe that then you're deluding yourself." Spinning around, I found Kendrick watching me with empathy rather than sadness. "He wants you. I've seen it as clearly as you have. You can't deny it."

My lips parted then shut. I didn't want to get into the nitty-gritty of Ty's attraction for me. We were like moths to a flame, knowing we'd get burned if we touched the fire. But physicality didn't equate to love. Ty couldn't love me anymore. He didn't.

"He does." Kendrick's response was without uncertainty or pain. My non-response had leaked through the bond. "And for the record —I was deluding myself, too. When I said I hated every second of it, it wasn't because of what you were doing with Ty. At least not entirely. Not even mostly. I hated the way you tortured yourself each and every time. I hated that you hated yourself for reacting in a way that was unstoppable to you. For doing what your heart and body desired and then regretting every single bit of it. In death I've seen what exists between you and Ty. I could never compete with that—"

"I never wanted you to." Now I moved like a flash back to the couch, standing just behind and kneeling to rest my folded arms along the backrest. This time I held Kendrick's gaze. "What we had wasn't less. It was different. I loved you—do love—"

"Amelia, please." Kendrick reached up to lay a hand over my scarred forearm. "Just listen, okay?" When I nodded, he took a deep breath, eyes doing a semi-circle as if trying to piece together what he wanted to say. With a nod, he took a deep breath. "I don't want to compete with what you have with Ty. And I'm not saying you don't love me or that I don't love you. I do. I always will. But…" He frowned, looking away before meeting my stare again. "Before you took off after Ty, I lied to you. Lied to myself, too." Now he peered over my shoulder to the window I'd been staring at, as if what was weighing on his mind was out there and out of his reach. "I had—have—feelings for Raven. It wasn't anything strong, and I felt like a total dog for using her to get back at you. Felt even worse because—I *liked* kissing her. I told myself it was payback. Told myself you deserved what little we did and that catching me out was your just deserts. But you didn't, and it wasn't just payback. I knew that the second you brought me back to life and I came to and saw what Raven had done. When I realized she was damned again…that you couldn't restore her…" His hand dropped from my arm and his eyes turned glassy. "I realized I was…"

Kendrick didn't finish the sentence, but then he didn't have to. I knew what he was scared to say. One, because he didn't want to hurt me. And two, because he feared he'd never get her back. I'd seen that look on a driven girl's face with her black, cropped hair and flashing wet eyes after learning of Kendrick's murder. "You realized you were falling for her."

"I'm sorry, Amelia. I never meant—"

"She was falling for you too." I didn't dwell on the fact that Kendrick was officially breaking up with me, or that he now held strong feelings for someone else. Instead, I clung to the truth that had just been aired between us and ran with it. There was no rosy end for Ty and me. That had already been established, despite our bodily reactions to one another. When this was all over, we'd part ways…forever. But that didn't mean Kendrick couldn't have his happily ever after. And after everything he'd sacrificed for me, I'd walk through hell to give him the existence he deserved. To return to him the girl who'd touched his heart. I stood with tall resolve. "And we will get her back. Whole and alive. One way or another, Raven *will* be saved."

In the lounge room, I avoided the twilight-glimpsing windows to pace back and forth past the boarded-up terrace doors. My stomach was in knots. After RVC meetings and damned research, sunrise was imminent. And Ty still hadn't returned. I shoved my iPhone back into my jeans. He wasn't answering, either. The line didn't even ring. After all he'd done to protect me, if something had happened because I hadn't insisted on tagging along?

I would never forgive myself.

In my state of pacing worry, I didn't hear my door open and close. Didn't know someone was closing in—until I scented his royal blood.

But it wasn't Ty.

Spinning with bared fangs, I saw Dorian's perfect dark hair, his anticipation, and his growing smile as his hand rose. "Time to sleep, sister."

He palmed my forehead before I could react, and the change was an instant shift that froze my batting arms at my sides. My head heated up and my eyes rolled back. I felt the colliding of my bones as they hit stone a nanosecond before my consciousness fled. The last thing I heard was Dorian whispering, "There's something you need to see."

Feeling like I was in a snow globe and being shaken, I watched my new surroundings float from fragments into a clear view. Outside a bay window framed by open drapes, I glimpsed a room I knew well. A glass-topped desk with a laptop, red briefcase, and neatly stacked folders. A framed photo sat to one side, collecting dust like it was invisible compared to the rest of the pristinely cleaned space. A photo of my mum holding Dorian and me as babies, because I'd compelled her to be happy and to never think of her children.

In a wrinkle-free blouse, the woman herself sat tall in her white-leather chair, focus trained at the open folder in front of her. Safe and, from her carefree smile, happy.

As I began to fear the reason I was seeing this, a loud crack decimated the quiet. Beyond her open office door, two thick jagged fragments of wood catapulted across the marble foyer. The front doors. And then a werewolf—smaller than most I'd seen and with rich auburn fur—pelted through the doorway and leaped onto the desk.

I cried out and bashed on the window as the wolf snapped its jaws and snarled. But every hit, although I felt the impact, made not a single sound and felt like I was bashing underwater at shark-proof glass.

My mom's carefree expression was long gone as she jumped up to race to the door—and stumbled back when two damned appeared through the opening. Lips curled up from their fangs, their red eyes glowed.

As they took slow steps forward, looking amused as Mom's eyes darted for a way out, I ran for the door—and hit an invisible wall not a yard ahead. Behind me and to my other side, everything was blocked, too. I was trapped in this vision and left with only one option. Watch the horror unfold.

Praying this wasn't already happening, that I could still stop this from playing out, I darted back to the window. I kept up the bashing, voltage escaping my tight fists that did nothing to get me to her. The damned were closer to my mom now, hissing and laughing as she threw books from the shelf behind her. And like watching a fatal car crash about to happen, I couldn't look away. One grabbed her as I screamed out, "Mom!" Then he threw her to his fang-baring side-kick.

"If you hurt her, I'll kill you all!"

My threat went unheard as the damned pulled my mom close and clutched her around the throat. Before either could sink their saliva-dripping fangs in, the wolf on the desk howled and then snapped its jaws. The damned both hissed and their eyes glowed lava-hot, but they didn't abandon my mom to attack the wolf. Instead, the first damned punched out fast, cold-clocking my mom in the face. Her legs became rubber, and as her eyes rolled, the damned clutching her throat threw her over his shoulder.

I bashed harder on the force field, screaming as the wolf trailed after the damned—

"I'll kill—" My words cut off as my lids flung open. Red clouded my sight and I registered the scent of blood a second before I felt his heated skin as he cradled me on the ground. Not lycan hot, but vampire warm compared to my chilled skin. I twisted to get away then stalled. My vision turned from hazy to clear, but the red remained. "Kendrick—" I snapped my mouth shut as my fangs punched free.

"Shh," he soothed, cradling me beside the boarded-up doors, his hold gentle but firm. His worry cracked with rage as he glared up at my watching brother. "What the hell did you do to her?"

"Delivered a vision."

"The damned—" I rushed, pushing out of Kendrick's hold and scrambling to stand up. And from the pleased look on Dorian's face, I knew my next words were fact, not a yet-to-occur scenario. "Two damned and a wolf. They've got my mom." I shot past him, coming face to face with my brother. Using my rising hunger to fuel my anger and the threat in my voice, I bared my fangs. "Where's our mom? I swear, if you fucking hurt her…"

"She's safe and sound." Dorian shrugged. He made no effort to retaliate or protect himself. "For now."

Kendrick had a dagger in his hand that I hadn't even seen him draw as he edged closer. He didn't want to hurt Dorian, but he wasn't about to let anything happen to me.

Dorian hiked up his brows. "The ever-protective bestie. Though I doubt the RVC would look fondly on the assault or injury of one of their own," he said, glancing purposely over his shoulder to the closed door that evidently his and Kendrick's guards waited behind.

"Where is she?" I demanded, jaw clenching to keep myself from attacking my brother. "What are you going to do to her?"

Dorian stepped backward, once, twice, his stare almost daring us to make a move. "I get to make the demands here. Dorian's release from my control and your mother's life—so long as you bond with me. Tomorrow. At Hope."

As he continued stepping backward, a plan formed in my mind. One that could give us the element of surprise and the upper hand. "Fine."

"Amelia, no."

"I'll be there. You'll get what you want, Marcus." And now for the condition. "But only if Raven's there too."

Dorian grinned wide as he bypassed the foyer table and opened the door. "Then I'll see you at ten-thirty p.m."

"No," Kendrick said for the millionth time. Stalking after me down the shadowed corridor, he caught my elbow and spun me around. God, the fear across his entire face was palpable. "You can't do this. I won't let you."

But his worrying wasn't going to change my mind. Nothing could, since my statement: *I'm going to bond with Marcus.* And Kendrick knew it as I twisted out of his grasp. "I'm saving my mom and I'm freeing Dorian. Nothing you say is going to change that. She will not die because of me." I narrowed my stare. After the bottle of Ty's blood I'd downed, I was still thirsty as hell. My flickering conscience removed my understanding of what my actions would do to him, Ty, and even Dorian after the fact, while resolve to protect the people I loved soared. "I am doing this. And don't you dare stand in my way."

Stalking off, I knew he was following right after me. At least we'd ditched his four guards. Listening ears were not what we needed right now, with the subject matter.

"What happens when Marcus uses you like he's been doing to your brother? His aim is to free the damned of their weaknesses, and you're the missing piece to his *free-the-damned* puzzle."

Kendrick was less than a yard behind me as we rounded a bend. The fear that seeped through the bond was a red flag, because I was doing my best to block him out. Still, there was enough slipping through that I knew his concern wasn't just for me, my mom, or Dorian. If I joined Marcus's side and he forced me to break the curse the way he intended, Raven would remain a monster forever. Unless my secret plan—which he hadn't stumbled upon in my mind yet—paid off. "You can't risk becoming Marcus's ally. Our race won't survive much longer if the damned are let off their leash. We'll never be safe."

I paused at a door along the corridor, fingers curling around the wrought iron handle. "Which is why we're here." I pushed inside and smiled at our own personal alchemist. "Vanessa's going to help me."

Vanessa's flushed pixie face—like she'd been rushing before our interruption—shot up. She rose from her crouch between torn-up books and broken vials and beakers. "Wow, Kendrick. I mean I knew, but to see you alive…" Her joy at the first living sight of him diverted. "What's going on? Is this about Raven?"

The bench centering the room was upright, but from the gentle lean, it was clear it had been broken when her den was raided and trashed. We'd come down to help after the incident, but the door had been bolted shut. A quick call had revealed Vanessa was out sourcing replacement equipment and materials. Guess she hadn't gotten to any cleaning before she left. Had she only just returned?

"Sort of. I need your help." Speaking quickly, I filled her in on the threat against my mom and on my plan to save her and free Dorian. "There's no other way to break Marcus's hold over Dorian. Only a stronger bond can release him. And that's me."

Vanessa looked torn, like she wanted to agree with Kendrick's viewpoint, but couldn't bring herself to do it.

"I haven't found another way yet. But, that does not mean it's impossible."

Waiting back by the door, Kendrick cleared his throat. "The deadline's been set. Unless you can come up with a solution to sever Marcus's control before tomorrow." Even as he spoke, his hope of actually achieving this was little to none.

I shook my head. "Even if we found a way, Marcus still has my mom."

Vanessa righted a stool and maneuvered through the mess of broken glass, Bunsen burners, and various pieces of wood and metal to reach me. Grasping my hands with a squeeze, her flesh was warm on mine. "I want there to be another way, but…" She winced as if remembering another time and place, before returning her eyes to me. "I know first hand how ruthless the damned can be. Pets are kept only so long as they're useful. Death is the punishment for disobedience. And Marcus? He's the most ruthless of them all. It won't matter that she's his mother. He'll…"

Unable or unwilling to complete the sentence, and knowing the 'punishment' she was referring to, I filled in the blanks. "He'll kill her." Thinking of Ty, I was now glad he hadn't returned from his lead. Had he been here, I could imagine the look across his face of pure condemnation, because he'd killed—or at least thought he had killed—Vanessa when I'd refused him. She'd almost died because of my disobedience then. And I wasn't about to let the same happen to my mom or to Dorian.

Kendrick came forward and braced his hands on the workbench, arms straight and stiff, the lean muscles along his arms twitching. "And how many will die when Marcus uses you to free the damned? If he can control you like he does Dorian, you will be powerless to refuse his plans."

"Which is why you're here," Vanessa stated with sudden clarity.

It wasn't a question, and I smiled at my brother's girlfriend. "Can you do it? Mark me to boost my ability to block Marcus out once we're bound."

Vanessa was all smiles that said, *hells yes. Who do you think I am?* "Absolutely. Especially since you're not already bound to him. I'm certain that's why it failed with Dorian."

Kendrick let out the breath he'd been holding in a long exhale. Part of him despaired at the thought of no longer being bound to me once I severed our link to bond with Marcus. Yet as he saw the larger plan I had swimming around in my mind, my harder-to-be-killed reasoning that could make my plan worthwhile, another part of him held anticipation for exactly the same reason. We'd have the chance we needed to get Raven back. "If he can't control you—"

"He can't force me to free the damned." I smiled, happy to have at least these two now on board. Though for my larger plan, I had a feeling Ty would be hard to convince. When he finally returned, that is. Make note—call straight after for ETA. I shucked off my hoodie and pointed to the side of my ribs. "I'm thinking somewhere out of sight."

Vanessa was around her bench and pulling her homemade tattoo gun from the side drawer. "It wasn't wrecked in the raid." A pot of black ink followed. "And neither was this."

CHAPTER 31

The next morning I sat on the edge of my bed, running fingers down the individual lengths of silver that were laid out on the purple covers. Each stroke singed my fingertips, and I was glad at the thought of confronting Marcus with this deadly silver strapped to my body. But it was only a backup. I had another plan, too. Another weapon that would be invisible to the naked eye. I met Ty's watchful eyes across my bedroom. "So, I'm going to bond with Marcus. I have to."

"Not gonna happen." Ty shot before me and pulled me up by my elbows. Breathing rough, he stared down at me. "We'll find another way." He shook me a little. "Okay? This is not how it ends. This is now how *we*..." He trailed off with a blink of his eyes as his head turned away. His strong hands released me and my butt hit the mattress with a clatter, missing the surrounding silver. With a deep sigh, he glanced back to me. "This is not how we stop him. This is not how we get them back."

Lost for words, I could swear Ty had been on the brink of saying something else. Like, *this is not how* we *end*. Except there *was* no "we." Wishful thinking much? Hanging on to hope for something that didn't exist. A way out of the cards of life I'd been dealt. "I'm out of time. Please, Ty. I need your help."

Since his return not even ten minutes ago, after he'd informed me of his success in saving those humans and picking off some damned, I'd laid everything out. My mom's abduction. My intent to bond with Marcus. My mark to keep my mind safe from my twin's control. My risky plan to get both my mom and Raven back.

Now as I watched Ty pace, hunting boots clapping stone, then quieting over the rug, I feared his refusal. The long coming, *screw your crazy plan and death wish, I've had enough.* The corded muscles along his arms, neck, and chest were trapped with uneasing tightness. That muscle in his jaw had been ticking since my statement: *I'm going to bond with Marcus. I have to.*

"I want it to be you. But if you won't"—*or can't*—"I will take this up with Troy and Marika. This is my mom and Raven on the line here. My mind is made up. And it can work, right?"

Despite my real threat, Ty didn't say what I feared. He didn't try to talk me out of anything, either. Face now laced with serious concern and tinged with caution, did he regret his initial explosive shoot down? Did he feel he had no right to object or intervene now that Kendrick was back and, with the time to the leave closing in, had already signed off on my crazy?

Ty quit pacing and came to kneel before me, moonlight through the window bathing his tight muscled arms in luminous tones. With Kendrick off prepping for the big event, getting his own marks and weaponry, he dared to lay his hot palms on my thighs. "Yeah, but it'll have to be done now. So the effects are full-on by the time we arrive. And you need my blood. It needs to be live." Apology was written all over his face. "Before will mask the effects and give you strength. Once the deed's done, after will…"

"Keep me alive." My lips remained parted as I zeroed in on the thick vein up his neck. I licked my lips. Though death wasn't a given, with Caius's claims on my hard-to-kill body, I'd rather not discover one of my fatal flaws the hard way.

Ty cleared his throat and held his wrist up between us.

"Oh." I tried to hide my dejection and forced myself to take what was offered, hearing the quickening rush of his blood as I brought his wrist to my mouth. Wanting to get this over and done with so Ty wasn't stuck doing something he'd rather not for longer than necessary, I latched on with my fangs.

Ty's nostrils flared and his lips parted, a rumble escaping his throat. His other hand squeezed, fingertips needling my thigh like he was trying to hold his body's reaction to me back. My body warmed at his response, but I didn't give in to the sudden desire that had my heart thudding faster and faster. Attraction aside, Ty didn't want this, didn't want me. It was unfair to blur the lines as I watched conflict dance across his strained face.

But then, as he searched my eyes in return, something changed.

Conflict turning into desperation, Ty's rough hand slid higher up my thigh, his calloused hand squeezing around my slight hips. His breath was getting faster, and as he held my stare his eyes shone with want. He reared up from his crouch against my shins and ripped his wrist from my mouth. "I know I shouldn't, but—" He captured my nape and slanted his lips over mine. His tongue licked over mine, tasting his blood.

I should have stopped him. Stopped this before he could regret even more than what he had already done. But I didn't. I couldn't. With my new bond block, Kendrick was fully out of my head. And he didn't want me anymore. For the first time, letting go wouldn't be a betrayal. With what was planned—especially if I failed—it could very well be my last moment of bliss. Was it the one thing that killed Ty's restraint—to do this, with me—one last time, too?

Kissing Ty back with hunger, I let every desire and passion kindle my need for him. Releasing his wrist I still clung to, I caught the hem of his muscle shirt and tugged it up. Ty released my mouth only long enough to remove the cover, and then he reclaimed my lips.

"We shouldn't," he managed between the unending kiss. "I should stop."

I didn't pull away. Even though I knew I should. "I don't want you to."

With a snarl, his hand moved with pressure up the side of my body, lifting my tank until it too was gone. Flesh on flesh, he lifted me and swiped his arm over the duvet, sending weapons overboard with a clang. Then he pushed me back on the bed so we were on our knees and tangled in each other's arms. My bra was unclipped as Ty's lips broke from mine. As he pushed one strap off, he kissed my neck and collarbone, following the fallen material off my shoulder. His neck was bared to me, that vein plump and pulsing with invitation.

"Bite me," he growled as one hand cupped and squeezed my uncovered breast.

My fangs plunged in quick, evoking a sharp inhale from Ty. His body heat skyrocketed and he pushed me back on the covers, wedging his hips between my legs. He was ready and my hands shot down, squeezing between our bodies to get to his waistband. The urge to reveal what Kendrick and I no longer were surged within me. Was his attraction to me fed by the fact that he thought I was unavailable? Loosening my lips on his flesh, I popped the button on his jeans—

Ty yanked his neck from my fangs with a look of unmissable longing and regret. At the same second, he released my breast and then his mouth was on me—just below my breast on my ribs. The penetration was quick and painful, teeth breaking flesh with his poisonous bite before he scrambled back on the mattress. Breathing hard, he groped for and flung me my discarded tank from the end of the bed. That regret didn't leave his sad face, not for a second. "I—I'm sorry. I don't know what came over me."

I fumbled to get my tank back on, super conscious of the fact that my nipples were hard below the black material. Ty didn't want me because he thought I was unavailable. He didn't want me at all. He lusted after me. Nothing more. A hybrid stuck in a vampire community, what other options did he have?

I slid off the bed and met his eyes as he got to his feet. I wasn't sorry. Not when that could have been our last encounter. My last moment of weightless passion and mindlessness. Of doing what deep down my heart wanted while I still had the chance. Of getting lost in Ty and for those fleeting moments forgetting all the mess of my life. "Don't be sorry. I'm not."

Over three hours later, I pulled my Ducati to a slow stop behind the blinking-off taillights to Dorian's M5. Moisture made my head feel clammy, and just as I'd done for the past few hours, I tried to ignore the constant burning that had a hold of my veins. Ty's blood before his bite was wearing thin, and fear that Marcus on seeing me would know what we were up to challenged my still-beating heart. Made me scared for the retaliation he might take against my mom or Raven. The notion that this was finally happening, that I was moments away from bonding with my twin, made me mourn the connection I shared with Kendrick. My soul's mate. Once forever more. Soon…never again.

We had finally arrived at the same lakeside cabin in Hope we'd raided after Vanessa's lead. And there was no turning back now, because unlike last time, the rickety cabin wasn't empty. The lights were on and inside every window the outline of men and women were like black shadows. Damned. A whole horde of them. More lined the verandah, red eyes glowing under the moonlit sky.

We were more than outnumbered. We were dwarfed. Our only one-up? The poison that swam in my veins.

Dorian was out of his car then and staring blankly over my shoulder at the blue WRX that pulled up behind me. Like even now, Marcus was measuring up the reinforcements through his eyes. And with his slow smile, he looked like he couldn't wait to get this show started.

Behind the wheel was Ty, who exited first, sizing up the enemy. His determination, that look of an alpha who was unafraid and ready to tear it up, shifted as he once-overed me. That flicker of concern came as fast as it went. He knew how my condition, both hunger and poison-wise, was progressing, but he wasn't going to draw watching eyes to it.

Exiting the passenger side, Kendrick was out of the car last, armed like all of us to the teeth. The hatred he propelled at the unmoving damned fell as he glanced from Ty to me. After hours stuck in a car alone together, he hadn't revealed our lack of "relationship." Thank God. This was not the time to unearth that can of worms. Ty needed to be focused. We all did. With Kendrick's thoughts otherwise on no-access, I could only begin to imagine what they had been discussing during the drive to get here. From the look Ty returned to my best friend, it hadn't been a *let's be buddies and put our differences aside* chat.

"Hope your wolf and lap dog are leashed." Marcus strode out the front door, looking both glad to see me and suspicious of the extra company, fully expectant of our bonding to come and any spanner Ty and Kendrick had up their sleeves. "I won't be held responsible if they get themselves killed."

I shook off the dizziness that threatened to tilt the world upside down and clenched my fists. "If you dare—"

"Settle, twin. I mean only to give you fair warning." In gray pants and a black-collared shirt, Marcus descended the rickety front steps. "I have no intention of harming your beaus—unless they get in the way of our business."

"We're only here to keep you to your word, Marcus," Ty called out, hand on the butt of his gun. He hadn't moved from the side of his car, but I knew he wasn't just hanging back and doing nothing. As an alpha, every silent moment would have been spent scoping out our surroundings and the enemy.

On the opposing side of the WRX, Kendrick freed a stake and flipped it in one hand. "We've delivered Amelia to you. We've kept our word so far. Where's Amelia's mother? Where's Raven?"

Marcus smiled. "*Our* mother." He strode over to me, ruby-red gaze sparkling with anticipation. "Will be free to leave—if that's what she wants—once you are bound to me, my twin."

My fangs grew long and deadly. "Show me she's safe first. Show me Raven's here, too."

Amused grin. Then Marcus snapped his fingers. A cry had my gaze shooting through the surrounding trees to a wide maple. Hanging from the thickest limb by her silver-chained wrists was my mother, her bare toes scuffing the dirt and grass below. Red welts marked her skin where the silver burned, and blood and dirt smudged her torn blouse. She'd fought her captors when she'd come to?

She wasn't alone even now. A figure in a long black robe stood right beside her, holding a silver-bladed dagger. From here, it looked identical to Marcus's and had a red smear down the blade. From where they'd just cut into my mom's arm. Their form was slighter than most, shorter. Female.

"Raven," Kendrick gasped out as my mom found us through the deathly still trees.

"Amelia? Dorian?" Face partly obscured by leaves, Mom's recognition of us shook me. Marcus had removed my compulsion. It was the only explanation. Which meant she remembered who we were, who I was, and what I'd almost done to her. She thrashed but the chains were unyielding. The terror in her partly obscured expression didn't propel at me, the daughter who'd almost drained her to death. Through the trees, it was directed at Marcus. "Not my son—not after what Caius did. Amelia, Dorian, get out. Please. Run. You can't—"

Raven cracked her in the skull with the butt of her dagger, knocking Mum's lights out.

"Marcus!" I barely held back the urge to lay into him, to make him pay for everything he'd done to me and everyone I loved. A few feet away, it would be so easy to let my hunger feed off my rage. But I had to be smart. I grappled for control. "She's your mother. Your flesh and blood. You don't really want to do this to her. You can't. Just let her—"

"Not my son," Marcus snapped, ire alive like fire in his blood-red eyes. "She said it herself. Only *your* deplorable actions are redeemable." At my surprise he said, "Removing her compulsion was a learning curve for us both. Amelia the golden child. Why would I ever compete with that? Why would I want to—when I can make you who you were meant to be. Just like me."

I gritted my teeth, fangs pressing into my lower lip. So that was it. His conscience was non-existent, any real emotion or care or love never existing. But I wouldn't be like him. Ever. The mark on my ribs was my fail-safe. Ty's poison a backup. And now it was time to play this out. "Me bound to you for my mom's life, Raven's restoration, and their safe release. That's the deal."

Marcus's amused smile grew wider. "Before this goes any further, there is something you should know…" He hiked his chin in the direction of my mom and Raven who guarded her. A gust of wind picked up. "I have an insurance policy."

Raven nodded from beneath her robe and that dagger disappeared into the black folds. Then she fisted my mom's hair and yanked her drooped head up. A hard slap jogged my mom's consciousness as I cried out. Her lids sprang open and her eyes met mine through the waving trees.

As I registered what was clear as day, even in canopy-shielded moonlight, I focused my hearing. Graying skin blemished with black forking veins, pulsing red irises, and…a single heartbeat that wasn't repeated as her head lolled forward again.

"You fucking monster!"

I went to lunge at my twin and, behind me without warning, Ty hauled me back. "This can be fixed," he grated into my ear as the damned on the verandah crept closer. A rumble vibrated the house and earth beneath us. Ty's power—which didn't stall their approach. "We still have the upper hand."

To my surprise, Marcus stalled the closing-in of his minions. "No you don't. You never did. You see, twin, our dear mother is not simply in transition, infected by blood and bite. She's marked, too. In the same way Dorian is, but not with the same symbol. In her current state…" He rubbed his hands together like he was gearing up for something big. "If you restore her, she'll die."

I freed a dagger and pressed the sharp edge to my twin's throat.

The need to kill for more than blood was like a boost to the poison swimming in my veins. "I swear to God, I'll take your head."

Almost imperceptibly and without concern, Marcus sent a nod through the swaying trees. His fangs flashed from his mouth, long and pointed. "Then how about I put our dear mother out of her misery now."

From that concealing robe, Raven's dagger reappeared. With my mom still fully unconscious, she put up no fight as the tip pointed straight at her heart.

Abandoning my need to kill—because Dorian's life was at stake too—I hissed in threat and went to take off to her.

Ty and Kendrick moved too, but none of us got far.

Marcus caught my arm and yanked me back. "Think before you act." He snapped his fingers and the sound of two bodies suddenly collapsing made me freeze.

I pulled free and spun to see Ty and Kendrick on their hands and knees, both spitting blood as scarlet leaked from their eyes and noses. Dorian hadn't moved an inch, still standing by his M5, but his hands had risen. As shadows from gathering clouds swarmed over them like wraiths, both shook as he worked his ability on the two guys. There was only one thing I could do to save them, him and Raven, and…my mom.

I tried to cool my anger in hopes of stopping the venom-sweats I felt about to burst from my pores. I holstered my dagger. "I'll give you what you want—only if you spare them and my mom. Call off Dorian and Raven over there." I held up my wrist for the taking. Ready for Marcus to drain me almost dry to initiate our new bond. "Do it. Now."

Another finger snap had Ty and Kendrick sagging on the dirt beside the WRX, gasping and spitting blood. Dorian remained stationary, the alien look on his face focused, ready to restart the blood expulsion in an instant. Rain started to fall from the sky, pattering on the ground as more damned exited the house to follow the others in forming a circle around Marcus and me. Ty and Kendrick struggled to their feet, the wolf rearing to break free as Ty began to tremble, and Kendrick palming a dagger—to throw at Dorian.

I shouted out before either completed their planned actions. "Don't. Please." To Marcus I said, "We're not here to fight." I held out my wrist again, praying he assumed the track of darkening veins up my arms and the mist over my forehead were due to hunger over anything more sinister. "Take your price and give me my family back."

Marcus's nostrils flared as if my comment had hit a nerve. His lips curled back from his teeth and fangs and the circle of damned around us tightened. With Ty, Kendrick, and my mom out of sight, Marcus caught and squeezed my wrist, bringing my pale skin to his mouth. He struck like a viper, fangs punching in and jaw clamping on. Sudden pain inundated my body, spearing backward from where Marcus bit me and through my veins, tracking back further and further, spreading like acid through my entire body. It made the pain of Ty's poisonous bite feel like a prelude to the main show. My mouth gaped to cry out, but I didn't let a sound escape. I didn't want to encourage Ty or Kendrick to take action that could work against us. Even now I could hear their elevated heartbeats and Ty's constant growl through the crowding damned. Was that the clicking on and off of the safety on his silver-loaded gun?

"Is she okay? What's happening?"

Ty was talking to Kendrick, demanding answers from the one person who was connected to me in body and mind. For now…

Dropping my blocks down, I let my best friend in just enough to send out a message. *I'm okay. Just don't do anything stupid. Don't let Ty, either.*

"He's draining her," Kendrick's voice carried through the hardening rain that pattered over us and the circle of damned. He knew I was blocking my physical pain from him. "She's still—"

My hearing lost track of Kendrick's voice then as my manufactured heartbeat sped up in my chest and pounded through my ears. It slowed dramatically, dwindling until the beats were so slow, no living vampire would have still been alive. But I didn't pass out dead, even as my body turned limp and my legs lost feeling. I couldn't. I was already halfway there. A transitionee. Still, the agony was brutal—the feeling of being drained alive, of dying without the hope of release because this couldn't kill me. Caius had already failed at that. As my eyesight darkened and a buzzing took up residence in my ears, my sense of smell soared.

"I've got you." With the releasing of his fangs, Marcus's arm snaked around me and then we were in the mud-turning dirt.

Feeling a squeeze around my neck, the sound of a strong pulse reached me. Marcus's, because his arm was hooked around my neck and his wrist was an inch from my mouth. I parted my lips in wait, and then I didn't have to. His pale wrist met my fangs, pressing down to force those sharp tips to break his flesh. Intoxicating blood welled in my mouth, spilling down my throat. A never-ending stream that kept up a steady flow. As my ability to move returned, I created a seal and drew on those two punctures hard, taking his blood as fast as he had taken mine—

An explosion of white light suddenly erupted, striking out from our bodies and vibrating the air. The rain stopped dead and the damned were thrown back into the surrounding trees and the cabin. Torture cut through me like I was being sawed in half, more light shooting out in pulses from my chest. I fell back, my head smacking the softening dirt—at the same time as Marcus. Floored beside me, another flicker of light propelled up from the near distance on my other side with a shout of pain. Then another from the direction Dorian's car had been parked. The severing of old bonds?

And then it was all over.

Feeling like I'd been fried through on the inside, I clambered to sit up as someone splashed through growing puddles to rush my way. Ty's hot hands cupped my face, shaking as he looked me over. "Are you okay? God, tell me you're okay."

With a nod, I saw two bodies lying on the ground as Ty helped me up. One beside the M5 and the other by Ty's WRX. Dorian and Kendrick—but they weren't dead, they were breathing.

A groan tore my worried gaze away from them as Marcus let out a tortured sound. Levering up on his elbows, his eyes darted up to me then Ty. Sweat sprouted across his forehead. His complexion paled. "What have you done?"

Ty bit into and offered me his wrist, which I took without question. The residual burning I felt through my veins died off. Ty's venom-filled wolf bite from earlier was being cured with his hybrid blood. Not that it would have likely killed me anyway. Damned didn't die from wolf bites, and being a transitionee, I was much closer to that than I was living.

Marcus seemed to guess, or perhaps remembered when he'd last felt this burning drain on his body. When Mr. Malau had bitten him and Marcus had returned to his hotel to have Ty cure him. "Wolf venom."

CHAPTER 32

The damned that'd been thrown by the blast staggered to their feet. In slow uneven movement they skulked toward us, recreating a loose circle just outside the cars—where Dorian and Kendrick still lay unconscious, breathing shallow but heartbeats steady.

So long as the damned didn't pounce.

One of Ty's hands splayed and both gold and silver flashed in his eyes. The ground beneath us began to rumble and shake, thin cracks fracturing out from where we stood to the feet of each damned. "We'll be leaving now. All of us." Keeping up the earth tremor, he fished into his pocket and pulled free a cork-plugged vial topped with his vibrant blood. "With Dorian, Raven, and Amelia's mother too."

Through the trees and still fully concealed, Raven was behind my unconscious mom. The same dagger—the one that was so alike the blade Vanessa had given Marcus when he'd been using her through Dorian's compulsion—was pointed at her heart as Mom's body began to tremble. From this distance, I couldn't scent her blood. Thank God. But it would only take a little downward pressure or for those tremors to turn violent to remedy that. To kill my mom.

In a flash, I imagined her waking suddenly with a fitful seizure and red froth spraying from her mouth. Like I'd seen happen to Ty when he was transitioning—when he'd died a mortal death. How long had she been in this state? Thirty hours? Forty-eight? If this wasn't the start of her convulsions, how much longer did she have left?

I snatched the vial of Ty's blood and held it up. "A cure for the wolf bite for our freedom. We restore Raven and you release my mom. You tell me where she's marked."

Still on his butt with sweat beading down his face, Marcus smiled wide, flashing his pearly white teeth. After a few seconds of silence, his expression turned from contemplative to considering. "I see you've more than prepared for our little meeting. You've been marked—to block me from your mind. Too bad the mark doesn't work."

A sudden gust of sensation almost floored me, and Ty's strong arm hooked around my waist to keep me up. The venom that spread through Marcus's body felt like hot acid, burning brighter with every passing second. Brighter than I'd felt before Ty's blood cured me. Marcus wasn't lying. The mark was doing nothing to keep his agony from me.

Instead of wasting time on questioning, I stuck to my guns. Using Ty's strength to stay vertical, I relied on his blood in my veins to get me through this pain that wasn't my own. Bound by blood? I was fully connected to my twin. "That doesn't change…anything," I bit out. "We're…leaving, Marcus. Your life…for theirs."

Amusement highlighted Marcus's damp, angled features. "I don't need your blood, wolf."

The damned started to creep in and Ty amped up the earth tremor in warning. He glared down at my twin. "You do if you don't want to die. You may be as cold-hearted as a damned, but you're still alive. My venom *will* kill you."

One hundred percent factual or not, with our hard-to-kill status? It didn't matter so long as my twin believed the threat.

Marcus bit back a grunt and got to his feet, planting them on the ground to keep from swaying. That fire was spreading up into his skull—into mine—I could feel it searing through the bond, the one I no longer shared with Kendrick. But he didn't react—because what he'd claimed so long ago was true. I could feel it. The pain he felt wasn't a debilitation. No pain ever was. Not entirely. For the most part, it fed his ambition. Fed the big reveal I felt on the tip of his tongue.

Marcus nodded toward Raven. She dropped the dagger from my mom who'd stopped quaking. Her cloaked arms and hands reached up to remove the hood covering her face—or not. Beneath all those folds of black material was not that rounded face framed by cropped blue-black hair. Instead of Raven, the girl who was revealed had long red hair and pixie-like features.

"Vanessa."

Ty growled as she waved like she was greeting friends.

She had returned from Marcus's captivity after managing to mark herself to repel his compulsions. But with Dorian's and now my marks failing miserably, it looked like hers had as well. Her story of escape and belief in her free mind had been a compulsion too. "Marcus is still compelling her."

Marcus's choked but amused laughter filled the surrounding woods and damp air. But it was Vanessa who spoke. "I'm here because I choose to be. I want to be." Her sapphire-blue eyes pulsed with red as her pale skin darkened to gray.

But there was still a heartbeat. And she couldn't replicate that without blood from a restored damned. "You're not damned." I'd heard her heartbeat on every occasion since her return. Been drawn to her human-scented blood more than once. "You can't be."

As if to prove me wrong, she stopped drawing and exhaling air. Hiking up the sleeve of her robe she remained otherwise perfectly still, flashing her inked-up arm. She grinned at my mom like she was pleased with herself. Only enough air passed through her lips to speak. "All signs of life and so, so much more manufactured by these marks."

Ty's hold on me tightened, his earth tremors rising to keep the damned at bay. Or was that just a reaction of the shaking in his power-directing hand? "But—but in the den, Dorian almost killed you. He attacked you too."

"A good actor knows how to play their part," Marcus said, sweat now sticking his shirt to his toned chest.

"But my visions…" As Marcus staggered a step at a time, I had to understand this. "I saw your escape. Saw the times you were injured when we'd left you behind to spy."

"All a ruse." Vanessa shrugged. "A ploy to gain your trust. A fail-safe to keep you from knowing whose side I was really on."

Kendrick groaned then and I swear I heard Dorian twitch. Both were waking up, which was good. Ty's fading earth tremors weren't. I had a terrible feeling things were about to get messy. And my mind was running one hundred miles a minute. Mum transitioning. Raven MIA. Vanessa damned. We needed a way out of this. We needed to get my mom back to the Armaya. We needed to find Raven. I needed to restore Vanessa. But I knew I couldn't do it all. At least not now. Not with the damned surrounding us and all the obstacles. At the very least there had to be a way to reverse what had been done to my mom. Whatever it took, I'd find a way to keep her alive.

And even with Vanessa's revelation, we still had something Marcus needed. "Mom comes with us. Ty's blood for her, a clean swap. You need this to live."

Backing up toward his circling damned that he signaled to stall their approach, Marcus shook his head. "No, I don't."

Panic tightened my chest.

"I don't need his blood. And not because of our immortality. After my last wolf run-in, I made sure of that."

Ty was still watching Vanessa, studying every inch of her from where we stood. "Marks can't change your appearance. Definitely not like that, turning on and off at will."

"Clever wolf who killed me." Vanessa stood in front of my hanging mom and rolled one shoulder back after the other. "And you did kill me, Ty. At least the living me. But it wasn't Harper's blood that I was fed. It was yours. A total infection of damned after your wolf bite had taken root. For all of my markings, I may as well be a natural born."

As I puzzled over what she meant, trembles inundated her body and she fell on all fours in the wet grass and mud. Loud cracks rang out as her body warped and morphed, twisting and growing by the second beneath that robe. Her hair receded as shorter strands sprouted over her body, sticking out in tufts as the covering was shed and fell away. And then it was done. The auburn wolf who'd been a traitor in disguise this whole time, who'd abducted my mother and foiled our every move—was Vanessa.

"That's not possible." Ty actually looked like his legs were going to give out as he stared at his old friend through the easing rain. Like he was seeing her still body the second after he'd attacked back at the damned hotel.

There was movement behind me as Kendrick got vertical and rushed our way. His mouth gaped, eyes disbelieving the sight. The shock across his face as Marcus gained more distance screamed, *we're fucked!*

And despite it all, I had to know. *Are you okay?* But beyond the tightening of Kendrick's lips and a nod, I got no response. He was no longer my soul's mate, I realized with a strike of deep loss that hit me even harder than Marcus's physical pain.

My loss for him split for Dorian's well-being. He was pushing himself up now too as the waiting damned eyed him. But he only had eyes for Vanessa, and a look of rapt fear for what she now was —because he cared, because he loved her, because he was free of Marcus and was himself again. *"Vanessa."*

"Humans can't be turned damned," Kendrick added, redirecting my loss and Dorian's return to reality. "Infection kills them."

Ty saw Marcus's retreat and shoved me at Kendrick to take chase. Too late. With a burst of effort, Marcus darted across the mud-puddled dirt, motioning his damned to close ranks on either side of him. Making a barrier between us and them and…my mom. "Not if they're also turning into a werewolf, it seems." His smugness was earned. Bound to him, he had my mom, Vanessa, and Raven somewhere. "A wolf bite isn't fatal to a damned, and even though the damned can't be turned into wolves—believe me, I've tried—it seems simultaneous infection can achieve both in the right circumstances."

The proof was there, which meant he now had the means to create his hybrid, undead army—using Vanessa. And whether or not they were all freed of their damned weaknesses, he'd control the most dangerous and unstoppable creatures on this planet. Our newest and greatest threat to survival. Damned werewolves.

Beside Marcus, Vanessa let out a growl, her four paws clawing at the mud. Cracks preceded the jab of bones at her skin as her form shrank and shed its fur. And then it was done. A full reversal of the wolf she'd been only seconds ago. Rising pink-skinned, dirty and naked, she flung the muddy robe around herself and tied it at the waist. As the poison in Marcus peaked, hitting me just as hard and making my knees fail, her wrist was offered up. With a hiss of pain and looking like death, Marcus took it, drawing hard on her vein. One. Two. Three… I felt the agony flee my body like a wave cleansing my insides. Licking his lips, it was impossible not to see the instant transformation from sickly to strong. As Marcus straightened, I stood on my own two feet again.

Our upper hand was gone. Marcus was cured.

"Now for the real show." Marcus strode through his parting damned, leaving Vanessa behind, who, with the protection of those long billowy sleeves, began untying my mom's chains. He sneered to the damned that edged in beside him with their staring red eyes and puddle-sloshing steps. "Amelia's coming with us."

Free of his pain I stalked forward, hissing my disgust. "Like freaking hell I am. Give me my mom. Or so help me—"

"You'll kill me?" With his smile I saw the carnage he had planned before his spat interruption. "Too bad that's not how this story goes." To his waiting damned he said, "Apart from Amelia, kill them all."

"You son of a—" Ty lunged for Marcus, freeing a stake and his gun from his utility belt. In mid-air an animalistic bark raked from his throat. A command to take action. An order to attack. He landed with a splash, staking the damned who'd shifted to block his target, while firing off a round to debilitate another.

My twin was now free to be killed. Bound only to my mind and not my body like Dorian had been.

With an explosion of ash and spurt of black, a voice jarred Ty and the rest of us to a halt. "Incoming!" Raven burst through the trees, red eyes wild with the need to kill as she landed right in front of Kendrick.

Already on task to attack and kill, Kendrick's hand brandishing a dagger shook as shock widened his eyes. *"Raven."*

"It's not her anymore!" Dorian yelled out too late.

She cracked her skull into Kendrick's face and spat, "You're still outnumbered."

At the same instant, two wolves tore around the side of the cabin, canines tearing flesh off bones and limbs from bodies. Troy and Marika. Our last line of defense. And given the situation, our added muscle if we hoped to get any of us out of this alive.

The damned responded at once, baring their fangs as half came at us, and the remainder continued to keep Ty off Marcus.

Dorian dodged through the damned to help Kendrick, and kicked Raven back before her wide jaw could claim flesh. "I've got this," his words rushed at me. "Let's end this."

Wanting to stay and keep them safe, I hesitated for only a second. With Troy and Marika stuck to one side lashing out, and my brother and best friend centering the lot, Ty was on his own. Still cutting damned down in a desperate attempt to get to Marcus.

And he was already injured. I could scent his blood on the frigid air.

Mind made up. Freeing a stake too, I went to assist Ty. To take on our biggest threat and put it down once and for all. To get past his body once we succeeded and ensure my mom's safety, who'd just been dropped to the ground behind the gathered horde. With my freed stake flashing as it caught the moonlight between shifting clouds, I didn't get far.

Four damned blocked my way. Lashing out, I met backlash as warring hisses, cries, thwacks, and grunts joined the scrabbling of feet through softening dirt. One damned caught my free arm and twisted it behind my back. At the same time, another shot right before me, forehead cracking into my nose. All four hissed at the spurt of blood, nostrils flaring at the sudden scent. Unlike every other time since I'd been declared protected, they weren't holding back. They wouldn't take me out, but to do as commanded, they'd get close enough. With this realization, I got my ass in gear and focused my assault. Releasing voltage into the damned behind me, I threw my head back. Pain ricocheted through my skull, but I refused to teeter as the damned released me and stumbled in the mud. Instead, I thrust the stake straight into the heart of the one who'd head-butted me. But I didn't waste a second. As its combusted body exploded into live ash, I sent voltage at one of the two still standing. He went flying as the female damned launched at me—and met the black-stained length of my stake. Jumping through her instant airborne ash, I buried the tip in the chest of the one I'd just zapped. I spun, the puddle I'd landed in spraying out like a sprinkler—and got caught in a tangle of arms by the first damned I'd electrocuted.

As I summoned voltage, trying to stream it to everywhere he touched me, I saw my surroundings.

Closest to me, Kendrick had his hands full, twisting his dagger in a damned's chest as Raven circled, ready to strike. I scanned for Dorian, eyes darting to the other side of the clearway in front of the cabin. Dismembered bodies littered the ground, pieces strewn between nearby trees. And so much blood. Mostly black. Centering the carnage, Ty and Marcus were both bloody. Both full of rage as they handed out their weapon-driven punishment. Behind them there was no sight of my mom or Vanessa.

There was more scrambling, but it wasn't them or even Dorian. Still in wolf form, Troy and Marika were cut up but unstoppable as Troy flattened a damned and Marika snapped its head clean off.

And I couldn't help any of them.

Voltage failing like a flame being doused by rain, the damned restraining me shifted. His arm trapped my chest, while the other twisted around me to grab my chin. He was going to break my neck? Just like Marcus had done to Kendrick. A death sentence. But not in my transitioning state…unless full decapitation followed. But it would render me unconscious.

Good as dead and easy to cart away.

I sent out sparks as his hold tightened, but only tiny bursts erupted. I was tapped out. I couldn't reach behind and between our bodies to stake him. But I could— I let the damned tug my chin sideways, holding back a cry as vertebrae crunched—and chomped into his fingers. His tugging hand flung away and I spun, driving the stake between us—

I never got there.

The damned hissed and his body turned hot, becoming live coals that singed my tank and skin. He fell to ashes, leaving a clear view of— "Dorian!"

Flipping a dagger, he almost smiled. "Got your back, Sis."

With a cut leaking blood down his face, more of the stuff covered his torn skin and clothes. He'd fought the damned to get to me. He'd saved me from becoming Marcus's for good.

But even as I wanted to hug him, I knew there wasn't time. While keeping himself alive, Ty had dispatched so many damned. Troy and Marika were fighting back the others that kept them from their alpha. Vanessa and my mom were still MIA. And Kendrick had Raven on her back in the mud, his dagger over her heart being held off by her hand and his inability to kill the girl he was falling for.

"Amelia." His voice cracked as the tip bit into Raven's chest while she snapped her fangs and hissed. "Do something."

I vaulted over ash and bodies to help restrain her—to save

Kendrick from having to follow through or lay down his life as Dorian murmured, “I’ve got this.”

As Kendrick released her and she sprang up, I trapped her arms from behind. But her resistance was short lived. With a cry, her knees buckled as a grunt drifted from the tree line.

Ty’s arm slung around Marcus’s neck as my twin too fell to the muddy grass. Blood streamed from Marcus’s eyes down his red-smudged face as Raven in my hold coughed a spray of black. Kendrick joined the wolves to hold the startled damned back from us. Dorian kept one quaking hand pointed in Raven’s and my direction and the other in Ty and Marcus’s.

“It’s over,” Ty snarled in my twin’s ear as Marcus’s eyes bugged. With his rain-soaked muscles popping around Marcus’s neck, he was blocking his air supply. I felt it as my own head became airy in response, experiencing what he was now suffering. My mouth parted even though I wasn’t weakened at the feel of vertebrae being crushed. As Ty’s other hand came up to grip his jaw, I knew he was a moment away from doing to him what Marcus had done to Kendrick.

“Ty.” My voice was a warning to slow down. “Marcus, order Vanessa back here with my mom and reveal where she’s marked. Call off your damned. Restore Raven with me and…”

In my hesitation, Marcus coughed blood, then smiled. His teeth and fangs were covered in crimson. “And what, sister? You’ll let me live?” Blood dripped from his nose and ears, faster than the water dripping from his hair. His smirk was full of confidence. “If you can’t speak your own lies, why should I believe them?” His lips pulled wider, but his next words weren’t vocalized. *Besides, I’m not the real threat here, now am I?*

Like a switch being flicked, my conscience shut down. My sense of right and wrong vanished. I was too weak to stop it.

"Amelia, what's happening?"

"Amelia, speak to us."

But I wasn't listening. All I could think about was blood and how much of it came with taking life. How good it would taste once I hit my target. My prey. And this damned, quaking and leaking black in my hold? Not my kind of meal. But Dorian, my brother?

Not for long, Marcus's voice inside my head was all that registered, all that gave me my direction. Heart still beating? Not for long.

I dropped Raven without warning. My name was shouted, but I didn't care. And then I flattened Dorian with a splash. My fangs found that sweet spot before his wet hands could stop me. And then there was movement all around as Marcus yelled, "Hold them off!" Half in his mind's eyes, I felt him spin and throw his elbow up into Ty's jaw. Free. And then Raven was there, throwing the alpha back into the fray to be caught by the damned.

And I didn't care. Not as they clawed and bit flesh. Not as I lost sight of Kendrick behind the masses. Not as Dorian fought to free his neck from my bite.

Marcus's voice rose in my mind as he and Raven took off through the trees. *I'll be in touch when I'm ready.* And then he was gone.

Listening as the damned did their bit, I heard the slowing of Dorian's pulse as his fight weakened. He spluttered blood as he coughed, "Sorry—"

And drove a stake between my ribs.

Chest on fire, my bite released just before his fist to my face had me seeing stars. But I wasn't going down. Bracing for the sting, I yanked the stake free—and went to plunge it into his slow-beating heart.

Bang. Bang.

I froze on top of him as agony exploded beneath my ribcage. Blood leaked from two…bullet holes. On either side of my heart. Liquid silver spread like fire through me as Ty holstered the smoking barrel.

And then I fell.

Ty was right there, skidding in the mud to catch me as everything turned black.

CHAPTER 33

W*akey, wakey, Sleeping Beauty.*

The voice as my lids fluttered was cold and detached, a taunt more than a welcoming. It wasn't Kendrick's and it wasn't Ty's. It was in my head. Marcus.

Heart jacking into overdrive, I ratcheted up and scrambled back—hitting soft pillows and the stone wall.

"Hey, it's okay. It's just me."

I froze at the change in voice, its tenderness, its rational reasoning as heat neared me. Blinking wildly, I saw with total clarity—Ty. One knee on my bed—my bed back at the Armaya—his hands were raised like he was approaching a grizzly. Weapons at his waist flashed from the lamplight on my bedside, but he made no move to draw one free.

And he should have. I wouldn't have blamed him. As I peered through a crack in the drapes, the deep navy sky was darkening. A new day was arriving, since the last one ended with me being shot after trying to kill my brother. "How? Where?" I shook my head to clear the cobwebs. "Is everyone—"

"All alive. Even Dorian."

Until we meet again. Unless you'd like to do me a favor...

My hand went to my chest that was tender from where I'd been shot. Marcus wasn't here, but he was loud and clear in my head. I felt his need for other's pain and destruction as I tried to block him out. But his totally lacking conscience didn't make me forget who Ty was and lunge at him. And I knew why, as I noticed the live feed that was taped to my hand, the one I'd torn from Ty's inner elbow in my scramble back. Like when I'd shot myself after letting my transitioning self go, he'd cured me of silver and returned my minimal self-control.

But it wasn't more than a Band-Aid. I knew it as my eyes scanned his held-up wrists, his neck. As even with my hunger satiated a simmering need to take life bubbled inside of me.

Just give in. It could be so easy. You and me, we can be a team now.

"No!"

Ty frowned and straightened from the bed, hands close to his weapons as mine cranked into fists. "He's in your head. Isn't he?"

I nodded and scooted off the mattress. I couldn't go on this way. I wouldn't. Not when we'd all gotten so far and had so much still to achieve. Kendrick alive. Dorian free. Raven re-damned. Vanessa, the alchemist we'd never had, lost. A hybrid damned. And the curse... "Not for long."

With Dorian free of Marcus, I could take action now. I could restore my own conscience—

So long as you don't mind me taking our dear mother's head.

I ground my teeth, cementing in my mind the only other option I could come up with. *Fine.*

I darted around Ty through the foyer, but his hot hand tugged me around before I could escape through the main door. "Where're you going? *Amelia*, talk to me."

You can do so much more than that.

I tugged free as the image of ripping into his jugular flooded my mind. My back hit the door. "I can't be like this. It's worse than before." I held my head with my hands, squeezing my eyes shut. Still able to smell him and salivating in spite of the live feed that had only moments ago been detached, I gritted my teeth. "I need him out of here. I need to get to her. To the cells."

"You think Erzsebet can help."

Oh God, if she couldn't…

Ty's calloused hot hand caught mine and I was yanked off the door that was flung open. Then we were sprinting, down the back corridors, down stone stairwells, through the prison's iron gates and down to the landing as we reached the circular room.

"Open it. Now."

For once the guards moved without my insistence after Ty's demand. Which was good for them, because right now I was reminiscing over all the humans and guards Marcus had drained in *The Pit* like I wanted to stage a rerun.

And then we were closed inside, bleach remnants doing sweet-f-all to block the scent of blood, and Ty refusing to relinquish his hold on my hand—because I was tugging to get closer to…

The chained meal behind that desk. Come on, twin. You know you were thinking it.

And I had been.

Standing up at the fang-flashing sight of me, Erzsebet's chains rattled. She scanned me over, seeing something wrong despite the lack of transitioning traits. "What is wrong with her? What happened?"

"She's bound to Marcus."

"He's in my head," I snapped as his voice goaded, *Two for the taking. Don't pretend you don't want to.*

"I do." I hissed as the thought of using one of Ty's daggers on him—to cut off his arm and get to Erzsebet—made my free hand twitch. Instead, I grabbed the hem of my tank and all but ripped it off to expose the mark Vanessa had given me. "It doesn't work. I need it to block him out."

"That's because it is not complete."

As my mouth fish-gaped, Ty took up the verbal. "You know the mark. You know what's wrong with it? What's missing?"

Erzsebet planted her hands down on the books that crammed the table. Her sigh was a hope sucker. "Yes, I do…"

Even my questioning "but?" sounded like a threat.

"I need the equipment. I have naught but books—"

"I'll arrange it with the RVC." Aside from planning her murder over all those age-worn and stained pages, I still had enough mind to know that I now had the votes to get what was needed. Which was so much more than re-leashing my self-control.

"That is all well and good." Erzsebet went and sat on her tidy cot, toying with her long skirt. "Though I cannot say that it will be enough."

"What do you want in return?"

Ty's accusation had the Countess's brows popping up into her unbound hair. "Nothing more than I have already proclaimed. To stop the damned once and for all. And I demand nothing now."

Her laser-like eyes turned on me as Marcus grated, *Put her down and I might let one of your beaus survive our plans.*

But what Erzsebet said next stripped my twin's threat and the impulse to follow through from my mind.

"Since you are already bound, the mark—the complete one—

may not work one hundred percent. His ruminations, his compulsions...until we try, there is no way to know if you will be able to block it all out."

And this was my best bet to stop myself from killing everyone I cared for and joining my twin in his evil plot to free the damned? The backup was clear. End my life.

And leave Raven and Vanessa damned.

My dangerous urges spiked. I clenched my fists to keep from tugging Ty to me—so I could pin him to the glistening wet stone ground and attack with my fangs. If push came to shove, there'd be no choice but to leave Raven and Vanessa damned. At least the damned wouldn't be free. But before all of that, I knew I at least had to try option one. "Then we'll deal with that when the time comes."

And unlike the times past, if this failed miserably, I wouldn't chicken out. *For the greater good,* as Caius would say. A father's intuition from a man who had known my soul better than I had ever thought.

I SAT on my throne in the boardroom with the other royals, drinking from a bottle filled with Ty's blood. Each sip kept my fangs—along with my encouraged and violent urges—in check as I faked the in-out routine.

And I needed to keep it together. With enough votes, my mind would at best be safe from Marcus. Be blocked from his—

It won't work.

Being two a.m., the only light source came from the wrought iron chandelier. Its yellow hue suddenly spotlighted the recreated portraits in gilt frames that had burned when Marcus outed himself. Heat spiked in my palms like they were about to burst into flames too, as images of leaping over the marble slab to make paintwork of the royals inundated my mind. Fingers needling my thighs, I ground my molars. Feeling his hatred, I wanted—needed—to understand what drove my twin's actions. *Why are you doing all this? Just for power? To rule over everyone? To be hated?*

Marcus's hatred of the people around me bled to shock. A sense of his unease told me I'd struck a nerve. *All my life I've been alone. Wearing a mask with two faces. Even our father never understood me. Never really wanted me.*

From my left, Kendrick saw my bear-trap grip on my thighs and squeezed the top of my hand. Without our bond, I'd filled him in verbally, and for now he was with me in revealing Marcus's motives, his end game to the RVC. It was a necessary step to get me marked. It was also a step to figuring out an alternative to break the curse. The right way. Not that he was ready to sacrifice me to save Raven, but his hope that the Countess would come through with a solution for all of us ran deep. After being dead and coming back to life, he needed to believe there was hope for us all.

"I..." I addressed everyone. "I have some..."

He saw through the guise sometimes, our father. Marcus's continued words stalled my own. *He wanted me to be like you: someone who leads with their heart, is honest to a fault, who puts others first. Someone who would want to save the world. I hid my darkest ruminations from him, my secret plan to free the damned over curing them.*

Despite feeling a pang of sadness for him and the life he'd been dealt, my growing hatred for who and what my twin was lit ire within me. *So you could rule above all?* Demand *acceptance?*

Not alone. With you. And not solely. If the damned were free, a whole race would be like me, understand me and my motivations. I'd never be the odd one out again. The one to bring shame to his *family. I'd be a ruler. Over all. A king to everyone like me.*

He was already their king. They all operated under his instruction without challenge. *And feared by all who weren't.*

"Ahem." Lord Strigon cleared his throat, and as I focused beyond Marcus's words, I saw he'd filled all the crystal glasses and had handed them out around the table in wait.

By the open drapes that framed a clear, star-glittered sky above treetops, Dorian watched me, sympathy and guilt across his face. He knew what was tying my tongue. Or should I say who. He'd been living with it before I'd severed Marcus's control over him for long enough to know where my head was at. Addressing the room, he spoke for me. "We have important information about the damned commander you all need to hear."

"About Amelia's twin?" Lady Rasputin narrowed her eyes at me. "This should be interesting."

They'd have no need to fear me. Not with you by my side. You'd make them understand. You'd be my reasoning voice. You'd level the balance.

When I couldn't even control his thoughts and dark ruminations in my own head? When anything beyond his compelling voice was locked from my access?

Taking a hurried sip from my bottle, I spoke fast to get the sentence out. "My twin means to break the damned curse. It's the reason he kept me alive when I was a prisoner."

"I cannot believe that." On my other side, Uriel tabled her glass. "Curing every damned would lessen his threat to us and our people."

Murmurs of agreement came from Rasputin and Strigon, and I aired a quick response to my twin. *Level the balance? Not if I'm damned—which is what you want.*

I felt his fists clench as mine tightened, breaking flesh beneath my Under Armour tights. *Especially if you're damned! Even then you'll still be you: good to your core, though rough around the edges. Like you are now, even bound to me, the darkness. The best of both worlds. Everything I envy.*

Like he had when he was just a confused boy being raised by Caius's iron fist.

"Amelia didn't say Marcus wishes to *cure* the damned." Aware of my internal struggles, but remaining on track, Kendrick pushed his throne back and walked to the portrait of his mother. He sighed as he touched the intricate gold frame, shoulders rising and falling slowly. Any sorrow was gone from his expression as he turned to face us all. "He wishes to free them."

"Of their weaknesses," Dorian added, meeting the Vladimir throne, but not moving to take a seat—because doing so would remind him of Marcus and who he'd forced him to be for so long?

A twinge of desperation tainted Marcus's anger. *The people love you, despite your power and volatility.* He dragged in a long breath and blew it out. *Despite where you came from. They believe in you. You alone can sway their loyalty. Make them see both races can co-exist.* A flood of sincerity almost drowned me. *Because that is what I truly want.*

But I couldn't believe it. I felt his true desires that resonated in his black heart. In spite of the flickers of honest emotion and even jealousy at wishing he'd been the 'loved' child, he was too much like the damned. The kills he'd ordered, and especially the ones he'd executed by his own hand were a memory form of trophy. An accomplishment. One he'd never lose his will to continue.

Thinking of how close I was to being damned myself turned my stomach. It also stirred that little voice in my head that taunted, *you would be free, too—to live as the thing you were always meant to be. A monster.*

Like you believe I am, Marcus added with a sigh. *I'm not all black and white, Amelia. Like you, like everyone, I only wish to be accepted. For all that I am and will forevermore be.*

Slamming the voices down, I stood up abruptly. It wasn't fair. What Marcus was or how he'd become that way. Still I couldn't back him. I couldn't try to control him. I wasn't strong enough. "In the way Marcus intends, breaking the curse will remove their allergy to sunlight. It will cure them of insanity. Only Erzsebet has the knowledge and her past failures to stop this from happening. She believes the damned can be cured with the right environment and tools. She *wants* to help us."

"She wishes to be freed," Uriel added, getting a nod and grunt of agreement from Strigon and Rasputin.

As fresh images of bloodshed scoured my mind, I blinked past the imagined sight of Uriel with scarlet pouring from her cut neck. "I don't believe that."

"Chain Erzsebet in the den," Dorian added in a rush to cover my hissed words. "Keep her under twenty-four/seven guard."

Kendrick's hand on mine as I clawed at the table, was now tense like talons, ready to hold me back from taking someone down. "Don't let your fear of one restored cloud your judgment over what needs to be done to stop the rest."

"We need her help," I pleaded around fully extended fangs before draining the last of Ty's bottled blood. And not just to get Marcus out of my head. "This is our best bet to stop the damned once and for all. To bring safety back to our people." If it was even at all possible.

It's not, Marcus's detached voice was certain. *You're fighting for something that doesn't exist, twin. But by all means, waste what little time you have left before the big event. Nothing will be the same afterward.*

Silence rose as Marcus's consciousness and voice left me, all eyes on me as I held it together and acted 'alive.' While I pretended his unwavering statement hadn't struck fear through me.

"If the Countess is so honestly inclined, she can achieve this from her cell," Rasputin stated.

Where there was no power to plug that tattoo gun in to mark me. Where bringing portable electricity down to be marked by the noisiest gun ever would draw too much unwanted attention.

"I agree," Lord Strigon said, tipping his head.

With only one vote left to tip the scales, my look to Uriel was pleading. After the longest moment she nodded. "This is what my father sacrificed his life for. To see our race free of the damned threat—once and for all. As long as the security measures are enforced…" She sighed long and hard. "I vote yes on Erzsebet's location change so long as she delivers on your beliefs, Amelia."

EXHAUSTION WREAKED havoc on my body a few hours later, and I could barely keep my lids open. Or concentrate past the distant sounds of beating hearts beyond my suite. I scratched through my tank to the mark Erzsebet had completed on my ribs after her guarded relocation to the den. So far so good. Marcus seemed to be blocked from my head. Locked out along with his enticing imaginations of destruction and death.

But that didn't mean I was in the clear.

After failing to secretly invade his mind, I was left with only one option to find anything to help us. An option I'd been working at for, oh—I glanced at the wall-mounted clock between the bedroom and foyer archways—about fifty-two minutes.

Empty bottles messed up the coffee table and more littered the couch's adjoining chaise beside my stretched-out legs. Like Kendrick would say, *that bottled crap isn't cutting it.* Yeah, like that wasn't the theme of my life these days. But I wasn't taking straight from Ty's vein after our last interaction—where only Ty's bite to infect me had cooled the escalating passion between us. At least not yet. Seeing him suffer just to feed me—just to go along with my plans—was torture. Seeing how much he had to fight his body's reaction to my proximity was like hearing those horrible words over and over again. *I so badly want to ask if we can start again. But I can't do it. I can't get past all the things that have happened. I just... can't.*

My diet wasn't the only thing draining my spiraling vitality.

With Dorian now back on our side, and both Ty and Kendrick safe, we had new life-threatening issues. Raven was with Marcus—unrestorable without his help. Mom was in transition, and Marcus's biggest bargaining chip. And then there was Vanessa—damned and a werewolf.

With our group on different tasks, Erzsebet was solidifying the steps to cure instead of free the damned. When Ty had seemed convinced that the mark was keeping Marcus's non-existent conscience from sapping my own weak one, I had been left alone. Now I had to conjure the right vision to help us get to them. Or at least get a head start on what we were going to be up against. So far, I'd uncovered jack-diddly-squat. I was still no closer to finding Marcus or saving my mom, Vanessa, or Raven.

The polar mirroring wasn't lost to me. Three guys alive and free—returned to their real selves. Three women damned and fighting for the enemy.

Following the vote on Erzsebet, the RVC had been shocked to hear about Vanessa, but I'd had to tell them. With her knowledge and position here, it was too risky not to. For Dorian's sake though,

I'd managed to get the others to agree to capture over kill if she returned or was found.

I gritted my teeth. Exhaustion, diet, and failing visions. My fingers squeezed around the full bottle I held. There was too much at stake. I wouldn't give up. And no one was here right now to tell me to stop. Meeting the cool glass rim, I tilted another bottle and let Ty's chilled blood slide down my throat. My tired heart picked up its pace. The painful throbbing through my fangs died off yet again. My brain focused past those far-away but never-ending heartbeats. The bottle clinked against the other discarded ones piling up beside me.

Pile of how many? It didn't matter.

Leaning my head back on the cushion, my lids didn't need encouragement to fall. The darkness was heaven, the almost-quiet released the tension that tightened my limbs and ligaments. I squeezed my fist around blood-spotted tissues. I'd need them soon. Already, as the black caved in and the pure darkness rose, I felt the pressure building up in my head. But for now I ignored it. Pinned my eyes shut and pushed through until the starbursts gave out. The slimy remnants slid in, just like in all my other attempts. They were moving quick, slinking around and around my body like a carousel of ghostly spirits.

A damp trickle dripped from my nose. Already?

No. Too soon. I hadn't even grabbed onto anything tangible yet.

Refraining from lifting the tissues to plug my nose, I kept my focus. Too much distraction would tear this void away, and I wasn't letting the last hour of trials end on a fail.

I struck out with both hands, strangling a shadowy eel between my palms. It fought like a bass out of water, and I held tight, willing the slimy length to sink in through my skin. And then it did—

And shot up my arm and through my chest to escape out through my other hand.

I screamed in frustration. The first one I'd managed to absorb and it had escaped.

Thinking fast with the black starting to flicker—like I was on the precipice of passing out—I came up with a plan. Striking out again, I captured two remnants, one in each hand. But instead of forcing them to absorb into my palms, I smashed them into my chest. The ball of electric twine that contained the spinning voltage beneath my ribs, expanded for a split second, loosening to create a cavity. Forced through my flesh and bone, the ball of twine closed around the remnants, caging them.

Then the void erupted like a balloon of spinning black nothing bursting around me. Now standing on my balcony with the sun safely below the horizon, the wailing of the alarms struck fear through me before I saw the horror that was about to set upon the entire community. Countless damned scaled the walls like a black sea, pouring into our warded perimeter. Leading them was—

That's cheating, twin.

Marcus's cold voice tore me out of the vision and slammed me back into reality. Scrambling up, the bottles around me clanked and two rolled off the chaise, shattering with a spray of red-stained glass. I whipped a dagger free and sprang upright, spinning and scanning. Heart pounding and head airy with the trickle from my nose, I saw only inanimate objects and no movement. My ears confirmed the facts. I was alone. Only the sound of the guards' heartbeats down the corridor was audible.

Cheating? Even with the bond block and supporting mark, in my blood-deprived state, Marcus had slipped through. He hadn't had access to my thoughts, but he'd implanted his voice. And…

You may be able to keep your thoughts and visions from me, but I can steal them from your memory.

I dabbed my nose with the back of my hand and my eyes

widened. I remembered every second leading up to the void and the shattering of that black carousel. I remembered my triumph—because I'd succeeded in bringing on a vision. About…

If I can't see the future through your mind, neither will you.

And then he was gone. But as I fought to remember, I couldn't see the reenactment. Had it been Marcus's new location? A play out of the curse-breaking ritual? Something about my mom? Before outing himself as the damned commander, Marcus had touched me during my conjured visions to remove them from my mind.

Now he didn't need to be here to steal my visions away.

Through our bond, he'd entered my mind and stolen the prophetic insight. And just like those earlier times, I had no way to get it back.

The only upside was that Marcus hadn't seen what he'd stolen from me, either.

Before I could even think of anything to do to try to get what I'd seen back, my gut squeezed so tight I teetered on my feet. Sweat sprouted across my forehead and my body felt suddenly hot as goosebumps rippled across my skin. The loud racing of my pulse drummed through my ears, striking out any and all sounds. My sight reddened and swam as the world went topsy-turvy, the ground rising up and then rushing away.

I fell, barely catching myself before my skull hit stone.

"How's the vision conjuring—Amelia!" A deep male voice broke through the pounding as someone rushed my way with a clank and smash of bottles. Their hands were warm but not hot on my shoulders, their scent familiar and tempting. "What happened? Are you okay?"

My heart gave out and a squeal of starvation burst from my mouth. I pounced, barely missing blurry furniture to flatten my prey onto their back. He grunted at the sting of shattered glass, but with everything spinning and stealing my visual clarity, it was easy to ignore any familiarity. Easy to let go and give in to the roaring hunger that was tearing my insides apart. Mouth gaping I snapped for flesh—

"Amelia, stop!" The toned body beneath me fought back, holding me at arm's length. "It's me. Kendrick. Just hold up. I'll let you—"

A knee came up between us and booted me off. I hit a table, but landed on my feet, clinging to a falling lamp pole and stumbling as the world's axis shifted. Knees scraping stone, I blinked frantically to get a bead on my meal. Not retreating, but on his feet before the coffee table and coming closer. "Your funeral." The hiss that raked from my throat was a threat and a promise. One I would make good on.

Right. Now.

I leaped and drove him down onto the couch, glass clanking as I snapped to claim my prize.

"Been and gone," my prey retorted, hands cupped around my head to hold my fangs back. "And I don't plan on dying again." One hand released and bone cracked into my jaw. An elbow, driven like a roundhouse as he rolled up and out of my hold.

My sight leveled out, the hit bringing clarity out of the fog as I rose. A lounge room with new and old white soft seating, scattered and broken red-tinged bottles, and…*him*. Golden-brown hair, slender muscled body under a Burton T-shirt, and an understanding expression that begged for recognition. "Kendrick."

A worthy meal to start your new life, Marcus's voice taunted inside my head. Even though none of his visualizations or lacking conscience backed his words, I felt no impulse to let this feed go. To let *Kendrick* live. My hunger was stronger than my knowledge that he was the one I was hunting. My bond with him was gone, my previously borrowed conscience through that lost link as dead as —*he soon will be,* my inner voice added with glee. "Then our plans differ, *Kendrick.*"

Disbelief parted his lips and I lunged before he could react—

The body that shot between us was piping hot and all muscle and raw strength. My fangs hit just above his collarbone at the base of his broad neck as iron-strong arms came around me. They didn't fight or push me away. They trapped me, held me close as hot blood flooded my mouth and filled my stomach. "Take what you need. It's okay."

I clung to my substitute prey, nails breaking skin, clinging with murderous need. I drew hard and fast, gulping down my fill. Releasing my bite, I repositioned higher along his neck, getting a stronger stream.

And then everything slowed down.

Blinking as the blood rushing in my ears quieted, my head lost that airy feel. The red bled away from my sight. New sounds replaced the old. Two heartbeats, one quicker than normal. The other was right up close to mine and racing sporadically. Other senses registered, too. Blood of a Pure Blood and one of…

Lids flinging wide, I saw Kendrick standing just out of the way, leaning against the back of the couch. His lips were pressed into a thin line, his stare was locked on me and…

I tore my fangs free and shoved Ty away. Not because I'd just turned ripper and attacked to kill. And not because Kendrick was watching. But because Ty had just had to offer himself up like a bloody steak to a guard dog.

Ty staggered at the sudden release, red torrents streaming from where I'd bitten him to stain his muscle shirt. "Are you…" He kept stationary, not moving an inch closer as one hand dipped into his pocket. His frown lightened. "You're okay now?"

He wasn't asking about my well-being. He was asking if I was still a danger to anyone with a pulse. He glanced to Kendrick as if waiting for him to confirm my danger status.

Kendrick didn't lose that strained expression and shrugged. "We're not bound. I can't read her."

Talking about me like I wasn't even here. Well, that was fair, I guessed. Neither of them knew if the me I used to be had replaced the monster living inside of me. "I…" I shook my head but couldn't move. Instead, I looked to Ty then Kendrick. "I'm sorry. The vision attempts." My teeth enhancements were still on full show, still pulsing with greed. I spoke around them. "They failed, except for one. But Marcus got into my head. He stole the details through our bond." After what I'd just done I knew one thing for sure. "I can't get it back."

"I'm sorry, too."

My eyes shot from Kendrick to Ty, but he wasn't looking at me.

"I'll, um, leave you two." Ty walked the long way around the couch rather than through the space separating me from Kendrick. "I'll check in with the wolves, tell them something could be up."

Then he was gone, through the foyer and out the door.

Kendrick pushed off the couch and rubbed at his head like he'd hurt it—or I had, when I flattened him to the ground. "Have you told him about us? That we're not…" He shrugged instead of finishing the sentence.

Beyond the shock at his sudden change in subject, and even without being bound to his mind, I knew the words he hadn't said. "That we're not *us*." I put my hands up to my face and pressed my fingers into my forehead. Dropping them back down, I shook my head. It felt so strange to be talking like this to my best friend and former boyfriend. Especially now that we weren't bound. I didn't have to cop to anything. But I owed him honesty. He'd given me that one-million-fold. "There's no point. He doesn't want—"

"Like hell he doesn't." Kendrick came close, gripping my elbows. "Dead *and* alive, I've seen how he feels about you. Nothing that's happened has changed that." He drew a long breath in then let it out. "You have to tell him."

I pulled free of his grasp and stepped back—and not just because his heartbeat and the scent of his blood was still affecting me and the monster I barely contained within. "Why? Why encourage this?"

For the first time in so long now, Kendrick smiled. A real smile, one that held hope rather than masking upset and grief. "I can only give you so much. And I don't want what we tried to make work. Your heart wasn't in it, and mine isn't anymore, either. I'm falling for Raven, no matter where or what she is. And you're in love with Ty. You always have been." Ignoring my rigid stance, he slung an arm around my shoulder. "You're my best friend, Amelia. I want you to be happy. That's all I've ever wanted."

CHAPTER 34

With only minutes of evening twilight left until darkness took over, I stole down the corridors and back stairwells alone to reach my destination. Quickly passing the guards, who smelled too enticing even after a bottled top-up since my monstrous attack yesterday, my nod was a directive to keep out. Shutting the heavy door to the den on them was met without argument. I faced my grandmother. The only person who could have the answers I needed after my stolen vision. Who could lay out the possibilities of what my future—and everyone else's, for that matter—could hold. With my thoughts safeguarded and minutes and hours forever ticking on, it was time to take action. "What have you found so far?"

The inked quill in Erzsebet's hand froze, no longer scrawling black script across the open page of the book before her. With the beakers and Bunsen burners pushed to one side of the bench, stacks upon stacks of books surrounded her. "Hello, Granddaughter." Her eyes slid up, her brows rising in surprise. "You came alone? Where is your protective entourage?"

"Your guards are waiting in the corridor." After Marcus's invasion and our beatings, which I blamed on him to keep Dorian's name clean, I'd argued to keep my previously arranged protection only. "They won't come in."

"Not what I meant." Erzsebet's ankle chain that bolted her to the ground rattled as she placed the quill in a pot of ink. "Lord Baldassare and the hybrid. I've never seen you without one or the other. They are your protectors."

I averted my gaze as guilt settled in my gut. "They're…busy."

Since the RVC commissioned Erzsebet to research breaking the damned curse yesterday, and my failure to do anything to help our causes, I'd been itching to steal down here and pick her brain. And since her proclamation to help days ago and the deliveries to her before Marcus's book-killing bonfire, I hoped like hell she'd been able to tease out facts from past beliefs. Right now, Ty was on wolf detail and Kendrick and Dorian were off training to re-hone their skill in anticipation for all that was sure to come. Waiting for them all to be busy had been a drain in itself. Like me, Kendrick and Dorian knew what the rumored price was to cure the damned. And if that was the only way, I didn't feel like having to argue to give my own life to save hundreds, maybe even thousands. At least, not until I'd cemented an argument to back up my plans.

"You ditched them." Erzsebet sighed at the many books and journals surrounding her, most of which were the ones her daughters had sent over. Her hair was half up and half down with long stands dangling out. Her ink-stained hand dabbed at the page before her, testing to see if the scrawl was fully dry yet. With a frown as more black stained her hand, she glanced up from the brand new book she'd been writing in. The same one she'd detailed the resurrection to bring Kendrick back in. "Then you are here for answers. For my musings over all Caius's and my experiments and experience." At my nod, she continued. "Breaking the curse will nullify your ability to restore the damned. Once free, they will remain damned—forever."

Yet another reason not to fail. If there was even a way to cure them over that outcome.

I went to sit on the stool opposite her. "So were you right? Is there an alternative to cure the damned over freeing them?"

A clipped smiled was returned.

"Two halves of a whole need to join to lift the curse. Black and white. Night and day. Good and evil. They are as opposite as they are alike."

"Yin and yang…" Marcus had called me the yin to his yang. "Does that mean…?"

"Yes. There is another way. The damned can be cured. Every single one of them."

"At what cost?" The words accompanied the door swinging open as Kendrick strode inside. He shook his head at me. "I knew the second I left you…" He broke off, concern riddling his face as he came toward me while looking pointedly at Erzsebet. "The cost? Lay it out in black and white."

"Very well." Erzsebet flicked back a few pages in the book she'd filled and spun it around so we could see. "But you must know everything." On the page was the same symbol Caius had used to try to steal my power when he drained my blood. A circle with a lightning strike through the center. "To channel the powers for our cause, this symbol must be present at the ritual site. Painted in the blood of one or both of the powers will work best."

"The powers? As in more than one?" Ty came through the open door and shut it behind him on the loitering guards. He measured the thin gap separating Kendrick from me and kept his distance. But that did sweet-f-all to keep his scent from me. And yet the lack of confusion in his expression was a tell. He'd been informed of what we already knew, or at least suspected—by Kendrick. "That is what you're saying, right?"

I stiffened at his presence more than his words. My almost forgotten hunger suddenly reared its monstrous head, and I couldn't stop the image of me sinking my fangs deep into his neck from entering my mind. My fangs tingled, the smell of his, Kendrick's, and Erzsebet's blood becoming potent rather than a dull background smell. Reminding me of the live taste I'd stolen from the alpha after trying to use my best friend like a living blood bag. And the reluctant top-up he'd offered before I'd gone to sleep. How many hours had it been since I drank from Ty?

"Your perceptions are correct, hybrid." Erzsebet's reply distracted my one-track thoughts as she turned a page to reveal another sketch. Except this one wasn't of a symbol, it portrayed a scene. Standing together in the circled mark were two people. A male and a female, hands joined like they were holding something. "If the powers of light and dark unite during the ritual within *this* symbol, I believe what I hoped for all those centuries ago will result. The damned will be permanently cured rather than freed, and the curse will forever be broken. Creating new damned will no longer be viable."

"Light and dark." Kendrick tensed by my side, and not because he could sense my hunger rising. The ambient wrought iron light above painted his toned arms in sinewy muscle. "You mean Amelia and Marcus."

Erzsebet nodded, lips pressing together and eyes casting down. "Only the most selfless and pure offering can restore order from chaos." Her silver-blue eyes met mine, a glimmer of sadness weighing down her expression. "Only you can cure them, Granddaughter. Return them all to what they once were. To bring peace to our race. But to use your powers in this way, it cannot be returned to sustain your mortal bodies. With great power comes great sacrifice."

I'd heard this before, from my father who, even though he hadn't raised me as such, knew what I'd decide if given the choice to protect so many over myself. "To cure them all, my twin and I must die. It's the only way to stop the damned."

"Unfortunately, yes." Erzsebet stood, her thick chains clanking. "Drinking of your combined blood from the chalice will connect your flesh and blood. Together you two are the key, the combined power I never attained to achieve this with Lord Aswind."

I stared blankly at the pages in front of me, slowly sliding the freshly inked book closer. The sketch of the blood twins joining their powers of light and dark were Marcus and me. The key ingredients. Our actions alone could finally stop the damned from killing off our races. A triumph for all who were endangered. All who were on the damned's cattle list. And yet I felt despair cling to my broken soul. To have what I'd suspected all along confirmed? To know that only my life along with Marcus's would pay the price to achieve this end? My cruel fate. One I couldn't escape or run from. The sense of loss I felt for everyone I'd be leaving behind brought crimson tears to my eyes. "So this mark needs to surround us both to complete the circle? Once we're joined physically it'll take our lives in order to cure the damned?"

At Erzsebet's solemn nod, I stared down at the sketch again. The place I'd seen myself standing side by side with the damned commander—Marcus, my twin—in a vision so long ago. With everything I now knew, my lack of fear in that future glimpse now made sense, because I'd given in, decided to go along with his plan, all the while hiding my own to help rather than hinder our race. To remove the threat of our greatest enemy…forever. But there was one thing I was stuck on, a hurdle I couldn't mentally figure out. "How are we supposed to mark the site before the ritual? Marcus hasn't revealed the location."

"He doesn't need to," Erzsebet said. "There's only one location this ritual can take place."

Kendrick, face morbid and arms crossed over his chest, looked like he'd just watched Raven become a rabid monster again, pulled his mother's corpse from that fountain, and watched me die when Caius had drained me alive. He looked like he'd just lost everything. In a raw voice he said, "A place of great power."

The words he'd said so long ago now rose in my mind. *This is a sacred site—a beacon of power. Where the Dawn of Reckoning took place. And where the damned were cursed to darkness and insanity.* It made perfect sense. It had to be. "Mount Major, in the clearing. It has to happen there."

Kendrick came to stand at the end of the bench, hands resting against the cool metal edge. So much strain was visible up his lean, muscled arms, but I couldn't read him anymore. "The place where the curse was forged from the beginning."

Ty hung back, stare focused intently on his boots as he leaned back into the door. After feeding me late last night, except for his questions to Erzsebet, he hadn't said a word. During the feeding he hadn't said anything beyond, *Let's get this over with.* He'd fulfilled his duty and done so with perfect professionalism.

And I'd hated every second of it. Using him. Needing him. *Wanting* him. Seeing the detachment across his gorgeous face.

At least I wouldn't have to put him through it for much longer. Soon he'd be free again. Free to live his life. To move on. From me.

Moving closer, Kendrick flicked back a page to that lightning symbol. His deep sorrowful frown ironed out as his eyes lifted to me with determination. "Marcus will likely have damned watching the site in case we try anything. Getting that mark done and in the exact place you end up standing with him to complete the circle is virtually impossible."

My worry about Ty's demeanor, Kendrick's pain, and my limited lifespan dulled. My mind took off racing as I tried to come up with an instant solution. But even if we got to Mount Major and it was unwatched, or we disposed of any lurking damned, Kendrick was right. Short of marking every clearing regardless of its size, I couldn't pinpoint the exact spot I'd end up with Marcus. And even if I somehow could, and managed to somehow conceal a sizable blood symbol, he'd freaking smell it.

Slumping onto the stool, small sparks danced over my arms and down to my fingertips. This volatile power now had a larger purpose. After all the havoc and conflict this ability had brought to my life, my sight became internal, remembering beyond the good of restoring caught damned, the infected, Uriel, and Ty. There had been so much more bad. Electrocuting innocent bystanders and the people I loved, failing to save Ty after blasting Caius and his heart-spearing sword off him. Failing to cure the damned part of my twin. Failing to give Raven back her life for the second time. I'd sealed my fate when I sought out the lightning at Mount Major. When I'd become half the puzzle to this damned curse, a livewire until I learned to rein in the voltage. I'd hurt Kendrick, floored him and burned him from the inside out. Even in Ty's dreamscape—

Ty's dreamscape.

I'd zapped him there, too. And that's not the only sub-reality my electricity had the power to work in.

I gasped as a solution dawned on me, then coughed at the unwanted rush of air that filled my lungs. Kendrick gripped my bicep like he'd caught me about to topple off the stool, his hand slightly shaking. "What is it?"

"A vision." I pulled from his hold and stood, gaining a few needed steps from his blood-circulating body. My sparking hand came up. "My power transcends time and space."

No longer in the doorjamb, Ty stood tensely at the end of the bench. He looked like he'd just been punched in the kidney. "Like it does in dreamscapes."

Erzsebet stared at me in open curiosity. Then understanding dawned across her youthful, pale features as she touched her forearms—where I'd zapped her centuries ago. "You can use it in past and future. But—can you direct it with exact precision?"

I knew what she was asking, even as confusion crippled both guys' faces. Could my idea overcome the obstacle that stood in the way of my death and everyone else's survival? To answer, I stepped back again, making sure I was clear of everything and everyone, a few feet away from Ty and Kendrick, the bench, wooden crates, surrounding shelves and all that stacked glass and metal. I kicked off my Vans. Concentrating my power, I didn't stream it down to my hands. Instead, I forced the gathered spinning ball of electric twine from my chest cavity down like a beacon, focusing on the two paths that needed to erupt. And then they did. Striking out from my toes on one foot and my heel on the other, a jagged bolt of blue singed a streak of black into the stone ground. Then it changed course, splitting left and right in an arc until the circle was fully formed.

With the blue light fading fast, the outline of the circled lightning bolt was a black symbol that encompassed where I stood.

It had worked. "I don't even need to be there. I can mark the site in a vision. One that occurs right as the ritual's taking place." Now my eyes, wide and hopeful, shot to Erzsebet. She'd said the mark painted by one or both of the power's blood would work best. She hadn't said it was the only way. "So long as a mark by my power can replace the blood mark?"

Erzsebet's nod was curt and without hesitation. "A mark forged by one of the powers itself? It can't fail."

BACK IN MY LOUNGE ROOM, I paced to the mended terrace doors and threw the thick new drapes open. Just for something physical to do. Forcing my hands not to shake, the replaced panes of glass swung outward. The cooling evening breeze fanned over my face and through my loose hair. But not even it or the view and subtle scents of all that green and gold down in the gardens could distract me from the two figures I hadn't been able to shake on my escape back up here.

"You can't," Kendrick grated at the same time Ty said, "Don't do it."

The latter was back by the foyer archway, keeping his distance like he had down in the den. His muscles creaked with rigidity I could perfectly imagine without having to turn around. The former was nearer. Right behind me. The gentle warmth of his body so close it warmed my back. The suffocating despair of loss in Kendrick's voice hit me like a physical blow—because stopping me would ensure Raven's eternal damnation. The girl he was falling for.

Facing him, I stepped back onto the balcony, needing the space to clear more than the strong aroma of his blood from my senses. Ty watched my retreat but his face was like stone, unreadable as he remained statue still. I could barely believe my words as they flowed from my lips. "It's what I was born to do," I choked out as the door to my suite opened and shut.

Dorian appeared around the foyer table and stalled beside Ty. The slight strain across his face dissolved to horrific expectation at the sight and expressions of all three of us. "Born to what?"

Ty seemed unable to look at anyone as he rifled through his pocket. "She's…" A soft pack and his Zippo came out. A click, roll, and a chink later, and the smell of burning tobacco stained the clean air. He made for the door, pausing with it open. "I…" Smoke curled from his mouth. "I gotta go."

As the door all but slammed behind him, Kendrick was the first to speak, his voice deadpan and expression lost. "Amelia can save the damned. Cure them. By…sacrificing her own life."

As Dorian's jaw dropped, my repeated words made me feel like a taunting broken record. "It's what I was born for."

Kendrick moved with desperate speed, gripping my elbows with a shake. "Born to die—because your asshole father traded your life for his cause? Well, fuck that. I won't—"

"Trade my life for hers?" I gritted my teeth, forcing my punching-free fangs to retreat. Despite the lid he'd kept on his deeper emotions since I'd brought him back to life and before our bond had been severed, I knew Kendrick still loved me. Still, I couldn't lie to myself. I knew he held deep-seated feelings for Raven, too. The widening of his silver-blues at my candid words proved that in volumes. He was falling for her. The girl who'd saved his life when I couldn't.

Unwanted ire fired through my veins and I tugged free of his tight hold. "Well guess what? I'm not asking you. This is my life and my choice. And if it's the only option to break the damned threat, I'll take it. For the greater good," I added, repeating what

Caius had warned I'd eventually do. How ironic that he'd been right all along.

"What if there was another way?" Dorian came to stand behind the couch, his fists clenched by his side. His jaw was tight and his teeth ground together. With Mom in transition and in Marcus's hands, I was all he had left. But I could get her back. The woman who'd raised him as her own. Who loved him even now as her flesh-and-blood son.

I shook my head, hating what I was doing to these two guys who held pieces of my heart. My brother. My best friend. "Dorian, there isn't. Erzsebet—"

"Has told you her conclusions after a few day's worth of note compiling," Kendrick snapped.

"There must be another way." Dorian shook his head. "A loophole to keep you alive beyond the ritual."

"But right now there's not. And we can't wait forever. The damned need to be stopped." I began pacing on the balcony, hair flowing back and forth with each about-face. I dared my mind to find an alternative. A ray of hope. A sliver of something. But there was nothing. Like Kendrick had said when he'd been dead, life and death was a balance. My one life to save so, so many. It was a done deal. A no-brainer. I quit pacing to face both of them with utter certainty. "If Marcus forces my hand, if the damned start coming at us and our community again, I won't stand idly by and let it go on. I will stop—"

I was falling before my vision melted. Both guys rushed at me, Kendrick closer and arms outstretched to catch me. But I was out before I felt his rescue or the hit of the hard stone balcony.

With a single blink, I was standing in an enclosed concrete room. No windows and only one door to the side that led upstairs. Old blood—human, vampire, and damned—stained the air as much as the ground. But it wasn't the main attraction. On the long table right in front of me, the convulsing body was. Her mouth and chin were bloodied, her eyes wide and terrified. Her blouse was stained with red and torn, revealing black forking veins. Only a single heartbeat reached my ears. Still transitioning.

Mom!

As my voice rose only in my mind, any attempt to get to her, to remove the straps that tied her to the table, hit a mental brick wall. "If you're seeing my delivery, twin, my threat should be clear…"

Marcus. Stuck inside his unflinching body beside our mom, he made no move to help her. And his words made a few things very clear. He'd used our bond to implant this vision, this already happened event into my mind. But with the bond-blocking mark, he had no way to tell if I'd received his *special delivery*.

"Two days, at Mount Major. Shortly before twilight dawns. Agree to come? Our dear mother lives until then. Fail to show? That day will be her last."

The vision was gone as fast as it came and I found myself in Kendrick's arms with Dorian kneeling right beside us. My fangs were already free and I scooted away from both of them, swaying as I gripped the balustrade to get vertical.

"What happened?" Kendrick questioned at the same time Dorian said, "What did you see?"

I tried not to track them as they both stood upright. Tried to ignore the tingling of black veins growing beneath my clothes and forking up my arms. I spoke quickly, fangs sliding over and poking at my lips. "Mom's not doing well. And the deadline to break the curse is set. For two day's time—shortly before the sun rises. He'll keep her alive only if I agree to show."

Dorian faced me, frown lifting from the veins now tracking over my shoulders. "So you're doing this? You're going ahead with it all?"

I nodded, sending out the only decision I could make. *I'll be there, Marcus.*

Hearing only what I let through, Marcus's reply was expectant. *I knew you would, twin.*

To Kendrick and Dorian, I said, "For Mom, Raven, Vanessa, all the damned, and our race. I have to. There's no other way."

"You don't know—"

"Even if there was," I said, cutting off Kendrick's rebuttal while feeling the stab of his piercing eyes, "we don't have time. I don't. The deadline is set. And I won't put my life above theirs. I won't let Mom die so I don't have to. I've made my decision."

Kendrick's silver-blues dropped to his DCs and his shoulders slouched. "Don't do it." When I said nothing, his tear-filled eyes lifted and his brow furrowed with deep thought.

With my hunger rising, I felt my sinister side growing, gaining power by the second. Transition traits surging, their blood made my mouth water as the beat of their elevated hearts became like drums in my ears. But there was another sound too. His voice. Ty's. Down in the garden's outskirts, blocked by tall hedges. He needed to know about my plans. The deadline. And I needed his blood.

And to get away from Kendrick's and Dorian's suffocating grief and their full, pulsing veins.

Going inside, I couldn't meet their unyielding stare as I swooped my hoodie up off the couch. Back out to the balcony and it was on, covering up the veins snaking down my arms as I kicked a leg over the balustrade. Just before I dropped over the edge, I met their misty eyes. "I'm sorry."

~

Less than a minute later, I moved quickly through the gardens, following Ty's deep voice and the scent of his blood and burned tobacco. Leaving behind all those beating hearts inside the castle as the forking black peeked over the backs of my hands and up my neck. Knowing what I had to do with him and what I had to reveal at the same time made me want to turn back. The reddening of the tall manicured hedges and gravel path as autumn leaves crunched under my shoes kept me going.

The safety of others came before my discomfort and fear of his response.

Darting left then right through the maze, his voice became clearer. Carried on the breeze it was nothing short of a snarl. "Do you have it or not?"

As I found him through a hedged arch in the same clearing below that draping willow, he spun to face me and paused. His phone was pressed to his ear. "I'm on my way."

"Where are you going?"

Ty saw the veins and my red stare. He didn't answer my question, instead striding closer through the delicate dropped leaves from the willow. Freezing in front of me, he clasped my neck with one hot, scarred hand and tilted my face up. "A vision?"

I tried to focus past his scent. Past the heat of him so close. Past the rush I felt inside to have his bare skin touching me. My words rushed, "The deadline's set. Two day's time. Mount Major. My mom's dead if I don't go."

With a flash of white-gold in his eyes, his hold relented. Hand bending back, his wrist was offered, hovering an inch from my lips.

It took everything in me not to strike then and there. To focus on the phone he still gripped in his other hand and the words he'd barked into the speaker. "You found something? That's why you're taking off."

His nostrils flared as if annoyed. "I restocked your fridge when you were still in the den. There should be enough until I return."

He was annoyed I'd come down here to use him over the nearby alternative I hadn't been bothered to look for upstairs? Clearly. But as the red lens over my sight flourished, I turned off the fact that I cared.

"Just feed."

My heart chose that moment to peter out, the pumping muscle turning dormant. The tone of my voice changed as I clutched his wrist. "Exactly what I had in mind."

But I wanted all I could get as fast as I could get it.

Tugging Ty forward, my other arm crowbarred around his neck—and met no resistance as my fangs hit that sweet spot between his jaw and shoulder. The flood into my mouth was fast and as hot as his body up against mine. The red retreated all too quickly, as did the veins as they reversed up my arms and legs with fading tingles.

When the rising moon above cast down on us like a spotlight, I heard something over the rustling of leaves and the jackhammering of Ty's heart.

Clicking.

No. A sort of ticking.

Keeping my viper grip on his neck, I angled only enough to see the source. Ty holding his phone—and texting. My normal thoughts returned from my now-dwindling transition side. He's so over me, over an act that used to rev up his body and actions so explicitly, that he's casually texting? Although, casual wasn't quite right. His whole body was tense, almost trembling with his key-hitting thumb.

Which was probably because I, the human-sized leech, was still attached to him like the parasite I was.

I withdrew my fangs fast and stepped away, fresh air striking the stale smell of smoke on his skin and clothes, along with his blood from my sinuses.

"You won't have to—"

"Here you are." I whirled to see Troy at the opening, tall frame barely fitting through the gap in the hedges. As usual, he was equipped to fight with silver decorating his belt. "Got your text."

Marika appeared beside her guy, similarly equipped and dressed in tight black gear. A look of mixed anger and sorrow crossed her face as she glanced from me to Ty. "Ready to go?"

"Yeah—"

"Go where?"

Ty began walking their way while Troy's expression hardened at me with such severity it kept me from following. "Wolf business," Troy snapped.

"Where? For how long?"

"I've said all you need to know, Blondie."

Ty placed a hand on Troy's shoulder and nodded. "I'll be right behind you." His voice was warning, but also empathetic. "Go."

With a huff, Troy was gone, Marika tailing with a last backward glance through the moonlit maze of hedges, their boots crunching gravel and leaves in their wake.

Ty turned back to face me, but he didn't close the space separating us. The look on his face was a mask I couldn't decipher. "I'll be back tomorrow. In plenty of time for the deadline."

Right now that was the furthest thing from my mind. If anything happened to him—to any of them… "That's not why I was ask—" I stopped myself, needing to know, feeling a strange hunch I couldn't put my finger on. "What's the wolf business?"

Ty's eyes darted up to the sparkling stars like they held the answer. He shrugged and re-met my gaze. "Just a damned lead. See you when we're back."

And then he too was gone, leaving me alone below the willow, the flutter of his heart at his last words branded across my memory. A tell. Like he'd taught me to pick up on so long ago.

A lie.

That he had no intention of coming clean about.

CHAPTER 35

I paced before the night-sky-gazing windows in the boardroom, unable to release the corded strain of every one of my muscles. And not because the room was fast filling with living bodies full of what I craved. Already two a.m. The end of this vampire day fleeting as every minute and hour passed. One full day existed beyond this one…before the next, when I offered myself up on a silver platter. In two day's time, the curse would be broken. The damned would be cured—not freed. Raven would be alive—and so would Vanessa, though there was no way to make her human again. She'd be a hybrid forever more. And Mom? As long as Marcus stuck to his word and kept her alive, she'd be okay too.

And I'd be dead.

Three souls, plus thousands of damned ones saved in place of two. Mine and Marcus's. Our lives and souls for theirs.

Less than forty-eight hours. Oh God. It wasn't enough. It would all go too quickly. But even as my legs quaked at the thought of ceasing to exist, I knew I couldn't change my mind. This is what I'd been born to do. Born to die. Saying goodbye to everyone I loved would almost kill me.

"Amelia?" Kendrick's voice jarred me to a stop and my legs cried out in protest. His glassy eyes watched me with unmasked despair. "Everyone's here now."

From the Vladimir throne, Dorian watched me, sadness straining his face. He didn't say a word. But I could hear his feet bouncing his legs below the marble slab and see the way his hands shook despite how hard he clasped them together.

Glancing around the rest of the table, Uriel, Strigon, and Rasputin watched me with avid curiosity. Reading my anxiety and both guy's depression made it totally clear something was going on. But they'd never know. Not until it was too late. I didn't move from my spot. I couldn't cage myself in my throne and go through the usual reports and suggestions of how to stop the damned. With the doors closed and no knowledge of where Ty was right now, I already felt like a caged animal.

I nodded my head, mentally ordering my lips to lie. "Erzsebet is still—"

"The date is set for two nights from now. Marcus expects to free his minions, but he won't get to."

"Kendrick, no!"

He kept on talking right over me as I rushed toward him. "A sacrifice will divert his plan, it could cure the damned over freeing them. If it works it would eliminate them for good."

Uriel looked past Dorian to me with hope and confusion in her eyes. "A sacrifice?"

"Amelia's and Marcus's lives." Dorian sounded dead as he spoke. "To cure the damned permanently, they both must die."

Discussion erupted at the bombshell, the other royals speaking over each other in shock and argument of the act. My ears started up buzzing and I barely heard what they were saying, only catching snippets of each argument for or against. Losing both their Oracle and another crowned royal, the possible end of a threat to our race. Stunned mute by my best friend and brother's betrayal, I couldn't summon the energy to berate them. What good would it do anyway? The cat was out of the bag. Staring blankly at the gilt-framed portraits around the room, I didn't bother to argue or plead my case. There wasn't any point. This was happening with or without their agreement. I wouldn't allow the rest of them to become just another face on the wall. I just had to figure out my next move if the vote went against me.

Seconds, minutes, it could have even been hours later, the din quieted down. The buzzing faded from my ears and Kendrick stood. His warm hand touched my elbow. The look on his face was pure hell. Even without the bond, I could feel his ultimate agony. "I'm sorry, Amelia. We…we couldn't let you do it. Our race can't lose you. We can't."

Yanking free of Kendrick's touch, I panned over the other royals and my brother still sitting around the table. Uriel was on her phone, expression tense. Dorian looked like he'd just staked me himself. He'd argued for them to veto my plan. He'd chosen me over our mom and Vanessa. I felt his desolation in the unshed tears that welled in his eyes. The other royals looked resigned, agreed on their decision as Uriel said, "Thank you, Alpha," before hanging up her phone. To me she added solemnly, "There is no guarantee this process will work. We can't risk the damned being freed if it doesn't."

"We've all agreed you're grounded." Dorian pursed his lips, unable to meet my accusing stare. "You can't leave the compound."

"You'll be assigned a full guard detail to keep you safe," Strigon said with regret.

"And as for the damned…" Rasputin twirled the glass in her hands as she nodded across the table.

"We will have a contingency of wolves and vampires organized to meet the damned commander at Mount Major. Mr. Malau will appoint his best," Uriel informed as a matter of fact. A decision that wouldn't be revoked.

"Their order will be to kill Marcus and any damned who stand in their way," Kendrick added. He gripped my upper arms and squeezed, gulping as a tear escaped his eye. "With him gone, we'll have a better chance at stopping the damned."

"Better than curing them all?" As the smell of his blood and the sound of his pulse reached me, small stray currents escaped at his hold, but he didn't let go until I tore my arm free. My heart shattered at his and Dorian's betrayal. And, because in the end, it wouldn't matter. With or without their support, my plans would go ahead. In my silence during their heated discussion, I'd been conjuring up a plan. And right now I had an idea. Which had to work. To save my race. To save them all. I shook my head. "Then I guess you'll all have to live with the consequences."

BACK IN MY SUITE, I paced beside my bed, shoes hitting stone then rug. Stone then rug. Outside my suite, two guards kept watch in the corridor. If I tried to leave, they'd be right on my tail. I glared at my uncovered windows and the terrace doors. More stood watch out there, armed with swords, stakes, and inked to repel any compulsion I might try on them.

I was trapped. A prisoner.

But I wasn't about to let that stop me.

I glared down at my iPhone again, seeing the back and forth.

'I need your help.'

'Still off the grid on wolf business.'

The one person I had left to call on and Marika was off with Ty and Troy. I was running short on time.

'Need to talk. Without ears. Dreamscape me. Please. I can't do this without you.'

Minutes had passed with no response as I forged a beaten track in the rug. I had to hit her where she cared. '*There will be casualties. Wolves will die.'*

A sudden response flashed on the screen with a repetitious buzzing. '*Get comfortable.'*

Knowing what was about to happen, I fell cross-legged to the rug, back propped against the side of my—

My head didn't touch the mattress before my eyes rolled. And then I was no longer in my bedroom or even my suite. Head cranking upright from cold glass, I realized I was in the back seat of Ty's WRX.

In the same fitted black clothes she'd left in, Marika faced me from the other side. That mixed emotion was still across her tan face, visible in the shadows of the leather-seated car from the moon that shone through the rear window. "Get talking and do it fast. I've got shit I need to do."

That she would clearly rather not be dealing with. To do with Ty? I didn't waste breath on asking. I had one objective here, and one alone. "I'm grounded…" I laid out everything and how it had come about, ending with, "The damned will still exist. Wolves will die in the crossfire. And who knows if Marcus will be stopped. I'm the only sure bet. But I need you, just one last time. I need you to be me."

Gold eyes falling to stare vacantly, Marika seemed to be piecing it all together. The risk. The advantage. The pros and cons of keeping out of it over helping me. A battle raged across her strained face. Like the choice she was deciding on ran deep within her. Like it hurt her personally.

"I know Ty isn't all on board with my plans..." Her expression changed to impassive at the mention of him. "But I know he would do anything to rid the world of the damned. To make it safe...for everyone."

With a deep and unsettled sigh, she finally nodded. "Oka—"

A loud chiming suddenly cut her off. A phone.

Like an old movie reel being burned on the big screen, I found myself back in my suite, tipped sideways on the floor. I sat up abruptly, disoriented and confused. Raising my phone I still clutched, the interruption hadn't been from my end.

My thumb sped across the screen. '*What happened? R U OK? R U in?*'

As I waited and waited, my wide eyes burned as I stared at the screen. When I was about to give in and call her, my phone vibrated with her reply. '*Wolves are being redirected to Portsmouth. Apart from Ty, we're not allowed back onsite.*'

They'd all been barred? And Ty would never take my place and leave me to challenge Marcus without him. Despite his could-care-less attitude, I knew that deep down in my marrow.

Shit. I needed a new plan. A new out. All those wolves and vampires. I glanced through the windows where each guard stood facing outward. Like they were guarding me over an outside threat, rather than the threat I posed to myself. A whole contingency was being arranged to leave the compound tomorrow, leaving only enough to guard the community—and me. I wouldn't let them die in my place. None of them. I just need to think—

My phone buzzed, the screen lighting up. '*Got a plan. I'll get to Mr. Malau. I'll hold the wolves back from acting.*'

My thumb moved like lightning. '*How? What can I do?*'

'*With the truth,*' was her simple and unhelpful explanation. '*Just be ready when the time comes. And don't tell Ty. If you do, our deal's off.*'

I ENTERED the alchemist den and closed the door on my babysitting entourage. The familiar person I hadn't expected to see down here made me freeze. I mean, I'd been looking for him. To ensure he'd returned safely after Marika's text on saving more humans. To relive my worry that he might have figured out whatever his pack mate was up to and planned to stand in our way. To know that the one person who could control and strengthen me still had my back in my quickly declining hours until the main event. But this was the last place I'd expected to find him, even after that tiny earth tremor I'd moments ago disregarded as the real thing over anything elemental. "Ty, what are you doing here?"

I frowned as he spun around, holding something behind his back. "Amelia…uh…" Over by the shelving and cabinets, he shook himself. "I was delivering a blood sample for your grandmother to test."

Close by at her workbench, Erzsebet picked up a rubber-capped vial topped with red from beside a microscope. "So I can confirm if the change in my cells is restore related."

Before I could question what the change was, Ty's shadow-circled eyes darted to the door—hearing my loitering guards. With clear stubble across his face, it looked like sleep and shaving had been skipped for his recent excursion. He glanced over my exposed arms. "Are you hungry or something? Who's in the corridor?"

Erzsebet's eyes slid from Ty to me. Her lips twisted in contemplation. "You've been reassigned guards?"

"Uh, yeah." And now for the lie. "Extra protection until I take off for the ritual."

"So the RVC knows about everything?" Ty leaned his weight from one leg to the other. "Is that why they're organizing wolves to gather in Portsmouth?"

Marika hadn't told him. Neither had his father. He wasn't aware of the change in plans. The utter refusal of my sacrifice. "Uh huh," was all I could force from my lips. I felt like crap for lying so blatantly, but there was an inkling I couldn't shift. One I needed to get to the bottom of. Something wasn't quite right, here. I eyed them both, my suspicion unmovable as I came to stand before Ty. Even after a bottle of his blood before my search started, I couldn't ignore his scent or the beat of his, Erzsebet's, and the guards' hearts. But I could keep it together. And after his reaction to my sudden entry, my focus was elsewhere. Without touching him, I spoke softly as my grandmother busied herself at her workbench. "What's behind your back?"

Ty sucked in a deep breath, looking to the side rather than at me. His eyes met Erzsebet's for the briefest second. "I've been tying up loose ends." He held out a sketch of the amulet between our bodies, forcing me to back up. "Double checking to make sure everything goes as planned tomorrow."

I frowned down at the charcoal drawing, seeing the ghost tracks of swirling lines below the heart-shaped bloodstone. "The inside of the stone is marked?"

Ty shrugged, folding up the page. "It's always been there. Not usually visible to the naked eye—unless you're looking for it."

"Oh." A tiny detail I hadn't ever noticed in all the time I'd worn the amulet or even after I'd returned it to Ty before Marcus had stolen it. "The marks are needed for the ritual then, to break the curse?"

"Among other things…"

I went to take the page from him and Ty jerked his hand back, shoving the folded sketch into his leather jacket. "Ah, I need to show you something. A memory of mine."

Frowning up into his eyes, I sensed his caution and unease. Like he didn't know how to act around me after everything that had changed and changed again. But I wouldn't deny him, not when there was so little time left. And I knew what he was asking permission for. The only way to make me relive one of his memories—just like Marika had done when the wolves had defended The Seven from Marcus and his damned. "Sure."

As I glanced over at Erzsebet, I just caught the nod she directed at Ty from behind my back. She smiled at me before busying herself by tipping concoctions from one test tube to another. Had I missed something? "Um…" Though even as I frowned, my thoughts returned to Ty. There was only one marginally private place I could think to go. "Should we go to my—"

"Don't mind me, Amelia." Erzsebet nodded to two crates cornering one wall across the other side of the large den. "Use that quiet space if you so wish. I'll alert you if there are any unwanted interruptions."

Which would bring Ty and me out of it like Marika's phone interruption had. And which was a better alternative. I didn't want to take Ty up to my suite. Too much had happened up there with him. And the risk of Kendrick or Dorian showing up was too great. I wasn't ready to deal with them after what they'd forced into place with the RVC.

I shrugged and began walking. "Alright, then."

Ty followed and sat after I did on the crate beside me. He made no effort to touch me as his lips curved into a tight smile. His brows hiked. "Ready?"

Knowing I was about to be knocked unconscious by Ty's ability to warp reality alone didn't concern me. Not even after the times when he'd forced me into his dreamscapes and from reality when damned. Unlike then, this Ty wasn't dangerous. Not anymore. I'd made sure of that. And I trusted him. With everything that I was and would ever be. With my life. Completely. "Sure."

The next blink of my eyes had me jolting back. I was no longer in the den with Erzsebet across the room. Ty was gone, a young boy replacing him that was much smaller but had his same satin-black hair, and what had been his golden eyes. "Ty?"

The boy gave me a somber smile and shrugged.

A woman's scream made him flinch and forced me to take in our surroundings. Tucked into a hidden compartment in a built-in closet, I could see beyond the cracked open door and through long hanging clothing. Movement caught my eye as grunts and the sound of hissing followed. The woman's scream had come from out there. A boy's room with car pictures on the walls, and a model airplane that spun from its hanging position from the ceiling. The woman was thrust down onto a single bed covered in red and blue bedding. She clawed and bared fangs and canines at her attackers. Two individual sets. A hybrid just like Ty. The modern setting and knowing Ty had witnessed this as a boy, made who she was horrifically clear. Ty's mom.

The man on top of her backhanded her face, making her hiss louder. "Tell me where it is." The others pinned her arms and legs.

The woman spat in the man's face. "It's not here. You'll never get it."

Her reply was met with a left and right to the face. "Find it!" the man screamed to the others. "Tear this place to shreds." Five more rounds of fist flying followed as the three others began ransacking the place. The boy next to me tensed, his canines sliding free. He gripped the door's edge, as if ready to jump out and take on the group of men. But then he froze.

I looked back through the gap he stared through. His mother's head now hung off the side of the bed. Her pleading gaze was set on the boy. On Ty. *"Stay,"* she mouthed as tears glistened on her bloody cheeks. *"Stay there. Please."*

The closet door was tugged open and the boy pulled the hidden door behind all those clothes shut with a start. I heard things being tipped and hanging clothes being dropped. "There's nothing here," a voice beyond announced.

Boots retreated away and the boy dared to inch the door open, even as I said, "Ty, don't."

The woman was bucking beneath the man on top of her. Trying to break free. Fighting until the end. Convulsing as loud cracks and a roar rang out.

Before she could shift forms, he whipped out a switchblade and drove it down into her chest—straight into her heart. Her mouth gaped and her body fell slack. Crimson welled from where the blade came free, waterfalling over her to add to the red of the covers and stain the blue to black. The man dismounted and booted her head. "Good-for-nothing bitch. Let's get outta here."

Their treading boots faded and a door slammed out of sight. Then the boy burst from his hiding spot, scrambling to get to the woman. His mother. Ty's mother.

Somehow now beside me in his current age and form, Ty watched with me as the boy pleaded for his mom to get up, for her to be okay, for her to stop bleeding so much. He cried for his father, screamed for help. When he broke down sobbing, the woman's hand lifted, trembling as she cupped his rounded face. "You—still have it?"

"Don't leave. Please, Mom."

"Ty, do you"—her quivering lips that were turning purple-blue by the second struggled to form words—"still have what I gave you?"

The boy sniffed back his tears and uncurled one small clenched fist to reveal the bloodstone and silver chain. "I kept it safe. Just like you asked."

"Good, good, my son." Blood trickled from the side of her mouth, dripping from where her head hung and down onto the wooden floors. She faked a smile. "Keep it safe…always. It holds great power to save—to save a life." Her face pinched for a moment, then released as if the pain of death was suddenly fleeting. Her voice didn't give up, forming hoarse whispers. "One day it may save the world…from great evil. Don't let…it fall into the wrong hands. Promise me?"

"I—I promise, Mom. But please don't—" His plea cut off as her expression fell slack. Her entire body went still.

His mother was dead.

The view of him as a boy, covered in his mother's blood, blacked out. Only Ty and I remained, alone together in the closet. "I failed her that day, but I never stood by again and let someone die when I could act. They wanted that stone. Vampires. Renegades. They'd heard rumors about the amulet being needed to free the damned. They wanted that control, possession of something they could use or bargain with."

I felt like someone else was speaking even though I knew the words were coming out of my mouth. "How do you know all this?"

Gold blazed in his eyes, burning out the silver for a heartbeat.

"After years of forcing my father to train me, to make me as deadly as they had been, I hunted every one of them down. I forced them to tell me why they'd killed her. And then? I repaid the favor."

Ty had been a boy, not even a teenager. To have seen all that—I understood so much about him now. His harsh treatment at times, his drive to save anyone in danger. The regret that killed him at all the heinous things he'd committed while damned. And now I was going to sacrifice myself, force him to stand by and watch while I did the noble thing. "I'm so sorry."

Ty cupped his hands over mine, the depth of resolve and sadness in his eyes drowning. "Now her amulet, passed down from my grandmother, will finally do what it was intended for. Because of you."

I CAME out of Ty's dreamscape hearing the drawer below the bench Erzsebet sat at rolling shut with a bang. She darted a look our way, and at seeing my open eyes she slid two beakers filled with what I could scent was vampire and damned blood away and busied herself by burying her nose in a book.

Strange. Plus the vial of Ty's blood was still untouched beside her. I went to question what else she was up to and what she'd already found out—but stalled as Ty's hot hand came down on my scarred forearm. He let go just as fast, his voice gruff and brow furrowed as he spoke. "Ah, about the vision marking…"

I stood abruptly, certain an argument was coming. Ready to stand by my choices. To defend them. "Ty, look—"

"I'll replenish you afterward. Before we leave for Portsmouth."

"Ah…" I didn't know what to say as his eyes fell. He wasn't

going to stand in my way like Kendrick and Dorian had. He was standing by me. All the way. “Thanks.”

As my eyes pricked with emotion, I had to turn away. I didn’t want him to see the sadness and fear in my eyes. I didn’t want to give him any reason to revoke his help. And one of the last times I’d get to be at his vein, feeling his warmth and strength as it filled me.

With my back to him, I reached the end of Erzsebet’s workbench, toying with whatever was in front of me that my distant stare refused to focus on. “It’ll be later. Closer to take-off time.” So long as Marika pulled through for me, and no more obstacles were thrown my way. “I’ll…”

I frowned as my sight cleared. The rustle my shaking hands had created by curling the edges of an open-paged book stalled. I couldn’t look away from the calligraphic heading on the tattered old page.

Conscience Sharing. A blood bond alone can influence a conscience to great lengths…

Just like Kendrick’s had done for me when we’d still been bound. Before my twin’s lacking depth to feel any empathy had replaced it. Despite my anger at him and my brother, I couldn’t hate either of them. I understood all too well the lengths people went to in order to protect the people they loved. But to risk everyone else just to ensure I lived? That wasn’t either of their choices to make.

Reading ahead, the passage went on about the reasons a conscience boost might be needed, detailing the struggles a spirit-gifted was faced with when drained or when using any of their abilities. *But to truly share one’s conscience, the burn of silver infused with heaven’s light must enter the heart of the conscience challenged.*

Exactly how I’d restored all those damned and transitionees. All those times I’d been giving pieces of what little I had left away.

When the one person I'd needed to fix, my twin, Marcus, had failed miserably.

It wasn't because I was in transition. I'd proved that with each monster I'd returned to sanity and life. It was simply and horribly down to an anomaly. A result of what we'd been made to be.

"I have something for you."

Erzsebet's voice brought me out of my depressing thoughts. Out of a past I couldn't change. I frowned at what she held out, bathed in yellow below the suspended, wrought iron light. Perching on my toes to lean over the bench, I took hold of the velvet-wrapped offering. The soft material slid from the top to reveal the hard object I gripped inside. My eyes widened. Within the velvet folds that shielded my hand from burning, a long silver length lay cocooned. Similar to a stake, but unlike any I'd ever seen before. At least twice as long and pointed on both ends, it had the same Greek inscription, meaning *deliver back unto hell,* engraved in the center of the long shaft. "What's this for?"

As Erzsebet shot a fleeting glance back to the open book before me, I hoped she wasn't about to reveal some now important and horrible thing I had to do to pull off curing the damned.

"A backup," Ty offered, still seated on the crate behind me.

"A parting gift, Granddaughter," Erzsebet said, her suddenly hardened face softening. Her silver-blue eyes dotted with maroon chips glinted with something I couldn't decipher as she rubbed her palms over her black-veined arms as if feeling a chill. "Should anything happen…should all our plans fail…" She shrugged. "Two birds with one stone…"

I understood straight away. This wasn't a weapon to fight with. It was a fail-safe. Not a stake. Not really. An impaler. Long enough and twice pointed to *kill two birds.* Marcus and me. Simultaneously. By my hand.

I gulped as I wrapped the silver length back up, misty red wetting my eyes—in acceptance. Nodding, my voice was steady despite the whirlwind spinning through my mind. Hey, it was better than decapitation. And now bound, we were weaker. "No matter what happens, Marcus and I won't come out of tomorrow alive."

CHAPTER 36

Back in my suite, it was hours later and almost five a.m. My minutes were numbered, and after Marcus's vocal reminders since I'd left the den this morning, my head was quiet. My headspace, in stark contrast, was screwed. Every time I blinked I saw Ty's mom, her face slack and bloody, her mouth gaping. And she wasn't the only one. Serafina soaking and cradled in Kendrick's arms. Ty run through and bleeding out over my lap. Kendrick twisted on that compacted-dirt cavern flood. They'd all died for what they'd believed in. For love. In protection. Out of vengeance.

Now it was my turn.

It was time to seal my fate.

And if I didn't do this right? By tomorrow at sunrise Marcus and I would still be dead, but the damned would be free—to kill and hunt without the drawback of daylight or insanity. I couldn't fail this.

Reclining back on the cloud-soft duvet, I kicked off my Vans and heard the thump, thump and a clank as they hit the ground and my discarded utility belt. My lids shut out the shadows of my four-poster bed and the unlit crystal chandelier right above. Focusing past the distant sound of guards' heartbeats out on the balcony and through the foyer in the corridor wasn't easy. But the empty bottle of Ty's blood I dropped beside me helped, and soon enough pure black rose up. The gliding and twisting remnants replaced every other sound: heartbeats, wind batting terrace doors, the gentle creaking of the old stone castle. They spun around me like a black twister, thick and tangible. The most I'd ever seen in a single void. And this time, when I caught the right one, I wasn't letting Marcus steal it from me.

But now that he was gone, his voice and presence, I had to be fast. He wouldn't be able to see what I was visioning, but he could cut my attempt short—stopping me from achieving the last thing I needed to ensure the damned's cure. And then I'd be up shit creek again.

Watching the swirling mass of black, I tapped my foot with impatience, waiting for one to stand out. I tuned my senses for some inkling that pointed to the one I needed. None made my breath catch —because I wasn't breathing. But one did call attention. Looping in and around the ones that swarmed around me, this one small shadow seemed to be playing. Taunting, even. I caught it without much effort and it didn't fight as it absorbed into my palm.

The black and swirling mass around me fell like a circling sheet being dropped. Behind the lost cover was vibrant green, yellow, gold, and red. The clearing at Mount Major. The time of year was right. Autumn.

The guy who materialized before me wasn't a shock, and yet my heart back in my here-and-now body mimicked mine in this future-to-come me. Only a split-second out of sync, like lips with sound on a bad TV recording. Centering the clearing of trees, Marcus looked ready and triumphant as he stared into my eyes. And the timing was right. Standing right there before him, both our bodies glowed, his red-hot and mine electric blue. Our hands were joined, feeling like they were locked together somehow. Not that I could feel anything from my future body. No power, pain, readiness, emotion at being about to succeed—or fail. All of that would be reserved for the real event.

The live show.

But there was no time to wonder about any of that now. At any moment, our powers would stream into the amulet we held between our bodies.

If I didn't act fast, I'd lose the opportunity to do what I needed to do. Even if Marcus didn't suddenly intervene. And once this vision was used up, there was no way of getting back to this time and place. I'd learned that with past visions.

As our mingling powers turned purple, I didn't waste another second scanning my surroundings. I didn't hesitate, either. Acting on impulse, I released the explosive ball of electricity I'd contained within my chest in the here and now and rocket launched it down to my bare feet. Just like I'd tested in the alchemist den, the power erupted from my feet in twin jets of identical but opposite tracking shots of blue. The same scorching path of a circled jagged bolt was singed thick into the healthy green grass, ending only when the circle was complete.

Nothing interrupted my actions, and no recognition came from the future Marcus and me centering the field. His voice didn't rise in my head and what I'd just done wasn't stripped from my memory.

I'd done it. Really?

The symbol to close the circle around light and dark, to redirect our powers and take our sacrifice was complete.

Tomorrow the damned would be cured—and I would die.

I came awake with anticipation and unwanted despair, the darkness of my room mirroring half of how I felt. I'd done it. Accomplished my task. Even now as I levered up on my bed, not really registering the shadows that made up my surroundings, I could remember my vision and what had happened. What I'd achieved by using my power that transcended space and now…time. I'd shocked Ty in dreamscapes before. But this, this was a new leap.

The one thing I'd needed to work.

Wetness rolled from one nostril down to my lip and I wiped it away. Invisible hands captured and squeezed my stomach—

Are you up to something, twin?

I jerked, legs swinging over the edge of my bed before I realized the voice had been Marcus's and it had been inside my head. He could still talk to me, but from the irritation I could feel through our link, I knew that was all he could do. Yet his sudden suspicion had panic feeling like a second set of squeezing hands around my dying heart. *I said I'd be—*

No backup. And don't be late. If you do anything to cross me… mother dearest will pay the price.

"Marcus—"

His consciousness faded from my mind and a blink took the blank haze from my sight, returning clarity to my bedroom with its dark shadows. Alone, but the threat was clear. Except it didn't matter. Marcus wouldn't have a moment to react. After my vision, I was ready to pull this off. I recalled Madam Rosalie's words. *Others hold the possible future of the lost in their hands.*

My reply had been confirmed. *Combining my power with Marcus's?*

But she'd never been talking about Kendrick and resurrecting him. She'd been hinting at mine and Marcus's combined power to save the damned. My twin and I held the power in our hands.

To save them all.

Including my mom.

And now I'd ensured our end. He wouldn't be able to hurt her or anyone else once we were dead.

My forgotten hunger returned with sudden intensity. The silence was stripped away, megaphoning the sound of heartbeats through my ears. So close, the balcony where two guards stood, their backs to me. *Easy prey.* And two top-ups that, if I feigned distress, would come running right into a trap.

Quick as a flash, I raced around the bedroom and lounge, pulling shut all the drapes, blocking the sight of them—but not the sound of beating hearts. "Rein it in," I chided myself, jaw clamping shut as I scooted back on my bed. "Focus." Still, everything that was sure to happen tomorrow became a distant second thought. My hunger was in control.

My gaze darted through the gap to the lounge, wondering if I could make it to the fridge inside that long, dinted cabinet. If I could get hold of one of the bottles of Ty's blood. Before I changed course and decided on a tastier living alternative.

Nails clawing into my sheets, I—

Like he'd sensed the danger in me growing, Ty rushed in through the foyer then, flicking the light on over that central table as he passed. He tracked over the black veins covering my arms, neck, and face, gaze settling on my eyes that as I watched him bled to vivid red. He rolled up his sleeve and even though I licked my lips, I didn't budge as he came to sit on the edge of my bed. Bending one leg over the covers to face me, his expression was blank as he held his wrist out to me.

Perfect timing. As usual. And that wasn't the monster in me talking. The surprise of his sudden and convenient appearance brought some rationality back to my mind. Some suspicion. An alpha's intuition? Or was there more to it?

The depressed look on his face kept me from prying.

"I hate using you like this." Despite the sliver of true sincerity I felt, the gravel in my voice surprised me. Saliva pooled in my mouth as the *thump, thump* of his pulse sent waves of his scent at me like an assault. My stomach twisted as if being wrung out like a wet towel. "I know you do, too."

Ty's jaw remained clenched, his lips twitched. "I don't hate this…"

He indicated the shortening space between our bodies—because I was leaning into him. And I was struck by the gleam of sudden hope in his eyes. My lips parted to spill what Kendrick had urged me to come clean about—

"I mean, I…I volunteered. I knew what the deal was when we started this. For the greater good."

My lips snapped shut and disappointment paled my stupid, should-never-have-felt-it hope. He didn't hate it, because keeping me in check served a purpose, one bigger than what he actually wanted—or should I say didn't. When he lifted his wrist closer to my mouth, I accepted it, trying to ignore his scent, his eyes trained on mine, and the heat radiating off him. Along with my sinister impulses to turn his offering into a bloody and lethal act. Averting my eyes to help maintain my thinning control, I bit down with my fangs and drew gentle but swift pulls. The quicker this was over for him, the better.

Seconds passed in slow-mo, me hating every one as I despaired in the knowledge that this was close to the last time I'd be near him like this. The red faded from my sight gradually, and as it cleared out I saw the photo I still kept propped against my more-than-once-replaced bedside lamp. Moments before boarding the cruise together, Ty looked so happy. Smiling, his white and straight teeth showing through his lips. A sparkle of gold glittered from his irises, so intense, so unique. And so different to how they now looked, in color and in emotion.

Ty reclined on the bed then, keeping his arm held out as I drank his blood. His lids were hooded, his expression dazed, relaxed.

Blood deprived.

With the twisting of my stomach releasing, I went to disengage my fangs.

"Another restored," Ty murmured, lids blinking more and more shut with every slow close and open. "I think another restored should take my place. It will be easier—"

Now I removed his wrist from my mouth and my fangs shot back into my gums as if on spring retractors. There was one, maybe two more feedings between now and when I arrived in New Hampshire, where I'd offer myself up to cure the damned and…die. After that, there'd be no need for a blood donor. Was the act of giving me his vein so bad that he couldn't stand to do it even one more time? I dropped his arm and Ty stirred. "If that's what you want…"

"What?" Ty went from stirring to bolting awake. Lurching upright, his heart pounded lacking blood around his body. He glanced around at the shielded windows and peering archways to the lounge and foyer as if gathering his bearings. He rubbed at his eyes —because he'd actually been asleep. "Did I say something?"

I wasn't going to bury this, pretend he hadn't said it. If this was what he wanted, even in my final hours, I wouldn't deny him. Not after all he'd done for me. For everyone I loved. "You want someone else to feed me."

Ty's mouth gaped, then shut. He sighed deeply and scrubbed a hand down his face. "I…I was dreaming. About you. About tomorrow." He blinked slowly, mixed emotions I couldn't read changing his expression. "In my dream, you lived. In my dream, tomorrow wasn't your end. And…and I knew after that, something between us needed to change."

He'd already made it clear he wouldn't be around anymore. The plan all along had been to part ways when all of this was said and done.

Ty squeezed his eyes shut, torture resonating over his tired and handsome features. His fists clenched. "But none of that matters, does it. After tomorrow, this"—he indicated between our bodies—"it won't exist anymore. *You* won't exist anymore."

CHAPTER 37

I didn't know what to say, couldn't find a single word to utter. Nothing I could say would change my fate. I wasn't backing out now, and Ty was right. After tomorrow, the need to have a restored damned feed me to hide my transitioning traits and cull my dangerous side would be null and void. Tomorrow I'd be gone, leaving everyone I loved behind. I cringed at the memory of my vision, the one where I'd fallen dead beside my twin. There was so little time, and so much I needed to come clean about, but Ty beat me to it.

"In my dream, I couldn't continue to be your donor. Not with our past. Not with Kendrick now back alive." The pain that resonated across his stunning face was torture, the only light from behind in the foyer painting every line in severe shadows. The clenching of his fists showed his anger at being out of options. And kept my confessions from passing my lips. "It wouldn't be right to either of you."

Thoughts of coming clean, tomorrow, and my end fled my mind.

My lips parted at his words, shocked at what I couldn't help interpreting. *Not right to Kendrick and me?*

Ty's clenched fists cranked tighter and a snarl escaped with his words. "I just don't get it. How he can let you sacrifice yourself. How the hell can he stand by and watch while you give your life up? To watch the second when the light vanishes from your eyes and you fall—*dead*." Gold blazed in his irises, striking out the silver that now mingled with that characteristic lycan color. His canines peeked through his lips and he scooted off the bed, pacing back and forth on the rug. His weapons clattered with each forceful step. "If you were mine, I would never let you go through with this. I would a find a way to stop you. To keep you alive. I couldn't live with myself if I did nothing."

Crawling up onto my knees on the mattress, my fingers clawed into the duvet on either side of me. My reanimated and strengthened heart drummed with emotion. If I'd needed air, my breaths would have been coming in hurried disbelief. I hadn't heard him wrong. I hadn't mistaken all the words he'd just said. "If I were yours?"

Ty stopped dead, startled as if just realizing I was right there and had heard his every word. His eyes flicked to the photo of us, then scoured over my bed, seeing the way I knelt at the edge while fisting the sheets. He shook his head, then sighed, canines receding back into his gums.

In a flash he was right before me, stare intense as his tight, calloused fingers cupped my neck, forcing me to look up into his eyes. "I shouldn't feel this way. I shouldn't say what I'm about to, but the hell with it…"

As he breathed hard and kept my gaze locked, I tingled at his touch, drawing shallow breath despite not needing to. Despite the way my lungs fought the sharp inhale and exhale of air. *"Ty?"*

"I want to be with you, Amelia. Damned, alive, after Kendrick, even though you're intent on killing yourself. I want you. Only you. Always have. Always will. Even after you're gone, I will still love you." He dropped his hold and frowned as if just realizing he'd stalked over and held me in that way. He stepped back, expression full of guilt. "It's not something I can turn off. And even if I could… I wouldn't choose to. You're it for me. If all I have left is the memory of you, your taste, your scent, how it feels to kiss you, how being with you has ruined me for anyone else, I'll take it. I'll savor every second I can remember…for as long as I will now live."

Ty, the guy I'd fallen head over heels for, who'd been my mortal enemy, a rogue vampire hunter, and so much more than that, wanted me. Would love me for the rest of his living days. His potential one thousand years being a Pure Blood and restored damned vampire. And I was *it* for him?

Ty stalked back across the room to the curved bench between the foyer and lounge archways and slumped down onto it. Leaning forward with his elbows on his knees, he held his head in his hands. "I'm sorry. That was selfish. I shouldn't—"

"I'm not with Kendrick."

"—have said all—" Ty's head whipped up and his nostrils flared. "What did you say?"

I watched as a shudder traveled down his body and couldn't miss the growl that came up his throat. Like he'd subconsciously heard exactly what I'd said, but his rational mind refused to believe it. With my heart about to burst from my chest, I clambered off the bed and over to Ty. I knelt and clasped his hands, so masculine and tracked by black veins, reveling in the feel of those callouses and his radiating heat. All this time, I'd been deluding myself. Pushing him away when there'd been no reason to. Deep down I'd known Kendrick wasn't mine. And I wasn't his. I'd been protecting myself. Ty too. Telling myself he didn't want me. That he couldn't get over our past. When all along I'd known it was a lie. A lie I'd made myself believe because I didn't feel worthy, and because I didn't want to hurt him. But I couldn't stop myself now.

On my knees before him, my gaze was unwavering and my voice escaped in a whisper. "I'm not *his*. We're not…together."

A mash of emotions hijacked Ty's features: confusion, desire, uncertainty, and *hunger*. "Why…why are you telling me this now?"

Because I was selfish. Because I wanted him too. Loved him with all my heart and soul. Always had. And always would. Tomorrow I'd be no more and this was it, our last and only chance. Even though I knew it would make everything that was set to happen infinitely worse, I couldn't stop myself. "I want you too, Ty." I leaned up, wedging my body between his strong thighs. Neck craning up, my parted lips neared his. "I never stopped wanting you. Not ever."

Silent frozen moments passed as Ty searched my eyes, his expression unreadable. As I worried that he was regretting his honesty, his hands pulled free of my mine. He slowly reached up to cup my face, bringing my lips to his. And with that gentle touch, I was lost to him. Forever more.

Mouth slanting over mine, Ty growled as my tongue lapped over his. Heat spiked from his body and mine tingled with growing need. A quick maneuver had his utility belt unclipped and falling with a heavy clank as I launched it away. I tugged at his T-shirt and he gripped my waist. Lifting me up, I straddled him on the bench, knees pressing into the soft cushioning on either side of him. Fingers riding up the ripples of his chest and abs, the cotton covering came away in a heartbeat. My tank followed more slowly, Ty's hands exploring their way up my stomach, over my ribs and squeezing as he cupped my breasts. I gasped at the contact, the tightness of my lungs adding to the dizziness his kisses evoked. And then I was topless, my black lace bra pressing into his chest as I kissed over his cheek stubble and down his neck. Licking and sucking without breaking flesh, a growl rumbled from his throat in response. "I want you, Ty. *All* of you."

Ty shuddered under my touch and his hands came up, gripping my biceps hard. Eyes vibrant gold, he spoke through ragged breath. "Are you…sure?"

All of a sudden he seemed so vulnerable. Half undressed, the look on his face was hope and despair. Was he remembering what he'd compelled of me in his dreamscape when he was damned? To want him and need him—all of him. To join him *forever*. I almost cringed at the memory, but for once, I wouldn't let our rocky past get in the way. This man before me was the real Ty. The one who'd owned my heart from the second I saw him. The one who'd ruined me for anyone else from the very start. Just like I had him. I smiled, tomorrow and anything beyond here and now forgotten. We were finally getting our shit together. Finally arriving at the exact place we needed to be. After all this time. "With every heartbeat."

Ty's smile was relief and desperate need wrapped up in a seductive smirk that fell too soon. "I wish we had longer."

I knew how he felt. "Me too." But I wouldn't have our future spoil the now. Our last chance. I took his bottom lip between mine and sucked. Grabbing his scarred forearms, I directed his hands to my sides, sliding them up and around my back. Diversion working, our kissing quickly re-escalated, and then my bra was unclipped. Ty's mouth broke from mine to trail down my neck and along, working the straps from one shoulder as his fingers slid the other side off. When his mouth brushed over my collarbone and headed south, I raked my fingers through his hair. Not to hold him back, but to urge him on. I cried out when he reached my uncovered breast, sucking one tip into his mouth. My other hand dropped down his abs to his pants, working the button of his jeans, dizziness climbing and breath rushing as the button popped free and the zip slid down.

Ty released his sucking kiss then and rushed to take my mouth with his. Rising to his feet, my legs tangled around his back. A few stumbling steps had the denim strew across the floor and brought us to my bed. Laying me down as if I were the most delicate thing in the world, he hovered above me, so different now, with those black restored veins down his neck and chest and the maroon chips to his now silver-gold eyes. But still the same Ty I'd known from the start. The one I'd fallen so deeply for. His breath refused to slow and he didn't look away from my face for a second. "I love you, Amelia."

Crimson tears sprang to my eyes but I wouldn't let them fall. Our first and last time. There's no way in hell I was about to ruin this. Taking hold of his wrist, I directed his fingers down to my waistband. "I love you too, Ty. *Always*."

Arching up, I claimed his mouth and kissed him deeply. Ty responded just as I wanted and made quick work of unbuttoning and unzipping the denim. Lifting my pelvis, I wriggled as he worked my jeans off. Anticipating where this was heading, I gripped the elastic around his muscled waist. When I pushed down his boxer briefs, I couldn't stop my mouth gaping at the clear sight of him. Equipped, proud, and ready. Despite my usually cool body and flesh, I warmed at the thought of what we were seconds away from doing.

Breathing hard, Ty curled his rough fingers around the sides of my lace underwear, keeping his eyes on mine as he slowly began to pull them down. Like he was waiting for me to stop him. A cease and desist. Waiting for me to change my mind.

But I wasn't on the fence about this.

About him.

Again I arched my hips up. Ty kissed my mouth, my chin. As he worked the lace down my legs he trailed kisses down my neck, through my cleavage, over each rib. He licked my belly button and kissed my hip as the material slipped off one foot then the other. Kissing his way back up my body, he leaned down into me.

I gasped at the feel of him between my legs. I was so ready for this. Finally.

Fingers curling around his neck, I kissed him hard, tasting him, savoring this feeling. Breaking away I stared up into his blazing eyes. My fangs tingled with so much more than hunger for his blood and they slid out in readiness.

But then Ty lifted off me, feet hitting the ground as he strode away.

"What are you—"

Before I could finish, he'd picked up his discarded jeans and spun back to face me. Standing buck naked he held—I had to blink, and again—a condom between his fingers.

"I've had this since the cruise. Not because I expected anything then. Really, I didn't. I just wanted to be prepared for when the time came. If it came. But then…"

Still proud and ready, straining from the hips, his luminous eyes that were all the light I needed in this room fell. "But then you died," I whispered. "You were damned."

Frowning, he came back to sit on the bed's edge, toying absently with the gold wrapper. "I was never with anyone else." As my heart skipped he met my stunned eyes. "Even damned, you were it. And I know it isn't necessary…" He sighed hard, not saying the why was because any protection was useless when I'd be dead tomorrow. "But this means something to me."

Legs folding under my butt, I leaned closer to touch his scarred forearm. Fresh tears made me sniff as I took the packet and tore it open. "Me, too. You, us here and now, it's everything to me."

As Ty plucked the condom free, I reclined on the bed. Slow

seconds later, he climbed back over the duvet, lips brushing mine as I directed his reclining body up and over the top of me.

Ty smiled down at me. "I will love you, Amelia…forever."

Lips meeting, our kisses were soft but sensual, rekindling our former heat until I could barely take a second more of it. Legs parting further, the upward tilt of my hips was the green light. The point of no return. "I love you, Ty."

With a chest-deep rumble, he pushed up gently, meeting my flesh. I gasped through the kiss, struck by the full sensation as we became one. Halfway inside, Ty paused and levered up, face sweating with restraint. Worry creased his forehead. "You okay? I can—"

"No. Don't stop." My body felt like it was on fire, parts of me awakening that I had never experienced before. "I'm fine." Half dead and with my future set, here and now I'd never felt more alive. "I always am, when I'm with you."

To prove my words true, I claimed his mouth and moved below him. Ty smiled against my lips and pressed up all the way before retracting. And then we were moving together, the gentle pat, patter as rain fell outside lost to our quickening breaths. With our bodies perspiring, the intensity soared. Nails scraping down Ty's back, I felt every scar and bunching muscle. Ty's hands were everywhere. My thighs, waist, around my nape, on my breasts. When his lips broke from mine his fangs were long and sharp. A thrill ran through me, knowing what he wanted.

Before he could gasp out the request, I tilted my head, elongating my neck. Eyes blazing at the invitation, Ty leaned in, still keeping our escalating rhythm. And then his fangs sank in deep. I cried out at the shock of pleasure and pain that shot through me, setting my hot skin on fire. And it wasn't because he was injecting vampire venom, or poisoning me with his canines. With only his vampire fangs embedded, this is what he'd felt every time I'd fed from him. His vitality stripped from his veins into me with a flood of dopamine to cover the pain. Pure ecstasy in the form of blood. Even without our attraction to one another, I understood his bodily reaction to me. Understood why he'd been powerless to control each and every time we'd crossed the line between donor and lover.

Drawing hard on my vein, I felt immense pressure build in me. Like a trail of gunpowder set alight and cracking along, getting closer and closer to a giant box of TNT. When Ty's lips and fangs released my flesh with a hiss, I claimed his mouth, tasting myself on his tongue. Keeping us joined, Ty levered up on the bed, one arm around my back pulling me up with him to his knees. Wrapping my legs around his waist, my thighs gripped as he moved against me. I gasped as that crackling gunpowder in me neared a massive explosion and plunged my fangs down into the base of his neck. Ty moved faster, growling as he held me hard against him. The taste of him threw me over the edge and my entire body clenched as a tidal wave rode me. The sudden bliss I felt of being shattered apart accompanied Ty's groan as every one of his muscles popped and his rhythm went from in-time to strained.

My first and last time with the love of my life.

And every second was worth it.

Still held in his strong arms—like he'd never let me go—I released my fangs as Ty exhaled a gush of air. With a kiss to my cheek, my forehead, and then my lips, he inched back, keeping us connected below. Face red and beading sweat, his smile was magnificent. "Wow."

I lingered in the moment. In him. In what we'd just done. Together. What I wished didn't have to end. What I mourned already, having finally experienced it. With *him.*

Finally, I kissed him sweetly and, letting my legs unravel from his taut waist to break our connection, I reclined on the bed. Ty followed to lie beside me, both of us facing each other and still catching our breath. The breath that, for me, had nothing to do with actual breathing. As the sweat on my body dried in our after-sex silence, everything we'd just done together began to feel like a dream. The words Ty had said when I'd first seen him after restoring his life rose and swirled inside my mind.

Ty brushed my hair back from my face, concern striking the spent passion from his expression. "What's wrong?"

I frowned, feeling the rejection from that day. "Can we start again—you didn't want to then."

Ty's complexion paled and he gulped, rolling onto his back to stare blankly through the four posts of my bed at the chandelier. "Back when I was damned…everything I did to…" Another gulp. "My brother…" Then another. "You." His eyes squeezed shut so tight and frown lines creased his forehead. "Vanessa. Fuck. There isn't a day that passes, a night where I don't loathe myself for that… for all of it." Now he looked at me, the grief and guilt across his features heartbreaking. "Getting you back would have been a dream…one I didn't deserve then, and still don't now."

"Ty, no." I rolled onto my knees, grasping the purple comforter hanging off the bed's end to cover my nakedness. With the end tucked around me, I cupped his face, forcing him to really look at me. "You're not responsible for any of those things. It wasn't you who did them."

"Soul or not, it was my body. I had my brother kidnapped from boarding school. I taunted you in dreams. Blackmailed you to let me turn you. Not because I needed your permission, but because I enjoyed watching you fight with your conscience. I killed Vanessa—at least I thought I had. But she's even worse than that. And for what?" Rolling sideways, Ty struck out to grip my forearm, teeth grating as he glared at the burn scars. "To get back at you for refusing to submit. Then I turned you and tried to tempt you into killing my own brother to make you just like me." In the blurt of words, he'd swung upward so he no longer rested on his arm. He noticed his nakedness then and, looking disgusted with himself, he gathered up the tousled sheeting to cover himself below the waist. "I did all those fucking things, and I remember every single detail… because part of me, the real me, was always still there. I just didn't fight hard enough to stop myself."

Ty's fist drew back like he wanted to hit something and I caught it in mid-air. I squeezed. "That. Wasn't. You. Are you hearing me? Not. You." Watching the anger fade back to guilt in his eyes wrecked me. I released his fist and as it fell to his side, I cupped his strong jawline. "I never stopped loving you. Not when I thought you were dead. Not when you were damned. Never." I released his face as the recognition of my limited living hours resurfaced in my mind. Tomorrow I'd be dead and gone. Forever. "Do you wish we didn't?"

"Never," Ty growled, fierce certainty blazing gold in his eyes. "I meant everything I said before. Every single word. I've wanted this, wanted you, ever since the moment I first saw you."

Goosebumps prickled my skin as my body grew colder by the second. I didn't want to push this any further, but I couldn't stop the word vomit. The time for the truth was here and now. I should have come clean before we… "The guards aren't extra protection," I rushed before I could swallow back down the words I needed to say. "They're protecting me from myself. Kendrick and Dorian had me grounded. The wolves being arranged in Portsmouth aren't backup. They're the plan. Kill over cure. But I won't have it. And they can't cage me. Marika's got a plan to bust me out." Now I hesitated as fear of Ty's reaction made my racing heart pound. "You said, *if I were yours…*" I let rest of the sentence hang in the air unsaid.

Ty slid off the bed and a minute later he'd pulled his boxer briefs and jeans back on and discarded the condom in the bathroom. Returning, he sat back down, knee bent to get close to me. Running his calloused hand up my arm, I shuddered as he clasped my neck and tilted my head up with his thumb. To think of where his hands had been and what we'd just done…and now this. "I'm yours and you are mine. But you don't belong to me, Amelia. I don't own you. I love you. God, I love you. I will do anything to keep you safe. I will protect you as long as you'll let me. But I will *never* restrict you."

"But you said—"

"I was angry—furious—because of everything I hadn't said, and for everything I wanted for us and knew I'd never get to have. A bit of it was jealousy. Well, a lot was." His hand dropped from my neck and he sighed, eyes falling from mine. "I will always have your back. But me, the real me that you saved, has never wanted to control you. I will love you forever. And I will be everything you need me to be…until your last and final breath."

My heart shattered in my chest and I gathered his face in my palms. My lips pressed to his, praying I could somehow take this one sensation with me to the grave. To my existence beyond the living. Crimson tears tracked down my face as I pulled back. "I wish it didn't have to be this way."

Ty smeared the twin tracks away with his thumb, one after the other. "Me too."

CHAPTER 38

I stole a glimpse at Ty across my bedroom, muscles bulging as he paced back and forth beside the tall Gothic windows. "Good, make sure they hold back," he barked into his phone. Fully redressed, his utility belt held stakes and blades around his waist. More were hidden in holsters at his ankles, and one along each forearm was concealed as he tugged on his jacket and shoved his phone inside. "The wolves won't tempt Marcus. They'll wait for a cue."

His face was still as flushed as mine from our intimate encounter, but tipped with sorrow, like he was mourning our end too, as he looked away. I could barely believe we'd done it. Finally. We'd been together in flesh and blood, joined in a way that I had never been with anyone before.

And never would again.

"That's good. Great."

Stealing this glimpse of him now while I fumbled to arm up beside my open weapon crates, I felt the deep burdening loss of knowing we'd never be like that again. That in less than twenty-four hours I'd been dead and gone. The sound of booted strides and clanging weapons out in the hall and down on the ground outside my suite through the shielded terrace doors made this too freaking real. Too definite. Guards. Swarms of them. Armed and readying to take off in town cars to the private jets that awaited them at Anchorage International.

But only one jet was getting airborne today. And we were hijacking it first.

Ty's gaze found me then, strained and frozen, not letting the devastating emotion that glazed his eyes shine through. His lips parted as if about to say something, but nothing came out. I had no words, either. Just a drowning sense of being cheated, out of time, a future—when we'd finally gotten our shit together.

The creak of my suite's door opening broke the silence and our stares. Kendrick strode through the foyer, armed to the teeth in shiny silver. He was going with the vamps? Seeing something between Ty and me even though we were no longer soul bound, he pulled up short. Then he registered the disarray of my bed through the archway. A flash of something passed over his face, but then it was gone.

Cheeks burning, I darted from my bedroom into the lounge, pacing like I'd done something wrong. "What do you want?" God, I hated being cruel to him. Especially since this was the last time I'd ever see him. But I couldn't let anyone stop me. Couldn't act like this was the end when as far as he knew, my days, or should I say hours, were far from numbered.

Following me into the room, Kendrick gave a single nod to Ty and came my way. I froze as his arms came around me with a tight hug. The breath through his nose fanned over my head, but then he let go, holding me at arm's length. Unable or unwilling to hold my confused stare, he glanced away at the terrace doors as if he could see the commotion going on outside. "We're sorry we went against you."

I stepped back. "We?"

Dorian appeared from the foyer—he'd arrived with Kendrick?—but stood back, leaning into the archway, his crossbow slung over his shoulder. "Me too. I just…couldn't lose you. You're my sister." Like when he'd revealed we weren't related, he looked out of place…lost. "We'll find another way to get Vanessa back."

Kendrick nodded, and I didn't miss the green hardcover novel that had belonged to one gutsy, black-haired, restored damned that he clung to. "And Raven."

"And Mom?" I shook my head, hurt resurfacing as I bypassed Kendrick and went over to my brother. I sensed Ty and Kendrick meeting gazes again and with the larger subject at hand, I easily ignored the elephant of Ty's and my recent activity in my viewable bedroom as I faced Dorian. "What about her?"

Dorian shook his head, his dark hair hanging over his forehead. "I couldn't agree to lose you to get Mom or Vanessa back. I mean, I don't want Mom to…" He sucked air like he was trying not to hyperventilate. "Or Vanessa to stay like…"

As he gulped, I curled my arms around him. "You don't have to choose." I was going to do that for the both of them.

As my phone buzzed from my hoodie, I could guess who the text was from. Time was up. Releasing my brother, I went to hug my best friend—for the very last time. Releasing him too fast, I turned away as fresh tears welled. "Look, can we talk about this later. I just need time—"

"What's going on?" Kendrick demanded.

"Why are you and Ty armed to the teeth?" Dorian added, pushing off the wall as he eyed my shiny waist-visible attachments sticking out from below my hoodie. Which included that seriously long double-pointed stake from Erzsebet.

At that second a shout was heard outside. A guard. Kendrick and Dorian made it to the terrace doors at the same time, each flinging one side of the drapes open.

"What the hell," Kendrick uttered as Dorian gasped, "Impossible."

With guards out on the balcony leaning over the balustrade, I saw movement amongst the thinning trees and in the main street. My vampire sight focused like binoculars. All girls. Same height and build, with vampire pale skin and long blond hair billowing as they darted about. At least twenty of them. Twenty of me.

Marika's plan. A diversion.

The jig was up. They knew it as they spun from the doors, letting the drapes fall back in place. "I've made my choice. And it is mine. My life. Neither of you are swapping me for Vanessa or Raven. You're not even swapping me for all the damned lives that'll be cured. I know you want there to be another way. I do too. But there isn't, and I'm okay with that. I'm…ready. I—"

"Okay." My jaw fell slack as Kendrick twisted back around to face the balcony. He poked his head out as a guard yelled his incoming. "She's not here. She's one of them. Track 'em all down. And do it fast."

"We guessed you'd take off anyway." Dorian came further into the lounge as that door clapped shut, boots meeting the edge of the rug where I stood.

"We knew you'd find a way." Kendrick spared a glance at Ty who hung back in the bedroom archway. "Which we can see you have. We just wanted to set things right before we lost the chance. Before it was too late."

"We want to help." Dorian touched my hand. "If you'll still let us."

My eternal supporters. The three most important guys in my world. "Oh, God. I'm gonna miss—"

A sudden and horrible sensation tugged at my insides, and Ty, seeing my knees wobble, rushed to my side before my legs gave out. But for once, it wasn't hunger. It was so, so much worse. I staggered to gain footing and rushed, tearing open the terrace doors. The guards were gone, rushing down on the ground through the maze-like gardens, while more tracked my doubles down in the street and surrounding trees. My insides felt like they were about to be pulled through my flesh. "Oh…shit."

Was this the vision Marcus had stolen from me?

Ty, Kendrick, and Dorian were right there with me, scouring the darkened, pre-twilight landscape of the town, trees, and mountains for something they couldn't yet see but that I had no doubt was on its way. "The damned are coming."

Ty shot into the foyer and pulled the manual alarm, speeding back to my side—where he belonged—so fast the wailing erupted with his return. Eyes like lasers, I followed the pull optically. Glimpses of the boundary through trees, houses, and buildings revealed only the guards' confusion as they chased my doubles. I caught and squeezed Ty's hand, waiting for the horror that was seconds away from being unleashed.

Dorian geared up his crossbow with the CO2 cartridge and a canister of silver bolts. "At least the guards are armed for their take off."

And then I saw her.

Through the main entrance, strolling in like she owned the place with her grayed-out skin. Her ruby-red irises glowed, the half moon nearing the mountainous horizon shining light up the street to the castle like an invitation.

And she was far from alone.

As the entry guards—knowing what was arriving from their cameras—braced against the swarm of black-clad damned shadowing her, their ready swords weren't enough. With a flick of her wrist, ten moved to cut down the vampires where they stood. Their swords and bodies hitting the cobblestone road were soundless over the screeching alarm.

On my other side, Kendrick's voice was hollow. "Raven…she's leading them."

I went to fly out to the balcony and over the railing, needing to act before any more lives were lost.

A strong hand hauled me back. "There's no time." Ty's jaw was set, his expression torn. "We need to leave for the jet."

"Ty's right." Kendrick spared me a look of hopeless loss. Then he returned his focus to tracking Raven as she led the running assault of damned that flooded through the main entrance and spilled over the surrounding walls. "This is just a diversion."

Understanding almost floored me. My twin was enforcing his demand. "Marcus is stopping us from bringing backup."

Screams rang out then as the damned took to the streets, vampires running back to their houses getting caught before they could get armed or to safety. That horrid feeling of déjà vu made me want to heave up Ty's blood that still sat in my stomach. I was suddenly sure I'd seen this. Even though I couldn't remember the details, I was certain this was the vision Marcus had stolen from my consciousness. The only consolation was that every guard was fully armed and prepared to fight, so close to leaving for Mount Major. But now…

They'd have to stay. To protect our people.

As a bonus, my diversion doubles hadn't scattered. Now exploding into wolf form, they fought to protect the vampires, too.

Dorian bared his fangs and took aim over the balustrade, firing a few rounds of bolts from his crossbow. His glance back at me said so much more than his words. "There's never been this many before."

As the whizzing sound of metal sliced the air at speed, armed guards flooded in through my main door. In a nanosecond my mind was set, fully armed with all my stakes and blades and that long double-pointed silver length, it was time. "Get out there and defend our people and the castle. They won't survive long enough if you don't. Stay until the community is secure." With their swords drawn, there was no argument as they all about-faced and fled my suite to battle. To my three guys I said, "I'm going after Marcus. I'm ending this once and for all."

Kendrick was still staring out over the balustrade, still tracking Raven as she directed an undead army on deadly assault. "Amelia, I —" He balked when the girl he was falling for tore into a man on the main street like a savage beast. He tore his gun from his holster but didn't aim or fire at her.

"I know, Kendrick." The look on his face reminded me of the many looks he'd given me when the monster in me had broken free. He loved that girl down there. Feared he'd lose her for good, too, even if I did succeed. Guilt was a personal torment not all could live with. "You stay. Keep her from killing." Pinching his chin, I forced him to look at me. "But don't you dare get yourself killed, okay?"

"I would say the same, but…"

Nail on the head. "Yeah. I know."

With a nod, his wrist flicked. A gust of wind had Raven's hold yanked loose from her prey. Kendrick took aim and fired. One shot into her chest. She dropped her victim but it hadn't been a kill shot, she was stunned but not out for the count. Eyes misty, he took the fleeting seconds we had left and trapped me with his arms. "Fuck, I'm gonna miss you."

I thanked Ty's blood swimming in my veins that kept me from turning our goodbye into something spoiled by my sinister impulses. That let me fully feel and linger in this one last moment with my best friend.

Too soon he let go and I could barely utter, "Me too," as he swiped at his tears.

Dorian removed the empty bolt canister from his crossbow then and smacked a fresh one in. "If I go, they'll have the castle in minutes. And there's too many to bleed out or freeze. But Mom, Vanessa…"

Down on the ground the castle's guards were storming through arched entries into the royal gardens, but they were outnumbered. As with the streets, darkness swarmed in like black water filling the hedge maze. If the damned took the castle, The Seven would be no more. Firing up, I sent blue forking volts down at the ground. "I'll save Mom, and Vanessa will be restored." One stunned. Two. "I promise I won't fail them." Three. Four. "The curse will be broken."

A spay of fresh bolts left his crossbow. His glance at me was full of sorrow as more damned flooded over the ones we both hit. The time for last embraces was long gone. And we both knew it. "I love you, Sis. Give 'em hell."

More bolts were loosed with a single tear and Ty's sudden hand around my wrist was possessive and protective. "I'm going with you."

I hadn't expected anything else, and I didn't argue. Ready and adrenaline pumping, I unraveled my whip from my back. To cut a path through the swarms, I'd need it. "I love you guys. Now and forever. Don't ever forget it."

I didn't stick around to watch my brother and best friend fire another shot, or to see the pain of loss across their wet faces. I couldn't. I couldn't bear another second of goodbyes because I feared I'd change my mind. Taking Ty's hand, together we jumped over the balustrade and down to the ground. There was no more time to waste. "Race you to my Ducati."

CHAPTER 39

I revved the engine of my Ducati, focusing on the wind in my hair and the vibration between my legs as I got airborne over a sloping embankment. The shocks took the beating, squeaking as I twisted harder on the throttle. Red and gold leaves swirled in our wake, but I didn't let our destination as I sped through the trees enter my mind. Instead, I focused on the call from Kendrick and Dorian reporting their success in securing our community since we'd left. On my last goodbye. On Ty's built frame as his strong muscled arms held tight around my waist. At the memory of tasting his blood one last time when we'd vacated the jet at Boston International.

And the fan of his warm breath over my neck as he said, "You will always, *always* be a part of me."

The long trees holding back rising twilight came to an abrupt end too quickly. I skidded to a stop, twisting to take Ty's mouth with mine one last time. "I love you."

And then I was off my bike and kicking my feet free of my Vans, body coming away from Ty's strong hold on my hips with his scraping release as we both stood.

The clearing—the place where the Dawn of Reckoning had taken place centuries ago—was just as I remembered it. And yet so very different. Knowing what would soon come to pass here, this place seemed more ominous than I'd ever cared to notice. The trees seemed to shiver with the sharp breeze, their leaf-dropping branches looking like deformed arms as the ghostly dawn moon edged below one side of the clearing. An altar was positioned dead center, black marble with gold veining. The chalice sat atop, its jewels twinkling as it caught the low moonlight. I imagined the drip of blood that had pattered down from its edge in my vision as if I could see it here and now. The surrounding horde of watching red eyes should have scared me. Should have made me fear for Ty and what would happen to him if I failed. Instead, the sight of them seething with anticipation tore a hiss from my mouth—because I couldn't see my twin. "Marcus! Where is she?"

The damned squeezed in on us, pushing us into the center of the clearing. Ty growled deep in his throat, eyes flashing and fangs lengthening. Tracking and even hearing his muscles creak, I saw him free two stakes before he lunged. Moving as fast as I'd seen him do when damned, he nailed the tip into one damned's heart. A spin and flip back rendered a second to ash. "Stop hiding behind your minions and show yourself, you coward!"

The damned went on the attack and I palmed my rubber-handled stakes to back Ty.

"Stand down!"

At the shout of that cold, commanding voice, the damned disengaged as one. Even the one who'd had the nerve to catch Ty around the throat. Ty didn't show the same restraint and reduced the damned to dust with a quick stab. Then the circle of damned widened, parting on one side as leaf-cracking strides neared. Marcus, smug as hell in the same dirty jeans and white shirt I'd seen him wearing in a vision before I'd known he was the damned commander. "I knew you'd come."

My mom appeared beside him, red-eyed and snarling, covered in black veins and snapping her long fangs.

In human form, Vanessa's wolf claws held her around the throat, her dagger-ready arm around my mom's torso, pointing that sharp tip to her heart. Mom fought against the restraint, eyes glowing with starvation and gaping mouth dripping saliva. Blood bloomed through Mom's dirty and torn blouse, and it was crimson.

Marcus had kept his word. Kept her alive and in transition.

"Damn you. Let her go." I clenched my fists around my stakes, glaring as Marcus came our way without concern, making for the altar.

His smile to me was pure mischief. "Of course." Mom stilled as his eyes pulsed back across to the clearing's edge where Vanessa held her. With barely a sound, his lips spelled out his command. "Kill the lycan."

"No!"

As my voice echoed around us, Vanessa's dagger swung away. But she didn't attack. With a cry of starvation, my mom flew at us—

And flattened Ty to his back.

He bucked her off as the damned stood their ground. As Vanessa watched with the eyes of a spectator observing live sport. But she came at him again, nail-striking hand hitting Ty's silver as he defended himself while holding back from taking her down. "She's ravenous. Lost to the hunger." Apology was all over his face as he backhanded her to the grass. "I don't want to hurt her."

Mom sprang right back up and Ty dropped his weapons. Palm

driving up, the connection to her nose reverberated a crack around the clearing.

She still didn't stay down, surprising Ty as she dove for his legs.

This was worse than compulsion, worse than the times I'd been compelled to kill my *boyfriend*, even worse than when Marcus had compelled Kendrick to attack me until I killed him. "Dammit, Marcus, what did you do to her?"

Goading shrug. "Damned blood. A little kick-start I'm sure you've experienced before, twin."

Which had made me as bad if not worse than a damned. A creature in need of being put down. But we hadn't come with silver bullets. And even if we had, I'd only survived because of what I was.

I stormed over to my twin who leaned into the altar with his elbow, casual and unconcerned. I had to play a part now. I couldn't let on to what I had planned. And I had to act before Ty killed my mom in self-defense. Or before he let her kill himself. "I kept to my word. Now it's your turn. Restrain our mom and let me restore her."

Marcus blew air through his nose as if amused. "And let you drain your power before the big finale? I don't think so." Whipping his dagger from his waistband, he held it out between our bodies. The same one I'd stabbed him with. And the same one I now wished I'd had the nerve to end him with, back then. "Time to bleed."

Ty went to race our way when Mom, just flattened, clawed his ankles and tugged. Reclaimed weapons in his hands and pointing up as his back hit the grass, my mom launched as I cried out—

Vanessa caught my mom around the throat and waist, holding her suspended just above those silver tips. Mom thrashed then screamed as those deadly silver points bit into her flesh.

"Ty, stop! Wait."

Vanessa hissed in delight. "Shall I let her go *now*?"

"Marcus, stop this. *Please.*"

My twin smiled as my hands clasped, pleading. "I keep to my word. Always." The look in his eyes was a deadly promise waiting to be delivered. "Once you've played your part, you will have all the time in the world to restore *our* mother."

Marcus didn't know we'd never make it out of this ritual alive. I'd be able to restore no one. But by then it wouldn't matter. The curse would be lifted and the damned would be cured. "Let's get this over with, then."

Marcus tugged my arm between our bodies and sliced the sharp edge over my wrist. Once. Twice. I didn't wince. Didn't try to pull away. The time had come. Twisting so the wound faced down, he held my trickling flesh over the chalice on the altar. As the level reached half full, he released me and cut himself, filling the gold cup all the way to the top. Crimson spilled over the rim, gliding down to the black marble to drip from its edges.

Just like in my vision.

Marcus raised the cup between us and arched his brows. "Soul and body, we are one." He drank half of our mingling blood and forced the cool gold into my hands. His teeth showed as he almost hissed the words, "Say it."

My nostrils flared with irritation, wanting so badly to challenge him. To chuck our combined blood away and tear him to pieces. If only… But that was a gamble that wouldn't pay off. I knew it as I glimpsed the way Vanessa restrained my mom. Still thrashing and hissing, more damned had stepped in to hold her back. From Ty. Still fully armed, he'd gained space from them and was now closer to me. But the resignation in his eyes painted our future in black and white.

There was only one solution here. Only one way to stop all of this horror and bloodshed.

The look I gave him was my final goodbye. Any words would give my chess move away.

Turning away—I couldn't bear to face him as my life expired—I flashed my fangs as I raised the rim to my lips. I was ready. I had to be.

"Soul and body, we are one."

The blood slid down with ease, the taste electric and full of power. I felt its steady descent into my stomach, felt it spread instantly through me as if the blood had been a tree and it was now rooting through my entire body.

Marcus began to glow red, a circuit system forking out all over his body. Less than a minute later I mimicked the reaction, electric blue lighting up my skin. The power was consuming and unstoppable, a fire burning out of control that I needed to let free.

Marcus tore the amulet from his pocket and caught my hands, squeezing to keep me from pulling away. His expression was focused and determined.

I was so ready to wipe that look off his face. So ready to take our fates into our own hands. To make up for all the horrible things that had resulted because of what we were made to be.

Behind me, among the sound of wind-creaking branches and rustling leaves, there was shouting. Ty. It was him. But a buzzing had taken up residence in my ears. I couldn't make out the words. Was he saying goodbye? Was he in danger? Was my mom? There wasn't any way to know, and there was no way to stop this. In seconds I'd be dead. As the power from our bodies streamed down to our hands and into the bloodstone, the blue and red stands turning purple, I spoke my last words, knowing my time was up. "Tell my mom I love her. And never forget—you were my *everything*."

A secondary culmination of power coalesced in my bare feet and broke free. At the same time, Marcus snarled, "I didn't miss your vision. I only pretended I couldn't see it. I know what you did." The focus across his face turned severe as those twin jets burned a circled lightning bolt around us.

I tugged to break our channeling power and cried out, feeling like the bloodstone had seared into and was now part of my skin. "Marcus, no!"

With a wicked smile, he stomped one shitkicker down on the ground. A fireball exploded out from beneath us, spreading like wildfire as it ate up the symbol my power had created, burning the soles of my feet like I was standing on a bed of hot coals. And then it was gone, the fire, and my fail-safe. Nothing but a black scar on the earth beneath us as my burned feet tingled with instant healing.

The circle was broken. My plan to die and cure the damned destroyed in a heartbeat.

Purple power erupted from the amulet then, striking out in a million-pointed star. I went to pull away again, even as I knew it was too late. But the power was already on course, now being sucked from our bodies rather than us sending it out. Remaining upright, the unending waves of purple hit every surrounding damned—even my mom. It streamed through each of them, penetrating them like a prism and sending countless rays out into the world beyond. An epic pulse vibrated the air, making my ears pop as purple lit up the dawning sky. Then in a rush, violet split from the heavens down into our joined hands and back into our bodies.

The power had returned. Come back into our vesseled bodies—without killing us.

Every pair of red eyes flared bright as rubies, then faded, turning black and glossy.

The bloodstone turned cold and the force that kept my hands joined with Marcus's relinquished. I stumbled back as dawn receded and the light chased away the lingering darkness. The damned grew edgy. Even my mom who Vanessa no longer restrained had lost her one-track lust for blood. I blinked against the growing light and raised my hands as if they could shield me from the sun's ability to incinerate. "Oh God, Marcus. What have you done?"

My twin took a deep breath of satisfaction as the sun edged higher. "What we were born to do."

Unfiltered sunlight crawled over the canopy of trees, growing nearer and nearer. The damned shrank to one side of the clearing, evading the brilliant light. And then there was nowhere to go unless they turned and ran. Sunlight hit the boots of the front row of damned first, then their legs, arms, and finally their unsheltered faces. Each damned looked down at themselves as if seeing what they now were with total clarity. Monsters unbound by insanity and weakness.

"Welcome to a new world," Marcus announced. "One where *we* hold the power. The ability to dominate at our discretion. Welcome to freedom!"

The curse had been lifted.

CHAPTER 40

Too many things happened in the next instant.

"Restrain her!" Marcus screamed, crowbarring my neck from behind. His rasp in my ear was deadly. "I warned you not to cross me."

Dread invaded my entire being as I fought to get free. "Marcus, no!" My voltage fed his, his red power draining me instantly, turning my arms to liquid as I groped for a weapon to lash out with.

At the same time, Ty responded, racing across the clearing—only to get blocked by damned that lashed out to kill. Black blood spurted up, glistening in the golden sunlight as he hacked bodies to reach me.

But even as his blood joined the scent of rotting berries that stained the air, my sight was frozen.

My life wasn't the one in jeopardy.

Across the way before the sheltering trees, two damned had hold of my mom. On either side of her, they clawed into and strung out her arms. She hissed and snapped, black obsidian eyes frantic.

"Amelia!" She could think through the bloodlust? A moment of clarity, of her conscience breaking through.

"Marcus," I pleaded. "Stop this. *Please*."

Vanessa's hair billowed over Mom's shoulder as her arm snaked around her torso. "Stop him," Mom cried. "Don't let—"

The punch of Vanessa's dagger through my mom's chest stole the words from her mouth as a tortured cry broke from me.

"Marcus. No. No!"

I fought harder, but his power made every command I gave my limbs useless. The smell of blood thickened the cool morning air. For every body Ty beheaded—because his silver weapons no longer incinerated—another took its place, tearing into him and adding to the lacerations that covered him.

"I gave you fair warning. Now a lesson must be taught." As my fight and screams failed me, Marcus's hold relented. Then he was across the clearing before I hit the scarred earth. With his red-glowing hands he yanked my mom forward by her hair and took position behind her.

Mom didn't cry out, her stained blouse turning crimson in a growing patch from where she'd been stabbed. Though her eyes welled with blood, not a single tear fell. "I love you, Amelia. Stop him. Stop them all. I know you can—"

Her voice cut off as Marcus gripped her shoulder and jaw like he had done to Kendrick.

Oh dear God.

"Marcus!" I choked out, struggling to my knees. Too late.

Marcus ripped her head sideways. And he didn't stop. Full circle. The crack and tear silenced the thumps and smacks of where Ty fought off the damned. My mom's suddenly lifeless body fell. Her head dropped beside where she lay, a pool of red flooding out to swallow green blades of grass.

I couldn't speak. I couldn't move. This wasn't real. It couldn't be. Not again. Not fully detached. Resurrection…was it even possible?

But I could—I would—give my life.

I just needed to get her away. Get her body—

My every desperate thought exploded in a ball of flames.

Literally.

One flinch of Marcus's hands sent a fireball at my mom's remains. And then it was too late. The hungry, licking flames consumed my last hope.

Consumed my mom.

"No. How can…why…?"

I couldn't string words together. I just…

Brain fritzing, all I could do was stare, taking in my surroundings as shock kept its talons hooked in me.

All around, the damned seethed, visibly waiting to be set upon the unsuspecting world. Humans, vampires, and werewolves, everyone would be fair game and there would be no safety. My mom just died. As wet drops hit my shaking hand, I realized I was crying. Silent devastated tears. Her last words, *Stop him. Stop them all. I know you can,* pulsed through my head that thumped with pain. Her dying wish.

One I needed to come through on.

For her. For our people. For the world.

I floundered for something to do to stop them, to end this like I'd planned to all along.

Over my left shoulder, Ty was bruised and bleeding, his tan chest bare and slick with black-tainted blood. On his knees, one damned held him by his hair, others strung out his arms while more kept a close circle around him. With a roar, he threw his head back, head-butting the damned that fisted his hair. With a howl up into the brightening blue sky—a call, a command to act—he went for a dagger.

But he never got there.

I screamed, stumbling upright, but the damned didn't finish him off. They just held him again, black eyes watching Marcus. Vanessa stood by, red-bladed dagger ready to strike his heart. Like every damned, she waited on a command.

"I'll let your pet live, Amelia. He doesn't have to die like our mother. Not if you both join me. Become what you were meant to be. I don't want to be your enemy. Together we can find a balance."

Hate burned like formaldehyde in my veins. I was alive and so was Marcus. Only because he deemed it so. But I could never change him. The heinous act of him slaughtering our mom proved that in spades. There was no saving him. And I couldn't beat him, not anymore. I'd failed, and now the damned were free with no way to stop them. More than anything I wanted to save Ty and our races. I blinked back tears as that body bonfire burned out, leaving a charred pile of remains. For Mom, I had to. But if I was just like him? The only balance there would be would turn every vamp, wolf, and human into a commodity. A controlled food source. Livestock waiting for the slaughter.

The stiff nod Ty managed and the blaze of gold from his irises matched his words to Marcus, "I'd rather die, you piece of shit."

Throwing up his hands, Marcus blew air. "So be it." Vanessa took her place behind Ty with her dagger, the damned holding him with his arms strung out as Marcus addressed every damned as a whole. "Go. Have fun. *Kill.*"

All of them bar the ones restraining Ty spun and took off through the trees. That silver blade drew back, red—my mom's blood—almost glowing in the intensifying sunlight.

"Come on. Come on," I muttered, scanning the swaying trees, ears straining past the whooshing wind and creaking branches.

Vanessa's blade drove down as Ty bucked and trembled. The point headed straight for his heart—

Snarls and shouts erupted and Ty's lengthening snout and long tough teeth snapped up Vanessa's blade. With a roar his arms came free and then her weapon was in his hand as his snapping mouth reverted to human. The beating sound of fast-approaching feet and cracking branches from all angles rushed in around us as Ty threw the redhead across the clearing. Damned broke back through the tree line as Vanessa jumped up. Right on their heels?

Leading the assault, Troy in full wolf form burst into the clearing and clamped onto Vanessa while Ty attacked the damned who'd restrained him. Lycans appeared behind the beta. Scores of them. All in wolf form, they forced the damned back, keeping them from setting upon the world beyond this forest.

All hell broke loose.

And like a pit bull set on its target, Marcus was coming for me through the fray, dodging lunges and attacks as his minions cleared a straight path to me.

"Amelia!" Ty screamed, stuck fighting off damned with the wolves, being forced back as he tried to get to me first. "Stay away from him. Restore yourself. While you still can."

I stalled, mind racing as bodies collided all around and hisses and snarls filled the air. Not in readiness to do what Ty wanted—if it could even still work with me being in transition rather than damned, now that the curse had been broken—but because *I* had a way to control the damned. I couldn't die without Marcus dying too. We were joined, our minds, our bodies, our souls. We were bound by blood. My arm brushed against the double-pointed silver stake at my side. The lack of sizzling surprised me. Until I remembered what freeing the damned had taken from us. The ability to execute them with silver. But before I could dwell on the added weakness breaking the curse had afforded, images flooded my mind.

From my twin.

In achieving his goals and with the surprise of the wolves, the impenetrable block around his thoughts had cracked. What I saw wasn't clear. Not even close. A page in a book. Calligraphic scrawl. A symbol. *Cure damned. Instill conscience.*

It was all gone too quick as Marcus reached me, taking hold of my arm. "Fun snooping? You may as well give in. It's too late—"

Letting my rage go, I uppercut his nose and leaped back. Like a Godsend, I remembered the open book I'd seen in the alchemist den. On conscience sharing. Protected as the damned kept wolves and Ty away, my plan to control the damned changed. This was our last real shot. To stop my twin and to hopefully stop the damned.

Silver. Blood. And, in the end, death. But first…

Marcus caught on to my threat, seeing my hand hover near my many deadly weapons. He chuckled as he shook his head and faced me. "You'll just make a mess, Amelia. Staking won't kill you or me. Not even with our life forces joined."

"Exactly," I said as I whipped out the double-pointed stake, palm wrapped around the center and that inscription. Shoving the silver length between our bodies, I yanked Marcus forward. And released my returned voltage. Heaven's light. A gasp parted my lips as one end plunged straight into my heart. The other bullseyed Marcus's.

Light exploded from our bodies in a boom, throwing Ty and the damned he'd just gotten through as well as nearby wolves battling damned back. My knees gave out and Marcus and I both fell to the scarred earth covered in blown-in leaves. Blood seeped as the silver came free of our hearts.

And then it happened.

My heart thudded beneath my ribs and I flopped onto my back. Spine ratcheting up, I gasped in a breath, my heart drumming as the hole in my chest shrank. Through the gasping, I heard bones crack. Not from Marcus, but from across the field. Ty was shifting forms with Troy MIA after the blast. Vanessa was gunning for him, shifting as she sprinted. But Ty was faster. Fully transformed he attacked, halting Vanessa mid-form and throwing her partly clothed body down. A clamp of his jaws around her neck pinned her. Then he picked her up and threw her across the clearing. The tree she hit cracked and there was a thump as her limp body hit the ground. Not dead, but out for the count. For now.

A nearby groan had me scrambling upright. Feeling like my lungs were on fire, I watched as Marcus sat up beside me. Ty padded closer, but Marcus didn't flinch or even prepare to fight or arm himself. Instead, he looked down, brow creased with confusion as the hole in his chest shrank to nothing. Lifting one hand, he pressed his palm over his heart and the red smear that was all that was left of my actions. His wide eyes shot to me. "What did you do to me?"

I knew what he was feeling because I felt it, too. Not just in my restored self, but in him. That ingrained sense of right and wrong I'd been born with. My humanity and my conscience. Everything I'd been losing while in transition, but had now restored the second I reanimated my dead heart. "If I bleed, then so do you. If I feel…" I almost smiled. "That's my conscience coiling inside of you, attaching itself to every fiber of your being." I knew the words I said were true, because I felt the phenomenon myself. "The one you should have been born with. So I guess I was wrong. I *am* your moral compass."

CHAPTER 41

Marcus sat in silence, knees propped and expression one of shock and something so much more deep-cutting. Resounding understanding fueled by pain. His head snapped up suddenly, registering with horror the battle that forged on as black and red spurted and new bodies fell, joining the already cooling. Seeing for the first time, the damned for what they truly were. The monsters he—not just here but all over the world—had released upon humanity. The look on his face was one of morbid realization. "What in hell have I done?"

Ty snarled, snapping his canines at Marcus like he didn't believe for a second my twin's sudden change in personality. But I did. I felt it in the shock and pain that resonated in my twin. In my empathy for my flesh and blood that had been dealt a bad hand that flooded back. In the pity that mingled with my disgust for what he'd done to our mom. In my hope for a change. A way to make all of this right. I stepped between them. "It's not too late."

Through the bond his mind was open to me, everything on

display, all the horrible things he'd succeeded in achieving while he felt nothing. That switch had been flicked now. I felt it in the total devastation that swamped his soul. In the true tears that glazed his view of the battle being fought around us. At his sight of our mom who he'd decapitated without a second thought. He felt…like a monster.

And he had been one. I couldn't deny it. I couldn't alleviate the hate he now felt for himself after all his heinous acts. Or the hate I still felt, despite my pity. But I could—

A wolf darted through the attacking damned and lycans, larger than most and one shade lighter than black. Their jagged teeth aimed for Marcus's throat and body. Ready to kill.

Marcus made no attempt to shield himself, and there was no question on who the wolf was.

Troy.

Ty blocked the way with a snarl, hackles shooting up in warning. Any injury Marcus sustained, including being torn to wolf bite-size pieces, would be inflicted on me too. A few moments of barks went back and forth and then Troy surrendered his dangerous need to attack Marcus. Now he swung around and defended us, keeping the attacking damned and wolves back just as Vanessa appeared through the fray. Troy responded in midair, colliding with her to knock her back.

With one threat forfeited for another, I fell to my knees beside Marcus and gathered up his hands. "We can still cure the damned, right?" Trusting what I felt through the bond, I let everything I'd hidden from him go. The mark keeping my secrets was a fail-safe, but it couldn't stop me from sharing what I chose to. Now along with my conscience, what I'd glimpsed in his mind was exposed for him to see. "We can put an end to this, once and for all. You know how. Don't you?"

Marcus's eyes became vacant, seeing into his own mind to the steps he'd known all along had existed. Moments later he shook his head. "In your vision to mark this site"—he brushed his hand over the scarred earth he'd burned to foil my plan to cure them all—"I knew your aim was to cure them. That's gone now. There's no curing them. But there is a third way. A backup." He nodded, lifting his gaze to me. "A price must be paid. Only life can restore order from chaos. And if I die..."

I laced my fingers through his and squeezed, ready to do what I'd come here to do. Ready to stand by my twin as the man he should have been, and make a change. "Then so do I. It's the only way." I glanced around at the battle, cringing at the sight of wolves falling between the damned who fought on. The dropped damned writhed, not dead but torn beyond any ability to attack. Lycan bodies added to the carnage, some still as death, covered in blood and reverted to human form, others twitching or straining to gain footing. Their comrades tried to keep the damned from feasting on the still living. Time was precious and running out for so many. "Our lives for all of theirs."

My twin gathered up my hands, certainty and despair in his red eyes. "Then we'll leave this world the way we came into it...*together*."

Marcus jumped up as Vanessa broke away from Troy, who must have been holding back from killing his friend. Before she reached me, my twin grabbed her and chowed down into her neck. Releasing his hold, Ty latched on with his jaws and threw her like a doll back at Troy amongst the battlers. The alpha didn't join the colliding of bodies, but kept any stragglers back as Marcus spat her black blood into his cupped hand. With his other he tore open his white shirt. Dipping a finger, he drew the lightning bolt symbol on his chest. Then he held out his palm with the pool of black. Regret at all his kills stained his soul that he didn't try to ignore. "Now that they're free, we need a way to channel them. To bind our power to them."

Ty barked like he didn't trust Marcus's motive, but for the first time, I did. I could read him like a book. "It's okay. We need to do this." Wetting my finger, I traced the mark over my chest above my tank. But there was still one necessary thing we didn't have to perform the ritual. I saw the similar need in Marcus's train of thought. In his step-by-step to pull this off. I looked down at the scorched grass beneath our feet. "The circle…"

Marcus retrieved his dagger and tugged his white sleeve up to score his forearm. When the tip came my way, Ty tensed, growling, but my twin held up the dagger in non-threat. He looked to me and handed the blade over, hilt first. "A new circle for a new cause. Two halves of a whole and our blood to keep the circle intact."

A blood circle, like the original cure had called for.

I took the weapon and stood tall with Marcus who then dripped crimson in a semicircle behind him.

The damned around us hissed, sniffing the air. They could smell my twin's blood. And they weren't the only ones. "They're going to cure you of your free—" Vanessa's voice in the distance cut off with a thump as Troy lunged.

But it was too late.

Knowing our plans, every damned changed trajectory, throwing off wolves to get to us. I sliced my arm, completing the circle around us as Ty joined Troy to fight back Vanessa and the launching damned. Around them, pockets of dirt erupted as Ty's ears flicked back and forth. In wolf form, his earth ability was in action. He was, as I'd always known, a force to be reckoned with.

A warrior.

The still-standing lycans shifted their attack too, creating a barricade to keep the damned out. As they forced the damned back,

Marcus threw fire at any he could safely hit. Knowing time was limited, I bled over the lightning bolt Marcus had already painted from the top to the bottom of the circle. The last trickle had the mark complete—

A transparent cylinder shot up around us, and I went to leap through as Ty barked. This was it, the end. Of me, of my life. I needed to wrap my arms around his massive wolf body and hold tight. Just for a moment. A second. I needed to say goodbye—for the last time.

The crackling cylinder zapped me as I went to penetrate it, and I cried out as the force threw me back.

Marcus caught me before I hit the opposite curved wall. "The circle protects us. It keeps us contained until the sacrifice is complete."

I was trapped.

Tears sprang to my eyes and I pulled from my twin's hold. Nearing the force field, I put my hands up, getting as close as I could without touching the barrier, feeling myself break inside at the cruelty of it all. To draw strength, I thought of Ty's hands on me as we sped here on my Ducati. Of our last and final kiss, the heat of his lips on mine across this body-littered field not even an hour ago.

That had been our goodbye.

The one I'd take to my grave.

Right outside, Ty padded closer, almost as tall as me standing before him. He pawed at the dirt and grass outside, oblivious to the chaos still waging all around him. His head dropped and then lifted, a howl splitting the atmosphere. A tortured farewell.

Tears falling, I lowered to my knees. "Don't let our races become enemies again. Keep them aligned. Make them keep the peace. Bury…my mom?" At the fall and rise of his muzzle, I knew he'd just made me a promise. Knew this was our last moment to say goodbye, too. Faster tears muddied my view of him and I swiped them away in anger of my cruel destiny. "I'm glad I knew you. Even for the short time we had. I love you, Ty. Even when I'm dead, my soul will still love you. Forever."

Ty barked then howled, refusing to turn away. Then Vanessa broke through the barrier, nails penetrating furred skin as Ty spun to meet her attack. Ty threw her off without getting bit, but I knew this was the end.

Time was up.

For the evil we'd unleashed. For Marcus and me. For everyone who fought on as well as Ty if we didn't hurry the hell up.

With my heart tearing in two, I rose and spun, unable to watch the guy I was leaving behind for a second longer. I had all I needed and all I hoped I could take to my grave. The memory of him and everything he was and would continue to be.

My hero.

Holding one of my hands, my twin surveyed over the evil we were moments away from stopping. His grief at everything he'd done and unleashed paled to his total drive to do what was right. What would save them all. And what would kill us.

Standing right beside me here and now, this exact moment stirred my memory. With his shirt parted to reveal the mark on his pale and slender chest and the lack of unease I felt over my total readiness, *this* was the moment I'd seen in my vision of the two of us. The one from so long ago where I'd been pulled away before I saw the damned commander's face. The Sight had foretold of this exact moment, of the sacrifice we would take—together—to rid the world of an evil it may not survive. Even then the future had been set. My actions since that day cementing this moment in time.

Focusing on my twin, I swallowed down my loss and squared my shoulders. "It's time."

Clasping both my hands, Marcus prisoned the amulet between our palms once again. "You sure you're ready for this?"

I didn't hesitate. I didn't bite my tongue. I didn't look back at the man I was leaving behind, either. Not because I didn't want to. God, it killed me not to. But I'd said my goodbyes. Our time was gone. Now and forever, lost to the memory only he would carry the moment I stopped breathing. I sighed, feeling the weight of the world on my shoulders bearing down as blue forked down my arms. "It's what we were born for."

With a sad smile from my twin, red streaked over his skin, racing to meet mine. Reverberating hits sounded as damned broke through the wolves—and got catapulted back by our protective cocoon. The veins of our pure energy gathered faster and faster, streaming from our cores, over our shoulders, and down to our joined hands. Once again the colors mingled, red and blue turning to violet.

But this time was different. I felt it.

Our power wasn't the only thing being sucked from our bodies. Our essence, our life forces were, too. Vitality drained from us as fast as if we'd been human and shot through the heart. The bloodstone turned hot, burning with scorching heat.

I grimaced as torture invaded me, striking through my veins, making them squeeze like constricting barbwire around my bones that felt like they'd shatter at any moment.

Marcus's mouth gaped with a gurgle of blood as more leaked from his eyes. But he didn't cry out; instead he spoke through the agony. "Though it all—I'm glad it was you. No one else c-could have done this." His teeth screeched as his grip on my hands cranked tighter. "You saved me, Amelia. Saved me…from myself."

Feeling mirrored wet tickles from my nose and eyes, I went to speak. To say I forgave him for all the horrible things he'd done. To say it wasn't his fault. Even our mother's death. That who he'd been hadn't been his choice. But I never got the chance. Violet light split from our bodies and shot out, not in a million-pointed star, but in a complete wave. The blinding sonic boom blasted through the barricading cylinder like a nuclear bomb.

Power fled my body and all sensation did too. All the pain was suddenly gone, total peace overcoming the torture of dying. As my bleeding eyes froze, my final view was of the damned and wolves being throw down by the force. My heart seized and my lungs hitched—then released the last of my breath.

Together, my twin and I fell.

CHAPTER 42

The world was a place I no longer recognized. And it had nothing to do with the damned forfeiting their attack at Mount Major when Amelia's shared conscience had been instilled into every single one of them.

In my arms lay the lifeless body of the girl who owned my heart. Legs dangling and head swaying, I could barely contain my need to scream as I climbed the stairs to the Armaya's main entry. This had to work. My very existence depended on it. I wouldn't live without her.

All around, the smell of death and the early stages of decomposition hung in the warm air. Vampires moved around me and fluttered down on the grounds. I could hear them all the way out past the winding roads to the perimeter. There had been casualties. The most killed in any attack on vampire turf. Cleanup was a messy task. And while I cared that lives had been lost, I refused to let my focus shift from the one thing I had to do.

Now that Troy and Marika were transporting Amelia's mother's remains and her twin's body to the Bathory tomb to be laid to rest, Vanessa followed close behind, ready to witness the impossible task I'd relayed. After being freed and then saved, her sad, black irises shimmered with gold glitter. Both werewolf and conscience-filled damned, a manufactured hybrid that would never be a threat unless she chose to be. The first in existence. "It's like I've skipped the transitioning vamp phase. All the blood smells around here are muted compared to…"

At her trailing words, I filled in the blanks. "When you had no conscience." I knew how she felt. Knew her relative silence on the long journey back here had been because of the many regrets spinning through her head.

Passing through the tall doors I'd not long ago barged through to set upon the town's people with Marcus's damned, I slowed my steps. Vanessa did too. The entire hall was lit up with white candles of all sizes, clustered on the stone ground, on tall candelabras, on the Gothic windowsills of battle-broken and intact windows, and all over the vacant stage. Two concrete platforms sat side by side where the pews would normally take up space. They were each big enough to stretch out a body on.

Kendrick stood at the head of one, looking like he'd just taken a walk through hell. In a fresh T-shirt and cargos, the remnants of battle showed on his healing skin. What would have been nasty grazes and gashes were now new, pinkish scars. Though the hell-bound sight of him had nothing to do with recovering. I could tell by the way his watery eyes watched Amelia as I carried her forward. Could see it in his cringe or wince at her swaying head that I tried to keep still.

Getting to the concrete block on my left, I stalled in laying Amelia down. In letting go of her chilled body that I cradled.

"Where is he?" I blinked at the sound of my voice, the way it broke. The fear. The unmasked devastation.

Kendrick seemed like he had to tear his gaze away from Amelia's lifeless face. He glanced over his shoulder at the door siding the stage. His eyes met mine for only a second, then returned to her. After my phone call, he knew every detail of my plan. "They should be—"

The door creaked open then and that damned girl, Raven, stepped out. I knew what had happened from Kendrick. He'd tranqued her shortly after I took off with Amelia, kept her from killing until the battle had run its course. Being twice infected hadn't kept her from being freed and then receiving a shot of humanity. Like all the other damned who hadn't fallen in battle, she had been cured of murderous hunger and given a deep-ingrained sense of right and wrong.

Her shock at seeing Amelia limp in my arms, morphed into worry as she glanced at Kendrick. Emotions no damned had honestly felt before the most amazing girl in the world had sacrificed it all. With one hand behind her, Raven tugged on a chain, bringing Caius out from the shadows and into the light. He looked to his dead daughter, vacancy taking control of his face like he was recalling another time. "It all went to plan, then?"

For the first time, I didn't want to kill the bastard. I nodded. Whether he delivered now that the time had come or not didn't matter. I'd take his place if I had to. Like I'd planned to in the beginning. For *her*. "It did…in the end. Marcus's body is being delivered to the tomb, along with…Lamayli."

The old vampire's eyes shut at the mention of Amelia's mother, and his lips pursed. As his eyes opened, he nodded to his daughter's body. "She is all I have born of my own blood. This must succeed."

"It will—"

A clatter of dropped chains stalled my assurance as Dorian materialized from the corridor. He looked driven and consumed as he glimpsed his sister. Guess Kendrick had filled him in. Then he saw Vanessa and his expression changed to total relief. He sprinted to lift and spin her around. "You're okay."

Vanessa laughed a little, squeezing him tight. As he lowered her she caught his face and kissed him. "I am."

Erzsebet appeared from the corridor Dorian had come from then. She came to stand beside her son, the chains joining her wrists and ankles trailing and jangling with each step. Emotion showed in her eyes, but she said nothing. She simply took Caius's hand and held tight.

Kendrick cleared his throat, demanding attention as Raven stood by his side. "Can we do this already?"

God, I knew how he felt. Seeing Amelia dead, no breath passing through her pale lips, and hearing no beat from her restored heart, was torture. Hell on Earth. My future was set if this failed. There was no life for me without her. Even when damned, I'd known that. Even in my driven, twisted way, I'd known then that I could never exist without her. The most selfless girl who'd jump off a high-rise if it would save someone. Who'd stolen my heart from the first second I saw her in that alley. Even before she begged for death. I'd been watching her in that club. I'd seen her struggle, her hate for herself, her fear and horror as the guy she'd attacked started to die. She was like nothing I'd ever seen in my life. And now she'd stopped both our race's biggest threat. She'd saved the damned. She'd even re-allied our races. Made peace between the vamps and wolves. A feat I never thought would come to pass. Not in any lifetime.

She was amazing. Unique. One of a kind.

She was mine.

I'd only just gotten her back, and I wouldn't stand by and let her go. Even if we hadn't sorted *us* out, if I hadn't had her in a way that would forever be imprinted on my brain, bodies naked and perspiring, lips on flesh, fangs buried deep, joined as one? I'd still be here doing this. Pulling off the impossible. Giving my life, if that's what it took. My plan had been arranged long before that memory-imprinted day, because even if she wasn't mine, the world needed her. Even if they didn't deserve her. We all did.

With a deep sigh, I kissed Amelia's forehead and forced my body to respond to my brain's commands to lay her out on the concrete. A shudder tracked down my spine the moment I let her go, and I gathered up her hand. My head craned up and I leveled my eyes at her father. "Are you ready, old man?"

Caius's answer was the action of him propping himself up on the siding platform. Chains jangling, he unbuttoned the top of his unraveling collared shirt and looked to me. "Tell her I love her. I never meant for any of this. I only pray one day she will have it in her heart to forgive me."

I nodded and Kendrick handed me a clean dagger from his utility belt. Walking between the two platforms, Caius held out his chained arm and I cut him quick and clean. Gathering his blood onto my fingers, I turned and painted a symbol over Amelia's heart. The same one I'd had Erzsebet mark him with using a mix of the damned and regular marking substances. The same one she'd tattooed into Amelia's shoulder blade when I'd brought her into that dreamscape and showed her my mother's gruesome death. If my mother's clues and my research were right, their life forces would be joined, because one of them—Amelia—had died.

Stage one complete.

Now it was action time.

Repeating the cut on Amelia, I stopped breathing at how slowly her blood welled at the slice. So cold and without a pulse, the blood was still and turning bad by the minute. I grimaced as I worked her arm with my bloodstained hands, coaxing what was congealed in her veins down, down, down to the gash. Travel hadn't been our friend, and I didn't know if there was a time limit to this.

Soon I would, though.

With enough blood on my fingertips, I painted the same symbol on Caius's chest, the one needed to transfer what I hoped I'd caught in—this. I plucked my mother's amulet from my pocket, feeling heat in the bloodstone that had always been cold to the touch. A talisman to direct the life force from a living marked being into the vessel of another—after it had trapped the essence of someone who'd been marked and holding the stone when they passed. If it worked.

Everyone else circled around the platforms, no one saying a thing. I spared a few words for the man who'd offered up his life. "She will know what you did for her, Caius. Anything else is up to her."

Caius smiled, head twisting to keep his daughter in view as he reclined. "Let us not waste a moment longer, then. I have never been more ready for something than I am for this. Watch out hell—here I come."

Holding either end of the silver chain in opposite hands, I leaned over the girl of my dreams, life, and future, and fumbled to join the clasp at her nape. A kiss brushed her forehead as the clip found the loop, and I breathed in her dying scent as I straightened. Everything I'd put in play would all come down to this. If it didn't work—no. It had to.

Grasping the warm bloodstone from where it dangled on the platform in the dirty tangle of her hair, I moved it so it was dead center over the mark on her chest. Over her silent heart.

Nothing happened.

After seeing the miracles she'd performed, I'd expected a flash of light, an expulsion of power, something, *anything*. But there was nothing. No change. No color to her graying cheeks. No sound of a heartbeat. No passing of breath through her lips.

"How long does it take?" Kendrick's voice was a croak. "Why isn't anything happening?"

"I don't know." I studied Amelia, frown so deep I felt like I'd be frozen in stone at any second. Like I'd shatter to pieces if I moved. "This was a hope. A long shot. But…" I glared up at Erzsebet, fangs and canines flashing, anger rising to cover my pain. "You said when I came to you that this would work."

The Countess ignored the challenge in my grated words and smiled sadly down at her son. "You did good. Really good. My strong boy, all grown up. My pride and joy." Then she released his hand. "Goodbye, my son."

The split second her flesh left his, every intact window around the hall burst out and every candle flame shot toward the Gothic ceiling. The chandeliers exploded and black crystal rained down over everyone. I leaped on top of Amelia, covering her from the debris with my body, hovering above her until the shower stopped.

Quiet grew like a plague as I stared down at the face of the girl I couldn't live without. Only the sound of beating hearts and quick breaths from the others were audible along with the still sky-high crackling of burning candles. I whispered, feeling my world implode in this very moment, "Come back to me, plea—"

Amelia's lids flung back from silver eyes, making me flinch as she jacked up to gasp in a lungful. Her body went suddenly limp and my arm wrapped around her neck, catching her before her skull cracked on the concrete. A groan and a release of breath had my sight snapping sideways to Caius as life fled his body. Then the candle flames snuffed out.

In my arms, Amelia shifted—her body that had been stone cold a moment ago, filled with heat. She gasped again and began coughing as if choking. I levered her upright, scared shitless that these signs of life were fading fast. That I'd lose her all over again.

But then the gasping coughs turned into labored breath. Her wide eyes with vibrant red whites gained focus, seeing everyone that surrounded us. Then she saw Caius, lifeless and still, eyes open, head tilted our way…and a smile on his face. Her hand on my forearm squeezed and she gasped another breath as she looked into my eyes. "Ty. W-what…happ—"

Her eyes rolled back in her head and her limbs turned to liquid as I caught her. My fear died as the gray receded from her face and neck down her body and the beat of her heart went from jack-hammer to quick but steady.

With complete disbelief, relief, and a thank you to my mother in heaven and her secret knowledge, I stuttered, "It-it worked."

I CAME to with corpse-worthy grace, lids cracking and blinking, muscles around my bones responding slowly. Head lolling sideways, I saw the figure on the edge of my bed. I felt his hot hand on mine. Ty. He couldn't sleep now that I was dead? Was he watching my corpse, unable to make himself leave?

But no. The smile as he watched me was too warm. Too happy?

And then I heard it. Over the erratic beat of his lycan heart, over his gentle words, "Hey, you," as his smile widened to flash teeth.

Another heartbeat. In this room. On my bed surrounded by four material-wrapped posts and all that stone and the Gothic windows, with the smell of stale smoke rising from a crowded ashtray on my bedside. My heart, strong and steady, was beating in my chest.

I ratcheted upright with a horrible gasp. Sudden panic made me want to bolt. "It failed. The damned…"

"Shh," Ty soothed, now holding my biceps to make my darting eyes abandon their erratic scan through archways and unshielded terrace doors. "You did it. You saved us all."

Everything came flooding back. The clearing. The damned and lycans. Marcus. The circle that trapped us. The moment we… "I—I died." All of a sudden relief hit me like a semi. By some miracle I was alive. Here. With… I flung my arms around Ty. I didn't know what was happening or how, what this here and now was, but I wasn't wasting a second of it. Not when it could fade at any moment.

Ty captured my face between his palms and kissed me like he'd never get to again. "You're alive," he said between kisses. "Free. I'm never letting you go again."

I pulled back, seeing the blush over his lips from our kisses, the hopeful sparkle in his eyes. Reaching out I touched his warm face, trailing down to cup his jaw, his neck. His pulse raced beneath my palm, as fast as my own. This was real? Tears sprang to my eyes—and didn't turn my sight of him rose-colored. The drops I wiped away were crystal clear. Restored and alive? "H-how?"

Ty reached into his jacket and pulled free…his mother's amulet. "This held the power—to save your life."

He turned my palm up, lowering the stone as I recalled his mother's words in the dreamscape of her death. *Save the world from great evil.* The damned. But Ty's statement was true. She claimed the stone could *save* a *life.*

Suspicion and sudden fear gripped my settling heartbeat, jacking it right back up. Life always came at a price. "Oh, no. Ty—"

As the bloodstone made contact with my palm, I felt my body

lose control and fall only for a second before my surroundings shifted.

Down in the gardens under that willow tree, Ty paced. With one clenched fist around the phone at his ear, his other was balled up at his side. "She's going to die. Give her life to save them all." More booted strides as the fleeing of twilight over the surrounding hedges painted his expression with morbid severity. "Dammit, Father. This is not an us or them thing." His canines flashed as he snapped, "I pay the price. It's my choice. Just be straight with me. The book. Do you have it or not?"

He spun to a hedged archway as I appeared. Not now as a spectator in this past memory. But as myself back then, after hearing his last sentence and interrupting.

"I'm on my way," Ty said as he hung up the phone.

The scenery changed with blink. Not that my wide-peeled eyes had moved.

Now in the alchemist den, Ty was all about pacing as he moved back and forth before the central workbench. His stare shot up to Erzsebet. "Can it work? Save her. Can it bring her back? Say no and I'll try anyw—"

"It can." My grandmother peered up from the piece of paper she held in her pale hands and pushed her unbound hair back. "But only a life sacrifice—"

"I know. I don't care."

I saw the sketch of the amulet on the sheet she held. The one I'd caught Ty with before the dreamscape of his mother's murder. Had this been just before I'd stumbled upon him down here?

"Then you'll both require marking."

Now Ty came to a halt, snatching back the sketch. "Amelia can't know. She'll never allow it. But I can knock her out. Make her oblivious."

He planned to die. For me. That explained why Troy and Marika had been pissed with me down in the gardens. They'd known of Ty's plan to give his life to save me. Which meant? When Marika had backed me to save the damned by jail-breaking me, she'd done so knowing she was securing Ty's demise. His death—because that's what he'd chosen. Saving the innocent and me over himself.

But he hadn't died.

Ty came around the workbench, and with the trembling of his hand the ground shook. The tremor I'd felt. The stone Erzsebet's chain was anchored to cracked in four places. Weak enough to tug that anchor free. "I'll get her—"

As the door opened and shut—with my arrival back then—the scene warped again. But not the place. The flesh and bone me was no longer there as Ty planted his hands on the stainless steel workbench. "You wanted me? You ready to do the marking?"

Erzsebet shook her head. "I have a detour."

"I don't have time for this bullsh—"

"My son wishes to see you," she spoke over him. "You will get your mark if need be *after* you meet with him."

As Ty all but yanked the den's door off its hinges to leave, he was no longer anywhere near the alchemist den as the door slammed shut behind him.

Caius's cell.

"A visit from the hybrid." My father by blood alone lifted his chin as he regarded Ty with clear scrutiny. "Without the company of my daughter. I see you received my summons."

Ty bared his fangs and thick canines. "We both know why I'm here. So let's cut to the chase. What the fuck do you want?"

Leaning into the wall, Caius didn't react as Ty stalked closer. "Amelia will not survive beyond her plan to break the damned curse."

"No shit." Ty looked like he was about to explode with rage. "She's already outlined her plan to die to the RVC. To lay down her life—because you, asshole, engineered her for this cause. And because she's a girl of honor and integrity, of care for others, even when they don't deserve it." His snarl and the look of murder in his white-gold blazing eyes screamed, *like you, you sorry excuse for flesh and bone.*

"So my mother's message was true." Caius slid down to the damp stone. "I knew all along she would end up at this. That she would take the weight of our world on her slight shoulders and carry us to victory." He almost seemed distraught at the thought. "And now it is my turn to make things right."

Ty crouched before Caius, eyes leveled at the old vampire. "What are you talking about?"

"In my own way, I care for my daughter. I never wanted to see her die. I still do not. Not when there is an alternative."

Ty rose, stepping back. "Erzsebet told you my plans."

"I love Amelia." Now the salt-and-pepper-haired vampire stood, rising without the help of his hands. Despite his aged appearance, he was strong and able. "I always have. My own daughter. I banked on the wrong child from the start. Thought I could control Marcus's impulses and mindset. But I was naive. I was following a plan I had not executed before. I never had control over my son."

"You never had any over Amelia, either."

Caius chuckled, harshness draining to lighten his expression. "Right you are, boy. Right you are. Controlling my daughter would be like controlling the sun. Demanding it not rise and fall each day. Impossible. And yet you tame her. You, a cross-breed, keep her in check."

Doing a one-eighty, Ty strode a few feet away then turned back. He shuddered as if far away, lost in a memory. The look of regret a moment later cemented my suspicion after his words, "Not just me. Kendrick." He still believed I was involved with my best friend. He gritted his teeth, fangs and canines growing longer, pressing into his bottom lip. "He's her moral compass."

"Young love." The old vampire sighed, striding to the far wall to lean into it with his arm outstretched. "Blind and painful. When it is true love, that is. But pleasantries aside, you should know…" His free and dirty hand scrubbed down his face. "You cannot die to save her. I need you alive…to keep her safe."

"If she's dead there'll be nothing to protect."

"Then let me…die in her place."

Caius, the father who'd tried to kill me, had just volunteered to save the guy I loved. To die in his place so that I could live on.

Ty almost staggered, running a hand from his neck and over his collarbone, dropping it as if he'd been reaching for the amulet chain before realizing it was gone. "Are you saying—"

"I am all in." Caius didn't flinch, didn't backpedal. He came forward and held out his hand for Ty to take. "Do your worst, hybrid."

As my father's determined face melted away with the past, Ty returned. He helped me lever up from fluffy pillows, hand still over mine and the amulet. "You saw it? What I did?"

I nodded, tongue-tied at the flood of emotions that raced through me like a train wreck about to happen. My mother was gone. My twin. "Caius," I choked out.

"Your father died to bring you back. He took your place in death. It was his choice. An act to make up for all he'd done to you. All he'd put you through."

"Mom, Marcus, Caius's body, where…?" I couldn't make my tongue cooperate but Ty got it as he slung his arm around me.

"In the Bathory tomb."

As I stared blankly around the suite that had been his, at the white furniture and plain materials that replaced his cherry wood pieces and antique sofas and seating, I felt a sense of grief. Of loss. Of being cheated. Not by Ty or anything he'd done. Having him alive, Kendrick and Dorian too, was right. But the rest of my years without my mom who'd fallen for the wrong man, my twin who'd been himself for such a short time, my father who, in the end, had done the noble thing? To save me? "I want to have a funeral. For all three of them."

Ty hugged me close and kissed my forehead. "We'll make it happen. Today."

I ENTERED THE GRAVEYARD, hand clasped tightly by Ty's as the rising sun bathed our pale and tan skin and warmed my flesh. He hadn't let me out of his sight since I'd come awake. Had barely let go of my hand when I'd dressed in the ceremonial gown I now wore. I think he feared I'd disappear, feared that at any moment the miracle he'd pulled off would vanish in the blink of an eye. I could barely believe I was alive myself—because of Ty and everything he'd done. For the plan that, without my father, he would have died to bring about. His love that ran so deep made my heart want to burst with happiness. I hugged my free arm around his bicep that bulged from his hand's grip on mine. "I'm not going anywhere. I promise you."

Ty's steps stalled and he pulled me aside down a laneway between tombs, bathing most of our bodies in shadow. Hand going to my neck, palm cradling my jaw, he kissed me passionately. I kissed him back without any restraint, mouth parting to take his tongue. In seconds I was dizzy and breathless. In another few, we were breathing for each other. When he broke away, his eyes shone with brilliance. His kiss-swollen lips widened with a smile. "Just making sure this isn't a dream."

I wrapped my arm around his waist and couldn't help but smile too. The chattering of others reached my ears and I tugged him forward. Despite the painful reality of our gathering, I couldn't wait to see everyone. "C'mon. The others are waiting."

Back out on the path of pavers surrounded by white gravel, we walked on until we came to the line of twelve royal tombs. Outside the Bathory one, three black marble coffins stood elevated on stands in a row, their lids open. Seeing the first kept me from acknowledging the small crowd that stood waiting. *"Mom,"* my voice cracked as tears fell freely. Skull aligned with her burned body, a sheet was draped over the charred tear that separated her head from her shoulders and covered her entire body. But I could see straight through the opaque weave with my memory of the second my twin had broken her in two. Taken her life in rage. Burned her beyond repair.

There was no undoing this. I'd already been told the harsh reality by Erzsebet. The other reason the resurrection of her daughter, Ursula, had failed? Unlike a broken neck in Kendrick's case, full decapitation was a dead end. Even without the fire.

Moving to the body in the coffin beside my mom, I couldn't feel hate for my twin anymore. Even with our mother that he'd killed right beside him, I just… I'd seen the person he would have been if unchanged by our father's experiments. I'd seen the good in him. The utter shock and despair in him at the heinous things he'd done—like in the slaughter of our mom. In the end, when he'd been the real him, the guy he should have been all along, he'd done the right thing. He'd stopped the evil he himself had unleashed on the world. He'd given his life.

In the last coffin before the steps up into the open tomb, lay my father. Eyes now shut—because someone had closed them—that smile I'd glimpsed for only a split second before passing out after coming back to life, still remained on his face. The one he'd died with. He'd been glad to give his life up for a chance to save mine. Tears glazed my eyes at the thought, the knowledge that he *had* loved me. In spite of everything, he had saved me. My life for his.

No consolations. No hidden agendas.

"She's at peace now. Your mom. They all are. You did it." I sniffed as Kendrick came to embrace me and Ty reluctantly released his hold on my hand. Through my hazy tears I saw his kind face, his golden-brown hair, the look of respect he directed at Ty, and the relief as he peered down at me. "Even for just a day, the world wasn't right without you."

That's how I'd felt when he'd been dead. When Ty had been, too.

Ty re-clasped my hand the moment I let Kendrick go, and my best friend smiled at him so genuinely I had to do a double take. "You did it, lycan." He held out his hand. "Frenemies?"

Ty grasped firmly and shook. "Wouldn't have it any other way."

Kendrick returned to his spot beside Raven, slinging his arm around her shoulder. "It's good to have you back," she said to me. Then she glanced up at Kendrick with a hesitant smile. He met her lips with his as if in reassurance.

A tear escaped my eye then, and not because I was jealous or upset. I was happy—because he was happy. Finally. And without me. We'd finally come to the place we'd been on the road to for all the years we'd known each other.

True best friends.

Erzsebet stood beside Caius's coffin where she held his pasty hand, free after my impromptu meeting to force the RVC to release her chains and remove her security watch. I mouthed *thank you* to her, to which she smiled, glassy eyes somber yet not regretful. She'd lost her son, but she'd helped him save her granddaughter, one she'd now have the chance to get to know. I wanted to know her too. And all the other secrets she hid. "No." Her smile though saddened, was genuine. "Thank you."

Crunching over gravel from behind had me twisting around. Dorian and Vanessa joined our small group, my brother's footfalls now rushing as he came to embrace me. Face in my hair he said, "I keep thinking I'm dreaming. That I'll wake up and be Marcus's puppet again, or that you'll still be dead. I'm so sorry for trying to stop you. For not believing in you."

"Shh." I smiled at Vanessa who stood mute behind him, eyes downcast with shame. "We all played our parts. Whether we had a choice or not."

I wriggled free of my brother's tight embrace and said what I felt in my heart. "I'm alive because of Caius. He took Ty's place. He saved me—twice." My voice was quiet as I forced myself to look at my mom's covered body. "I see now why she loved him, our mom. He wasn't all bad." I knew from experience how trapping the loss of the people you loved was. Knew the lengths I'd gone to myself to bring the people I loved back to who they were meant to be. "Like Marcus, who had to live as something he was never meant to be, he was just…stuck."

Tears escaped Erzsebet's eyes, streaking her cheeks wet. She sniffed to rein them back in and failed. "Caius really did love you. I hope you know that."

The thing I never thought I'd believe was now undeniable. "I know he did." I walked a few paces to Raven, who held the bouquet of black calla lilies I'd asked her to arrange. I plucked three out and breathed in their beautiful scent. Tracing my steps back, I laid the first over my mom's chest, the second over Marcus's clasped hands. Then I peered down at my father. The one I'd wished I'd never had…and the one I was now glad I had. In the end, I'd saved our people. Saved the damned. There had been losses, but I couldn't regret all we'd gained. The uniting of vampires and wolves. The safety of both races and the world. Seeing the people I loved happy. Finding and being allowed to love the guy who owned my heart.

"Despite everything, I'm grateful for you." I laid the last flower down across Caius's chest—like he'd done after draining the life from my veins. I let go of every bad feeling I'd harbored toward the man who'd brought me into this world. Who'd predetermined my twin's and my fates and what we'd be. "I forgive you, Father."

CHAPTER 43

Sitting in my throne on stage the next day, I watched as the entire hall filled with people, vampires, restored, and the saved that had returned, gathering as one. With the crescent moon low and rising steadily into the twinkling night sky beyond the Gothic windows, I felt the grief of losing my mom, twin, and Caius all over again. The mother I would always love. The twin I never thought I'd understand. And the father I never thought I'd ever miss. His gold cloak was draped around my shoulders, the one I'd inherited now that he was dead, and the one I would gladly pass on when my day with death returned.

And yet, none of that was what spiked my pulse now and sprouted moisture over my face and constricted my body beneath the white and gold gown I'd been advised by the RVC to wear. It wasn't what kept me toying with the handle of the dagger I had holstered to my forearm, either.

Where was Ty?

After sleeping away the light hours beside him while my body fully repaired from death, I'd woken late. Well after sundown. And alone. Advised of this *public* gathering that I'd barely had time to dress for.

Grabbing my braided hair, I worried the end over my shoulder. Had Ty fled? Been ordered away? Or…worse. Ty was a hybrid, a wolf by nature. With the damned threat gone, the vamps had no reason to allow him access to our world. Even if the truce stood, this was vampire turf.

Oh God, if anyone had so much as tried to hurt him—

The movement of two figures quickly down the grand arcing staircase brought my head up and to the right, and stopped my vengeful and panicked train of thought. Kendrick had a look of triumph across his face as he descended hand in hand with his *girlfriend,* Raven. It was clear in their close stride and every glimpse I'd seen of them since returning that they were together. That they were happy too. Which instantly calmed my about-to-lose-it panic. He'd never look so at ease if something horrible were about to happen, or had already taken place.

After placing her in the front row of pews with a tender kiss, he climbed the stairs to the stage and placed—the chalice?—on the cloth-draped table I hadn't noticed before this second. He smiled as he took his place beside me. "Hey."

Trying to keep calm, I reached out and squeezed his arm. "I'm so happy for you. Both of you. I really am. But…do you know why we're here? What's with the chalice? Have you seen Ty?"

"He'll be here," was all he said as the other crowned royals, except for Dorian, mounted the stage and took their thrones. With a wink, Kendrick rose from beside me and strode to the front of the stage, quieting the full audience. "You are all invited to a formal ball this evening…" His strong voice carried louder over the packed hall as they started to cheer. "But first! Today brings our race to a new beginning. One where we are not hunted. One where our biggest threat is now extinct—for good."

A roar of applause accompanied multiple cheers as our mingled race stood up from the pews. And that's when I spotted Dorian—dressed in a formal suit, the Vladimir cloak molded over his broad shoulders, and a look of readiness in his eyes as he stood down by the iron-braced doors. Across from him, Vanessa was all smiles and dressed in a glittering red gown.

Together they lifted the door-length latches and tugged the doors wide. Werewolves in human form and a few transformed lycans stepped over the threshold and into the hall. Troy and Marika led the way, unarmed but looking fierce nonetheless. Ready to act and defend if needed, but somehow hopeful at the same time. The vampires down in the pews tensed, whispers rising with their fear of an enemy they'd had for so long now. One that they still clearly didn't fully trust, even after the times they'd been defended by the once guardian race.

Their reaction made something as clear as the night was dark. They had no idea why they'd been gathered here, either. All they knew was what they could see. That a massive pack of wolves had gathered without warning, with no common enemy left to fight, and with canines that could kill with a single bite. As the wolves suddenly parted down the middle, the guards around the hall were unworriedly still.

And then I knew why.

A young but solidly built man passed through the middle of the muscled mass, heading the group as they stalled before the standing and fearful vampires. Ty—in a suit? His unique-colored eyes lifted to me with anticipation, then swept over the crowd. "You have nothing to fear from us. Not now, not ever. Damned threat or no, we are your ally. Not your enemy."

Leaving his wolves, he passed through the pews and mounted the stage in a single bound. The whispers and caution persisted, but nothing and no one stopped him. Meeting my side as I rose on numb legs, breath left my lips in a rush with my whispered words. "You're okay. They didn't… What's happening?"

Ty kissed my cheek—in full public view—and smiled. "The future." He faced the crowd as Kendrick returned to his throne and Dorian took his on my other side. His voice rang true and strong, echoing around the Gothic hall with its cavernous ceilings. "I have a story to tell you…of a lycan who dared to love a vampire." He took my hand then and squeezed. "Centuries ago, a lycan fell in love with the young Lord Ruthaven. The heir to the throne. When their love was discovered, your race reacted out of fear and prejudice. The heir was burned at the stake. The lycan who caused the revolt for his death was my grandmother. Born to Selina Malau-Ruthaven, I am the grandchild of that lycan and Lord Ruthaven."

He was instigating a war? No, he wouldn't. My grip on his hand squeezed tighter. "What are you doing?"

Ty let his canines and fangs slide free. "Trust me?" The crowding vamps grew even more anxious and the guards moved in to block them from fleeing.

But my worry dissipated like a receding wave. I did trust Ty. Who he was. What he stood for. He was my hero. Our race's. "With all I am."

Ty's smile shone brighter than the candlelit chandeliers above. He addressed the crowd. "But I do not want retribution!"

The many vampires stalled in their attempt to escape, heads twisting and eyes glancing back to stare at the hybrid in between looking to the other crowned royals for a cue. In each of their thrones, they showed no concern, but rather, total acceptance.

"I do not want payback for my grandfather's death, or the lives that have been lost because our races chose feuding over acceptance. I want *peace*. I want the past to mean something. I want all of our futures to be just and deserved and honorable. Not stained by racism. By hatred. I want future generations not to be led into bloodshed, but to be lifted above it. To know that being different doesn't make you wrong. It doesn't make you bad. It just makes you —unique."

The watchers had fallen silent and it seemed that no one knew what to say or do.

But I did.

Suddenly I knew what was happening. Why we were all here, vamps, restored, and the saved amongst the wolves. "Are you sure?" I whispered. "You refused when they offered."

"I couldn't stand being so close to you when you weren't mine. Couldn't bear to watch you with Kendrick when we succeeded in bringing him back. But now…" His smile intensified, brilliantly white. "For the rest of our days, I want only to rule and protect our races, both worlds side by side—with you."

Heart bursting at his choice and what the future could hold, I addressed the crowd. "We have seven of the thrones we once ruled with. Seven from twelve. The damned took the majority, but so did our rigid beliefs and ways." Collecting the waiting chalice from the table, I freed the dagger from my forearm sling as Ty held out his arm without question. With a quick, diagonal slice, blood bloomed from the cut. Holding the chalice below, I collected the red current. When the trickle stopped, I held up the offering and glanced to the crowned royals. The ones who'd known all along what was coming —but who probably weren't all on board with what was ready to take place. "Will you look past your ingrained grudges and accept a new way?"

In a wave, each crowned royal stood, starting with the last

crowned, Dorian, moving to Kendrick, and then Uriel who smiled, and even Strigon and a tight-lipped Rasputin. They held out their arms inner wrist-side up, no words needed to cement their total agreement. Their readiness to offer their blood in full support and acceptance.

I faced the crowd and let the decision fall on them. After all, they were our people, and without their acceptance, this would never work no matter what the crowns wanted. "Will you accept the rightful heir to the Ruthaven throne? The grandson of the burned Ruthaven and the rebellious lycan? The man who was willing to give his life to save vampires, even after he was sentenced to death in Portsmouth? The man who joined our people to save us from the damned? And the man I love—Ty Malau-Ruthaven?"

There was a long moment of silence, then a *clap, clap* broke the quiet. Raven in the front row clapping her approval, of me, of everything I stood for, of all we'd achieved and our potentially happy futures. Kendrick and Dorian behind us followed suit a split second before Vanessa joined Raven up front. Wolves behind the vamps joined in too, and then one by one, so did the vampires.

Every single one of them.

As their applause clapped on, I moved swiftly from Dorian and down the line of crowned royals, collecting their offered blood to fill the chalice. Once brimming, I returned to my hybrid hero. Stepping on my toes, I kissed his cheek without worry of the many watching eyes. "It's all you."

Then I handed him the offering.

Taking it with both black-veined hands, Ty lifted the gold edge toward his lips. With a pause he said, "To a new beginning. To being equals. To living in peace." Then he swallowed the blood down—every single drop—and raised the chalice above his head. He called out over the erupting cries of support. “To wolves and vampires united once again!”

STANDING on the balcony in my suite, I reveled in the feel of Ty’s pecs under my palms beneath his black collared shirt. My neck craned up, bringing my lips to his. “I can’t believe you’re staying. I just can’t believe…” I trailed off, basking in his warmth as I turned, long skirt swishing, to glance past the gardens to the streets. Both races intermingled, sharing what was now even ground, existing in peace as they shopped, dined, and walked down Main Street under the crescent moon’s light.

Ty stepped closer behind me and hugged his arms around the gold and white bodice that covered my waist. I heard his inhale as he breathed in, his nose in my hair. His forearm tightened, cording around me…with nerves? “You made this happen.”

I held on to him as he kept me close, loving the feel of his rippled chest against my back while wondering what might be playing on his mind. “I’d never have done any of this if it hadn’t been for you.”

Pulling one hand from me, Ty tensed with a quick inhale. Then he shifted to dangle something before my eyes. I gasped at the sight. “The amethyst pendant. Where did you—”

I cut myself off and spun to face him, leaving the glittering stars and busy streets behind me. I already knew the answer to the question I’d been a breath away from asking. Ty had been the one to strip me of my weapons and anything I could use against him when he’d imprisoned me while damned. Which included this stone that I’d worm around my wrist, gifted from the fortuneteller as a warning of approaching threat. I shook off the little chill at that too-close-for-comfort memory of what Ty had been. What I'd come so close to becoming. Not enough time had passed. And I didn't want to dwell on all the bad we'd had to overcome—or committed. I wanted to live, finally. To be free in my own skin.

To be…happy.

I looked away from the stone he now held between our bodies and up to him. "You kept it all this time. Why?"

Ty sighed and glanced down at the amethyst with a frown. "After you saved me, I wanted you to have it back…but then something happened. That day when I saw you through"—he glanced over his shoulder—"these terrace doors, I hadn't been on my way because I'd been allowed access. Your vote hadn't been relayed to let me in. But I couldn't wait."

My heart had picked up speed. I dared to ask, "Why?"

"I knew I'd let you down. When your pendant heated up in my hand, I knew it was alerting me to you. To what you were doing…"

"Killing my mom," I breathed. I saw a flash of Marcus and the moment he'd twisted our mom's head clean off her shoulders. Stone cold… But not before I'd compelled her and gone to suck the life from her vital veins. Feet from where I now stood beyond these terrace doors in my lounge.

"Giving in to what I'd turned you into." Ty took my hand and pressed the amethyst with its leather cord and swinging gold clasp into my palm. "I vowed when I saw you about to kill yourself that day, that I would find a way to save you back. To free you from your guilt and give you a reason to live on." Lifting my chin with his fingers, he almost smiled. "That one day, I'd return this to you—that I'd cure what I'd done to you even if it killed me."

Ty hadn't had to die, but his plan and drive had been the catalyst that brought me back to life. And all those times he'd been my protector—to keep me from killing—he'd gained insight to my sudden mood shifts from the very thing that had been my warning of danger. His perfect timing and appearances when I'd been on the edge, when I'd needed him most? The way his hand had so often dipped into his pocket when he'd seemed unsure of my stability, my homicidal urges? They all now added up—to this piece of jewelry. He'd kept his word, to himself, to me. Even without any hope of ever having me back, he'd done everything in his power to save us all.

Leaning up on my toes again, I smiled as he tilted his head down, bringing his forehead to mine. "You did that and so much more. You're my hero, the one you always were."

Ty's lips parted, in argument and hunger, I guessed from the speeding up of his heartbeat. But I refused to let him slide back to the horrible past. Bringing my mouth to his, my tongue took advantage and swept inside. Ty's groan and hands going around my back, toying with the bodice's satin ribbons, were proof of his lost guilt, and I wasn't about to let it back in. Pocketing the pendant, I pressed my body against his, one arm slinging around his neck, the other circling his waist below his formal black jacket. Ty growled in response, cupping my face with his rough hands to deepen his licking strokes over my tongue—"

"Hey, guys! Oh, uh. *Sorry*."

At the interruption and shift from excitement in Raven's voice, our kiss slowed, lips separating as we struggled for breath. The sight of Kendrick over Ty's shoulder had me jerking back a few inches. "Oh, hey." I wasn't embarrassed or ashamed, but with everything we'd all been through, being so openly passionate with Ty still felt like a giant hurdle.

Kendrick didn't look upset, his face didn't redden at the sight. Instead, he smiled, swinging Raven's hand that he held tight to. "We have some news…and I'm pretty sure it's good."

Vague and slightly ominous. “Pretty sure?”

With Ty now beside me, I followed his lead as he leaned back into the polished-stone balustrade. He arched his brows. “What’s up, Baldassare?”

Raven’s smile was infectious as she reached the open terrace doors and released Kendrick’s hand, clasping hers together with clear excitement. “Erzsebet’s been doing some tests. Oh my God, this is going to blow your mind.”

That ominous feeling in my gut intensified. Tests equaled experiments. In the past, so much harm and heartache had come from the causes that drove her to experiment. To others before me, and to everyone I loved. People had died and come back to life. Some had stayed dead. Like my mom, Caius. And Marcus. I thought of him and the clearing he’d died beside me in. The place where he’d been who he could have been if not for Erzsebet’s and Caius’s actions. I wasn’t ready for another round of ‘save the world.’ I needed a break. To grieve. To live. Had I made a big mistake by forcing my grandmother’s freedom? “I don’t like the sound of this.”

“Just hear us out.” Kendrick’s relaxed expression and the lack of tension in his body settled me a fraction. “It’s not something to come, or to fight or do. It’s just…facts.”

“Facts about what?” Ty seemed on edge too, nostrils flaring as if testing the air—or maybe the scents coming off the other two.

“About being brought back to life, of being a cured damned, or a saved one.” Raven hugged an arm around Kendrick, looking up at him like she wanted him to spill the news.

I felt like I was going to explode. “For the love of—”

“Erzsebet tested her blood and Ty’s, as well as mine and Raven’s cells, and a few other cured and restored damned to confirm what she found,” Kendrick interrupted, stalling my words.

A memory tickled my subconscious and I recalled the moments

before the dreamscape of Ty's mother. She'd been testing her blood and needed Ty's to confirm a change being restored had created.

"The saved, still being damned, will never die," Kendrick went on. "Neither will any you've restored. Raven's restored blood bringing me back to life changed me too. My aging has already slowed beyond the speed of a mature Pure Blood, at least ten-fold at this stage. And you..." He smiled at me. "Caius was right about not just your blood being immortal. The aging of your cells has almost completely stopped, too."

"So you're saying—"

Ty's cutting-in voice was choked, "I'm immortal..." Looking suddenly in shock, like his mind was racing as fast as mine, he almost tripped on his shiny black shoes through the doors as he bypassed Kendrick and Raven. With a distracted look back, I would never forget his words. "I—I need some time. I'll—I'll be back."

CHAPTER 44

I paced behind the couch, legs aching and mind spinning. Right after Kendrick and Raven's bombshell, Ty had taken off. He hadn't said where he was going or what he was doing, had only said he'd be back. But not when. Now it was one a.m. An hour short of the grand ball's kick off, with me still in my white and gold ceremonial gown from earlier because I didn't want to miss the moment he returned. *I'm immortal.* I heard his cutting voice in my head over and over. Saw the horrible realization that had frozen his features and widened his eyes. The almost frantic reaction that'd had him stumbling to escape. *I need some time.*

He'd just been crowned one of The Seven—now The Eight, once a Paole stepped up to fill the role. He'd promised to rule for the rest of his living days. By my side. An eternity. Was he re-evaluating the promises he'd made, to our people—to me? Was he freaking out that he'd be stuck with me forever? For all of time? Frozen in our early twenties by the time our cells completely stopped aging—while anyone who hadn't been damned, restored, or brought back to life aged normally? While his family and pack grew old and perished?

He'd said back on the cruise that he'd wanted a chance to compete with what Kendrick had to offer. He'd wanted to give me as many years as possible. But back then he'd known the most he'd get if we did reignite his vampire genetics was up to one thousand years. Again, not an eternity.

It was too much. Of course it was. We were young. In our late teens. Lifelong commitment was one thing, but eternal commitment?

I blinked and realized I was standing by my bedside. Snatching up the photo at the lamp's base I studied Ty's happy face. God I wanted him, all of him. Forever. But I wouldn't make him keep to what he'd promised. Not when the game had changed yet again. When he returned, I'd—

"Amelia, you still in here?" The main door opened and shut, and then I heard ripping cardboard and crumpling plastic. "Sorry I took so long."

The sound of drilling brought me to the foyer archway to see what Ty was doing. Facing away, he was driving screws into a metal plate on the door. "Is that a lock?"

"Strongest ones I could find." On one knee, still in that suit, Ty threw a glance over his shoulder then drilled the piece the metal bolt slid into. He repeated the action with two more latches, one up high on the door and another down low. When it was done, he bolted all three and spun my way with a smile. But there was something on edge about the look that hit my heart like a stun gun. "I think it's time people started knocking around here. I like my privacy."

"I thought…" I shook my head. Physical privacy. He still wanted what we'd reignited…for now. "It's fine. I get it. We can just live in the moment for as long as it lasts."

Ty saw my shifting glance down to the photo I held with shaking hands and frowned. He came around the granite table and rested a hand against my jaw, eyes studying mine. He must have seen something, because his hand fell away. "You don't want me to move in?"

I jerked from his touch as my jaw fell. That hadn't even crossed my mind—because before the bombshell I'd just kind of expected him to stay with me, like he had since coming back to life. But now he'd gotten these locks and secured our privacy. "You still want us, even after what Kendrick and Raven said?"

Ty swallowed and I heard the constricting sound his throat made. That vulnerability I'd seen so rarely in his features came alive. He patted the front of his suit jacket then dropped his hands as his eyes lifted, meeting mine with unwavering strength. "You don't?"

I understood his body language then, the nerves, the uncertainty, the vulnerability. Ty was scared *I* didn't want him back. Scared I'd changed my mind after learning of our never-fading lifespans. Placing the photo on the table, I laid my hands on Ty's chest. His desire wasn't a promise of forever, and right now I wasn't after one. I knew what I wanted, and for as long as he wanted me too, I'd take it. Rising up on my toes, I craned my head up, meeting his narrowed gaze with total certainty. "I want you—more than *anything*."

Ty's growl was instant. His arm snaked around my back and my feet left the ground as my body crushed against his. The second his lips parted mine, I was lost to him, all thoughts and worries melting away. Wrapping my legs around his back, skirts riding up, I threaded my fingers through his hair, deepening our kiss as our tongues tied. Swinging me around, my butt landed on the table and Ty's arm released, both hands working the satin tie up my back with fast fingers. "God, I'm so in love with you," he rasped, lips breaking from mine and kissing their way up my jaw and down my neck.

He broke away again only for as long as it took to slide the loosened bodice up over my head and to fling it away. Mouth reclaiming my flesh, my body came alive under his rough fingertips, and I couldn't stop the groan that escaped. "I want to taste you," I gasped.

Ty's mouth abandoned my neck and he tore the top few buttons of his collared shirt open. His head tilted, exposing that thick vein up his neck.

Overwhelmed by so much more than my physical hunger for him, I plunged my fangs in deep. Like I was marking him as mine and mine alone. Branding him with my bite. Ty hissed at the breaking of his flesh and his calloused hands released my bra. Tugging the straps down, the cool air hit my bare skin the moment before his hot palms covered my breasts. I moaned through my fangs, the pressure in my body escalating by the second.

Suddenly his clothes were my enemy. And they had to go. Shoving his black jacket off his shoulders, it hit the ground as I tore the rest of his shirt open, buttons popping off in every direction and bouncing as they hit the ground. Then our naked chests met, feeling the amulet pressed between our hearts as my fangs released. Looking up at me, I kissed Ty deeply, his blood on my tongue now shared between us. "I want you now," I broke away to hiss, dropping my fingers to the button on his pants and tugging. "All of you. Right now."

Ty's smile was both wicked and promising as he produced a condom from his pocket. "Anything for you. Always."

He reclaimed my mouth as I released the button and unzipped his fly. A push down with my hands then feet, as I kicked my shoes off, had him standing before me in nothing but his boxer briefs, his own shoes flying with his pants as he kicked them off. Ty made quick work of my now-wrinkled skirt, removing it only short of tearing the fine white and gold material to shreds. The hot kissing continued, getting quicker and making us pant for air. Hands feeling their way down the perspiring ripples of his muscled chest, I pushed his briefs down, releasing his ready manhood. Ty's growl in my mouth was met by his hot hands tugging down my panties, the cold table meeting my butt with the cotton cover gone.

I cupped his face and pulled from his kiss. Future unknown, I didn't care. When life was so unpredictable, all that mattered was here and now. A love I would kill for. A love I would die for. The guy who owned my heart now and forevermore. Taking the prophylactic from him, it was free of the wrapper and rolled over his readiness in seconds. I gazed into his stunning, brilliant eyes. "I love you, Ty."

Ty's snarl was animalistic passion that sent goosebumps over every bare inch of my flesh. Mouth parted, his fangs found my neck and slid in deep—like he was branding me as his own—at the exact same moment he pushed inside, joining our bodies. I gasped at the twin penetration, the feel of him as the ecstasy of his bite flooded my body. Undulating against him, together we created the rhythm, bodies so totally in sync as he moved inside me, drinking from my vein.

Lifting me, he supported my weight as we moved together, as our bodies became one in the same and our blood intermingled. My back connected with a cold wall and my hold around his neck tightened. "Don't stop."

Heat was growing inside of me, soaring by the second. Rising and rising like a bubbling volcano, ready to explode. Ty moved with me faster and faster, deep-buried fangs drawing hard. He gasped when they released and growled as he reclaimed my mouth. And then it was all too much. The lingering sting and fire of his bite. The feel of him inside me. The taste of what he'd taken from my vein in my mouth.

"Ahh!" I cried out as I detonated, my body breaking apart in ecstasy and shattering in ultimate pleasure.

Ty grunted as he jerked inside me, his entire body turning rigid as his arms around me squeezed the air from my lungs. His head buried in my hair at my neck, his chest expanding and contracting as we slowly caught our breath.

Still clinging to me minutes later, slow kisses trailed up my neck and jaw. A sweep of his tongue parted my lips with a deep breath. "I love you." Keeping me locked around him, he carried me from the foyer and lay me down on the bed. On top of me, he kissed me slow and sweet. "I will *never* stop." He stroked my hair back from my face, and eased down beside me, pulling the comforter over our naked bodies. "Not ever."

My eyelids became heavy then, the days, and weeks, not to mention what we'd just done, finally catching up with me. "Me neither," was the last thing I said as I turned toward him, the stroke of his gentle hand that could kill forcing sleep to claim me.

WHEN I FINALLY AWOKE, still sleepy but so content, my reaching hand as my lids slitted open felt…mattress. More mattress. My eyes opened—to find Ty gone. A quick listen and inhale revealed reality. He wasn't here in my suite. Not even in another room.

After his words and everything we'd just done, my mind refused to reconcile the facts. *He'd left?*

After being together for the second time, was he already regretting what we'd started?

Ratcheting up, then gathering the comforter to my neck to cover my cold naked body, I felt abandoned. Confused. I crossed my legs under the covers, hand going to the amulet Ty had re-clasped around my neck when he'd brought me back to life. Scanning around, like something would suddenly make sense, I froze—then snatched up the folded note from the pillow Ty had laid beside me on. Unfolding it with shaking hands, I knew it was from him.

Meet me at the Gazebo.

Vaulting out of bed, I reacted physically rather than on any thought-out conscious level as I darted for my discarded bra and panties in the foyer and almost fell trying to get them on. In and out of my walk-in with fresh clothes and tugging on my hoodie, I couldn't strip from my racing mind the last time we'd both been together—almost—in the location he was now waiting for me.

When he'd lured me there to witness me start something with Kendrick. Where he'd seen me move on and kiss my best friend. Where he was going to tell me it was over? That the past was too much to forget? Too much to move past? I recalled his nervous uncertainty when he'd installed those locks.

Feeling more scared than I had in my life—bar the times I'd seen the people I loved die—my shaking hands threw open the terrace doors. My run and jump with one hand's stability over the balustrade and down to the ground was fast as light. I wouldn't keep him waiting in hope he'd change his mind. I'd do anything for him. Even if that meant letting him go.

On autopilot, I was already through the nearest arched entry to the royal gardens. Running around bends and curves, being stuck in this confusing maze of tall hedges, brought me back to the night I'd chased Ty after finding him lurking. The sight of him, the red glow of his eyes. I'd had to convince myself it wasn't him. That I was losing it.

But now, as I found the exit to the mouth of Main Street, I

pushed the memories that struck my heart aside. This was different. This time, as I bypassed the closed-up shops and cafés—because everyone in town was celebrating in the ballroom—instead of taking to the backstreets, I knew I'd find him there.

The place I'd let him go.

The place I'd moved on.

With a haze of tears blurring my vision as I skirted around the gushing angel fountain, I didn't notice the change until I was halfway across the grass field. And it wasn't the regrowth of green blades over the scarred earth where so many bodies had been burned.

Pulling up short with a gasp, I had to rub the tears away and blink. In the distance was the gazebo, golden candle flames flickering in the gentle breeze from all around its octagonal edges. Fairy lights twined each post and made the raftered ceiling inside look like a starlit galaxy. And as I continued walking, that wasn't even most of it.

In the surrounding trees, glassed tea lights hung from every branch, making it look like they were decorated with thousands of fireflies. Thick white candles lined a path over the grass to the gazebo entry.

Where Ty waited.

In his leather jacket with one hand behind his back, he shifted his weight from one leg to the other. "I didn't want to leave you like that…but I had to…"

He glanced around at the lights and flames that had, in an instant, turned this place of hard memories and shadows of the past into the most beautiful place I'd ever seen. "You did all this?" Leaving the lit-up path behind, I entered the warmth of the gazebo. "For me?"

"I've known what I wanted from the very first moment I saw

you. Through everything, that one thing has never changed. Not for me." Ty reached up to palm the amulet that dangled between my now covered breasts with a shaking hand. "My heart in stone against yours…forever. If…you'll have me?"

As he released the stone, I stammered, "If I'll have you?"

Ty unbent his arm from behind his back—to hold a small velvet box between us. He popped the lid to reveal a pear-shaped diamond ring surrounded by a halo of smaller diamonds. "I can't imagine life without you. Not for a day. An hour. A minute. Not even for a second. You're everything I think of when I wake, and my last thought before sleep claims me each day. I need you. I want you. I love you, with everything I am and will ever be." He plucked the sparkling ring free, even as I stared in fish-mouthed shock. "Marry me, Amelia. Say you'll be mine…for all eternity."

Tears flooded my eyes and a few spilled free. I'd been wrong. One hundred percent. Ty did love me as much as I loved him. His nerves all day had been a clue to this. His eternal commitment. And whether I'd accept it. I gathered Ty's face up with my hands and kissed his lips, feeling his shallow breaths and hearing the rush of his beating heart. Mine was racing too. I'd never expected this. Never really thought I'd deserved such real happiness and love until this very moment. But Ty had taught me so much. He'd helped me accept myself and everything I was. He'd shown me the forgiveness I'd wholeheartedly given him and now my father and twin… because, like them, I was worthy too. Ty was my hero in every way. My warrior. My lover. My forever. Surrounded by beauty and where I belonged, my voice was as sure as my heart. "I am yours, now and forever."

Ty's smile was paramount as I offered my left hand and he slipped the ring onto my finger.

I smiled up at his handsome face, the one I'd get to wake up to for eternity. "With every beat of my never-dying heart."

The End

THANK YOU FOR READING!

Thank you for taking the time to read *Born To Die*. If you enjoyed it or any of the other books in the Blood Bound Series, please consider telling your friends or posting a short review. Word of mouth is an author's best friend and much appreciated.

http://bit.ly/reviewbtd

Thank you, J.L. Myers.

Continue reading for a sneak peek at the first book in my epic love story - the Fallen Angel Series.

MORE FROM J.L. MYERS

Fallen Angel 1 - Ashes of Eden

Gabriel writhed against the tree, flames entering her robe from the ground up. She cried out, the burn attacking her toes and climbing her legs, melting and burrowing through her skin. This was the end—her end—here in this grassy field. Here under a darkening sky before the eager eyes of all the human men who had captured her. Here—*alone.*

With agony consuming her on the outside, Gabriel retreated into her mind, away from the smell of her cooking flesh and the sound of her bloodcurdling screams. No longer able to feel the wet tears that forged tracks down her face, she conjured the memory of her last encounter with Lucifer.

He had come to watch her. To observe her down on Earth.

But of course she had known the moment he landed nearby. As always, she had felt him.

At first her heart had taken off in her chest, soaring like a bird's rapid wings on the breeze. But her heart did not make the rules.

"I want you to leave, Lucifer. Leave me be."

And he had, despite the tears she could not hold at bay. Despite how clearly his heart was breaking as he staggered away and took flight up into the twilight sky. Clinging to the image of his shell-shocked face, she remembered the sheen to his wide silver-blue eyes, the bunching of his tan brow, the way his lips trembled over clenched teeth as if he were fighting the temptation to refuse her demand. Her hand cupping his jaw had been their last touch, a touch that could never compare to the slide of his rough hands over her bared body or the hungry pressure of his mouth against hers. But that would never happen again.

"As you wish." Lucifer had surrendered to her refusal. He had granted her wish. And now…

She would die alone.

Gabriel's screams shattered her memories as the blaze engulfing her robe-clothed body licked even higher. Legs bared and bloody, flames now lashed her stomach and arms. Renewed panic made it feel like her insides were smoldering too. This couldn't be her end. It couldn't be *their* end.

Yanking her arms up to evade the burn, the lowest rope snapped around her hips, ripping skin away in its wake. Gabriel hissed at the sting, swallowing her screams. Raw hands snatching and tugging at the higher ropes, they refused to budge, her strength failing her.

Darkness fell, teasing her senses with the promise of cold that could never combat the inferno of flames that climbed ever higher and renewed her tortured cries. Wings trapped to the tree behind her catching alight rapidly, even escape from her bindings would not spare her. Those men stood by, spears in hand and murder painted in their eager gazes.

Strands of her windblown hair sizzled up to her scalp with flaming embers, and Gabriel's eyes pinned shut. The burn attacking her arms had a hold of her ribs, eating away inside her, breaking her. Her heart felt hot, *too hot.* Soon her screams would turn to fire—with her final shriek.

Unable to speak, parting words formed in her mind. A telepathic message, a goodbye…that would never reach its source. *Never blame yourself, Lucifer. This was not your doing. It was mine. I was wrong. I need you. I have always needed you.*

A sudden commotion sounded, a booming ruckus as the ground shook. But the cause mattered not. Nothing mattered anymore. Her end was imminent.

And then everything changed.

Gabriel's bindings suddenly released and she fell like the dead. A blanketing weight covered her, blocking the cooling breeze and dousing the consuming fires that coated her sticky body and wings. Skin stuck and peeled away, the sound joining her rattling sobs. And then she sucked in a choked breath—and smelled *him.*

Unable to believe her senses, Gabriel cracked her melted eyelids open.

Staring down at her was the one face she had never expected to see again. Tan, rugged, and filled with a fear of losing her that resonated in his eyes with silver tears. "Lucifer. You came—" she rasped, realizing this was real. Realizing Lucifer had returned to this field on Earth and was surrounded by murderous men. Tongue feeling like it was on fire, she gasped out, "No. Oh, no. Please. Leave before they get—"

There were screams, men barking orders out of sight that refused to break through the sound of rushing blood in Gabriel's ears. The look of relief across Lucifer's face morphed with animalistic fury. "No being will ever hurt you again. I vow it."

And then he was gone.

Chilled air swept in at his absence, fighting the burn that clawed at her bloody body and causing a fresh wave of agony to dance across her melted skin. Grunts and shouts rose up, and then wet thumps—bodies hitting mud. Dread hooked into her insides as if worms had suddenly risen up to devour her charred remains. Murder of men was a heinous sin. A sin so much worse than her forbidden interactions with Lucifer. She needed to stop him. She needed to—

With a gasp of pain, Gabriel rolled to her side, seeing movement through the long brown grass as men fell injured but still alive. Her eyes scoured through the mass of men screaming commands to kill. Finally locating Lucifer, she saw a dagger in his hands as he caught the throat of the man who had led this village of men and ordered her death. The man's face turned red then purple as he was lifted from the ground. Spit sprayed from his lips, but no sound escaped. The grip on his jugular was too tight. A death grip.

"You attacked the wrong angel, you disgusting excuse for a human." Lucifer's smile was a promise as he pointed the dagger at the man's wide eyes.

Gabriel struggled to her hands and knees, the grass ripping more of her raw skin away. About to fall in a heap, she grunted through the agony.

"And now you die."

Gabriel pushed upright, choked words flying from her bloody mouth. "Lucifer, no!"

Dagger freezing mid-air, Lucifer's head cranked sideways. His eyes widened and flung the man aside to run at her. "Gabriel, look—"

Something punched into Gabriel's back, stealing a gasp from her as it tunneled through her heart and exploded out through her chest. Her head fell forward, and a bloody spearhead gleamed up at her.

Get it here: http://bit.ly/1ashesofeden

CONNECT WITH J.L. MYERS

If you want to stay updated about my latest book releases and get freebies or exclusive review offers, join my VIP list!
Visit : www.jlmyers.com and enter your email address. You can unsubscribe at any time and your email will be kept 100% private.

Come check out my author page on Facebook. I'd love to hear from you:
https://www.facebook.com/author.jlmyers

Come say hi on twitter or Connect with me on Goodreads!
https://twitter.com/authorjlmyers
https://www.goodreads.com/author/show/7178370.J_L_Myers

Don't miss my new releases. Follow me on Amazon & Bookbub
https://www.amazon.com/J.L.-Myers/e/B00DK4P0EO/
https://www.bookbub.com/authors/j-l-myers

ABOUT THE AUTHOR

Jessica L Myers' vivid imagination and quiet demeanor as a child led her to the imaginary worlds of books. Even at a young age, her love for the supernatural was prevalent, with her first loved books being R.L. Stine's *Goosebumps* series. Following that she took an interest in other non-fantasy fiction, including Virginia C. Andrews series *Flowers in the Attic*.

In her teen years, Jessica spent many school hours writing poetry and dark short stories and took up sketching some of the terrifying things that came from the graphic night terrors she'd grown up with.

As an adult and after meeting the love of her life, Jessica got married and started a small construction business with her husband. With the birth of her son, Jessica suffered PPD and found escape in her books and their fantasy landscapes. It was during this time that her need to write flourished. In 2009 the decision was made and the first words to her YA novel *What Lies Inside* were written.

When Jessica isn't immersed in writing about extraordinary characters with dangerous and deadly obstacles to overcome, she likes to spend time with her two kids and husband, curl up with a good book, or watch anything and everything supernatural.

Contact J.L. directly:

www.jlmyers.com

facebook.com/author.jlmyers

twitter.com/authorjlmyers

instagram.com/authorjlmyers

ACKNOWLEDGMENTS

A huge thank you…

To the readers and supporters of the Blood Bound Series, my awesome editors and beta readers for helping to polish this book and make it shine, and to my cover designer for creating the amazing works of art for this series.

To my family—especially my husband, son, and not-so-little girl—your support, encouragement, and above all, your patience, helped me get through the marathon of this epic story I've had in my head for so long now.

I couldn't have done any of this without you all!

www.ingramcontent.com/pod-product-compliance
Lightning Source LLC
LaVergne TN
LVHW050909080826
845145LV00001B/24

* 9 7 8 0 9 8 7 5 6 5 3 9 6 *